Words and Wisdom

Wishes and Chances Series: Book One

by

Suzie Peters

GWL
PUBLISHING

First Published in 2018
by GWL Publishing
an imprint of Great War Literature Publishing LLP

Produced in United Kingdom

ISBN 978-1-910603-47-5 Paperback Edition

GWL Publishing
Forum House
Sterling Road
Chichester PO19 7DN
www.gwlpublishing.co.uk

Dedication

For S.

Chapter One

Four Years Earlier

Cassie

"Stop it." She moved his hand gently away from her hair. "It doesn't matter what you say, or do, I'm not changing my mind."

"C'mon, Cass." Jake's voice had that persuasive tone; the one that had talked her round so many times before.

"No, Jake. You know how I feel about this." She wasn't going to budge. Not this time. This was too important.

She stared at him until he looked away, but she knew this was no victory; the dark resentment in his eyes told her everything she needed to know. The argument was far from over.

"I'm gonna grab another beer," he said, getting up from his seat beside her. "You want anything?" She shook her head. "Suit yourself."

She felt like telling him to grow up, but what would be the point in that? Miracles never happened.

He moved through the throng of people toward Sean's kitchen and, looking at his back, she felt herself calming, just a little. Even from behind, he was gorgeous. Tall – a good head above most of the other people in the room – dark haired and muscular, Jake was stunning. His jeans hung perfectly on his hips, and his black t-shirt clung to his toned body. It was hard not to admire him, even when she couldn't see his face… the face that was usually so gentle, tender and caring, whenever it was looking at her. Except it wasn't at the moment, because Jake could also be childish and pig-headed, especially when it came to where they were going to live now that they'd graduated.

Cassie glanced around the room. As graduation parties went, this one was going… fairly badly. All she and Jake had done so far was fight – but then that was really all they'd done for the last three months. She hadn't even wanted to come here tonight in the first place: these were Jake's friends, not hers, and she felt really out of place. She'd wanted to go back to their apartment, finish packing and head straight home to Somers Cove, the small, coastal town in Maine where they'd both grown up together. She'd wanted them to settle down, maybe get a small place near to her mom, where she could write books, see her friend Emma every day and laugh over coffee with her. She'd wanted to stare out at the ocean, watch the sun rise and set over the still blue water, while the breeze played in her hair and Jake sat beside her, holding her in his arms… And she'd wanted Jake to want that too; maybe for him to work with his dad, Ben, fixing people's roofs and fences, helping out around the town, becoming as popular and loved as Ben was. And, one day, she'd hoped they'd get married, have kids and raise them in the quiet seaside resort she'd always loved and called home…

Except it seemed that wasn't what Jake wanted at all. Jake wanted them to take off for Boston. He had a friend there, who was happy for them to crash at his place until Jake could find work and then, he kept assuring her, they'd rent somewhere – maybe nothing much to start with – but they'd be together. And they'd go back to Somers Cove every so often to see her mom and his dad, and Emma could come to the city to visit with them. And it would be great. He'd made a point of smiling when he'd said that bit. He didn't want to work with Ben; he didn't want to be 'small town', as he put it. He wanted to make something of himself, to really *build* something, to create something more solid, more ambitious. Mending fences wasn't enough for Jake…

Clearly.

Cassie sighed. Mending fences had never been Jake's strong point. Busting down walls, and burning bridges… yeah, that was where his strength lay.

He wouldn't even think about going home with her for a few weeks over the summer while they worked out their future. She knew he thought that once they got back there, she'd never be willing to leave, and maybe he was right... but why couldn't he trust her enough to try it? It was asking too much to just take off to the city, with very little money, no prospects and no support behind them. Cassie wasn't that kind of risk taker. Even the idea of it terrified her, and Jake knew that... and that's what really hurt. He knew how she felt, but he didn't care enough to put her feelings first.

He came back into the overcrowded, overheated room and Cassie couldn't fail to notice that most of the female eyes surrounding her were turned toward him, following him as he walked toward her and sat back down again. He looked at her, his green eyes darkening just a little.

"We seriously need to talk this through, Cass," he said, taking a swig from his beer. "I don't wanna go back there."

"Not at all?" She felt cold fingers of fear inching up her spine. "Not even for the summer?"

He gave her a withering look. "No."

She turned and faced him on the couch, trying to ignore the music that some idiot had just turned up a little louder. "How can we just go to Boston, Jake? You don't even have a job." At least he was listening this time, even if it was hard to hear what he was saying.

"I've already explained, Cass. It'll be fine. Pete is happy to let us crash at his place until I find work. It won't take long."

"You don't know that."

He looked at her, a furrow forming on his brow. "Well, thanks for the ringing endorsement."

"Sorry, I didn't mean it like that."

"Why can't you have a little faith in me?" *Right back at you*, she thought, but didn't say out loud.

"I do... I just..."

"What?" He sounded impatient, like he knew exactly what she was going to say – which he probably did, because they'd had this same argument so many times it was like déjà vu.

"You know I don't want to go..."

"And you know I can't live back there. Everyone has to know everything about you. It's so… claustrophobic."

"But it's where our families are." And there they were, back on the same old turf again.

"I'm not saying we won't see them, just that we don't have to live right in their back yard. I want my own life, Cass; not my dad's."

"And what about *my* life? What about what I want?"

"You can write anywhere…"

"Yeah… because what I want to do isn't as important as what you want to do, right?"

"I didn't say that."

"You didn't need to." She could feel the anger and resentment building again, and the argument degenerating into the usual tit-for-tat. She took a deep breath, trying to stay calm. "My mom hasn't got anyone else," she said. Cassie had no idea who her father was. Her mom never spoke about him and she never asked. They'd been happy together and she wanted that to continue.

"Your mom has the whole damn town, Cass. She belongs to so many committees and clubs, it's a wonder she has time to work."

She glanced up at him. "What do you want her to do, sit around doing nothing all day?"

"No, of course not. I'm just saying, she probably wouldn't miss you as much as you think she would."

Cassie felt the sting of tears in her eyes. "Well, thanks for that." She went to get up, but he pulled her back down again.

"I'm sorry. That came out wrong."

"Really?" She wondered if the truth was finally coming out in the heat of their argument.

They stared at each other for a long moment, until Jake broke the silence. "Do you love me, Cass?" he asked quietly, so quietly she struggled to hear his voice above the crashing music.

"Yes. You know I do."

"Then come with me."

"I'm scared, Jake," she whispered.

"What's to be scared of?" He raised his voice a little and smiled... the smile that normally had her melting from the inside out. "It'll be an adventure."

"I'm not feeling very adventurous." *I'm feeling scared that, if we go to Boston and you really are as fed up with me as you seem to be right now, we'll break up, and I'll be stranded... well, not stranded... Boston isn't an island, but it's not home either.*

He sighed. "What do you want from me, Cass?" he huffed out angrily.

"You know what I want. I want to go home."

"Christ, you sound like a baby..." He moved forward in his seat and looked back down at her. "A fucking selfish baby." And he got up and moved into the crowd, soon disappearing.

Cassie bit back her tears. Even in their worst arguments, he'd never spoken to her like that. He'd never called her names... but then they'd never been arguing on the eve of having to make the actual decision before. Tomorrow they were giving up their apartment, and they were going to leave – either for Boston, or Somers Cove. They'd packed up most of their things already. The only question was where were they going.

Except that wasn't the only question anymore. Because now, Cassie had to ask herself whether they'd be going anywhere together.

Jake

"What's up, man?" Sean's voice calling out from behind him cut into Jake's darkening mood.

"Nothing. I'm outta here."

"What about Cassie?"

Jake hesitated for a moment, then shrugged and strode on through the open front door, dodging the few people on the front lawn, before heading for his Jeep. He didn't glance back, didn't want to see if Cassie was standing watching him – mainly because he knew she wouldn't be.

He slammed the Jeep into drive and took off down the street, knowing, even as he turned the corner onto the main road, that he was abandoning the woman he loved – and he did love her – at a party she'd never wanted to go to, with people she barely knew, and no means of getting back to their apartment, other than calling a cab. He pulled his foot back off the gas. He should go back and get her. Leaving her there on her own was wrong… But if he went back, all they'd do is fight again.

"Fuck it," he said out loud, and smashed his hand down on the steering wheel as he floored the accelerator.

Ten minutes later, he parked up outside Joe's Diner, went inside and ordered a black coffee from Marilyn, who was on the late shift. Although nearly thirty-five, even Marilyn wasn't immune to Jake's good looks and she smiled sweetly at him as she poured his coffee.

"You okay tonight, hun?" she asked.

"Fine," he lied.

"We don't normally see you here this late… or on your own."

"No." He wasn't feeling very talkative. Marilyn gave up making conversation and moved back to the counter.

He was sitting in a booth near the back, away from the other customers – not that there were that many of them. It was gone eleven thirty, after all.

He stared through the misted window, at the haloed lights outside and sighed deeply.

Why couldn't Cassie understand? It really wasn't that difficult…

Ben Hunter, Jake's dad, was well known in Somers Cove. He was always there; always ready to help someone out whenever they needed him. Mending this, fixing that. And if they couldn't afford to pay him that month, well… he'd wait… and wait… and usually wait a bit more.

For as long as Jake could remember, everyone in the town – his dad included – had assumed that Jake would take over Hunter's Construction, the small building and repair business that his dad ran from the office above the family garage.

And nobody, but nobody, had really understood why, when he left high school, Jake had wanted to go to college.

"You don't need to do that," Mrs Adams, the coffee shop owner, had told him. "What do you need with an education when you've got a job ready and waiting for you?"

Jake had tried explaining to her that he wanted to learn construction engineering technology, so he could design and build houses and office blocks, hotels and shopping malls... but he knew he'd lost her halfway through his first sentence.

His dad thought he was going because Cassie was. She was going to study English, which made sense, considering she wanted to be a writer and his dad was happy for them to go together, being as they'd been inseparable since they were six years old. Cassie had always been his best friend. Before she came into his life, he didn't even know such things existed. He had his friends from school, but Cassie was the person he confided in, the person he talked to. He remembered her being there when his mom died. He'd just turned nine and Cassie had been eight, and they'd spent that weekend sitting on the beach, while his dad made arrangements and cried quietly to himself in the bedroom he and his Jake's mom had shared for eleven years. Cassie had held his hand in hers and told him it would all be okay, and he'd believed her. And, eventually, it was – well, Cassie made it hurt less, anyway. So, when they turned eighteen, his dad said he understood that was why Jake was 'going with her' to college.

He took a sip of his cooling coffee and remembered that even Emma, Cassie's friend, who worked for Mrs Adams, had been surprised he was going. That had stung, because Emma had been going to college too – even if she had lasted less than one semester before returning to work in the coffee shop again. It seemed it was fine for everyone else to want to better themselves, but not Jake...

The thought of returning to that suffocating town, the small-town ways and the small-town minds, filled him with dread. He knew Cassie wanted to go back there and she'd told him they should try it, just for the summer, or until he found a job in Boston. Except, he knew that once she got back there, he'd never persuade her to leave… and he'd be stuck there, drowning, forever.

He finished his coffee, paid Marilyn, who winked at him, and left.

When he pulled up at Sean's place again, the party was still in full swing. There were a few more people on the front lawn – he guessed it was getting too hot and crowded inside, and was proved right as soon as he tried to barge his way in. There were even more people here than there had been when he'd left.

He looked over the top of the crowd of heads, trying to see Cassie. She was fairly tall, at around five foot nine, so he should be able to see her, assuming she was standing up, of course. He searched for blonde heads, but there were very few there, and none of them were Cassie. He moved around a little more. She'd been wearing jeans – tight, sexy jeans – and a white camisole top, which showed off her tan, and her soft, soft skin… the skin he liked to kiss, and caress…

"You're back then?" Sean said, coming up behind him and tapping him on the shoulder.

"Yeah. Where's Cass?" he asked. "I can't see her."

"She's gone."

"Gone? What do you mean, gone?"

"Just that, man. She called a cab and took off, about ten minutes or so after you left."

"Where did she go?"

"How the hell do I know?"

"Was she alone?" He was suddenly gripped with fear that she'd left with another guy… but even as he asked the question, Jake wanted to kick himself for even thinking that. Cassie would never do that to him…

"Yeah. She sat outside and waited for the cab and then, when it arrived, she got in and left."

"And you didn't try to stop her?"

"No. Why the fuck would I do that? She seemed pretty mad."

"*She* was mad?" Jake couldn't understand why she hadn't just waited for him. She must've known he'd come back for her. "For fuck's sake." Jake turned and headed back toward the door.

"Where are you going now?" Sean called after him.

"Home." Not that he really wanted to. She was mad… he was mad. It didn't look good for resolving their differences.

Outside, he climbed back into his Jeep yet again and was just starting the engine when a tapping on the window made him jump out of his skin.

Standing on the sidewalk, looking at him, was Alice. She motioned for him to wind down the window, which he did.

"Hey," she said quietly. "You couldn't give me ride home, could you? I don't have enough cash on me for cab fare." She twirled her brown hair between her fingers, her big hazel eyes looking up at him through her long, dark eyelashes.

"Sure, jump in."

"Thanks, Jake. You're a lifesaver." She ran around the front of the Jeep, opened the passenger door, hitched up her already short skirt, and hopped up beside him.

"You live over on Westfield, don't you?"

"Yes. How did you know that?" she asked, smiling.

"Because you live in the same building as Mike and Steve… and I play football with them." It was hardly rocket science.

He pulled away and set off toward Westfield, which was only a ten minute drive away.

"What are your plans for the summer?" Alice asked, trying to make conversation.

"I don't know," Jake replied, trying to avoid it.

"I'm going home," she said.

Alice also lived in Somers Cove, but nowhere near Jake, or Cassie. Her father owned a car dealership on the outskirts of the town and, although they'd all attended the same high school, they'd not really known each other that well. She had hung out with a much bigger, louder crowd… the type of people Cassie tried to avoid.

"Really?"

"Well, I have to see my folks," Alice said. "Just for a few weeks… I'll probably stay until the fall, and then I'll try and get a job."

"Where?"

"Who knows? Maybe Portland… maybe Boston."

"You don't want to stay in Somers Cove then?"

"Hell, no. Why would anyone want to stay there?"

Jake felt a surge of relief. He wasn't alone. There was at least one other person on the planet who didn't think Somers Cove was the best place on earth and who saw the small town for what it was… Stifling.

He pulled up outside Alice's apartment building, putting the car into park and relaxed back into his seat.

"This is kind of you, Jake," Alice said, placing her hand on his leg. "I'm real grateful."

"It's fine," he breathed. What the hell was she playing at?

"You know…" Her voice had dropped to a soft purr. "I've always liked you…"

What was he supposed to say to that? Her hand inched higher up his thigh.

She twisted in her seat, moved her leg to one side and, before he knew it, she was on his lap, straddling him, her skirt hitched up around her hips, revealing black lace panties…

"What the—" Her kiss interrupted his protest, her tongue delving deep into his already open mouth. The steering wheel at her back prevented him from pushing her away, so his only option was to lift her off of him. Just at that moment, she moaned into his mouth, and he became aware of her hands between them, fumbling with his belt, undoing it.

Oh, Christ. She was breathing hard, grinding into him with her hips.

There was nothing for it, if he was going to get rid of her, he'd have to touch her – even if she did misinterpret his intentions. He reached down and put his hands on her ass, then lifted her and dumped her back on her seat.

"What the fuck, Alice?" he said, glaring at her.

"Don't pretend you weren't interested," she murmured, peering up at him. "I could feel you."

"I don't know what you thought you felt, but I'm not interested."

"Oh, really?" She snaked her hand across and touched him… and he let her, just to prove that he wasn't aroused by her display. Not one bit.

"See?" he said. She pulled her hand away again. "Now get out of my car."

Embarrassed, she opened the door and quickly jumped down onto the sidewalk, running away into the building. She hadn't bothered to close the door and Jake leant across and pulled it shut.

He sat there, at the side of the road for a while. Nothing like that had ever happened to him before and he didn't really know what to think. The only girl who'd ever kissed him, or touched him, was Cassie, and he liked it that way. He liked – no, he loved – everything about Cassie and he couldn't imagine his life without her in it… except that meant he might have to face a life in Somers Cove, doing odd jobs and never realizing his own ambitions. He shook his head. He couldn't face it, he really couldn't… and, if he was being honest, he couldn't face Cassie and another argument either. He knew she'd be safely back at their little apartment on the other side of town by now. The inevitable argument could wait a little longer.

He pulled away from the curb, driving around aimlessly for a while. He wanted to forget about Alice, he even wanted to forget about Cassie, but only because he didn't want to think about what they were going to do tomorrow. They had to make a decision about whether they were going home, or going to Boston. They couldn't both win this argument, but losing meant either one of them being unhappy… or breaking up. After six years… well, a lifetime, really. Could they really break up over this?

He thought back over their time together. He remembered when everything between them changed. It had been a warm summer's day, they were both sixteen years old, and they were walking down the lane between his house and hers. His nerves had been jangling as he'd pulled her to one side, beneath the oak tree and asked her if she wanted to be his girlfriend. There was no point in just asking her out on a date, because they spent all their time together anyway, so he'd told her that he didn't want her as just a friend anymore, he wanted more… he wanted her to be his girlfriend. He remembered her reply, accompanied by a shy smile, that she would love to be his girlfriend, but that she would always be his friend. He'd leant in and kissed her then…

Now he *was* getting hard. Just thinking about Cassie could do that to him. Every. Damned. Time. She was like a drug… one he'd always been addicted to, ever since the day she and her mom had moved into the house right down on the beach and his mom had insisted they visit, taking a chocolate cake as a welcome gift. Cassie'd looked at him with those wide, baby blue eyes and asked if he wanted to go swimming with her. He didn't really, because she was a girl and he thought she'd be a bit boring… but his mom had pushed him forward and he'd reluctantly agreed and they'd spent the whole summer together, swimming, playing on the beach, walking, laughing – especially laughing. He smiled and slowly shook his head. Cassie had a way of making everything better. Even the things that you never thought could get better… His mind wandered back again to the day his mom had died. She'd been ill for months… no years. She'd had breast cancer and, at first, she'd seemed to beat it and, for a while, everything had been okay, but it came back and very quickly claimed her. He recalled his dad, sitting him down on the edge of his bed and telling him that he had to be brave, and that his mommy wouldn't be coming home again; and how he'd run straight down the lane to Cassie's house, and found her playing on the porch and how he'd cried when he'd told her, and she'd silently taken his hand led him out onto the beach and sat there with him, watching the sun slowly fall into the ocean… He wondered if he'd loved her, even then.

He turned the car in the direction of their apartment.

He couldn't ask her to move to Boston with him… not when he had nothing to offer. But he could go there himself. He could get a job, find them somewhere to live… and then come back for her. He wondered if she'd accept that as a compromise…

She wanted to live in Somers Cove. He knew that. He just hoped she wanted to live with him more.

By the time he put his key in the lock of their apartment, it was nearly three in the morning. He hadn't realized he'd been driving around for so long. He opened the door quietly, so as not to wake Cassie, and went inside.

It was a small studio apartment, with everything, except the bathroom, in one room. He knew she'd be asleep in their bed in the far corner, curled up facing the wall as usual, so he tiptoed over in the darkness and leant across the bed.

"Hey, baby," he said quietly.

Something was wrong.

Even before he knelt on the mattress, he knew she wasn't there. He couldn't hear her breathing. He flipped around and turned on the lamp on the nightstand. Cassie was nowhere to be seen.

"Cass?" he called out, heading for the bathroom… but the door was open and the room was in darkness. The apartment was completely empty.

His heart racing, pounding in his ears, he went across to the small closet where they kept their clothes, and slowly opened the door to Cassie's side. Even as the hinges creaked, he knew… he knew it would be empty. He stumbled backwards to the bed and held his head in his hands.

What the hell had happened to her?

Well, the answer to that was obvious… she'd left him. She'd gone home. She was done arguing. She wanted one thing; he wanted another. They couldn't agree, so she'd gone.

But why couldn't she wait and tell him? Why just take off like that? They'd always been friends, always been able to tell each other everything… and they'd never argued about anything until they'd tried to work out where they were going to live and discovered they wanted different things from life.

Did she want her own way so much, she wasn't even prepared to sit down and talk it through? Wasn't she even willing to try and find a compromise? Clearly not.

Jake got to his feet and went over to the closet again, opening the door on the other side – the one containing his clothes. Then, grabbing his bag from under the bed, he started to stuff his belongings inside, moving quickly around the room.

Within an hour, everything was packed and he'd loaded his bags and three boxes into his Jeep. It was too early to call Pete – it was still only just after four in the morning – but if he set off now, he'd reach Boston by around seven-thirty. He could get some breakfast and then call his friend, and go around to his place. And then he'd turn off his phone. He had no intention of speaking to anyone, not for a while. Not until he'd calmed down enough to be civil… and he had no idea right now how long that was going to take.

Chapter Two

Cassie

The road was a blur and if she didn't stop crying soon, she'd never make it home; she would become a road traffic statistic. It was a sobering thought and she gulped down the next wave of tears, reached across to the passenger seat, pulled a Kleenex from the half empty box and wiped her nose for the twentieth time.

Gripping the steering wheel a little tighter, she resolved not to cry again… at least until she'd reached Somers Cove. Then she'd cry… maybe for the remainder of the night, and tomorrow, and for the rest of her life.

Her mom's house was in darkness, but that was hardly surprising, considering it was three-thirty in the morning. She'd been as good as her word and hadn't cried again, but she was home now and, sitting in her ten year-old Ford Focus, she sobbed. How could he do this to her? After everything they'd meant to each other for so many years. It was only a fight; she'd have waited, and they could've talked it through. "Oh, God," she sobbed. How could he…?

"Cassie?" Her mom's concerned voice woke her with a start. "How long have you been sitting out here?" She looked up. It was dawn and Kate Reynolds was leaning over, looking into Cassie's car. Despite the early hour, Kate was already up and dressed, her hair neat and tidy. "Dear Lord, you look terrible, child. Get out of that car, right now and come on in the house." Her mom opened the door and Cassie almost fell into her arms. "What on earth has happened to you?" she said, half carrying her daughter up the porch steps and into the house.

Cassie sat on the kitchen chair that her mom pulled out and rested her head on her folded arms in front of her.

After a little while, she felt, rather than saw her mom sit beside her, and smelt fresh coffee close by.

"Talk to me, Cassie." Kate's voice was gentle. "Tell me what's wrong. Why've you been crying?" Cassie raised her head, stared at her mom for moment then, focusing on the mug of coffee in front of her, she picked it up and took a sip.

"It's nothing, mom." Even Cassie wasn't convinced by her lie.

"You gonna stick to that story for long?" her mom asked, frowning at her. "Because it's a Saturday. I've got nothing planned but housework, so we can sit here all day."

"Please, mom…" Cassie got to her feet, swayed slightly and sat back down again.

"You're not well," Kate said. "Sit here and I'll fetch you something to eat."

"I'm not hungry. I just need to sleep."

Kate stood. "Let me help you to your room then."

Cassie didn't argue and allowed her mom to lift her from the chair, and help her down the short, narrow corridor that led from the front of the house – where the large open plan kitchen and living room were – to the bedrooms and bathroom, at the back.

It felt good to lie down on her own bed and, before her mom had even closed the drapes and shut the door, she was fast asleep.

"Your mom called me," Emma said, perching on the edge of Cassie's bed. "She told me you were home. Well, she told me you'd driven through the night and got here sometime in the early hours, and that you'd slept in your car… and that you haven't stopped crying."

Cassie didn't deny any of Emma's speech.

"Wanna talk about it?" Emma asked. She'd obviously come over on her lunch break: her long dark hair was tied behind her head in a loose up-do, and she was wearing her black pants and white blouse – standard 'uniform' at the coffee shop.

Cassie stared up at her friend. She couldn't say that Emma was her 'oldest' friend, or even her 'best' friend, because both of those titles belonged to Jake… or they had done. Even thinking about him made tears well up in her eyes again.

"Hey, Cassie," Emma said, noticing her friend's distress. "What's happened? This isn't like you. Talk to me."

"It's Jake," Cassie muttered.

"What about him?"

"He… he… Oh, God, Emma… he cheated on me…" she wailed and started sobbing loudly again.

"Jake?" Emma was shocked. "Jake Hunter? Are you sure, Cassie. I mean… Jake?"

"We'd been fighting," Cassie explained, trying to compose herself.

"So? Lots of people fight. That doesn't mean he cheated. Tell me what happened."

Cassie took a deep, stuttering breath and sat up on the bed. Emma handed her another Kleenex and she blew her nose, wiped her eyes and took a gulp of the coffee that Emma had brought in with her. "We went to a party, last night," Cassie began. "I didn't want to go, but the guy who was having the party – Sean – he wouldn't take no for an answer. He's one of Jake's friends and he insisted we had to be there. It seemed weird and didn't make sense to me, but Jake went along with it. Oh, God… it was a disaster."

"Why?"

"We've been fighting for weeks, Em. Jake wanted us to move to Boston; I wanted us to come back here, and neither of us was listening to the other. Neither of us was budging. But we were supposed to move out of our apartment today, so we kinda had to make a decision last night. That's why I didn't want to go to the party. I wanted to stay home and talk… Jake said we'd just go for a little while, but a little while became a long while, and before I knew it, it was eleven o'clock and we were arguing again."

"At the party?"

Cassie nodded her head and took another sip of coffee, cradling the cup in her hands.

"He called me a 'fucking selfish baby'." Cassie could hear her voice cracking.

"What an ass."

"And then he stormed out."

"Just like Jake. Losing an argument, so he leaves."

"I know. I thought I'd sit and wait for him…"

"But?" Emma prompted.

"But his friend Sean…"

"What about his friend Sean?" Emma moved a little closer.

"He came on to me. He was making all kinds of suggestions and touching me, and telling me how Jake's always looking at other girls, and he'd only asked us to the party because he liked me so much."

"Creep."

"Exactly. I couldn't hang around there by myself, so I called a cab and left."

"Good for you." Emma nudged into her and gave her a smile.

"I'd only been home about half an hour," Cassie continued, "when my phone rang. I thought it would be Jake, trying to find out where I was, so I answered without checking to see who was calling."

"And?"

"It was Sean. I don't even know how he got my number. Someone else must have given it to him."

"What did he want?"

"He said he had a message from Jake, that Jake had said not to expect him back anytime soon, because he'd gone home with Alice." Cassie bit back her tears this time.

"Alice Hammond?" Cassie nodded. "And you believed this guy?"

"No. But I kinda believed Alice."

"Sorry?" Emma couldn't hide her confusion. "Alice called you too?"

"Yes. About another half-hour later, I suppose… maybe a little longer. I'd just finished up in the bathroom and was getting ready to go to bed. She told me Jake had sex with her in the back of his Jeep…"

Emma sat in silence for a minute. "So, this Sean and Alice both called you. Could they have been together – maybe trying to cause trouble between you guys for some reason?"

"No. Sean was still at the party. I could hear the music in the background. Alice was calling on her landline from her place. She told me Jake had offered her a ride home from the party and had come onto her, and they'd ended up in the back of the Jeep… I stopped her before she could go into too much detail."

"But their stories tallied?"

Cassie nodded her head. "Even down to the times they gave me. The thing is, I still can't believe Jake would do that to me."

"Then why did you leave? Why didn't you stay and have it out with him?"

"I couldn't face him, or another fight. I just wanted to be somewhere I felt safe and, short of being with Jake, coming back here was the only place I could do that."

"So, what are you going to do?"

"I'm gonna call him. I need to hear about it from him."

"You've reached Jake Hunter. Leave me a message and I'll get back to you."

That was the eighth time in less than four hours, since Emma had left, that his phone had gone straight to voicemail. He never turned his phone off. Cassie knew he'd turn it to silent if he didn't want to be interrupted, but he'd always check his messages and call people back, or return their texts.

Cassie didn't want to text him. She didn't want to leave a message either. This was too important for anything that could be misunderstood.

She wanted to hear his voice, listen to an explanation from him, and ideally arrange to meet somewhere so he could tell her what had happened face-to-face. She wanted to be able to look into his eyes and know he was telling the truth.

But first, she just wanted him to take her damn calls…

It was evening now and Kate was preparing pasta bake for dinner.

"I'm just going to look at the ocean," Cassie said quietly, going through the kitchen and out onto the porch.

"Okay, honey. Don't be long."

"I won't."

She walked down the beach and stood on the shore, letting the waves lap over her bare feet. It was still quite warm, but she hugged her arms around herself, wishing she could feel Jake's kisses on her neck, his hands touching her skin… and that she could hear his whispered words. Not just gentle, tender words of love, but his need, his desire, expressed between them, intimately, as only lovers can. Now, as the tears fell down her cheeks and she watched the bright orange sun blur into the horizon, she wondered if she'd ever feel any of that again. Of course she wouldn't… after what he'd done, she couldn't even be sure now that he'd meant any of it in the first place. As she'd listened to his voicemail greeting that final time, it had dawned on her that maybe – just maybe – the reason he wasn't taking any calls was because he was otherwise occupied… with someone else. Perhaps, having slept with Alice, he'd realized what he'd been missing out on all these years.

"It's been ten days, and you still haven't heard from him?" Emma asked. They were sitting in the coffee shop together, talking over hot chocolate – with extra whipped cream and sprinkles.

Cassie shook her head. "No. I've kind of accepted it's over."

Emma nodded, although she didn't look convinced. "What are you going to do?" she asked. "You'll need to look for work, won't you?"

"I've applied for a couple of jobs as a freelance editor," Cassie replied, "and I've been doing some research."

"Really?"

"Yeah… I decided, if I'm ever gonna write a book, I need to look at genres, styles, settings… character creation…"

"And?"

"And it would be great if I could focus on anything for more than ten seconds. My brain seems to have turned to mush."

"Maybe you need a day off. Why don't we do something, just the two—" Cassie's phone rang, interrupting whatever Emma was going to say.

Cassie picked it up from the table and looked at the screen. "Oh, God... it's Jake."

"Answer it then," Emma encouraged.

"I can't." The phone kept ringing, attracting glares from people at nearby tables. She turned down the volume a little.

"Why not?" Emma asked.

"I don't know what to say to him... not now."

The ringing stopped and they waited, staring at Cassie's phone for what seemed like forever... until it beeped, telling her she had a voice message.

"You've got to at least listen to it," Emma urged.

Cassie stared at her friend, then lifted up her phone, connected the call and put it to her ear.

"Hey, Cass." His voice was soft, just like the Jake she remembered. "I saw you'd called a few times. Sorry, I—I turned my phone off. We —we... um... we need to talk." There was a long pause. "I'm so sorry, baby. I screwed up and I really regret what I did and, if you'll just let me explain, I'll make it up to you, Cass, and I'll never do anything to hurt you again, I promise. Call me? Please? I love you."

Cassie let the phone fall from her hand and, as she tried to stand, everything went black.

"Doctor Cooper?" Cassie looked up into the light brown eyes of the town doctor, then glanced around at the white painted walls of his clinic. "How did I get here?"

"Nick Woods carried you," he replied, looking down at her. "He was just ordering his drink, saw you start to fall and made it across the coffee shop in time to catch you." He felt for her pulse. "Feeling better now?"

She nodded her head, wondering how many of the townsfolk would have seen Emma's older brother carrying her across the road from the coffee shop, to the doctor's office. She'd have been willing to bet that by now, even those who hadn't seen it first hand, would have heard about it. "What happened to me?" she asked, trying to sit up.

"Stay where you are for a moment," the doctor said, placing a hand in her shoulder. "I need to have a look at you."

"But I'm fine."

"Oh… really?" He smiled. She'd always liked Doctor Cooper. He'd been the town doctor for as long as she and, pretty much everyone else, could remember. "You think it's normal for a healthy young woman to faint for no reason, do you?"

"I fainted?"

"Yes." His face became more serious. "Can I assume this hasn't happened before then?"

"No, sir." Cassie shook her head.

"Anything been troubling you lately?" he asked.

"I was really sick a while back," Cassie replied. "Jake was too. It must've been a bug, but it took me ages to get over it…"

"Nothing else?"

"No."

He took her blood pressure, and checked her temperature. "We could run some blood tests," he mused. "I don't suppose…" He paused for a moment. "I don't suppose you could be pregnant?"

"Um… No."

"Because you're on birth control?" he asked. Cassie nodded her head, staring up at him.

"And because I had a period a few weeks ago, roughly on time. My next one's due any day now. I've even got sore breasts, just like I normally get just before it starts…"

The doctor smiled at her. "Even so, it's still possible for you to be pregnant."

"How?" Cassie barely heard her own voice, so she wasn't sure the doctor had, until he replied to her.

"You've just told me you were sick last month… well, being sick can make the pill ineffective."

"Okay… but I had a period."

"Did you though? Was it the same as normal?" he asked.

Cassie thought back for a moment. "No. it was a lot lighter," she told him. "And it only lasted a couple of days." She felt clammy and sick. "But the sore breasts…" She clutched at straws.

Doctor Collins shook his head, kindly. "Tender breasts can be an early sign of pregnancy," he said, his voice calm. Now Cassie felt the blood draining from her face and the dizziness returned. "Hey." He moved forward quickly. "Cassie. It's okay."

"No, no it's not," she mumbled.

"Look, why don't we do a pregnancy test before jumping to any conclusions? Then you'll know – one way or the other."

"O-okay," she stammered.

"Are you alright to stand up?" His concern was obvious.

"I'm fine." Despite her words, Cassie didn't feel fine at all and she let him help her to her feet, taking the packet he offered her.

"Take this to the bathroom," he said. "The instructions are on the inside. Bring it back here when you're done."

Cassie sat at the kitchen table in her mom's house, looking at the faces of her mother and Emma.

"You have to tell him," Kate said. "He has a right to know."

"No, he doesn't." Cassie was adamant.

"Emma…" Kate turned to Cassie's friend. "Will you talk some sense into her?"

"I agree with Cassie. I'm sorry, but I don't think Jake deserves to know about this."

Kate looked from one young woman to the other, her mouth slightly open and her blue eyes widening. "Excuse me? That boy – well, young man – is going to become a father sometime around Christmas, and you two have decided for some reason that he doesn't have the right to know about it. Who made either of you two God for the day?"

"Nobody, Mom," Cassie said. "But there's something you don't know."

"Really? Well, enlighten me then."

Cassie looked at Emma and nodded towards her mother. The one thing she couldn't face – especially now – was saying it out loud.

"What Cassie's talking about, Kate, is that Jake and Cassie argued. He ran out on her…"

"Well, that's nothing new. Jake always runs when things aren't going his way."

"Hmm… which makes him perfect father material, don't you think?" Cassie's sarcasm was so out of character, the other two women stared at her for a moment. "It must be the hormones," she murmured, shrugging.

Kate smiled at her daughter. "Get used to them… you've got them for a while yet." She paused, laying her hand gently over Cassie's. "I see where you're coming from, honey, but Jake being a bit unreliable isn't really a good enough reason not to tell him he's gonna be a father. Who knows, this could be the making of him. It could force him to grow up, be more responsible."

"Oh, but that's not the reason," Emma said. "At least it's not all of it… Jake cheated on her. He slept with Alice Hammond the night that Cassie came back here."

Kate turned in her seat and took both of her daughter's hands in hers. "Why didn't you tell me, Cassie?" Her voice was soft, tearful, and Cassie looked at her mother.

"I couldn't face it. I still can't."

"And how do you know he did this?" Kate asked. "It doesn't sound like something Jake would do."

"One of his friends told me," Cassie said. "So did Alice. And Jake left me a message earlier today, making it very clear how guilty he was."

"You do understand, don't you, Kate?" Emma continued. She and Cassie had talked about it on the long, slow walk back from the doctor's office. "Cassie can't trust him… not now."

"Yes… yes, of course I do. Once a cheat, always a cheat. I learned that the hard way."

"Mom?" Cassie twisted in her chair. "What do you mean?"

Kate swallowed hard and took a deep breath. "Your father," she said. "He cheated on me… the night I told him I was pregnant." Cassie couldn't hold in the gasp that formed in her throat, even though she moved her hand to cover her mouth. "He went out and slept with some woman. I don't know who she was… I didn't want to know. He came back and told me about it – to make himself feel better, of course."

"What did you do?" Cassie asked quietly.

"Fool that I was, I forgave him. I was pregnant. I was scared. I was a little younger than you are now. We weren't married and I assumed he'd propose when I told him… How stupid was I?" Kate let go of Cassie's hands, stood up and walked over to the kitchen sink, staring out at the ocean beyond. "I didn't forgive him the second time," she murmured.

"The second time?" Cassie stared at Emma.

"Yes." Kate turned around again, facing the two younger women. "The second time I was about four months pregnant… and I threw him out. Like I say, once a cheat, always a cheat."

Cassie got up and went across to her mom, putting her arms around her.

"What will you do if he calls you again?" Kate asked, patting Cassie gently on the back. "He's called you once, and knowing Jake, he's bound to call back, if you don't phone him."

"I've deleted his contact details from my phone, just so I'm not tempted…"

"Really?"

"Yes, Mom. He can call, but he'll come up as an unknown caller and I'll ignore him. He'll get the message eventually."

Kate hugged Cassie a little tighter. "You honestly had no idea you might be pregnant?" she asked eventually, smiling.

"I'd been sick, Mom. I didn't realize that affected the pill… and I'd had a period, or what I thought was a period. It wasn't."

Emma looked at her, concerned. "That bleeding you had, that you thought was a period… that doesn't mean the baby's in danger or anything, does it?"

Cassie shook her head. "No. I asked Doc Cooper about that and he said it happens sometimes. I should only worry if it keeps happening."

"You'll be just fine," Kate said, sounding upbeat and reassuring. "You've got me, and Emma… and we'll look after you."

Cassie pulled away again, looking down at her mother's face. "I can't stay here, Mom."

Kate's mouth dropped open. "What do you mean?"

"I have to move away."

"But…"

"Jake's dad lives here. How would I keep the baby a secret from Ben? He only lives down the road… Besides, as soon as it was born, half the town would know about it, and they'd start talking. Jake would get to hear sooner or later, wherever he is, and I don't want him having anything to do with me, or my child." Her voice gained in strength as she spoke. "Neither do I want him accusing me of trying to trap him into marriage, or forcing him to stay here, if that's what he felt obligated to do, which I doubt… He made his choice. Now I'm making mine."

"Where will you go?" Kate asked.

"Portland, I think. It's only about an hour and a half's drive, so you and Emma can come and visit me. "

"You've thought this out… already?"

"Not really. But one of the jobs I applied for is there. It's freelance, so I was planning on working from here, if I get the job; but that's where their offices are, so living there would make it even easier."

"And if you don't get the job?"

"There's bound to be another one."

"Where will you live?"

"I've just about got enough money saved for the deposit on a small apartment…"

"I'll help," Kate replied. "I've got a little bit put by."

"No, Mom."

"Yes."

Cassie didn't argue any more. She couldn't afford to.

"When are you going to leave?" Emma asked, tears forming in her eyes.

"The weekend, I think. I can't wait much longer, just in case."

"You think he might come back here looking for you?"

Cassie shrugged. "I don't know," she whispered. She genuinely had no idea what Jake was going to do… not any more.

On Saturday morning, as Kate packed the last of Cassie's belongings into the trunk of her car, and spoke to Frank next door about keeping an eye on the place while they were away, Cassie stood on the shore, looking out at the ocean, one last time.

She wasn't sure if she'd ever be able to come back here again. She'd have to bring her child with her; people would see, they'd notice and word would get back to Ben, and to Jake. She'd have to stay away from her home, from the one place she'd always felt safe… well, apart from in Jake's arms, of course. That had always been the safest place of all to be, until he'd put them around someone else.

Try as she might though – and she had tried – she couldn't hate Jake. She still loved him far too much to hate him. And she'd love their child too… enough for both of them.

Jake

"You're a miserable asshole, you know that, don't you?" Pete glared at him from the other end of the couch.

"Thanks." Jake, sitting cross-legged, picked at the frayed hem of his jeans.

"You've been here for two weeks now and all you've done is eat pizza and mope around."

"That's not true. I've got a job."

"Okay, all you've done is get a job, eat pizza and mope around."

Jake didn't answer. He didn't have an answer, because everything Pete said was true.

"It's Cassie, isn't it?"

Jake shrugged.

"Okay… don't talk about it." Pete got up and went toward the kitchen. "But take a word of advice from a veteran of many a fucked-up relationship." He turned as he reached the door and waited until

Jake looked up. "Go talk to her… because I guarantee you'll regret it if you don't."

Jake was due to start his new job on Monday morning. He'd be working construction on one of the many sites belonging to Eldridge Holdings, renowned in Boston for building executive houses… and when they said 'executive', they really meant 'palatial'. He knew it wasn't what he wanted to do; it wasn't what he was qualified to do, it wasn't even the job he'd interviewed for, but he had to start somewhere and Rich Eldridge, the boss, owner, CEO, or whatever he called himself, had made Jake a proposition: Jake lacked experience… and he needed to prove his work ethic, so Rich had said, if Jake could hold down a construction job, working long, hard hours, for six months, Rich would promote him. He'd let him actually use his degree, and move him off of a building site and into an office, where they both knew he really belonged. Rich, it would seem, had seen something in Jake that no-one else ever had… and Jake wasn't about to let him down.

But first, he needed to take Pete's advice, before he too became a veteran of at least one fucked-up relationship.

So, early on Saturday morning, he loaded an overnight bag onto the back seat of his Jeep and set off for Somers Cove.

It was a three hour drive, which gave him time to think, although that was maybe not a wise move, because he didn't really have anything positive to think about.

To start with, he still couldn't work out why Cassie hadn't returned his calls. He'd left her that first, long message, apologizing for walking out on her at the party. And he'd heard nothing back from her. He'd waited a couple of days and tried again, leaving two more messages… and still nothing. It wasn't like Cassie to hold a grudge. But then it wasn't like Cassie to run away either.

He wondered if she'd forgive him… if, now he'd got a job, she'd agree to moving to Boston with him. He'd even seen a couple of really small apartments he thought they could afford – well he'd seen them on the Internet, anyway. He was lonely without her, he knew that. He missed her company, her voice, her smile, and her laughter, more than anything… even more than he missed her body… and he missed her body so much, his own ached.

Thirty minutes out of Somers Cove, he started to get nervous. What if she wouldn't forgive him? What if she wouldn't even see him? He'd have to try and think of some way of talking her round, winning her back; because he didn't like the idea of driving back to Boston tomorrow on his own. He didn't like that idea at all.

He pulled up outside his dad's garage. Ben was working inside, sanding down a cabinet door. He was wearing ear defenders and goggles, but he looked up and stopped working as soon as he saw Jake's car.

"Hey, son," he called, walking over and brushing off the worst of the sawdust from his clothes. "I was starting to wonder if you were ever gonna come home."

"Yeah… sorry about that."

"No need to apologize. You're here now." Ben put his arm around Jake's shoulders and steered him toward the house. "We were surprised when Cassie came back without you."

Jake knew, without having to ask that 'we' meant 'the town'. He also knew his dad was waiting for an explanation.

"We had a fight," he said simply.

"What about?" Ben opened the door to the kitchen and let Jake go in ahead of him.

"The future." Ben didn't reply. He stood, waiting again. "Cassie and I want different things."

"I see."

"Do you, Dad?"

"No, not really."

"Cassie wanted to move back here…" Jake left the sentence hanging.

"And you didn't?" Ben completed it for him.

"I don't," Jake corrected. "I've got a job."

Ben's face paled noticeably. "Where?" he asked quietly. "Doing what?"

"Working construction, in Boston."

"Construction?" The color came back to Ben's face pretty fast. "Construction?" he repeated. "I don't understand…"

"I didn't want to work here. I never did."

"So why work construction for someone else?"

"Because it's a start, and it's all I know."

Jake looked at his father across the kitchen table. The disappointment in Ben's eyes cut through Jake, but he couldn't let that show.

"And you've come back now to… what? Get Cassie? Take her away from her mom?"

"No. I've come back to talk to Cassie and see if she'll change her mind and come to Boston with me, now that I've got a job."

"Got anywhere to live?" Ben asked, kicking his foot gently against the leg of the table.

"I'm staying with a friend at the moment."

"You don't think Cassie deserves better than that?"

"Yeah, she does," Jake admitted.

"And what if she says 'no'? What if she doesn't wanna go with you?"

"I don't know. I hadn't thought that far ahead."

"No, you never do, Jake." Ben stared at Jake for a long moment, then turned and walked out of the kitchen and into the living room, closing the door softly behind him.

Jake went back out into the yard and past his Jeep, into the lane that led down to the ocean… and Cassie's mom's house.

Now, more than ever, he needed to see Cassie. He needed to talk to her. He needed her to make sense of everything. She was good at that. She'd help him work it out. Hell, she might even help him explain it to Ben, because he was doing a God-awful job of that himself. He may have helped his dad out since he was old enough to pick up a hammer, but that didn't mean he'd choose this life – why couldn't Ben see that?

As he came up to Cassie's mom's house, he noticed neither Kate's nor Cassie's cars were outside. The house looked kinda closed up, too. Usually, when Kate was home, the door would be open, with just the screen closed. Neighbors were always welcome to walk right on in. Today, though, it was shut, as were all the windows.

He knocked anyway, and waited. And he knocked again, calling out to Cassie, just in case.

"Hey… Jake. Didn't know you were home," Frank called from over his fence.

"Yeah, Frank. I just got back."

"They're not there."

Jake walked over to Frank, rather than calling across to him. "Where are they?" He knew Frank would know, purely on the basis that this was Somers Cove.

"I don't know exactly." Jake was shocked. "Kate asked me to watch the place for the weekend."

"So they'll be back tomorrow… or Monday?" Jake hoped it would be tomorrow. He'd stay as late as necessary and drive back to Boston early Monday morning, if he had to.

"Kate will, but judging from all the stuff they were piling into the cars, I'd say Cassie's moved out. I'd say she took just about everything she owned. Didn't look too happy about it, mind…"

Jake wasn't listening anymore. He had stopped the moment Frank had mentioned Cassie moving out. He turned and walked slowly away, back up the lane.

Moved out? No… Frank must've got it wrong. Cassie would never leave Somers Cove. Wild horses couldn't drag her away from this place. Not even a wild horse with Jake on its back could drag her away… he knew that.

Who could he ask? Someone in this damned town had to know the truth.

He got back to his dad's house and jumped into his Jeep. He'd go into town. Emma would know.

He pulled into a vacant parking space outside the coffee shop. It looked busy, but then it would. The summer season was just beginning. The town would soon be livening up. Cassie used to hate this time of year. She much preferred it in the winter, when everything was quieter.

Maybe she hadn't gone away for good… just for the summer, while things were busy. Maybe she'd gone somewhere quiet to write? That was one of her arguments against living in Boston – that it would be too busy, too noisy for her to write. He nodded his head as he climbed out of his car. All he had to do was to get Emma to tell him where Cassie'd gone.

She was serving a young couple who were sitting at an outside table and, when she turned and saw him, her face blanched – it noticeably whitened, turning the same color as her t-shirt. What the hell was that about?

Jake walked over to her.

"Hi," he said.

Emma didn't reply, but nodded her head at him.

"Can we talk?" he asked.

"I'm busy." Jeez, she sounded cold.

"Okay. I'm trying to find Cassie. Can you tell me where she is?"

"No."

"What does that mean?"

"It means I can't tell you where she is."

"You can't tell me, or you won't tell me?" He looked down at her, but she wouldn't raise her face to his. "Which is it, Em?"

"Both. I don't know exactly where she is, and even if I did, I wouldn't tell you."

"Excuse me? Why not? What the hell am I supposed to have done?"

"*Supposed* to? Jake…" She fell silent and sucked in a deep breath. "It's nothing to do with me, and I really am busy." She turned but he grabbed her arm.

"Is she coming back?" he asked.

Emma glared at his hand on her arm until he let go of her.

"No," she whispered. "You've taken everything I had…" She was mad. At him? What was she talking about? "Apart from my brother, Cassie was all I had in this town…" Jake was startled by the tears forming in Emma's eyes. "You know what my parents are like," she sobbed. "Cassie was the only person I could really talk to, apart from Nick, and I don't always wanna talk to my brother. There are some things I'd rather not tell him. But Cassie…" she sobbed. "I've lost my best friend, Jake Hunter. And that's all your fault. Now, go away and leave me alone." And with that she turned her back on him and went into the coffee shop, letting the door close behind her.

Jake stood with his mouth open for a few minutes. He had no idea what Emma was talking about, but he'd never seen her that upset, and he'd known her all his life… Why was this all his fault? Sure, he and Cassie had argued, and he'd left her at the party – which he regretted, because he shouldn't have done it. But Cassie had been the one to run out on him; Cassie had been the one to pack her bags and leave the apartment – and now Somers Cove, it would seem. What was he supposed to have done to make her leave town? He hadn't even been here…

He sighed and turned, walking slowly down Main Street.

None of this made any sense at all. If Cassie didn't want to move to Boston, if she didn't want to be with him anymore, why couldn't she just tell him that? Why did she keep disappearing on him? And why was Emma, Cassie's friend – *his* friend, for that matter – treating him like an outcast.

"Oops… Sorry." He stopped just in time, before colliding with the door to the beauty salon, which had just opened, outwards, spilling two primped, giggling females onto the sidewalk.

"Jake?" He turned.

"Alice." He couldn't hide the dismay in his voice.

"I didn't know you were back," she said, linking arms with him.

"I just got here." Jake tried to pull his arm away, but Alice hung on and turned him.

"You know Rachel, don't you?"

"Um… I don't think—"

"We've never been formally introduced." The other girl's voice had a similar effect on his ears, to that of the sandpaper his father had been using on the cabinet doors. Jake found it hard not to wince.

"I can't stop," he said quickly. "My dad's expecting me back for lunch."

Alice nodded her head. "We'll catch up sometime soon," she called as Jake walked away. He turned back, nodding vaguely and, over Alice's shoulder, he saw Emma, standing outside the coffee shop, her hands on her hips. Even from this distance, he could see the look in her eyes and he knew, without a doubt, she wasn't his friend anymore.

By the time Jake got home, the garage and yard were closed up. His dad clearly didn't want to talk – well, not to Jake anyway.

He let himself into the house and went up to his room. It was still exactly as it had been when he'd left for college. There were posters of football players on the wall, a big closet and chest of drawers, a double bed and, beside that a nightstand, on top of which was a framed photograph of Cassie.

He lay down on the bed and picked up the picture, staring at her. Her face was perfect. She had the purest, softest skin, full kissable lips and baby blue eyes, behind which there was a vulnerability that she only showed to Jake. She'd always told him that even Emma and her mom didn't get to see the real Cassie; the girl who was often scared, wasn't as strong as she pretended to be. To other people, she made out she was in control… but, not with him. He was allowed to see her when her defenses were down. He – and only he – was allowed to help her, to protect her.

Christ, who was he kidding? Cassie didn't need protecting. And Cassie was very much in control. She sure seemed to be running rings around him, anyway.

She loved Somers Cove. It was the thing they'd argued about for months and months… the fact that she didn't want to leave either the town, or her mother. She'd refused to join him in Boston for the simple reason that she wouldn't leave this place. And yet, within two weeks of getting back here, for some reason, she'd upped and left and it would seem she had no intention of coming back, even though – according to Frank, at least – Kate would be back after the weekend.

So much for loving the town.

So much for loving Jake.

He glanced down at the picture once more. Had she ever loved him? Yeah, he thought so. Cass couldn't lie, not like that. And that just made it worse. She loved Somers Cove, she loved Jake, but she'd left them both, and he had no idea why.

The only thing he knew for sure was it was over.

Her image blurred before him.

Fuck it… He wasn't gonna cry.

He jumped up off the bed and walked toward the door, throwing the photograph across the other side of the room. He paused as he heard the frame hit the wall and the glass break.

He stood in the doorway. Should he go and pick up the pieces? Should he take the photograph back to Boston with him? He glanced over his shoulder, looking around the room he'd grown up in… the room he was about to leave forever.

No. He was done with all of it, and he was especially done with Cassie. Anyway, why did he need a photograph to remind him of her? She was etched on the pieces of his heart.

Chapter Three

❦

Present Day

Cassie

"I'm so sorry, Cassie."

She felt the tears falling down her cheeks.

"How… How did it happen, Em?"

"She had a heart attack."

"But there was nothing wrong with her heart. She was only forty-seven…"

Emma didn't reply, and Cassie knew it was because she didn't know what to say.

Cassie changed the phone from one ear to the other so she could reach over and take a Kleenex from the box on the small table beside the couch.

"Ben found her?"

"Yes. She was in the kitchen."

"Is he… is he okay?"

"I don't know. He was real shaken up when he called me. He wasn't sure how to get in touch with you."

"I'll have to come back," Cassie said, wiping her eyes again.

"Yes."

Cassie checked the time on her watch. It was still only just after eight in the morning.

"I'll shower straight away, then I'll have to call my boss and let her know what's happened."

"Is it going to be a problem with her?"

"No. She's really nice. Besides, I work from home anyway. I just need to let her know I'll be out of town for a while. I'll bring my laptop with me, so I don't fall too far behind. I've got to keep writing anyway, I've got deadlines to meet for my own publisher…" The thoughts rushed through Cassie's head, faster than she could speak them.

"Don't push yourself, Cassie. Your mom just died. I'm sure they'll all understand."

"I know. But I don't know how long I'll be there, and I've got my book coming out in a couple of weeks."

"Take a deep breath." Even Cassie could feel the panic rising in her voice, so she knew Emma would hear it too. "Okay now?"

"Yes, thanks. I guess I'll be there by late morning."

"There's no rush. Ben and Doctor Cooper have dealt with everything for now. I'll come over to your mom's place tonight after work," Emma said tearfully.

"Please… I'm gonna need to see you."

"Me too. Call me when you get here, just so I know you're safe."

"Okay. And thanks, Em… It can't have been easy calling me."

"Please don't thank me." Cassie could hear her friend crying.

"I'll see you later."

She ended the call and let the phone drop onto her lap, her head falling into her hands. "Oh, mom," she whispered as the tears fell down her cheeks and dripped onto her robe.

She felt a tugging at her sleeve and looked up. Her daughter, Maddie was kneeling beside her. She pointed to Cassie, then raised her right hand, making her forefinger and thumb into a circle, to signal 'okay', while tilting her head to one side.

"Yes," Cassie said, nodding her head and, at the same time, making her right hand into a fist, holding it about shoulder height and bobbing it up and down. Then she pulled Maddie into a hug. She was far from okay, but she didn't want her precious little girl to see her crying like this. It was going to be hard enough explaining to her that her grandmother was dead…

The journey was difficult. Cassie had showered quickly, while Maddie played on the bathroom floor. This was quite normal; she had to know where Maddie was, and what she was doing, so she'd gotten used to having her in the room, or even in the shower with her. Then she'd made a coffee and sat down at the small kitchen table, and explained, very slowly, signing out each word, that Grandma Kate had died, and that they were going to go to her house – a house Maddie had never even seen – and they'd be staying there for a while. She was fairly sure Maddie understood the words. Cassie had kept it simple and, even at three and a half, Maddie was a bright little girl. What Cassie wasn't so sure of, was whether Maddie really understood what the words actually meant. That would become clearer in the coming days.

Now, as she got closer to her home town, Cassie was becoming more and more nervous. She hadn't set foot in Somers Cove for four long years, not since discovering she was pregnant with Jake's child… with Maddie. She knew he wouldn't be there. Her mom and Emma had visited regularly during her years away and kept her informed of all the town gossip. Jake had only been back once in all that time. He'd reappeared just briefly on the same day that Cassie had left town; they'd missed each other by just a couple of hours. Emma told her that he'd come to the coffee shop and asked after Cassie. He'd seemed upset, and Emma said she'd wondered about calling Cassie and telling her Jake was there, then keeping him at the shop until Cassie could get back, so they could talk… but she'd then seen him flirting with Alice and her friend Rachel outside the beauty salon just a few minutes later. So, it seemed Kate had been right. Once a cheat, always a cheat. He'd left town again later that day and hadn't been seen since. He rarely even contacted Ben, just sending birthday and Christmas cards. He'd definitely washed his hands of Somers Cove, which was what he had always wanted.

Not for the first time in the last four years, she wondered if Jake was happy. She'd never stopped loving him, which meant she wanted him to be happy, no matter where he was, or even who he was with. There was no doubt about it, Jake was far too handsome to be alone for long and, although the thought of him with another woman made her heart ache, she hoped he'd found someone who shared his dreams, who could make him smile… make him laugh… Because if there was one thing she'd always loved about Jake, it was his laugh.

She sighed and checked her rear-view mirror. Maddie was sitting in her car seat, gazing out the window. Every time she looked at her daughter – which was fairly constantly – she was reminded of Jake. Maddie was the image of her father, and Cassie realized she'd have to keep her away from the town gossips while she was in Somers Cove. If Ben found out, he'd be bound to tell Jake…

With that in mind, she pulled into the parking lot of a grocery store in the neighboring town. If they were going to eat over the next few days, she needed to get some supplies. She had no idea how much food her mother had left in the house, and Maddie could be a little fussy. And she couldn't do her grocery shopping in Somers Cove – the store was a focus for tittle-tattle.

Signing to Maddie that they needed to buy some food, she carried her daughter into the store, then held her hand as they walked around and picked up what they needed, paying at the counter.

"What a darling little girl," the server said, winking at Maddie. "Would you like some candy?" she asked.

Cassie signed the question to Maddie, who nodded enthusiastically.

"Oh…" The server's voice took on a sad note. "She's deaf?"

"Yes," Cassie replied. "She was born deaf."

"The poor little thing."

Cassie wanted to ask why, but instead she took the candy the lady was offering to Maddie and handed it down to her daughter, who put her flattened hand on her chin and then moved it forward.

"Is she blowing me a kiss?" the server asked.

"No," Cassie replied, "she's saying thank you."

"How do I say 'you're welcome'," the lady inquired.

"Using baby sign language, it's exactly the same as thank you," Cassie explained. "So kinda like blowing a kiss, but put your fingers on your chin, not your lips."

The server made the sign and Maddie nodded her head, unwrapping the candy and putting it in her mouth.

"She's adorable."

"Yes, she is. Thank you," Cassie replied. She lifted her grocery bags in her arm, took Maddie's hand and exited the store.

She'd just strapped Maddie into her seat when she heard someone calling her name. She turned, closed the car door and her heart flipped.

"Ben," she cried out, tears welling in her eyes. She moved to the back of her car, drawing him away from the rear seats – and Maddie, of whom he still knew nothing. "How are you?" She put her arms around him and let him hug her.

"Pretty awful, truth be told. How about you?"

"Same."

"It's good to see you again, Cassie. I just wish…"

"I know. Me too. What happened, Ben?"

"I… I…" Tears filled his eyes. He tried and failed to blink them away, and they fell onto his cheeks.

"Oh, Ben." Cassie held onto him.

"It should be me comforting you, not the other way around."

"It doesn't matter who comforts who, Ben. We're all gonna need each other over the next few days."

"We sure are." He looked embarrassed now. "I've gotta be going," he mumbled. "I'll catch up with you soon… You take care now."

"It's so odd, being here without her," Cassie said, topping up Emma's wine glass.

"I know. The whole town's shaken up by it. No-one's talked about anything else all day."

"Oh, God. I suppose everyone knows I'm back."

"Yes." Emma took a sip of wine. "How did you get on explaining to Maddie?" She nodded toward the still open bedroom door. Maddie was sound asleep in Cassie's old bed. Cassie would be sleeping in there too a little later on – at least she'd be trying to anyway – there was no way she could sleep in her mother's bedroom. It was filled with happy memories… memories Cassie wasn't ready to face yet.

"I don't know," Cassie answered honestly. "It's not something I thought I'd have to sign to her at this age."

"Did she understand?"

"I think so. But she didn't seem sad at all, so I don't know for sure."

"Maybe it'll hit her later."

"Maybe… but then she's only three. The concept of death probably doesn't mean much. She'll probably only notice when Grandma Kate hasn't been to stay for a while. Right now, this just seems like a vacation by the beach. She's got no idea this was ever her grandmother's house."

Emma looked at Cassie. "And that bothers you, doesn't it?"

Cassie nodded. "It does, now I'm back here… I feel I cheated both of them."

"How?"

"They could have had so much fun here together. Mom loved this place as much as I do. Maddie could have loved it too."

"Are you saying you wish you'd stayed?"

"No. I couldn't have stayed, but I wish we'd found a way to visit. I wish I'd let them be together here. Mom would've loved that. And you should've seen Maddie's face when we got here. She took one look at the ocean and… she just beamed with excitement. It was beautiful, Em."

"*She's* beautiful."

"She is. She's just like her father."

Emma didn't reply.

Eventually she said, "You can still come visit though, can't you? You can keep the house and come up here on the weekends…"

"No, Em, I can't do that. I'm going to have to sell it."

"Seriously?"

Cassie nodded her head, then looked slowly around the old kitchen. "It needs work though, doesn't it?"

"Yes. It's strange; your mom lived here for years and it looked just fine, but now she's gone…"

"You can see all the faults, can't you? The broken cabinets, the leaking roof, the peeling paint… I could go on, but…" Cassie felt the lump forming in her throat yet again.

Emma reached across the table and took her hand.

"I know," she said. "The soul's gone out of the place, hasn't it?"

"She was the soul," Cassie whispered.

"Is that why you want to sell?"

"No… I don't *want* to sell. If I could, I'd keep the house, but I can't. I can't afford the luxury of a weekend house… and I could do so much with the money."

"So, are you gonna fix this place up, or sell it as it is?"

"I don't know." Cassie looked around again. "What do you think?"

"Well, you'd get a better price if you fixed it up a little. I guess a lot of it is cosmetic, really. Okay, the kitchen and bathroom have seen better days, but if you gave the whole place a coat of paint, got the roof mended, sorted out the garage and the porch… that would probably be enough."

"And how am I going to do all that?"

"Ask Ben to help," Emma said quickly.

"How can I? He knows nothing about Maddie. If I have him working here every day, he'll see her. I can't shut her in a closet, Em."

"I'm not suggesting you do."

"What then?" Cassie asked.

"I'm suggesting you tell him."

"About Maddie?"

Emma nodded. "Yes. You know your mom always wanted you to… Maybe now's your chance. He's her granddaddy, Cassie." Emma took a deep breath. "You say you regret not bringing Maddie back here, not letting her and your mom share this place… well, this is your chance to let Ben have that."

Cassie stared at her friend. Emma had unwittingly struck a raw nerve that had grated on Cassie since she'd left town. She'd never been happy about lying to Ben. It was only her fear of him telling Jake that forced her to keep the secret, and demand that same secrecy from her mom and Emma, too. "What if he tells Jake?"

"Explain. Tell him why you've kept Maddie from Jake. Ben's a good man. He'll understand."

"And if he doesn't?"

Emma sighed. "Jake and Ben don't speak, Cassie. I can't see why Ben would suddenly contact him after all these years. You've gotta remember, Jake ran out on Ben too. He just left that afternoon while Ben was out repairing the guttering at Mrs Shinfield's place. He got home to find Jake gone – no note, no message, nothing. He thinks Jake's just as unreliable as you do. I seriously doubt he's gonna put Jake before Maddie, especially when he knows all about her. He'll understand that she needs constancy in her life… and Jake is the opposite of constant."

Emma left at around ten-thirty, returning to her apartment above the coffee shop, which she now managed.

Cassie sat out on the porch, the door open, the screen closed – just like it had been when her mom was alive… so, just yesterday, and the day before… and the day before that. Days when Cassie could've been here, spending time with her mom, sharing her daughter with her, giving Maddie the benefit of her mother's wisdom and kindness.

She looked around the well-kept garden, just about visible in the light from the kitchen window, and smiled.

"Oh, mom…" she whispered. Her mother had tended to her flowers, kept the lawn immaculate, and let the house fall apart.

She got up and walked down the steps, looking out at the moon shining across the ocean. God, she loved it here, and she really wished she could keep the house, but she couldn't. It just wasn't possible.

But she could spend a few weeks here, fixing things up, getting the place as good as she could, so she could sell it and, just maybe, make enough to buy a place for herself and Maddie in Portland, so she wouldn't have to worry about making the rent anymore.

She smiled. She had a feeling her mom would like that.

Jake

He looked in both directions and pulled out into the traffic. He was pleased it was still early in May. The Saturday morning traffic was light… well, light compared to how it would be in a few weeks when the tourists started flocking to the coast.

Jake recalled the last time he'd gone home, almost exactly four years ago. Hell, had it really been that long? Like he didn't know… of course it had been that long. He knew the exact date. May 24th. He'd never forget it. It was the day his heart broke, and if he was being completely honest with himself, it had never completely mended. He cleared his throat. He wasn't going to dwell on that, not this weekend. This was going to be a good weekend… at least he hoped it was.

Although he'd not gone back home in four years, he had driven quite a large part of this journey several times in the past six months and each time he'd gotten to roughly twenty miles down the coast from Somers Cove, and then turned off to the plot of land his client had acquired. He'd had meetings there, gone over plans and sketches, discussed materials, layouts, designs and schedules. He'd spent hours… days… weeks working on the project from his office in Boston. This was a first for Eldridge Holdings. This wasn't an executive home. This was going to be a luxurious, high-class hotel. The owner – Mark Gardner – was insisting that his company's name be kept out of it until the opening. Gardner's Hotels had never built a property from scratch before, so this was a new venture for them too. If it didn't go to plan, he was prepared to lose money, but not his company's reputation – it was a reputation his father had spent years building and Mark was wary of risking it. Jake didn't plan on Mark losing anything. He liked the guy… in fact, they were friends. Nothing was going to go wrong. He'd make damned sure of it.

He had no intention of letting Mark down – or Rich for that matter. Rich had put his faith in Jake, and that was a two way street as far as Jake was concerned.

His boss had been as good as his word and, after six months of hard, slogging graft, Rich had promoted him, given him his own office and his first project to oversee and, when Jake had brought it in under budget and ahead of schedule, Rich had promoted him again... and again, until just before last Christmas, Jake had finally put forward his proposal to Rich, that they should branch out into corporate construction. Jake explained his idea for a hotel, built out of sustainable materials, on a plot of land he'd already found, not far from where he grew up.

Just as he had when Jake had first joined the company, Rich set him a target.

"Bring the project in and I'll give you free reign to run it... and the whole department. No interference."

"What department?" Jake asked, dumbfounded.

"The corporate construction department you're gonna be running..."

At twenty-six, Jake knew he'd be the youngest Head of Department in the company... and that was his next target. He smiled to himself at the prospect. He hadn't failed to realize any of his targets, or ambitions yet.

Well... as long as you didn't count Cassie.

Did Cassie count as an ambition? No, not really. She counted as a wish... a hope. Cassie had been a need, a desire, and a deep, deep longing. But now she was also just a memory. A beautiful, lost memory.

Jake shook his head. He wasn't going to think about Cassie – well, not much anyway. Being back home was bound to remind him of her, but this weekend wasn't about her, or him, for that matter. It was about his dad. Because he was going home to see his dad, for the first time in four years.

He felt bad about the way things had been left between them; about running out on him, without even an explanation.

Now, he was going home to tell him about the hotel. This project was going to give him the chance to stand back, when it was all completed, and say 'I did that'. And that was what he'd always set out to do. That was what he'd wanted when he broke away from Somers Cove... the chance to build something and then to say '*I* did that'. He really hoped he could get his dad to understand, to see how much that meant to him. He hoped more than anything that his dad accepted what he had to say – which he knew would have to start with a big apology on his part – because in three weeks' time at the beginning of June, they'd be breaking ground on the new site and Jake would be living up there for the whole summer. This project was too important to risk leaving it in someone else's hands, so Jake planned on overseeing it personally… every step of the way. He'd travel back to Boston when he had to, but from June to at least the beginning of September, when the main structure was due to be completed, he was going to be based permanently around Somers Cove. Of course, he could rent somewhere nearby, but he wanted to ask his dad if he could stay at home; if they could put the last four years behind them and be friends again.

He knew his dad's house wasn't really his home anymore – that was a one bedroom apartment in the Back Bay area of Boston, that he'd worked damned hard and saved damned hard to buy – but his dad's place would always be home in his heart, because it was where his fondest memories were.

He had no idea how Ben would react to seeing him; their exchanged birthday and Christmas cards were brief and to the point. They contained no news, nor even much sentiment, just the necessary greeting… and he knew that was his fault and no-one else's. He had a lot of ground to make up, lot of apologizing to do… and a lot of fences to mend. He just wanted the chance.

He turned his black BMW into Main Street, cruising along the shop-lined road. Nothing changed here, that was for sure. It was as though he'd only left yesterday. The shops all looked the same; a few people were sitting at tables outside the coffee shop, soaking up the lunchtime sun and, a couple of doors down, Raine's Flower Shop had the usual display of bouquets, plants, pots and garden ornaments spilling onto the sidewalk. Jake slowed down… *Wait a second*. He almost came to a stop. Now *that* was different. He smiled and nodded his head a little absently. Next door to Doc Cooper's surgery was Tom Allen's office, where Kate, Cassie's mom, worked as a secretary. The sign displayed above the door, which had always read, 'Tom Allen, Attorney at Law', had been taken down and replaced with one which read 'Allen and Woods, Attorneys at Law'. Nick had made partner. Jake was pleased for him; he still didn't understand why someone like Nick had ever returned to Somers Cove, or chosen to practice law here, when he could've done so much better for himself in Boston, but he was pleased he'd got his name above the door.

He indicated right between the boat yard and the realtor's office, and turned into the long, long lane that led down to his dad's place... and the ocean beyond. The ocean – and Cassie's mom's house.

Cassie. Memories of her were going to be everywhere. That much was obvious, being as he'd spent pretty much every waking minute of his time in this town with her – and quite a few sleeping ones too – right from the age of six to the age of twenty-two, when he'd fucked the whole thing up, by behaving like a six year old. Actually, he hadn't even behaved that badly toward Cassie when he was six.

As he pulled up outside his dad's house, he wondered where she was and what she was doing. He wondered whether she'd ever come back to Somers Cove, or whether she'd made a life somewhere else... He'd done this quite a lot over the last four years, although to begin with, when he'd got back to Boston four years ago, he'd tried not to think about her at all. He was too mad with her for leaving town to think about her, but after a week or so, the anger faded to a dull, aching hurt, as he realized it was his fault, not hers. He'd run out on her at the party, just like he always did when he wasn't getting his own way; he'd been juvenile, inconsiderate, and for the first time in their whole friendship, he'd been rude. He'd hurt her; he'd been able to see it in her face. She'd trusted him to never hurt her, and he had. He'd gone too far. At that point, the guilt had kicked in. And then, a while later, he'd started to wonder where she'd disappeared to, whether she was okay and what she was doing... and then, who she was doing it with. That thought had tortured him for ages. The idea of another man kissing her, touching her, making love to her – it didn't sit well with him, and for several months, he'd really struggled with that. Then, he'd won his first promotion at work, and to celebrate, Pete had taken him out to a bar, where he'd met Lorna. She was pretty, kind, fun… and she was the first woman he'd slept with who wasn't Cassie. He could still remember the look on her face when he broke up with her after a couple of months. She'd asked him why and he'd made up something about work and not having time for dating since his promotion. He'd known she hadn't really believed him, but it seemed kinder to say that than to tell her the real reason, which was simply that she wasn't Cassie. Still, four years was a long time, and although Lorna may have been the first, she hadn't been the last. He'd had a few girlfriends, but no-one serious… because they all shared the same problem. None of them would ever be Cassie.

The thought of Cass with another man filtered back into his mind. He didn't doubt for one second that she would be with another guy. Someone as beautiful as Cassie wouldn't have been single for long and he fully expected she'd have settled down somewhere quiet, and probably got married and had a couple of kids by now. He let out a half laugh as he climbed out of the car. Knowing Cassie, which he did, she'd have insisted on doing things the 'right' way. She'd have wanted to get married and then have kids, not the other way around… and she'd certainly never have been a single mom. He almost wanted to laugh out loud at the thought of her potential reaction to that idea, remembering her paranoia about getting pregnant when they were together.

He had to try and stop thinking back to them being together. They weren't anymore, and they wouldn't be again. As much as he regretted losing her, so long as she was happy, that was fine with him. Well, it was as good as it was gonna get, anyway.

One of the other things he was hoping for from coming up here for the summer was that he might just be able to lay Cassie's ghost to rest. He was desperately lonely… and he knew it was about time he admitted it to himself. The temporary relationships he had were fine, but he missed having someone special; someone in his corner, who'd take his side, listen when he needed to talk, let him help them, let him support them; someone he could share his life with. If he could just put Cassie behind him, he might be able to stop comparing every woman he met with her, and finding them always wanting. He might even be able to let himself love again.

As he opened the rear door to get his bag, his phone rang and he pulled it from the pocket of his jeans, feeling his heart sink as he checked the name on the screen.

It was Erica.

He let it ring out and replaced his phone in his pocket. He wasn't in the mood for Erica at the moment. He'd only spoken to her last night, and he'd told her then, for about the hundredth time, that he wasn't interested in her… he'd never be interested in her. Hell, if she was the last woman on earth, he'd still look the other way.

It wasn't that there was anything really wrong with Erica, except that she was annoying, and clingy and intense. She had no sense of humor, took everything at face value and had spent the last four years making Jake's life a misery. Well, that might be a slight exaggeration. She'd been away at college for a lot of that time, so it had only been the vacations that had been miserable. But she'd been back in Boston for the last year… a truly awful year. She worked just down the hall from Jake and used any excuse to come into his office, interrupting meetings and phone calls to ask mundane questions that almost anyone else in the building could answer. She touched him, simpered over him and generally behaved inappropriately around him. That was one reason he was relieved to be spending the summer away from the office… it also meant he'd be away from Erica. And hopefully in that time, she'd find someone else to fantasize over.

His phone beeped, telling him he had a voicemail. He pulled it out and let the message play.

"Hey, Jake," Erica's voice had a low hum. "I just wanted to catch up. Hope you're okay. Maybe you can call me back and… um… let me know if you'll be back in the office in time for the meeting on Wednesday afternoon." There was a noticeable pause. "Anyway, I hope you have a good weekend. Bye." The line went dead.

Jake deleted the message. It had been a feeble excuse to call him. She knew he'd be back in the office on Wednesday. She'd been there when he'd discussed it with Rich. And she'd made sure to be included on the meeting, even though it really had nothing to do with her. But, as Jake was learning damn fast, Rich could never refuse his only daughter anything…

He looked around the yard. It was closed up, which wasn't that surprising. His dad was often out on Saturdays, doing odd jobs around the town. Jake had always helped out on Saturday mornings, learning the basics, picking up tricks of the trade from his dad. They were good days… Jake still had his key, so he let himself in, dropped off his bag and locked the door again.

He'd take a walk down to the beach… Okay, so he knew that meant walking right by the beach house – Cassie's mom's house. And he also knew that meant he'd probably see Kate, but it had been four years. He was sure they could be civil to each other. He hadn't seen the view from there in years… and he needed to.

Chapter Four

Cassie

Cassie dipped the paintbrush into the tin again. "I'm still not sure about this color, Ben," she called out. He came around the corner of the house, wiping his hands on a rag.

"It works, Cassie. Just trust me on this."

"It's such a pale blue, though; we're not doing the whole house this color, are we? It's almost white."

"No, the rest of the house is gonna be the slightly darker blue I showed you yesterday."

"Oh yes, I'd forgotten about that. Sorry."

"That's okay. You've got a lot on your mind." Cassie crouched down and applied the paint to the railing, trying to forget the impending finality of Kate's funeral on Monday.

"I really appreciate you giving up your Saturday, Ben," she said, to distract herself.

"I told you I'd help out… I meant it," he replied. "Besides, if it means I get to spend more time with you and Maddie, I'll happily spend every spare hour down here." He smiled at Cassie as she looked up at him and then, seemingly embarrassed by his own words and maybe the memories they were evoking, he hurried back around the side of the house again.

Cassie sighed and turned to check on Maddie, who was sitting in the rocking chair near the front door, playing with her dolls… safe and sound. Sitting back on her ankles, Cassie recalled the whirlwind of the last few days.

Having decided to fix up the house, she'd had to speak to Ben and ask for his help, and tell him about Maddie at the same time. Although the thought of it filled her with dread, she had known it was the right thing to do, so on the next afternoon after her arrival, she'd called Emma at work and asked her to sit with Maddie. Unusually, Mrs Adams was there, so Emma could finish work early and agreed to come straight over, and Cassie had taken the short, ten minute walk down the lane to Ben's house.

He'd welcomed her quietly and they'd sat in his kitchen, which hadn't changed since Cassie and Jake used to sit there after school, drinking milk and eating the cookies her mom used to bake and drop in to Ben every couple of days – "so that Jake can have something home made, not shop bought," as Kate used to say.

"I—I need to talk to you," Cassie had said, floundering over her words.

"Would this be about Maddie?" Ben asked, his voice barely audible.

"You—you know about her?" Cassie was astounded. Ben nodded. "How?" she asked, fear coursing through her.

He hadn't answered straight away, but instead got up and went into the living room, returning a minute later with a small box, around the size of a shoe box, but flatter. He placed it on the table between them and opened it. Inside were dozens of photographs of Maddie, all identical to the ones Cassie used to send her mom by e-mail every few weeks.

"She told you?" Cassie had been unable to hide her disappointment.

"Don't blame her," Ben said, his voice a little louder now. "There's something I need to talk to you about too." He'd nodded toward the box. "And then this'll make more sense."

Cassie stared at him, but didn't reply.

"Your mom…" Ben began, then stopped, swallowing hard, his eyes filling with tears. "Your mom and I," he tried again, "we'd been friends for years."

"I know."

"She helped me so much when Amy died. I don't know how I'd have gotten through that without her... She cooked, cleaned, washed, ironed, mended... and she listened. Man, did she listen." He looked out the kitchen window into the yard for a moment, evidently gathering his thoughts.

"She was good at that," Cassie whispered.

"She was." Ben took a deep breath, turning back to her. "When you and Jake left, we both found it real hard. We turned to each other, and... well, we became more than friends."

Cassie stared at him. "You mean, you and my mom were..."

"We were lovers, Cassie," Ben had said outright. "We'd become close over the years and, if I'm honest, I'd wanted more than friendship from your mom for a while, but it wasn't until the night she came back from settling you into your apartment in Portland that she came to me. She was distraught. She told me that leaving you there all by yourself was the hardest thing she'd ever done. She said she couldn't face being on her own..." He'd left the sentence hanging and Cassie knew he was remembering that night.

They'd sat in silence for a moment or two before Cassie spoke. "I didn't realize," she murmured. "I never thought about her being lonely. I thought it was just me..." She stopped herself before she said too much. "She was always so busy..."

"It's one thing to be occupied, it's something else to come home to an empty house every night."

"Did you live together?"

"In this town? You've gotta be kidding." He managed a slight smile. "Who knows? In time, we might've moved in together. Hell, I asked her often enough... but Kate... well, she was reluctant."

"Why?"

"She was worried about how you and Jake would feel about it."

Cassie blinked a few times. "I can't speak for Jake," she said quietly, "but I think it would have been wonderful."

Ben smiled. "I told her that..." His voice tailed away to silence.

"So, how did you find out about Maddie?" Cassie asked eventually.

"She told me the day she got back here after Maddie was born," he replied.

"She kept it a secret all through my pregnancy? Even though you were… together?"

He nodded his head. "Yeah. I knew nothing about it. And then, out of the blue, she got the phone call from the hospital in Portland, and she took off. We'd had some bad winds the night before and I was out fixing the fences at Hal Watson's place, even though it was a Sunday… It needed doing. She left a message on my phone, just saying she had to go see you and she'd be back as soon as she could… and then she was gone… for nearly two weeks. Scared the hell out of me, that did. Every time I called, she'd make some excuse about why she couldn't come back yet. I knew she was lying, and I assumed she didn't want to be with me anymore. We hadn't been together that long. I guessed she was having second thoughts." He shook his head, remembering. "That was a pretty awful couple of weeks."

Cassie smiled, just a little. "We weren't having a whale of a time ourselves," she said.

"No. I can imagine." He paused. "Anyway, when she got back, she came straight round to see me. I told her I knew she'd been lying, and asked her outright what was going on. I think she could tell how scared I was of losing her, so she sat down, right where you are now and told me where she'd been… and why."

Cassie frowned. "But I'd asked her not to tell anyone… and especially not you."

"I know. But, like I said, she could see that not knowing where she'd been was tearing me up. And she hated lying to me, she really hated it. You didn't know it, but you put her between a rock and a hard place, Cassie." It was Ben's turn to look a little disapproving. "It wasn't an easy decision for her to make." He'd closed his eyes, remembering, and when he opened them again, Cassie could see they'd darkened a shade. "That was the first and last time your mom and I fought," he murmured. "I was mad as hell at her… and you."

"It wasn't her fault."

"I know…"

"I asked her – and Emma – to keep my secret."

Ben had reached across the table and taken Cassie's hand in his. "I understand that," he said gently. "I didn't to begin with, and I gave your mom a hard time. But once she'd explained why you didn't want Jake to know; once she'd told me what he'd done, I agreed to keep the secret too."

Cassie stared at him. "You mean, you've never told him?"

"We don't talk, Cassie. And even if we did, I don't think I'd tell him." He was echoing Emma's words. "He's an unreliable kid… well, I guess he's a man now, although whether he acts like a man, who knows. But he's selfish… always was and probably always will be. Maddie needs someone better than Jake."

Cassie swallowed back her tears. "Thank you," she muttered.

He'd let go of her hand. "Don't thank me," he whispered. "I may have agreed to keep your secret and Jake may be an unreliable, selfish young ass, but this is not something that sits easy with me. He's still my son, Cassie." They stared at each other. "Now…" He sat upright, squaring his shoulders. "Let's talk about this house…"

And so they'd talked, over coffee, for nearly an hour. Cassie explained her plan to stay for a few weeks, fix up the house and sell it. He'd offered to help as much as he could, starting with fixing the garage – which was the biggest job of all, being as it was all but disintegrating.

As she was leaving, he'd told her he wanted to help with Maddie too. He didn't want to be a stranger to his granddaughter.

"Would you like to meet her?" Cassie offered.

"She's here with you?"

"Of course." Cassie smiled. "We're never apart."

"I—I wasn't sure if you had someone… a man in your life that you might've left her with."

"I don't leave Maddie with anyone, except Emma… and… mom." Cassie swallowed down her tears.

"We're gonna miss her, aren't we?" Ben whispered. Cassie nodded. "So where's my granddaughter now?"

"Back at the house, with Emma."

"Then I'd love to meet her, if that's okay?"

They'd walked together, back to Kate's house, where Maddie and Emma were sitting together on the front porch. On the way, Cassie had taught him how to sign 'hello' but, when he saw her, he didn't say or sign a word. He just picked her up and held her in his arms, tears streaming down his face.

Early the next morning, Cassie had phoned her boss in Portland and explained she'd be staying in Somers Cove for a few weeks.

"I can't say how long I'll be here for yet," she explained.

"That's fine," Veronica replied. "You know it makes no difference to me where you are. And I've already contacted the two authors you're working with at the moment and told them there'll be a delay in getting the next edits back to them, because of what's happened. You don't need to worry about anything for a couple of weeks at least."

"That's really kind of you, Veronica. I've got so much to do, what with the funeral, and the house, but I'll still get the work done."

"I know you will. Let me know if there's anything I can do…" The kindness in Veronica's voice was almost her undoing. "And don't forget to call Teresa."

"That's the next job on my list," Cassie replied, swallowing down her tears and contemplating the call to her own publisher, in New York.

Teresa *had* made Cassie cry, but for a completely different reason. She'd tried – and failed – to sound sympathetic, and then explained that they were keen, despite her 'personal problems', as she put it, that Cassie shouldn't fall behind. Her first book was due out in two weeks, with the second part of the series following close behind. The third part was still going through its last edits, which Cassie would need to get back to them as quickly as possible, and then the manuscript for part four was due with them soon too. Teresa pointed out that they'd received such good pre-release reviews, they couldn't afford to lose momentum. Cassie could feel the pressure, like a physical force, bearing down on the top of her head.

She'd completed the edit on the third part of the series already and was just going through it again, checking for errors, and she only had a few more chapters to write on the fourth story. She wasn't sure she was in the best frame of mind for doing that kind of writing, but there was nothing for it, she'd just have to knuckle down and work in the evenings, once Maddie had gone to bed. But then she was used to that… It gave her less time to think anyway.

Then later on, Ben had arrived in his truck, which was loaded with pots of paint, wood, roof tiles and building materials.

"I can't afford all of this," Cassie had said. She'd only received a small advance for her books, being an unknown author, and she was reluctant to spend it, especially since she knew the publisher could ask for it back if she didn't sell enough books.

"I got everything at trade prices," Ben explained. "Besides, I'm not charging you."

"You can't give me all of this." Cassie waved her arms expansively as Ben started to unload the truck.

He turned to her, his hands on his hips. "How long did you know Jake?" he asked.

"Sixteen years," she replied softly, thinking about the last four years without him. "Why?"

"Ever known him back down on anything?"

Cassie shook her head.

"Well, he got that from me… so it's probably best if you just accept it, and maybe give me a hand unloading this lot."

She stepped forward and lifted down a large pot of very pale blue paint. "Thank you," she whispered, blinking back tears, yet again.

"You're welcome, Cassie."

Ben had stayed for dinner. In fact he'd stayed until Maddie had gone to bed, and then he'd sat out on the porch with Cassie and they'd discussed the plans for the funeral, until it became too much for both of them.

This morning, he'd arrived early again. Being Saturday, he had the whole day free. It was a warm, sunny day and, although Ben had intended to get started on the garage, he'd changed his mind and decided to fix some of the broken roof tiles first. The weather forecast said they were due to get some rain in the middle of next week. There was a really bad leak above the bathroom that needed work, so he said he'd get that done, and maybe deal with the garage next weekend.

Cassie, meanwhile, had decided she could paint the railing around the porch. She heard Ben climbing the ladder at the back of the house, and then his footsteps above her on the roof.

"You take care up there," she called.

"I do this every day," he called back.

Cassie smiled. It was good to have some company… someone to talk to. She checked on Maddie again. The little girl was still playing happily.

Cassie stopped, mid-stroke, her paintbrush paused in mid air. She could have sworn she heard footsteps approaching down the lane. She stood, wondering who could be calling; hoping it wouldn't be one of the neighbours come to pay their respects. She knew they meant well, but whatever they said, she'd only get upset… and then they'd get upset… and who would that benefit? The footsteps got closer. It couldn't be a tourist. This small section of the beach, around to the cove, was private, and a big sign at the end of the lane made that very clear. Besides, the lane was too long to really walk down; most people drove… so whoever it was had to have come from one of the nearby houses. She rested her paintbrush on the rim of the tin and stood at the top of the steps.

She saw him maybe a second or two before he saw her. Those couple of seconds were enough for her heart to stop beating, for her whole world to stop turning.

Before he could even focus on her, before he could open his mouth to speak, she turned, grabbed Maddie and fled into the house.

Jake

The walk down the lane normally took no longer than ten minutes, but Jake was taking it slow today. His hands in his pockets, he was enjoying the shade from the warm sun... but he was also reliving so many memories. So much of his past was centered around this lane and the house at the end of it.

Every day, after school, he and Cassie would stop off at his place for milk and cookies – baked by Kate – and then once they'd done their homework, he'd walk her back to her house. He stopped, staring at the gnarled old oak tree off to the left of the lane, before wandering across and running his hand over the rough bark. This was where they'd shared their first kiss. Even now, he could still remember the fear of getting it wrong, of losing her friendship in asking her for more – which was why he'd waited so long to ask her to be his girlfriend in the first place. He could also remember her soft lips, how she'd opened up to him, let his tongue explore her mouth, and responded gently with her own. He looked up through the green leaves to the blue sky beyond. God, could she kiss...

He shook his head and carried on down the lane until the ocean came into view, thinking now about the first time they'd made love. It had been during the summer break at the end of their freshman year and they'd been trying for so long not to have sex... until suddenly, neither of them could see a reason for their restraint. They often spent the long summer evenings on the beach, in the little cove just beyond Kate's house and that night, lying on the soft blanket, they did all the same things as usual... He'd touched her, tasted her, made her come on his tongue; she'd used her hands on him, and then they'd just kind of looked at each other and Cassie had lain down, staring up at him, an expression of such longing in her eyes...

Jake laughed inwardly, remembering how Cassie had panicked right at the last minute, because he didn't have a condom. He explained he didn't need one... Cassie was on birth control, so it was perfectly safe. Even then, she'd been worried. He'd reassured her everything would be fine and, eventually, she'd calmed down and he'd made love to her. It had been magical… no, it had been better than that. And it had gone on getting better over the years as they'd learned more about each other.

He took a deep breath. There was no point in looking back. No point in dwelling on all the 'what ifs' and 'if onlys'. And definitely no point in thinking that he'd never had it that good with anyone since. Cassie would have moved on. Again the thought made him uneasy, but he tried to face it. He was happy, wasn't he? He had a good life – just what he'd always wanted. Well, almost…

He was nearly at the beach and turned the final corner, the front garden of Kate's house coming into view. He fully expected to see her out there, tending her flowers. He half expected her to be angry with him and, although she was a fair minded woman, he was prepared to take whatever she wanted to throw at him. He deserved it, after all…

The garden was empty. There was no sign of Kate. He kept going, looking along the porch… And then his heart stopped. Surely, that couldn't be… Cassie?

He didn't have time open his mouth, let alone say her name. She turned, grabbed a little girl from the rocking chair by the door, and bolted inside the house.

What the hell? Why would she do that? He'd expected her to be married with kids by now… Okay, he hadn't expected to run into her this weekend, but with her mom living here and his dad living just up the road, it was inevitable at some point… So why would she react like that?

He stood still, running his fingers through his thick, dark hair. She'd definitely seen him. And he'd seen enough of her to realize how beautiful she still was, especially wearing those cut-off denim shorts and that skimpy gray top. Her hair was as long as ever, although she'd braided it loosely, and left a few strands hanging down the sides of her face. That always made her look real sexy when she did that. It would seem that was something else that hadn't changed in the last four years… He'd only seen Cassie for a few seconds, and his whole body ached for her.

What should he do now though? Should he leave? Should he go and knock on the door, say hello, ask after her. God, this was horrible. There was a time when they'd been so close, he'd known her thoughts, sometimes even before she did, and now he didn't even know whether to go and say 'hi' to her.

He glanced up at the sky and, just then, noticed his dad, standing on the very top of the roof.

"Dad?" he called, not thinking that hearing his voice might shock his father.

Ben wobbled, just slightly, before regaining his footing.

"Jake?"

"What the hell are you doing up there?"

"Fixing the roof." Ben stated the obvious. "Where's Cassie?" he added, sounding concerned all of a sudden.

Jake raised his hand to shield his eyes from the sun. "She's… um, she's gone inside." Jake glanced toward the front door and wondered if Cassie was in the kitchen, looking out.

"Wait there," Ben called. "I'll be right down."

"Take care, Dad."

Ben disappeared from sight. "I've been doing this longer than you've been eating hot meals." Jake could still hear his voice.

"I know." That didn't mean he wasn't worried. His dad wasn't as young as he used to be… and he'd been really high up.

Ben appeared around the side of the house.

"Jake," he said, the emotion obvious in his voice.

"Dad." Both men stood looking at each other for a moment.

"You're back?" Ben said quietly.

"Yeah…" Jake replied.

"For a visit, or to stay?" Ben's eyes searched his face.

"Both."

"Sounds complicated."

"It's not. Not really."

"Let's go home. You can tell me all about it." He put his arm around Jake's shoulder, steering him back toward the lane.

"Wait a second, Dad," Jake said, shaking himself loose. "I didn't know Cassie was back."

"Come home with me. I'll explain everything."

"Why can't you explain it here?" Jake asked, confused.

"Because this is complicated." Jake wasn't going to budge and Ben only took a moment to recognize that familiar stubbornness. He took a deep breath. "Cassie's mom…" he began quietly, "she had a heart attack."

"Oh God… Is she okay?"

"No."

"Dad… what are you telling me?"

"She died, son."

Jake could feel the blood draining from his face. "When?" he asked.

"Last Wednesday… real early. I found her."

"Oh, Dad." Jake put his hand on Ben's shoulder. He knew Ben and Kate had been good friends. It must have been hard on his dad, finding her body.

"Cassie's come back to arrange the funeral, which is on Monday morning, and she's fixing up the house."

"How is she?"

"You know how it feels, Jake. How do you think she is?" Ben stared at him.

"Do you think she'll see me?" Jake asked.

"I don't know. I guess that depends why you want to see her."

"Just to talk to her… tell her how sorry I am about her mom. I still care about her, Dad. I always did."

Ben nodded his head slowly. "Let me… let me go ask her," he whispered.

"Why don't I just go on in?" Jake said. "I'm not gonna do or say anything to hurt her… I promise."

"No." Ben's reply was quick… too quick. Jake raised his eyebrows. "Let me check with her first." Ben didn't wait for Jake to reply, but strode off to the house, up the steps and in through the door.

That was damned weird, Jake thought to himself, turning and facing the ocean. Whatever his dad thought of him, he'd never hurt Cassie, especially not at a time like this. He just wanted to tell her how sorry he was about her mom… to offer to help, if he could. He'd always just walked straight into Kate's house… hell, everyone had. Why was his dad being so protective of Cassie all of a sudden?

He turned at the sound of the screen door closing.

Cassie was standing on the porch, looking at him.

His earlier assessment was spot on. She was beautiful, crazily beautiful. She was exactly the same as she'd been four years ago… and yet she was different. She was more 'woman', and less 'girl'. There was another difference too. Behind the vulnerability in her eyes that had always made him want to protect her, was something else. He thought it looked like fear, but he couldn't be sure…

"Cassie?" he whispered. At the sound of his voice, her eyes widened and his throat closed… and he knew exactly what she was afraid of. He'd always been the one who'd kept her safe, made her feel protected from everything and everyone. But now, seeing that look on her face, he could barely breathe.

Why the hell is she so frightened… of me?

Chapter Five

Cassie

She sat in her old bedroom, shaking from head to toe and cradling Maddie in her arms. *He can't be here*, she said to herself. *He can't see Maddie.*

She knew that the moment he saw her, he'd know – in the blink of one of Maddie's deep green eyes – that she was his daughter.

She started rocking, not knowing what else to do. Maybe if she just waited long enough, he'd leave. Ben would persuade him to go, surely. She could hear voices, but not what they were saying, and she hoped Ben was convincing Jake to go back to his house.

The knock on the bedroom door made her jump, and Maddie startled.

"It's okay," Cassie whispered, and joined her thumb and forefinger into a circle, making the 'okay' sign.

"It's me… Ben," came the voice from the other side of the door. "Can I come in?"

"Yes, okay." Cassie's voice was quiet, barely audible.

The door opened, just enough for Ben to pass through and, once he was inside, he closed it again.

"Why's he here?" Cassie asked straight away. "Has someone told him?"

"No," Ben reassured her. "I don't really know why he's here. We didn't get around to that. He saw you…"

"Did he see Maddie?" Her voice was shaking.

"He didn't mention seeing her, no."

Cassie heaved out her relief. "So, what does he want?"

"He wants to talk to you. I told him about your mom. He just wants to see you, Cassie… to make sure you're okay."

"Can't you just tell him I am?" she pleaded.

"I don't think he'll take my word for it. Besides, that'd be a bit odd. As far as he's concerned, there's no reason why he can't see you. If you don't go out there, he's only gonna wonder why."

Cassie nodded her head. Everything Ben was saying made perfect sense.

"I'll have to go and speak to him," she said eventually. "Can you sit with Maddie?"

"Um… sure." Ben seemed a little doubtful. "I don't know a lot of sign language yet though."

"I won't be long." Cassie got up from the bed, signing to Maddie that she'd be back in a minute.

Ben took her place, sitting next to the little girl. As Cassie reached the door, he called out to her. "Are you sure about this?" he asked.

"No… but you're right, if I don't go and see him, he'll only start asking questions."

"That's not what I meant, Cassie." She turned and looked down at him. "I know I've only spent a few minutes with him, but he seems different – *very* different – to the boy who ran out of town. Maybe you should try giving him a chance?"

Cassie stared at him. "Ben, I can't make a decision like that on the spur of the moment… especially not right now." She sighed. "I'd need to spend time with him myself, get to know him again, work out if I can trust him with Maddie… and that's not going to happen easily, not after what he did." She glanced at her daughter. "I can't risk him coming in to find me," she said, opening the door. "I'll be as quick as I can."

"Just think about what I've said," Ben murmured as the door closed.

Outside, she wiped her palms on her shorts and went to the front door, passing through the screen, which slammed shut behind her. Jake, who was standing in the garden, a few feet away, spun around, staring up at her.

"Cassie?" His voice was quiet, but still ignited every nerve ending in her body.

It had been so long since she'd heard him speak; so long since those feelings had been awakened. If only she wasn't so scared of him now.

"Hello." She walked slowly down the steps and came to stand in front of him.

She knew it was impossible, but he seemed even taller than he'd been four years ago. He was certainly broader, more muscular, but she guessed doing construction work would account for that. He'd always said to her that was where he was going to start out. She dragged her eyes away from his toned body and looked up into his deep green eyes, and she knew exactly why she'd fallen so hard for him. He'd loved her completely and he'd always made her feel safe... well, he did, until now. If he found out about Maddie, he'd despise her, he'd change the life she'd built for herself and Maddie these last four years without him, and she'd probably never feel safe again.

"How are you, Cass?" he asked. She hadn't heard herself called that in so long. No-one else ever shortened her name... and his voice was so tender, so caring, she had to take a deep breath and blink back her tears before she could even think about forming a reply.

"I've been better," she replied honestly.

"I'm so sorry about your mom... Is there anything I can do to help?"

"No." Her response was so fast, it even took her breath away, and Jake's eyes widened in surprise. "I'm fine." She paused, trying to calm herself. "I'm just fixing up the house so I can sell it and then I'm going home again."

"Home?" he queried.

She nodded, not telling him where 'home' was.

He took the hint and didn't pry any further. "The little girl I saw," he said, "is she yours?"

Cassie could feel her heart constricting. Part of her desperately wanted to say 'yes, and she's yours too', but she didn't, replying simply, "Yes," instead. She nodded her head at the same time, just for emphasis.

"So, you're married?" She'd half expected him to ask more about Maddie, so his question was a surprise.

"No," she said. "No… I'm not married."

Jake

He waited for her to say something more, but she didn't.

Cassie… a single mom. That sure as hell was something different and nothing at all like the Cassie he remembered. But then, people changed, didn't they? He had. Well, in most ways, he had. It seemed he was still just as attracted to Cassie as ever, so he guessed a part of him hadn't changed in the slightest.

He smiled and moved a little closer to her.

"Why'd you run, Cass?" he asked. "When I got back to the apartment, you'd left. Then I drove back here to find you, and you'd gone again – why? I never understood it…"

She looked at him. He could see she was thinking about something. She closed her eyes for a moment and, when she opened them again, they were filled with tears. "It was too late, Jake. You'd already lost my trust. You'd already lost me."

"Sorry?" He couldn't hide his confusion. "I don't understand. What are you talking about? What had I done to lose your trust?" She stared at him for a long moment, but said nothing. Once it became clear she wasn't going to reply, he carried on, "Okay…" he said, "I ran out on you at the party. That was wrong; it was stupid of me. And I turned off my phone when I got to Boston – again, really dumb – but how exactly did I lose your *trust*, Cass? How did I lose *you?* Tell me… please…?"

"Does it matter?"

"Yes. It does to me."

"What? Right now? It's a long time ago, Jake."

"I know it is, but…"

"Jake… I've got work to do, with deadlines I'm not sure I can meet; I've got a house to fix up and… and my mom just died, which means it's her funeral on Monday, and I still haven't finished all the arrangements for that yet… because I'm finding it real hard to face up to the fact that she's—she's gone…" A single tear fell onto her cheek.

He took another step closer, so they were barely an inch or two apart. It was all he could do not to hold her, but he didn't dare.

"I'm sorry, Cass," he whispered. "I'm being insensitive."

"Now isn't the time to be thinking about the past," she added, as though she hadn't heard him.

"I get that. I'm sorry," he repeated. He hesitated for a moment, looking into her tear-filled eyes. "Don't cry," he said. "I remember when my mom died, you told me it'd get better, and it did. It just takes time."

"Time… and friendship. We had each other then, Jake."

"Yeah, we did. You helped me so much; you were always there for me, Cass. I've never forgotten that." Oh, to hell with it. He put a hand on her shoulder, feeling her bare skin, and he noticed her shiver at his touch. God, that felt good. "I'm not going anywhere," he added. He couldn't fail to notice her face paling as he said this. "In a couple of weeks' time, I'm moving back here, and I'm gonna be around for the whole summer. I'll help out in any way I can. I'll help with the house, and we can talk… well, I can listen. If you need me to, that is…"

The tears that had been brimming in her eyes started to fall freely and she pulled free of him, shaking her head and running back up the steps, into the house.

"Cass?" he called after her, but she'd gone.

A minute or so later, Ben came back out.

"What did you do?" he asked, glaring at his son as he stormed toward him.

"I don't know. I just told her I'm gonna be around for the summer and offered to help out. She burst into tears and ran."

"You're gonna be here for the summer?" Ben pulled up, surprised.

"Yes, if you'll have me. That's why I'm here… to ask if I can stay with you." Ben ran his fingers through his hair and Jake felt his shoulders drop. "It's okay, Dad," he said quietly. "You don't have to say yes."

"No, you don't understand."

"Yeah. I think I do." Jake turned and started walking back to the lane.

"Jake?" He turned and faced his father, but kept walking backwards. "Wait a minute; I'll go with you. We need to talk. I'll just let Cassie know I'm going."

Jake stopped. "Okay. Can you tell her I'm sorry I upset her? I didn't mean to…"

Ben nodded and went back into the house, returning within moments.

The two men walked side by side and in silence until they were halfway home.

"So… have you got a job working on a site up here then?" Ben asked all of a sudden.

Jake turned to face his father. "No, Dad. I don't really do that anymore."

"Oh? What do you do now, then?"

"Well, if this project I'm about to start goes to plan, I'll be Head of Corporate Construction."

Ben stopped in his tracks.

"You've gone from a site worker to… what did you say?"

"Head of Corporate Construction," Jake provided.

"Yeah… that… in four years?"

Jake nodded his head. "Four damned hard years."

They started walking again. "And what's this project?" Ben asked.

"Have you heard about a new hotel being built just down the coast?"

"Rumors, yeah… no names." Rumors didn't surprise Jake in the slightest; this was Somers Cove after all. But he was pleased his dad knew nothing about the client's identity.

"Well, it's that."

Ben whistled. "It's supposed to be big."

"That's an understatement. It's gonna be huge."

Jake couldn't hide his enthusiasm. And Ben couldn't fail to notice it. "And you're behind it?"

"Yes. Well, the company I work for is. But the project is my idea. We break ground at the beginning of June."

"Which is why you need to be up here?"

"I'm gonna oversee it myself. I can't afford for this to go wrong. There's a lot riding on it, Dad, and not just for me. The client has a lot invested in this... and I'm not just talking about money." They walked in silence for another few yards. "It's okay. I know things haven't been great between us and that's my fault. Staying here was always gonna be a big ask. There's a motel not far from the site – I'll book myself in there for now."

Ben cleared his throat. "I made over your room a couple of years ago, so it's nothing like it used to be," he said quietly. "But you're welcome to use it."

Jake swallowed hard. "You're sure?"

"I'm sure." They'd reached Ben's house by now and were standing outside. "This yours?" Ben nodded toward Jake's BMW.

"Yes."

"Enough room in the trunk to fit groceries?" he asked. Jake nodded. "Good, because I wasn't expecting you. You'll need to go shopping. May as well let the whole damn town know you're back... and the store's always been the best place to do that. At least you'll get it over with."

Jake let out a laugh. "I left my bag in the kitchen," he said.

Ben turned. "Assuming I'd say yes, were you?"

"No, not assuming. Just hoping." He opened the car door. "Anything in particular you want me to get for dinner?"

"Surprise me."

Just as he was about to climb into the car, Jake stopped and looked across at his father. "I'm sorry, Dad... for everything," he said. "I shouldn't have run away like that, not without telling you why."

"Oh, I didn't need you to tell me why. I got that. It was about Cassie. I'd have worked it out for myself, but the smashed photograph on the bedroom floor was a big clue."

"Sorry about that."

"It's okay. I got it re-framed. You'll find it by the side of the bed; where it always was."

"Thanks."

They stared at each other for a moment.

"You understood why I left then?" Jake said eventually.

"No, I didn't. Running away never solved anything, son," Ben replied. He came around to Jake, looking up into his eyes. "But I'm guessing you've worked that out for yourself by now, haven't you?"

Chapter Six

Cassie

"What am I going to do?" Cassie was curled up on the couch, cradling a cup of coffee in one hand and holding her phone with the other. Maddie had been asleep in bed for half an hour and, although Cassie knew she should be working, she couldn't even hope to think straight.

"Tell him the truth?" Emma said, after just a moment's hesitation.

Cassie paused, the cup half way to her mouth. "Did you just say…?"

"Tell him the truth," Emma repeated. "What choice do you have, Cassie? Someone else is bound to find out. You know what this place is like. And then how long do you think it'll be before it gets back to Jake? It's better if you tell him. You have control then. Besides, you can't expect Ben to keep it a secret… not if Jake's going to be living here for the summer. That's just not fair."

Cassie thought about what Emma was saying. She knew, deep down, that it made sense… but the very idea of telling Jake was horrifying. He'd be livid… he'd be worse than livid, understandably.

"He'll be so angry," she said out loud.

She heard Emma sigh. "Did you honestly believe this day would never come?"

"Yes… no. I don't know." She heard her own voice cracking.

"Oh, Cassie… don't cry. The timing sucks. You don't need this, not on top of everything else."

"No, I don't."

"But that's not Jake's fault. He wasn't to know."

"I know." She paused. "How do I tell him, Em? I can hardly just sit him down and say 'Oh, I forgot to mention, you've got a three year old daughter', can I?"

"No… because for a start, you didn't *forget* to mention it."

"No. I deliberately kept her from him… Oh God, Em. This is such a mess."

As she tossed and turned in bed, trying not to wake Maddie, Cassie tried to keep Emma's advice at the forefront of her mind.

"Remember to focus on Maddie," her friend had said.

Cassie was doing that right now, wondering how Jake was going to react, whether he'd fly off the handle, get mad at her, go silent… or run away, like he used to. She knew she needed to protect Maddie from Jake's reaction, in case it was negative; she couldn't let her daughter see him respond badly, even if she didn't yet know who he was. She'd find out eventually, and she'd probably remember his behavior, and Cassie didn't want Maddie to think badly of her father, or worse still, to be afraid of him. At the same time, she wondered how Maddie would respond to him. Apart from the last few days with Ben, she'd never had any male figures in her life. How would she feel about Jake's sudden appearance?

She decided that she'd speak to Ben first, maybe get him to sit with them when she told Jake, so his reactions were limited. She didn't think Jake would do anything to physically hurt her, but with Ben there, he'd probably behave better than without him. She'd talk to him tomorrow. He'd called earlier to check how she was. They hadn't talked about Jake – for which she was relieved – but he'd said he'd come down later on Sunday and carry on with the roof, so he could get it finished before it rained. She'd try and talk to him then. And she'd arrange a time to speak with him and Jake when Emma could sit with Maddie. It was the only way…

Sunday was another beautiful day. Cassie had still only painted half the railing and wanted to try and finish the rest of it today. She smiled at Maddie, who was playing on a blanket in the garden, and set to work.

Worrying about talking to Jake was bad… but now she was even starting to worry about how she was going to talk to Ben as well. Would he mind sitting there with them? There was always the risk that Jake finding out that Ben had known about Maddie, and hadn't told his own son himself, would cause a rift between them. Maybe Ben wouldn't want to take that chance and would refuse to help.

Not for the first time in the last twenty-four hours, she wondered how her life had suddenly become so much more complicated.

She tried, just for a moment, to focus on what she was doing and realized she'd dripped paint onto the porch. She stood and picked up the rag from the floor to wipe the drips before they dried. She really was making a mess of everything at the moment. She needed to concentrate.

She glanced out into the garden and felt her blood turn to ice. There was no sign of Maddie. She wasn't on the blanket. Cassie looked frantically around the garden, but couldn't see her anywhere. She dropped both the rag and her brush and ran around to the top of the steps, just as she heard Jake's voice calling from the lane, "Stop! Hey… Stop!" She thought he was calling to her and, just for a second, she stopped in her tracks, but then she saw he was looking toward the ocean.

Everything seemed to happen at once. Jake started sprinting in the direction of the shoreline. Cassie looked to where he was running and let out a scream as she saw Maddie, thigh-deep in the water, wading out into the sea, totally oblivious to the danger.

Cassie took off down the steps, hurdling over the flower bed and racing toward her daughter. Jake got there first though, charging through the shallows, still in his shoes, his jeans soaking, and pulling the little girl up into the safety of his arms.

Arriving just moments later, wading out to them, Cassie took Maddie from him and held her close. Maddie, still unaware that anything was really wrong, buried her face in Cassie's shoulder, shy of the stranger who'd mysteriously pulled her out of the nice cool water.

"Thank you," Cassie cried, unable to stop the tears from flowing down her cheeks. "Thank you so much, Jake."

"Hey... it's okay." He put his hand on Cassie's arm and led them both back up onto the beach, out of the water.

"No... I mean it. Thank you. I was... I was distracted. You must think I'm an awful mother, but I've never done anything like that. I've never taken my eyes off of her before, you have to believe me... Oh God, to have done it right by the ocean. How stupid... how neglectful could I possibly be?"

"Stop that, Cass. There's no harm done."

"Only because you were here."

"I'm sure you'd have seen her in time." Jake's voice was reassuring and Cassie calmed a little, remembering that she'd spotted Maddie's disappearance just before she'd heard Jake's voice and saw him running. He was right, she probably would have seen Maddie wading into the ocean in time... That didn't really make her feel any better though.

"I still shouldn't have let it happen in the first place."

"Stop beating yourself up, Cass. She's fine. I'll admit I know absolutely nothing about kids, but I can easily believe they're a handful at the best of times - and this is not the best of times. You've got a lot to deal with at the moment, so give yourself a break." He took a step toward her, but instead of touching Cassie, which she thought he was going to, he reached out his hand and, using the backs of his fingers, he touched Maddie's cheek. She turned her face to look at him, giving him a shy smile.

Cassie heard the breath catch in Jake's throat and forced herself to look at him. He was staring at her, his eyes darkening.

"Cass?" he whispered. And with that one word, she knew that he'd worked it out.

"I'm sorry." It was all she could manage to say before her knees buckled and she collapsed to the ground at his feet.

Jake

Jake didn't see how it could be possible. The little girl couldn't be more than two and a half, maybe three years old... and he hadn't seen Cassie in very nearly four years. The timing just didn't work out. It had to be a coincidence that she had his smile... *and* his eyes.

But then, why did Cassie just say 'sorry' like that, and why was she on the ground at his feet sobbing her heart out... *and why the hell am I just standing here watching her*, he thought to himself.

He sank to his knees beside Cassie, wanting more than anything to pull her into his arms. The little girl turned around again and stared at him and, this time, there was no escaping it. The darkness of those green eyes was enough to give it away. They were the same as his, and his own mom's, and the color was so unusual, people commented on it all the time. She was his.

"Cass?" he whispered again, and waited for her to look up. Her eyes were filled with tears, her cheeks red and puffy. She was still beautiful, but then she always was.

"You asked me yesterday why I ran... why I was gone when you came back to town?" she murmured. He nodded his head slowly. "I had no choice. You know what this place is like. Gossip is the fuel that lights the fires around here, and I didn't want to be gossiped about."

"Why would they have gossiped about you, Cass?" Jake asked, trying to keep his voice calm.

"Because I was pregnant... with your child."

He looked again at the little girl. "But..." he began, then found he couldn't speak for a moment. He took a deep breath and tried again. "She's not old enough."

"She'll be four in November."

He quickly worked things out in his head. "You mean you were already three months pregnant?" He knew that couldn't be possible, even as he said it.

"No."

"Then… I'm really sorry, but I don't understand."

She sighed. "Maddie was born early. They told me she'll probably always be a little small for her age."

"Maddie? That's her name?"

"Yes."

At that moment, the little girl turned toward Cassie and put her forefinger across her chin, moving it down toward her chest.

"I'm sorry," Cassie said, getting to her feet. "Maddie wants something to drink."

Jake stood as well, wondering how on earth she knew that, or whether she'd made it up, so she could escape from him, even if only for a few minutes.

"Okay," he muttered, watching them walking back toward the house.

He was struggling to take this in.

He was a father. He'd been a father for over three years. And he'd had no idea.

Chapter Seven

Cassie

Cassie knew Jake would be angry and she was just grateful that Maddie, unprompted, had asked for a drink at that moment, so she'd had an excuse to go back into the house for a while, and give them some time apart.

She fetched Maddie a beaker of juice and, while her daughter sat at the table drinking it, Cassie stood at the kitchen sink and looked out the window. She'd half expected Jake to leave, to storm off just like he used to, so she was surprised to see him sitting on the beach still, staring out at the ocean. His shoulders were hunched, his muscles looked taut and she could just imagine how dark his eyes were about now.

Over the years, she'd often felt guilty for keeping Maddie from him, but never more so than now. Her next conversation with Jake was going to be the hardest of her life…

She turned back to check on Maddie, who'd nearly finished her drink.

"Okay?" she asked, forming her thumb and forefinger into a circle.

Maddie screwed up her fist and held it at shoulder height, making a 'knocking' signal, nodding her head at the same time, to say 'Yes'.

Cassie held out her hand and Maddie jumped down from the chair, coming over and taking it. They went back outside together.

The sound of the screen door slamming made Jake turn and he looked back across the garden, climbing to his feet and walking toward them. They met each other half way, which Cassie hoped was a good omen for what was to come.

He stood, roughly a foot or so away from her and looked down at Maddie for a few moments, before returning his gaze to Cassie. What she saw in his eyes took away her budding hope. He looked empty. She thought she could have handled almost anything but this. Seeing and knowing how much she'd hurt him was hard to take, even if she did still feel her actions were justified.

"Why, Cass?" he asked, and his voice sounded devoid of any emotion. "You said you left because I lost your trust. You need to explain that, because this…" He waved in Maddie's direction. "This doesn't make sense."

"You hurt me, Jake."

His mouth dropped open. "I *hurt* you?"

"Yes."

He closed his eyes for a moment and she could see him sucking in a deep breath. "I hurt you?" he repeated, moving a half-step closer. "How the hell do you think this feels?"

"Please try and understand… I couldn't tell you, Jake. I couldn't trust you, not after what you did."

"What I did?" This time he didn't bother to suck in the breath… he let it out. "Jesus, Cass," he yelled. "I left you at a party for an hour or so… and I was rude to you. I regret both of those things, but all I wanted was for you to come live with me in Boston. I just wanted you to have some faith in me, that's all. It wasn't that much to ask. I know you were scared, but I'd have looked after you." He glared at her. "Name me one time I ever failed to look after you."

"That night… the night you abandoned me at a party, and went off—"

"Because you were being so fucking selfish," he interrupted, then stopped. "Sorry, I didn't mean to swear in front of Maddie."

Cassie ignored his apology. "*I* was being selfish? You weren't even listening, Jake. You wouldn't even try and compromise."

"Your idea of a compromise was to drag me back here for the summer, and then we'd never have left. You know that… I know that.

That wasn't a damned compromise, Cassie. That was just another means of getting your own way."

"It also wasn't a good enough reason to walk out on me. You have no idea what happened after you'd left."

It was like he hadn't heard her. "I didn't do the walking out, Cassie. I came looking for you and every time I did, you'd already left…" He stopped for a moment. "And you really think any of that's a good enough reason to keep my own daughter from me?"

"No, of course not. That's not the reason, Jake. What kind of person do you think I am?"

"Honestly, Cass? I have no idea. I don't even know you anymore. The Cassie Reynolds I used to know would never have done anything like this… So, I have no goddamn idea who you are."

He stared at her for a moment, then turned and started walking back toward the lane.

"That's right, Jake," Cassie yelled after him, her anger matching his now. "Run away, just like you always do."

He ignored her jibe and kept walking.

Cassie was watching him, angry that he'd judged her. He hadn't listened. He hadn't let her explain what Sean had done to her and how much that had frightened her, because Jake wasn't there to protect her. He hadn't let her tell him the real reason, nor had he admitted, or explained why he'd cheated on her, like there could ever be any justification for that.

The sound of Maddie crying broke into her angry thoughts.

"Hey, baby," she whispered, kneeling down and pulling Maddie into a hug. Jake was forgotten as she stroked her daughter's hair, gently rocking her from side to side. "No-one's cross at you," she murmured, even though she knew Maddie couldn't hear her.

She picked up the little girl and carried her into the house, vaguely aware that Jake was standing in the lane watching. He could watch, she didn't care. Maddie came first, last and always… One day, he'd stop running away, stop putting his needs before everyone else's, and realize that.

Jake

He heard the crying sound and knew straight away that it wasn't Cassie… this was a completely different kind of cry to Cassie's. It wasn't something he'd heard before, but it tore at his heart and he stopped immediately and turned around.

Maddie was crying, real sobbing tears.

Cassie wasn't even looking at him anymore. She was focused on her daughter – his daughter – kneeling down in front of her and pulling her into her arms, comforting her, stroking her hair and rocking her gently.

He had no idea what that felt like, but he knew then that – no matter what Cassie thought of him – he wanted to find out.

He watched while Cassie carried Maddie back into the house, waiting until the door closed behind them, before walking away again. He needed some time to think.

He slammed the kitchen door closed behind him, the glass rattling in its frame.

"Hey… careful, Jake." He looked up at his father, who was standing by the sink. "What's wrong?" Ben asked, seeing the look on his face.

Jake flopped down into one of the kitchen chairs and put his head into his hands.

"Cassie's little girl," he said quietly.

"What about her?" Ben asked warily.

Jake looked up. "She's mine."

Ben came and sat down opposite him. "She told you, then?"

Jake paused, just for a second. "You… you knew?"

Ben nodded.

Jake stood quickly, knocking his chair to the floor, then leaned over the table. "What the fuck is it that I'm supposed to have done that was so bad even my own father decided I had no goddamn right to know I have a child?"

Ben looked up at him. "You let Cassie down, son,"

"Jesus Christ, Dad... We had different dreams; we wanted different things. Yeah, I left her at a party by herself... is that really such a crime?" He didn't give his father a chance to reply. "I'm going out."

"Where?"

"Anywhere I don't have to look at people who've got no faith in me whatsoever... Around here, I guess that might take some doing."

He stormed from the room, went outside and got into his car.

Parking up outside the coffee shop, he got out and went over to the door alongside the shop, ringing the bell. Emma was the only person he could think of who knew Cassie nearly as well as he did. She didn't work on Sundays, but he hoped she'd be at home, and that she wouldn't slam the door in his face. Given the way his luck was going so far today, nothing would surprise him.

He didn't have to wait long. Emma opened the door, and looked him up and down, her face paling. She looked as though she didn't quite know what to do, and he wondered if she might be about to shut him out too.

"Em?" he said, putting his hand up against the door. "Please... I need to talk to you."

She paused, seemed to think about it, and then stood back to let him in. He followed her up the narrow stairs and into her small kitchen.

"I'd heard you were back," she said, offering him a seat at the breakfast bar while she leant against the countertop, facing him.

"Bad news travels fast?" he suggested.

"Something like that."

He raised an eyebrow, but didn't comment. He wasn't sure when he'd become 'bad news'.

"Why are you here, Jake?" She didn't hold back.

"Here at your place, or here in Somers Cove?"

"Here at my place. I'm guessing you're in town to see your dad."

He ignored her assumption. He didn't want to even think about his father right now. "I need to ask you something."

"Okay..."

He felt like asking why she was being so abrupt, but he had more important things on his mind. "Did you always know about Maddie?" The way her skin paled, and her eyes widened told him everything he needed to know. She didn't need to nod her head, but she did anyway… just once.

"I'm glad Cassie's told you," she said. "She felt bad about it."

"Well, that's a damn shame." His sarcasm wasn't lost on her. "And she didn't tell me, Em. Not really. I only found out by accident."

"What do you mean?"

"Cassie was painting at the house. She took her eye off Maddie and she wandered out into the ocean."

Emma pushed herself off the countertop in alarm. "Oh my God. Is she okay?"

"Yeah, she's fine. I ran out and picked her up. She'd only gone in a little way. It wasn't a big deal… although the way Cassie reacted, you'd have thought she'd taken Maddie to a crack den and personally introduced her to crystal meth."

Emma let out a chuckle. "Cassie went on a guilt trip then?"

"Just so's you'd notice…"

"So how did you find out… about Maddie being yours?" Emma asked, relaxing again.

"I looked at her," Jake said simply. "I mean, her eyes, Em…"

"I know. She's the image of you." Emma smiled.

"Cassie had no choice but to tell me after that," Jake explained. "And then…"

"Then what?"

"Then we fought," he murmured, looking down at his hands, clasped in front of him.

"Way to go, Jake."

"Why the hell is it my fault?"

"Because you're not the one who's just lost their mother, that's why."

Jake felt the enormity of her statement. Cassie had been there for him when his mom had died. Now she was in that same God-awful place, he'd just yelled at her and walked out on her – again.

"And don't tell me… you ran away again?" Emma added, like she'd read his mind.

He didn't reply – but then, he didn't need to.

They remained silent for a few minutes.

"Does everyone know?" he asked eventually. "About Maddie being mine."

"No, of course not," she replied. "Why do you think Cassie left?"

"But surely she's been back to visit. It's been four years…"

Emma shook her head. "No, Jake. She stayed away. The only people who knew were me and Kate. Cassie didn't even realize that Ben knew about Maddie until she came back the other day. We were sworn to secrecy. She didn't want anyone knowing… in case they told you."

"Excuse me?" He sat up, leaning toward her. "Is there something here I'm missing? When did I become such a villain?"

"Cassie trusted you, Jake. She trusted you more than she ever trusted anyone in her whole life."

"I know that."

"And you betrayed her."

"I did what?"

"You betrayed her, Jake. She didn't feel she could rely on you to stick around for your child." Emma leant back and took a breath. "Look, this isn't really anything to do with me. I'm just Cassie's friend. If you really want to know why she did it, you're gonna have to ask her."

Jake got to his feet and looked over at her. "Oh, I fully intend to, believe me."

He drove around for hours. The irony wasn't lost on him, that he'd done this that night four years ago… after he'd abandoned Cassie at that party, and his life had fallen apart.

So far today, he'd been told that he'd lost Cassie's trust, that he'd let her down, that he'd betrayed her… none of that made any sense to him. The only thing that did make sense was that look of fear he'd seen in Cassie's eyes. He understood that a lot better now. She hadn't been scared of him; she'd been terrified of him discovering her secret.

He drove out of town, not really knowing where he was going, but trying really hard to remember what he'd done four years ago. He thought back. What had he done that had made him feel bad? Maybe if he could remember all of it, he'd come up with something… He'd always felt guilty for ignoring her fear about moving. It made sense really, and he'd known that even then… he'd just been scared of coming back to Somers Cove and being trapped there. Cassie was just trying to be sensible, getting him to find work and somewhere to live before they moved. He'd also been really rude to her that night. Quite rightly, she'd always expected him to look after her, and protect her – not hurl insults at her. Then there was turning off his phone when he'd got to Boston. That was really childish of him, but thinking about how he was back then, he was pretty good at behaving childishly.

Still, being childish and rude and impatient weren't good enough reasons to deny him the first three and a half years of his daughter's life, or the whole pregnancy with Cassie.

At twenty-two, with no prospects, he wondered how he might have reacted to Cassie telling him she was pregnant. He doubted very much he'd have been overjoyed, but he'd have been there for her… surely she knew him well enough to know that. He was always there for her. He stopped the car abruptly, pulling over to the side of the road. Yeah, he was always there for her… except when he wasn't. Except when she'd needed him most…

He let out a long sigh and rested his head on the steering wheel.

He was due to pay a visit to the hotel site the next day. He had a meeting booked with the construction manager at ten. But, he decided, he'd leave early, get out of town and spend the day thinking things through. He needed some time alone.

Chapter Eight

Cassie

"Cassie?" She heard Ben's voice at the same time as he knocked on the door frame. "You in there?"

Wiping her hands on a towel, she went over and pushed the screen open. "C'mon in," she said.

"Are you okay?" he asked, hovering just inside the threshold.

She didn't really have an answer for him. She didn't know how she felt, so she just shrugged.

"Can I get you a coffee?" she suggested.

"I'd like that," he replied, appearing to feel more certain about his welcome. "I was worried you'd be upset, or angry with me."

She turned to face him, the kettle in her hand. "Why on earth would I be angry with you, Ben?"

"Jake." The single word hung in the air between them.

"He's a grown man," Cassie said, turning back to the sink and switching on the cold tap. "Or at least I think he is."

Ben came and sat at the kitchen table, where Maddie was coloring, using wax crayons. She handed him a blue one and pushed the book in his direction. He took the prompt and began to fill in the sky above the castle she was shading.

"He should be the one doing this," Ben said, wistfully.

"Well, first he'd have to want to." Cassie's voice was maybe a little harsher than she'd intended.

"I think he wants to," Ben reasoned. "He's just angry, and confused."

Cassie put the kettle on the stove and turned it on, then came and sat opposite him, smiling across at Maddie. "He's not the only one," she remarked, keeping her smile intact. When Ben looked up, bewildered, she continued, "I'm a little bored with being called selfish by him…"

Ben stopped his coloring. "Excuse me? He called you what?"

"If you want me to be precise, he called me 'fucking selfish'," Cassie replied. "I know he was angry and I understand that – he's got every right to be angry with me – but he wouldn't even listen to me, he just lashed out… and it's not the first time he's said it. He's called me that before."

She could see the anger rising in Ben's face. "I'm so sorry, Cassie," he whispered.

"It's not your fault."

"Well, it kinda is. I thought I'd raised him better than that."

Maddie reached over and nudged Ben with her hand.

"I think she wants you to get back to coloring," Cassie said.

Ben looked down at his granddaughter and smiled, then made his hand into a fist and rubbed it in a circular motion across his chest. Maddie smiled up at him, then leant up and kissed his cheek.

"I didn't know you knew how to say 'sorry'." Cassie was impressed.

Ben started coloring again, but glanced up at her. "I've been teaching myself on the Internet," he told her. "Sorry seemed like a good place to start… Considering Jake's behavior, I think I might be saying it a lot."

Cassie got up and came around the table to him. "You don't need to apologize to us," she said quietly as she put an arm around his shoulder and gave him a squeeze. The kettle started to whistle and she went and turned off the stove. "And please don't think we blame you for anything he says, or does," she continued as she started making the coffee. "I will try to work things out with him, when he's calmed down a little."

"I don't know when that's gonna be," Ben replied. "He's gone off again."

"Gone off where?"

"I have no idea. He came home, slammed the door, told me he knew about Maddie and, when I said I already knew myself, he stormed out, yelling at me."

Cassie brought the French press over, pouring two cups of coffee and placing one in front of Ben. She sighed as she sat down again. "It doesn't look good, does it?"

"How do you mean?" He glanced up at her again.

"Maddie doesn't need someone like that in her life. She needs someone who'll deal with things calmly and reasonably, not a man who's gonna storm off at the first sign of trouble."

Ben colored in silence for a few minutes. "I hate to say it, but I'm inclined to agree with you." He put his arm around Maddie. "No matter what happens," he said, kissing the top of her head, "I'll be here… for both of you."

"I know," Cassie replied.

"And if my son ever says anything like that to you again, Cassie, I want you to tell me. I don't stand for any man talking to a lady like that… not ever."

They sat for a while, all coloring in Maddie's book.

"I'd better get on with this roof of yours," Ben said eventually.

"Oh, leave it for today," Cassie replied. "I'm not in the mood to work on the house."

"I can come down on Tuesday… in the afternoon," Ben said.

"Okay." They stared at each other. "First, there's tomorrow to get through."

"Yeah… there's that."

"I thought it best I should let you know," Emma said quietly down the phone. "I'd have called earlier, but Nick came round after Jake left and ended up staying the whole day."

"Was Jake still angry?" Cassie asked. It was nearly nine o'clock. Maddie had been asleep for ages and Cassie was staring at her computer screen, getting nowhere with writing. She hadn't typed a single word.

"I guess… well, he was to start with. But then he told me you'd fought, and he seemed to feel guilty about that."

"I should hope he did. He called me fucking selfish… again."

"Seriously?"

"Yes." Cassie felt her eyes stinging and her screen blurred. Why did he keep doing this to her?

"Then I'm not surprised he looked so guilty."

"Where did he go?"

"When he left? I have no idea. He got in his car and drove off. Why?"

"Because Ben was here earlier and Jake hasn't come back home."

"So, he's just gone off again?"

"It looks that way."

"I don't think he'll be gone for long though, Cassie," Emma said, a note of worry sounding in her voice.

"Why not?"

"Because the last thing he said was that he's gonna talk to you."

"What about?"

"Maddie… why you kept her from him. He wants the truth."

"Well, I'll give him the truth, but he might not like what he hears." Cassie let out a deep sigh. "I can't do it with Maddie around though," she murmured, almost to herself.

"Did she get upset?" Emma asked.

"Yes. I'm not gonna let that happen again."

"Why don't you arrange to meet him on your own one evening before he goes back to the city. I can come over and sit with Maddie for you."

"Would you?"

"Of course. I love spending time with her."

"I'll talk to him tomorrow. I know a funeral isn't the best place to discuss things like this, but we can set up a time and place away from the house… maybe even out of town somewhere, so it's completely neutral and we can try and be civil to each other."

"Try and speak to him early, before the service," Emma suggested. "Otherwise you're gonna spend the whole day worrying about it, and tomorrow's meant to be about your mom, not Jake."

"You're right. I'll do that… and thanks, Emma."

Later, when she'd finished the call and was on her way to bed, Cassie wondered what she'd do without Emma. She was always there whenever Cassie needed her, no matter what. There had been a time when she'd thought the same was true of Jake… but she'd been so wrong about that, and about him.

Jake

Monday dawned just as bright and sunny as the day before, not that Jake really cared. He didn't need rain today, but other than that, he really couldn't have cared less about the weather.

He was up, showered, and dressed in jeans and a white button down shirt, and had left the house before six. He would get breakfast on the way to the site. He had no intention of running into his dad, having stayed out late and successfully avoided him the night before. He needed to spend the day alone, thinking things through… and then, later on, he was going to talk to Cassie. He wanted the situation resolved before he went back to Boston on Wednesday, but the issues with his dad could wait until he knew where he stood with the mother of his daughter.

God… was he really so mad at her that he could only think of her in those terms? He honestly didn't know, and that was one of the things he most needed to work out for himself during the course of the day. He had to try and figure out his emotions. If, when he'd thought it all through, he still felt angry with her, then fine, they'd just have to deal with it, but he had to learn to control it better, because behaving the way he had yesterday, calling her names and swearing at her… that wasn't acceptable.

His meeting with Mitch Kline went well. Mitch had made a few changes to the plans, which he was going to send through to Jake, but otherwise everything was set and ready for them to begin work on June 1st. Jake sent Mark Gardner a message confirming this and asking if he wanted to be there for the ground breaking. Mark replied, saying his diary was slammed, but he'd try and clear some space and he'd get back to Jake in the next couple of days, but he was happy with progress.

He'd just gone back to Mark, when his phone rang. It was Erica. He seriously wasn't in the mood for her right now, so he ignored the call. He'd let the voicemail pick it up. Except she didn't leave a message… she called again, and again. Fed up and exasperated, Jake switched off his phone.

He took a slow walk down to the private stretch of beach beneath the the site. He wasn't in the mood for seeing people, so this deserted shoreline was ideal. He just wanted time and space to think.

Standing on the sand, looking out at the ocean, he wondered if Cassie would ever have told him about Maddie, if he hadn't saved her, and then seen her smile and her eyes, and known she was his. He liked to think she would've done. Certainly the Cassie he used to know would've. She was incapable of keeping something like that from him. But the Cassie he argued with yesterday? He wasn't so sure. She seemed distant, very willing to keep him at arm's length… and that was an alien emotion when it came to Cassie. They'd always been so close. Well, they had in the past, anyway.

Maybe her experiences in the previous four years had made her like that – had made her more aloof, more reserved, harder. God, he hoped not. One of Cassie's most endearing qualities was her ability to open up to him, to let him see inside. Even if she couldn't with everyone else, she could always tell him everything.

He started walking along the beach, not even really seeing the scenery, just staring ahead and thinking.

He thought about what Cassie must have been through since leaving Somers Cove. He knew very little about pregnancy, other than how to avoid it. At least he'd thought he knew how to avoid it… but there was three and a half year old evidence in Somers Cove that proved he'd got that wrong too. He knew a lot of women got morning sickness... had Cassie had that? She always hated being sick. He recalled the few times she'd been sick when they were together. He'd always had to hold her hair back while she vomited, and rub her back to ease the nausea. Had there been anyone there to help her, he wondered? There would have been scans, he guessed, and hospital appointments... and the birth. He felt a lump rising in his throat. He'd have liked to see Maddie being born. In his mind, he painted a picture of himself and Cassie holding her together, their heads touching as they cradled their newborn daughter. God, what he'd have given to be there for that...

There would have been sleepless nights, dirty diapers, four am feeds, which sounded like hard work. But there would have been Maddie's first steps, her first tooth, her first words... He'd never heard her speak and he thought about how her voice might sound and what it would be like to be called 'daddy'. He stopped walking, and stared down at his own feet in the sand. "Oh, fuck," he muttered under his breath as it dawned on him that there might already be someone in Cassie's life who Maddie called 'daddy'. Yeah, she'd said she wasn't married, but that didn't mean she was single. Hell, the guy could even have been there at the birth, for all he knew...

He started walking again, the horizon becoming a blur as tears welled in his eyes. He didn't want there to be another man in Maddie's life... not until she was old enough to meet the man she'd share her own life with, anyway.

How could Cassie do this to him? What crime did she think he'd committed that was so bad he deserved this?

It was dusk by the time he returned to his car.

He wasn't as angry as he'd been when he started his walk, although he still didn't understand what had happened, and he still wasn't sure that he could forgive Cassie for keeping Maddie from him for so long.

He had decided that, first thing the next morning, he was going to call on Cassie and calmly talk to her. He wasn't going to lose his temper again, no matter what she said. He was going to see if she'd agree to him spending some time with Maddie. He really hoped she'd be reasonable, because if she wasn't… well then he'd have no choice but to fight her for the right to see his daughter.

Chapter Nine

Cassie

Cassie wondered if a funeral could ever be called 'lovely'? It would seem so, because that's what a lot of people had said to her at various points during the day.

"It's such a lovely day."

"What a lovely funeral."

"This is so lovely. Your mom would've been so proud."

She had to admit, once the service itself was over and they'd all gone back to the beach house for the wake, the somber atmosphere had lifted and the day had become more of a celebration of Kate's life, which was just how Cassie had wanted it to be. Guests had filled the house, and were spilling out into the garden and onto the beach. Emma had provided the food and Ben the drinks, and no-one was downhearted – except Cassie, whenever she had a few moments to herself, like now. She looked out of the kitchen window, onto the garden, where Maddie was sitting with Emma. God, she wished Jake was here. She knew he probably hated her, but she needed a hug, and the only person she ever wanted to hug her was Jake, but he wasn't here. He'd let her down... again.

Oddly, no-one had asked about Maddie. They just seemed to accept her. Cassie wondered if Ben or Emma had spread the word, and everyone had decided to say nothing for the day. Whatever had happened, Cassie knew that, from now on, the whole town would know about Maddie and who her father was – it was so obvious.

"Hey, beautiful lady," Nick's voice at her shoulder caught her unawares. "Don't be sad. Your mom wouldn't have wanted that."

"I'm not," Cassie lied.

"Yeah… you are."

She turned and looked up at him. There was something about Nick that just made you want to straighten him out, and yet to do so would spoil the effect. His dark hair was long and messy, and yet kinda stylish at the same time. He looked like he rarely shaved, and yet he wore his stubble with elegance. His clothes, even today, bordered on inappropriate, and yet he just came in on the side of acceptability.

"Nice tie," Cassie said, to distract him.

It was black, but undone, as were the top two buttons of his shirt. His trademark waistcoat was unbuttoned and his usual blue jeans had been replaced by black ones. He dressed like this all the time, whether at home or in court, and didn't care how many eyebrows he raised, and that was one of the reasons Cassie loved him – the other being that he was Emma's older brother, who'd looked out for them ever since she could remember.

"That's not gonna work," he countered. "Not today." He put an arm around her. "You've got a gorgeous little girl," he whispered, looking down at her. "I've always known about her, you know," he said. Cassie started.

"What do you mean?"

"Your mom called me," he explained, "when you went into labor."

"I thought she called Emma," Cassie said.

"No, she needed to explain why she wouldn't be at work for a few days – and she asked me to let Emma know. We talked for a while. I think she was packing at the time. She told me how early the baby was, and that she was Jake's – obviously – although I think I could've worked that out for myself. Kate was so scared, Cassie. Maybe it helped her having someone to talk to who wasn't gonna panic, or cry. I think she knew Emma would have cried." He smiled. "Emma did cry, if I remember rightly. I offered to drive your mom down to you, but she said she didn't want that. She just wanted me to tell Em, and to keep it to myself."

"You've known all this time?" she whispered.

"Yeah."

"And you've never told anyone?"

"Of course not. Your mom asked me to keep it quiet, so I did." He paused for a moment. "If you ever wanna talk… about your mom, or Maddie, or even Jake – dumb son-of-a-bitch that he is – well, you know where I am." He didn't labor the point, but wandered out through the door and onto the porch.

Cassie turned and noticed Ben, standing in the doorway, watching her.

"Now *he's* a good man," he said quietly.

"He is," Cassie replied. She stared at him. "He's not going to show up, is he?" They both knew they weren't talking about Nick any longer.

Ben pushed himself away from the door frame and moved closer. "It doesn't look like it."

"And you haven't seen him?"

"No. He came back real late last night and he was gone again before I even woke up."

"But he definitely came back?"

"Yeah. His bed was slept in, but as for where he is now, I don't have a clue. Hell, for all I know, he's gone back to the city already."

Cassie could barely hold back her tears now, although she wasn't sure whether she was crying about her mom, Jake letting her down again, or the fact that Maddie seemed to have come so close to having a daddy, only to miss out.

"He's too damn unreliable," Ben said. "I don't know if he's got what it takes to be a father…" he continued, then sighed. "After Amy was diagnosed, she was in and out of the hospital all the time. Jake was only seven then, and he didn't really understand what was happening. And then when she died, I don't really think it sunk in…"

"It did," Cassie interrupted. "He was devastated."

"Really? He always seemed so strong around me."

"He didn't want you to see." Cassie walked over to him. "He knew how upset you were. He told me he heard you crying at night, and he didn't want to make it worse. So in front of you, he pretended to be fine and then he used to come down here and sit with me. We'd talk for hours."

Ben blinked back his tears. "I thought you were just hanging out, playing. I wish… I wish I'd known," he whispered. "He shouldn't have done that."

"He was okay… in the end."

"Yeah, because you made it okay. But looking after him… that was my job."

"It wasn't anyone's *job*, Ben. Jake was my friend before he was anything else."

"You're a good woman, Cassie." He tried to smile. "Makes a mockery of what I was gonna say though."

"Why?" Cassie tilted her head to one side.

"Because I was gonna tell you that I found out when Amy died how much hard work and devotion it takes to be a parent…"

"You're not wrong there."

"And then I was gonna say, I'm not sure Jake's got either of those qualities… not anymore."

She could feel the tears welling. "Excuse me," she whispered and ran from the room and into her bedroom. She needed some time to herself.

She pulled a Kleenex from the box beside her bed and wiped her eyes. She was surprised by how upset she was. Of course, today was always going to be tough, but she wasn't crying about that. She was crying because he'd *really* let her down this time – he'd known the funeral was today. She'd told him, Ben had told him. Ben had helped with the arrangements. Jake couldn't not have known… and he'd still disappeared on her.

She'd been thinking during a fairly sleepless night, that when she met up with Jake for their talk about Maddie, she'd be prepared to let him see her. She knew she'd have to be there too, at least until he'd learned to sign, but she'd felt it would do both him and Maddie good to spend time together. Except he couldn't even be bothered to turn up to her mother's funeral. Kate had played an important part in his life too… and where was he on the day Cassie was burying her? Nowhere. So, if he thought he was going to be able to see Maddie, he could damn well think again.

Everyone hung around all afternoon, and into the evening, with the last guests only leaving at just before seven. Emma, Nick and Ben helped clear everything away, while Cassie gave Maddie a very quick bath.

When they came back out, the house was much tidier and her friends were ready to leave.

"Are you gonna be okay?" Emma asked her.

"I'll be fine." Cassie forced a smile. "I could do with some quiet time."

"You sure?"

Cassie nodded and Emma gave her a hug. Ben followed suit and Nick put his arm around her as she led them to the door. "I meant what I said," he whispered. "Call me if you need to. I'm happy to listen."

"Thank you," she managed to say.

"I'll come by tomorrow," Ben said from the top of the steps.

"Okay," Cassie called. She picked up Maddie and held onto her, carrying her out onto the porch. As her friends disappeared around the corner of the house, she sat down on the swing and let it rock gently, with Maddie in her arms.

"You're a tired little girl," Cassie whispered, running her hand over Maddie's soft dark hair. "I know you can't hear me, but I love you very, very much." Maddie's eyes slid closed and, within a few minutes of rocking, she was fast asleep.

Cassie didn't want to put her to bed yet. She liked the feeling of Maddie's little body in her arms. Without her, she knew she'd feel more alone than ever, so she held onto her for just a while longer, as she looked out over the ocean and let the tears fall down her cheeks.

Jake

It was nearly dark by the time Jake got back to Ben's house. He let himself in, surprised to find the house in darkness. His dad's truck was in the yard, so he knew he was at home… somewhere.

"Dad?" he called out, but got no reply.

He went through the kitchen, turning on the light as he passed, and carried on into the living room. His hand was on the light switch, when Ben's voice sounded out of the darkness: "Leave it."

Jake lowered his hand slowly and let his eyes adjust to the gloom. Over by the window, he could make out the figure of his father, sitting in an armchair staring outside. There was nothing to see; the garden was shrouded in darkness too. He took a few paces into the room and, as he grew more acclimatized to the shadows, he noticed Ben was wearing a suit, the jacket undone, the top two buttons of the shirt unfastened. It was a dark suit… and on the arm of the chair was a tie, which looked black.

It hit him like a wrecking ball. *The funeral…* he'd missed it.

He ran his fingers through his hair. He'd felt ashamed by his own actions before, a few times, but he'd never felt anything like this.

He took the last couple of paces across the room and sat in the chair across from his dad.

"I'm sorry," he said quietly.

Ben didn't even acknowledge his presence.

"How did it go?" Jake persevered.

His father looked up at him slowly. "What do you care?" The coldness of Ben's voice took Jake's breath away. "The only thing you care about is yourself, Jake. So I suggest you carry on doing that… preferably from Boston. It'd make everyone's life a damn sight easier. I wouldn't have to keep apologizing for you, and I wouldn't have to keep feeling so disappointed in my own son." He lowered his head again.

Jake swallowed hard. Ben had never spoken to him like that before, but he didn't argue... He felt the justification of everything his dad had said.

"I'm sorry," Jake repeated. "I should've remembered; I should've been there." He waited, then added, "How's Cassie?"

Ben raised his head once more. "It's no concern of yours, but she's fine. She's an amazing young woman. She's coped with worse."

"Worse?" Jake still remembered how it felt to stand beside his mother's grave as a grieving nine year-old. He couldn't understand how it could get any worse.

Ben didn't reply. Jake waited a few moments, then got to his feet. His earlier anger was forgotten. He owed Cassie an apology, if nothing else. But he also wanted to know she was okay.

"I'm gonna go and see her," he said quietly.

"Oh, are you?" Ben jumped up, coming to stand right in front of Jake, almost nose-to-nose. "If you're even contemplating upsetting her, insulting her, or hurting her again, then don't bother coming back here. Ever. You hear?"

"Upsetting her? Insulting her?"

"Yeah... Where the hell do you get off calling Cassie 'fucking selfish'?" Ben prodded Jake in the chest with his forefinger. "When you say things like that to the mother of your child, you show you're not worthy... of either of them. I didn't raise you to swear at a lady, Jake."

Jake could feel himself shrinking inwardly. He sighed. "I know. That was wrong," he whispered.

"You think?"

"But I didn't say she was being selfish *now*... I said she was being selfish back then – when we broke up before."

"Oh well, that makes it so much better. You've got no right calling anyone selfish."

"I know, I know. I was upset, okay?"

"No, it's not okay. For Christ's sake. Cassie's got no-one to turn to, Jake, not really. She never had a father, her mom's just died. She's got Maddie, and that's it. Well, she's got Maddie... and me. Because I'm gonna look out for that girl. I'm gonna do the job you should be doing, if you were any kind of a man, that is."

Jake stood up to his father. "I'd be doing that job myself, if Cassie had told me I had a daughter in the first place."

"I'm not talking about Maddie right now; I'm talking about Cassie. I'm gonna look out for her… But it's you that should be doing that, instead of which, you're leaving it to me and Emma and Nick. You should never have left that girl in the first place."

"I didn't. She left me. She broke my heart."

"And that gives you the right to keep hurting her… to keep letting her down, does it? You broke my heart four years ago, when you ran out of here without a word. Did you notice me behaving like a child when you came back?"

"No, sir," Jake whispered.

"No… because that's not what you do when you love someone."

"But I had a daughter… for all this time. And I never knew. I'd have been there for both of them, if she'd told me."

"You really think that? You think you'd have coped like she has? You should try getting off your career carousel and see how it feels to be Cassie for a day – hell, you wouldn't even last an hour. She can't just take time out for herself to nurse her own feelings, even though her mom's just died. If you need time to yourself, you get to take off and do that, like you did today. Hell, I get to do it too, if I want to… but not Cassie. She's with that little girl the whole time…"

"That's her choice, Dad. No-one made her leave here. No-one made her do this by herself."

Ben pulled himself up to his full height. He was still a little shorter than Jake, but he clearly didn't care.

"You think so? You think she *chose* to leave this town? She loved this place nearly as much as she loved you, and she loved you with everything she had, although for the life of me, I can't work out why. You think she wanted to live by herself, in a city she doesn't know, with no friends or family close by? Keep deluding yourself if it makes you feel better, Jake, but that *wasn't* what she wanted. That *wasn't* her choice."

Jake stared at his father for just a moment longer, then turned and left the room, going out through the kitchen door and into the lane. He felt belittled by their conversation. There was no justification for what he'd done. None whatsoever.

The beach house was still lit up and he spotted Cassie straight away, sitting on the swing, in the shelter of the porch. She didn't see him. She was gazing out to sea, rocking Maddie in her arms. It must be way past Maddie's bedtime and he wondered why Cassie was still holding her when his little girl seemed to be asleep.

He stood still at the corner of the house and looked at Cassie closely. She was wearing a black shift dress – presumably the outfit she'd worn to her mom's funeral – and she looked completely worn out. Still beautiful, still vulnerable, but so worn out.

He wanted, more than anything to go over to her and pull her into his arms. Yes, he was still mad at her, but he cared about her. He cared about her more than he'd ever cared about anyone… and probably more than he ever would.

He walked quietly up to the steps and, as he put his foot on the first one, Cassie startled and turned toward him. The look that crossed her face was anger – there was no mistaking it. He recognized it from when they used to fight, just before they broke up. But there was something else in her eyes. It was pain. He'd hurt her. And he knew it.

She didn't take her eyes from him as he climbed the remaining steps and walked over to her.

"I'm sorry, Cass," he whispered, crouching down in front of her.

She didn't reply, but shrugged her shoulders, still staring at him.

"We need to talk." She still didn't answer him. He took a deep breath. "We've got a lot to say to each other," he continued, "but that's gonna be hard work if you're not gonna speak to me."

"Fine. But I need to put Maddie to bed first." Her voice was cool.

"Okay." He ran his hand gently across Maddie's hair. Cassie looked from his face to his hand, then back again. "Can I help?" he asked.

"No." She dismissed him.

"Okay." He stood up and let her stand, then went back to the steps, sitting down on the top one and waiting, while Cassie went into the house and put Maddie into bed.

Chapter Ten

Cassie

Maddie didn't even stir as Cassie laid her down in the double bed that had once been her own, pulled up the comforter and kissed her gently on the forehead. She turned out the light and pulled the door to, but didn't close it.

She hesitated before going back outside. She wasn't really prepared for another confrontation with Jake, but he was here… so what choice did she have?

She let the screen door close behind her and went back to sit on the swing. He twisted round on the step, looking up at her.

"I'm really sorry, Cass," he repeated. "I know I should've been here. I had to work, and I needed some time to think. I mean… it's not every day a guy finds out he's got a three year old daughter he knew nothing about."

She stared down at him. "Most guys might like to be with their three year old daughter, when she's attending her grandmother's funeral. And maybe they'd spend a little time working things out with their daughter's mother too. But I guess that's not as important as work, and you having some private time." She saw him wince, but whether that was at her words, or her tone, she didn't know. She didn't care much either.

"It is important," he replied, calmly. "And I do want to spend time with Maddie. I was gonna come and see you in the morning. I wanted to talk to you about whether I could have her for a day – maybe at the weekend."

Cassie burst out laughing. She couldn't help it. She fought hard to control the laughter though, before it turned into hysterical tears.

"No chance," she said once she'd calmed down enough to speak.

"You're over-reacting." Jake raised his voice, just a little. "I missed your mom's funeral… and I'm sorry for that, but there's a big difference between that and you keeping the fact of my daughter's existence – before and after her birth – from me for nearly four years. You owe me an explanation, Cassie. Emma told me you did it because I betrayed you, but all I did was go off to Boston. That's hardly a betrayal. I came back for you. I came to find you…" he whispered. "But you'd gone. You'd taken off – permanently. Carrying my child, evidently. I think, at the very least, that warrants an explanation. Don't you?"

"You've forgotten something, haven't you?" Cassie asked him, leaning forward and resting her elbows on her knees.

"Forgotten what?"

"You took off for Boston. You came back for me. What about sleeping with Alice? Or has that conveniently slipped your mind?"

"Sleeping with Alice?" He stared up at her.

"Yes. That's the betrayal Emma was talking about; that's why I can't trust you… well, that and the fact that you keep disappearing whenever the going gets a bit tough. That's not what Maddie needs from her father."

Jake got up slowly and walked over to her, looking down into her eyes.

"Cass… I've got no idea what you're talking about. I never slept with Alice in my life. I never slept with anyone else while we were together."

"But you took her home from the party…" She heard her voice wavering. The absolute certainty in his tone was matched by her own growing uncertainty.

"Yes."

"And you're telling me nothing happened?"

"She kissed me," Jake said, crouching down.

"She kissed you?" Cassie's eyes narrowed just a little, and she leant back in the swing seat. "Is that all?"

"She might have touched me. I can't remember it very well. I stopped her, because I was in love with you, Cassie."

"I don't understand."

"No, neither do I." He looked closely at her. "Who even told you I'd given Alice a ride home?" She didn't reply, but stared down at her fingers, clasped in her lap. "Cass?" he urged. "Tell me, what happened when I left you at the party?"

She looked up at him again. His face was so sincere that, for the first time in four years, she really believed she might have been wrong – about everything.

"It was horrible," she began.

"Tell me." He stood up, turned, and sat down next to her. She could feel the heat from his body. It was familiar… reassuring.

"Sean," she continued, falteringly. "He came on to me."

"He did what?" Jake moved even closer. "What did he do?"

"He was touching me," Cassie whispered.

"Where?"

She turned her face to his. "You want me to tell you?"

"Yes."

She swallowed and took a deep breath. "My behind… my breasts." She felt his muscles tighten. "He told me you were always chasing other girls behind my back and you wouldn't mind if I went upstairs with him. He told me what he wanted to do to me – and I'm *not* repeating that, before you ask." She paused for a moment. "I was scared. He'd got me cornered, and you weren't there."

"I'm sorry, Cass. I should never have left you there. If I'd known…"

"I know. If you'd realized he was going to do that…"

"I've have kicked the shit out of him."

Cassie managed a half-laugh. "I was going to say, you'd never have left me."

"Well, that too." He leant into her, just a little. "But I am sorry." They sat quietly for a little while. "I still don't understand," Jake said, breaking the silence, "how did you know I'd given Alice a ride? And what made you think I'd slept with her."

"Sean called me." Cassie turned to him. "I managed to get away from him. I called a cab and waited outside. I'd only been home for a little while when he called and told me he had a message from you."

"What message?"

"That I wasn't to expect you back anytime soon because you'd gone home with Alice."

"Asshole. I hadn't gone home with her… well, not like that, anyway. She'd found me outside and asked me to give her a ride back to her place."

"To be honest, I didn't really believe him. I thought he was making trouble because I'd turned him down. If you'd wanted to let me know something, you'd have called, or sent a message, so it didn't make sense. I ignored him and started getting ready for bed…" She paused.

"But?"

"But then Alice called."

"What? When?"

"About half an hour later, I guess. I think I'd just got into bed. She told me she'd had sex with you… in the back of your Jeep."

Jake

"And you believed her?"

She was staring at him. "Yes."

"Why didn't you ask me?"

She got up and walked over to the railing, then turned around, leaning back on it, and looked down at him. "Because I didn't know where you were."

"I came back to the apartment for you, Cassie. All you had to do was wait."

"I was scared, Jake. Sean had gotten hold of my number from somewhere. He might have had our address too, and for all I knew, you were spending the night with Alice. What was I supposed to do?" She raised her voice. He tried to stay calm, sitting back in the seat and looking up at her. He understood that she'd have felt scared – and he hadn't been there to make her feel safe. He'd let her down.

"Okay. I get that," he said, "but why didn't you call me? When you got back here, I mean."

"I did. I called you over and over… remember? You didn't return any of my calls, not for ten days. How was I to know what you were doing, or who you were doing it with?"

"I wasn't doing anything with anyone. I was angry with you for leaving, and I turned my phone off for a while. But then I did call; I left you a message."

"Yes, you did. I can still remember it. You apologized. You told me how sorry you were for hurting me; you promised it was a mistake and you'd never do it again. It sounded like you were saying sorry for cheating, Jake. Hearing that, it was like the end of my world. I fainted…"

"You did?" He'd never known her to faint. Not once.

"Nick caught me and carried me to the doctor's office, and that's when I found out I was pregnant."

"Is that why you fainted? Because you were pregnant?"

"I don't think so – it didn't happen again. I think it was just the shock of your message. The realization that you really had cheated."

"But I hadn't."

"It sounded like you had though. Think about the message you left. Think about how it sounded to me, especially after Sean and Alice's calls as well."

He closed his eyes, recalling his own words. He could see how she'd easily have misinterpreted what he'd said. "I should've been more specific," he said quietly.

"So… so you didn't sleep with her?"

"No, Cass. I had far too much to lose to ever cheat on you. I mean, I lost you anyway… but I didn't cheat on you. What Sean said, about me chasing other girls, that wasn't true. I didn't even look at another girl when we were together. Why would I? I only wanted you."

He saw her close her eyes, her head tilted back and her shoulders dropped. It seemed like the years of misunderstanding and mistakes were rolling over her.

"Did you ever feel bad?" he asked after a while. "About not telling me, I mean?" It was a genuine question, not a criticism.

She opened her eyes and looked down at him again. "Only every single day."

That surprised him and it took him a moment to ask his next question: "And you didn't think to get in touch?"

She lowered her head still further and stared at the space between them. "All I had to do was remember how much you'd hurt me... how good you were at putting yourself first and running out on me." She looked up again. "Maddie comes first in my world, Jake. She needs constancy, not someone who disappears when they feel like it." She turned away, just for a moment, then focused back on him. "I nearly called you when I was in labor, though," she whispered. He sat forward. "It was real quick," she continued, "and I was alone. Maddie was early." Her voice faltered as she remembered.

"Tell me about it," he said.

She came and sat down next to him again. "I was at work," she began, "when my waters broke. There wasn't even time to call for an ambulance. My boss, Veronica, took me to the hospital in her car. But my mom couldn't get there in time. I was so scared, Jake... so, so scared I was going to lose her." She was holding back her tears, but Jake could see it was a struggle. "I had a nurse with me, and she was very kind, but there was no-one who really cared about me. That was when I wanted to call you most of all. I wanted you there with me... more than anything."

He hated seeing her like this. "I'd have come, Cass. If you'd called me, I'd have been there." She looked up at him and, in the light from the kitchen window, he could see the tears brimming in her eyes. "Why didn't you?"

"Because Maddie was early, all hell broke loose," Cassie explained, swallowing down her tears. "She was taken away as soon as she was born. I didn't even get to see her, let alone hold her. Not long afterwards, my mom arrived and, from then on, it was just awful. There were so many doctors to see, so many tests…"

He felt fear rising in his own throat. He hadn't experienced an emotion like this for a long time; not since that day, in his room, when he'd realized he'd lost Cassie, for good. "What happened, Cass?" he asked gently.

"She wasn't breathing properly, and then she had jaundice. She was kept in the NICU for weeks, nearly six weeks in total. Mom could only be there for ten days, but I stayed at the hospital until Maddie was well enough to come home. She got a really bad infection, and it looked like she might not make it." She looked up at him. "I've never been so scared, Jake…" Her voice tailed off to a whisper.

"Why didn't you call me then?"

"I came real close. But then I imagined you and Alice – together – and I stopped myself."

He sighed. None of this should've happened. None of it. "And what about when you took her home?" he asked.

"Then it got even crazier. When I wasn't changing her, feeding her, trying to get her to sleep for more than ten minutes at a time, just so I could do the laundry, or clean the bathroom, or eat a sandwich, I was worrying about how we were going to communicate; whether I was doing the right thing by her; then I was trying to hold down a job and meet her needs at the same time; add on the constant fear about how she was going to cope in the long-term, what to do about schooling—"

"Wait a second," Jake interrupted. "What are you talking about? Maddie's fine now, isn't she? I mean, it was obviously scary at the beginning because she was just born a little bit early and she was sick… but she's okay now…"

"No, Jake. Maddie was born six weeks early – which is more than a *little* bit. And, although she turned out to be a stronger than any of the doctors believed possible, one of the tests she had before we left the hospital showed that she's profoundly deaf…"

Cassie's voice broke on the last part of the sentence and she burst into tears.

That was more than Jake could handle. He got to his feet and pulled her up into his arms. She was stiff and resistant, to start with, pushing him away, fighting hard against him. But he refused to let go, even when she started raining punches on him and, without saying a word, he hung on to her. With every strike against his chest, he felt her anger, that he'd thoughtlessly been the catalyst that had led to her whole life changing; he felt her frustration that he'd let her down again today, putting himself first, just like he always did; and more than anything he felt her pain. Everything she'd been through by herself, for the last four years came out in each of those blows, and he took every single one, until the emotion gradually abated and she slowly started to soften against him. Then, exhausted, she lay her head on his chest and sobbed. He took a deep breath, as he held her close and stroked her hair, and let her weep.

Chapter Eleven

Cassie

When Jake put his arms around her, all she wanted to do was yell at him that if he hadn't left her at that party, none of this would have happened. Cassie would never have had to flee the house to get away from Sean; Jake would never have been in his car for Alice to ask for a ride; the phone calls could never have happened. They'd have gone back to their apartment by themselves. Okay, they might have argued, but they'd have been together. And she was convinced they'd have found a compromise eventually. Maybe he'd have agreed with her suggestion, the one she'd thought of in the cab on the way home from the party – that Jake should go to Boston until he found work, and she would join him once he'd got them somewhere to live. That they'd give it a year, and if she really didn't like it, they'd think again. That was a scenario she'd recreated over and over in her mind during the past four years. She wouldn't have had to find out she was pregnant by herself, leave town and move to Portland and live a lonely, isolated life. She'd have had Jake there to help her through the morning sickness, and the all-day nausea. He'd have been there to share the joy of the scans, seeing their baby for the first time, as a shadow on a screen. He'd have been there at Maddie's birth and in the weeks that followed, so she wouldn't have been so scared, because she was never scared when Jake was with her. And he'd have been able to help with caring for their daughter, learning to sign, watching over her, making the decisions. My God, the list was endless… and they'd had none of it, because he'd walked away from her that night. And he'd done it again today…

Her anger, her frustration, her fear and pain were so great, the words wouldn't form. Instead her hands became fists and she found herself striking blows against his chest. He didn't stop her; didn't grab her wrists, or flinch, or pull away from her. If he'd spoken, asked her why she was hitting him, or sought an explanation, she knew that would just have made it worse. She needed him to understand her, like he used to; she needed him to be able to read her thoughts, without words… because she didn't have any. But he didn't say a single thing. He just held on to her, and took her pain, until she had nothing left. Worn-out, spent by four years of sadness, loneliness and fear, she finally stopped, unclenched her fists and melted into him. His arms came tighter around her, he held her close and, as she lay her head on his chest, he stroked her hair, while she sobbed and sobbed into his shirt.

She calmed eventually, taking in gulps of breath. Now she wasn't crying so loudly, she could hear his heart beating, and she was more aware of how his chest felt harder and broader than it used to, his arms stronger. Melting into him was easy, but then it always had been. Being held felt good. She hadn't been in a man's arms since the last time Jake had held her, and she really needed to be hugged. She needed to feel safe. Would another man's arms have felt as good? She didn't need to think about it; she knew no-one could compare to Jake. No-one could ever make her feel like this… and although she knew he'd never forgive her for keeping Maddie a secret, although she knew any hope for a relationship with him was gone, he would always be Maddie's father and they'd always share that bond. She stuttered in a deep breath, pulled back from him and looked up into his face.

"Sorry," she whispered. His head tilted to one side, and she knew she had to explain. She wasn't saying sorry for all the years of hurt. That needed a lot more than just a simple 'sorry'. "For hitting you," she continued. "And for crying all over you."

"It's okay." The concern and understanding in his voice almost made her start weeping again. He pulled away, just a little, and looked down at her. "Do you have any wine?" he asked.

Cassie thought for a moment. "Yes," she replied. "There's some in the refrigerator, left over from today."

"Good." Jake smiled, just slightly. "I think we both need a glass." She went to move, but he turned her and sat her down on the seat. "I'll get it," he said, and went inside the house.

He was gone for a little while. Cassie sniffed. She didn't have a handkerchief on her. She'd used one earlier, at the funeral, but it was in her purse, which was in the living room. Hell, she didn't even have a sleeve she could use to wipe her face. She knew she must look a mess, not that it mattered.

Jake came back out, carrying two large glasses of white wine, already frosting on the outside.

"There you go," he said, handing one to her. Then he reached into his pocket and pulled out several folded Kleenex.

She took them and looked up at him.

"You always kept a box beside the bed," he explained, sitting beside her again. "I guessed you still would. I hope it's okay… I went in and fetched you some."

"Is Maddie alright?" Cassie asked, putting her glass on the ground by her feet, and wiping her nose and eyes.

"She's fast asleep… God, she's cute." She glanced across. Jake was smiling at her.

"Yes. She is. Everyone who's seen her says she looks just like you." She screwed the tissues into her hand and picked up her wine again. "Thank you," she whispered, taking a sip.

"She's got my eyes," Jake murmured. "And my smile… the rest is you, Cass."

"No, she's got your hair too."

He grinned. "Oh yeah. I'd forgotten that. Everything else is you, though."

They sat in silence for a while, occasionally taking a drink of wine and staring out at the dark ocean, listening to the waves lap on the shore.

"How do you communicate with her?" Jake asked eventually.

"Sign language."

"You learned to sign?"

"I had to."

"How? I mean, how did you learn?"

"The Internet. They told me at the hospital that sign language would be the best thing for Maddie, so right from the beginning, I spent every spare minute I had learning. She's starting school in September and they'll help her improve her vocabulary. And her being at school will give me more time to learn as well."

"And is there nothing else?"

"I'm doing everything I can, Jake…" She felt the tears rising again. Why was he finding fault? She was doing her best.

"Hey…" He put his glass down on the floor and moved closer, putting an arm around her shoulders. "I'm not criticizing, Cass."

She looked up and nestled into him, just a little. "Sorry, I didn't mean to jump down your throat."

"Don't be sorry," he whispered into her hair. "It's fine. You're tired… you've had a horrible day. I'm just interested, that's all. I don't know anything about this."

Cassie sighed. "When she was first diagnosed, I listened to the doctors at the hospital. One of them seemed to know a lot about profoundly deaf children and he really recommended signing. He gave me lots of advice and places to go to learn. And for a while, I settled on that route. But then I got to thinking, what if there was more I could – or should – be doing? So I did the research and I took her to see three more specialists about having a cochlear implant."

"And what did they say?" He leaned a little closer still.

"They all agreed it probably wouldn't help. She has no hearing at all, so any sounds she might pick up would only confuse her. She lives in a silent world and she knows no different. Confusing her with abstract noises won't help her. They all agreed that the best thing was to get her to use sign language from an early age."

"So she can only communicate with you?"

Cassie let out a half laugh. "No. Mom learned to sign too. I taught her to start with, and then she got herself a second-hand computer, so she could use the online guides. Emma picked up the basics from me and then taught herself the rest."

"And my dad?" Jake asked gingerly.

Cassie paused. "He only met Maddie for the first time last week. I've taught him to say 'hello' and 'goodbye', and he knows when Maddie's asking for a drink and when she needs the bathroom. He must've been teaching himself too. He said 'sorry' to her the other day. I hadn't shown him that."

"Why? I mean, why did he need to say 'sorry'?"

Cassie smiled. "Maddie wanted him to do some coloring with her. He and I were talking – about you – and he got distracted. She gave him a nudge and he apologized for neglecting his coloring duties."

Jake nodded. "I see." There was a hint of sadness in his voice.

"What's wrong?" she asked, leaning back and looking up into his eyes.

He released her. "Where do I even start, Cass?"

"At the beginning? It's usually best."

"It seems everyone else can communicate with my daughter, except me."

"It takes time to learn, Jake. And you have to want to do it."

"I do want to do it." He stared at her. "And my dad was coloring with her… but that should have been me."

"She's his granddaughter – he likes spending time with her. Even if you'd been there, he'd still have wanted to do that."

He sat back a little. "Emma told me you didn't even realize that dad knew about Maddie, until you got here last week."

"No. I swore Emma and mom to secrecy."

"So how did my dad find out?"

"You'll have to ask him about that." Cassie didn't feel it was her place to say. Jake was staring at her. "I'm sure he'll tell you, if you ask, but it should come from him."

He paused, then nodded his head. "Okay, I'll speak to him later."

Jake

Jake leant forward and picked up his wine glass, holding it in his hand. He swirled the golden liquid around a few times.

"I want to spend time with her," he said quietly.

"I know. I understand that."

"And I'll need you there, at least until I've learned to sign properly. I'll teach myself, like everyone else has, but I want to know Maddie's ways, Cass. I want her to feel comfortable around me, and only you can help with that."

She hesitated, staring at him.

"What's wrong?" he asked.

"I have to be able to trust you first," Cassie whispered.

"Is this still about Alice?" He twisted in the seat, turning toward her. "Nothing happened, Cass. I promise." He took a drink of wine. "Do you want me to tell you about it? Would that help?" Cassie shrugged and Jake took that as a 'yes'. "I stupidly left you at the party," he began slowly. "A decision I think I'm gonna regret for the rest of my life." He stopped, reflecting for a moment on everything that had changed for both of them as a result of that decision. Cassie looked up at him, like she was waiting for him to continue. "I drove around for a while," he said. "I went for a coffee at the diner, did some thinking, and came back to the party. Sean…" He paused again, his lips becoming a thin, angry line. "Sean told me you'd left and I was mad at you for not waiting. I couldn't understand why you'd gone without me." He held up his hand as she went to speak. "I didn't know what he'd done, Cass. If I had…" He didn't need to finish his sentence. He took another sip of wine. "So, I got back into the car, and then Alice knocked on the window. She asked for a ride home and I didn't see the harm. I know it wasn't exactly on the way back to our place, but it was only ten minutes away. She didn't have cab fare, and I could hardly leave her there, could I?"

Cassie looked down at her wine glass.

"Could I, Cass?" he asked.

She shook her head and he breathed a sigh of relief. At least she'd understood that much.

"We talked on the way back to her place – I don't remember what about, but it was nothing important. When I parked up, she put her hand on my leg. She told me she liked me… and before I knew it, she was on my lap, kissing me." He heard Cassie suck in a breath. "I didn't kiss her back, Cass."

"Did she do anything else? Did you?" she asked.

"She started undoing my belt," he replied, "and I remember thinking I had to get her off of me. So I lifted her up and dumped her back on the seat. I told her to get out of the car… and she ran. I waited until she was inside, and then I left."

Cassie looked up at him. "Why didn't you come straight home then? You'd probably have got home before she even called me."

"Because I was confused."

"Why were you confused, Jake?" He heard the uncertainty in her voice. "Did you like what she was doing?"

"Hell, no. I didn't want her in the slightest. You have to believe that." He was almost shouting, and he took in a breath to calm down. "Her touching me made me realize how much I wanted you, and how much I didn't want us to fight anymore. But I couldn't face the idea of coming back here, which was what I knew you really wanted. I could only think of two solutions: either one of us had to be unhappy, or we had to break up. I didn't want either of those things to happen. I needed to think, to try and work out a way forward. I thought you were safe at the apartment, so I drove around for a while. I thought back over our time together and, slowly I came to the conclusion that being with you was the most important thing."

"So you'd have come back here?"

"No."

"Then I don't understand…"

"I'd have gone to Boston by myself," he said.

"You'd have left me?" He could hear the heartbreak in her voice.

"Not for good, no, Cass. I couldn't have done that. But I knew you wanted to feel safe, and going to the city, crashing at Pete's place, wasn't your idea of safe. So, I'd have gone to Boston and got a job, and found us somewhere to live, and then I'd have come back for you. That's what I was coming back to suggest."

They stared at each other. "Oh, God," Cassie whispered. "That's what I'd been thinking too. I was going to put that to you as a compromise, when you got back. I came up with the idea while I was in the cab on the way back from the party. I had an extra condition, though…"

"Which was?"

"We'd give it a year, and if I really hated it, we'd think again."

"Sounds fair."

"Well, it would have been, if you hadn't slept with Alice."

"I didn't sleep with her, Cass." He wondered how many times he was going to have to remind her of that.

"Sorry, I know. I'm really tired and I've just gotten so used to thinking you did. And I'm sorry I didn't wait…" Jake felt the relief course through him, felt his nerves relaxing at her admission. "But I still can't trust you, Jake."

He was instantly on edge again. "Why not?" What was she talking about?

"It's obvious, isn't it?"

"Not to me." He moved away from her, putting some space between them.

"You're very good at just going off when things don't go your way. You can't do that when you have a child, especially a child like Maddie. You can't just decide – like you did today – that you're not happy, that you need some 'me' time, and take off to be by yourself. She needs stability. All children need that, but she needs continuity and constant attention."

Jake let out a long sigh. "It wasn't entirely like that, not really. I'll admit, I needed some time to think today. I was shocked, Cass. You threw me one hell of a curve ball yesterday and I think a lot of guys would need some time to think things through. But I had to go down the coast this morning for a meeting. I'll willingly admit that if I'd been less selfish and more considerate about you and Maddie, I'd have rearranged my meeting, fitted it around the funeral and I'm really sorry I didn't do that. I'm sorry I didn't put you first."

"I'm not asking you to put me first. This is about Maddie." He looked at her, and an overwhelming sadness suddenly washed over him. Did she really just want this to be about Maddie? Was there nothing at all left for them? "I have to be able to trust you with her."

"I know. I get that," he replied. "But that doesn't alter the fact that I've got a job… and I need to do it."

She looked up into his eyes. He thought, just for a moment, that he saw a hint of understanding. "So, when are you going back to the city?" she asked.

"I have to be back on Wednesday for an early afternoon meeting," he replied. The understanding in her eyes faded, and he saw something else… sadness, maybe? Hope flared in him that she might just be disappointed that he'd be going back so soon.

"You said you're spending the summer here?"

"Yes. I've got work commitments in Boston for the next few weeks."

"Oh, I see." She sighed and, again, he wondered if the thought of his absence might be making her feel downhearted.

"But I was thinking, I can spend my weekends here." He hadn't been thinking anything of the kind, but the idea of spending time with Maddie – and Cassie – was more than appealing. "And from the beginning of June, I'll be here permanently… at least until September."

Cassie nodded her head, seemingly thinking.

"I want to get to know Maddie," he added. "I'll be working during the day. I have to be on site and I've got commitments to clients." He sat closer again and waited until she looked up at him. "I won't disappear again, Cass. I promise."

Silence descended and he waited for her response for what seemed like an eternity. She was looking at him, evidently searching his face for answers.

She didn't take her eyes from his as she replied, "I'm not there yet with trusting you. I grew up without a father, Jake. My mom gave me everything I needed, and I never wanted for anything… and I can do that with Maddie if I have to. But, if she can have a daddy, then I want her to. I want her to have what I didn't. She's a very special little girl and if you want to be a part of her life, you've got to prove to her that you're worthy of being her daddy."

"I will, Cass." He felt his heart filling his chest, like it was going to explode. "I promise, I will."

"You can't run away from this, Jake. If you do, I promise you, there's no way back. I won't let you hurt her."

"I won't. I'm not gonna hurt her…" He took her hand in his. "Ever."

"Don't let her down."

"I won't let either of you down."

"It's not about me, Jake. It's about Maddie."

"I know." He stared into her eyes. "Thank you, Cass."

She nodded her head, just once, then leant back. She looked ready to drop. Today – this evening – seemed to have taken everything out of her.

"You need to get some sleep," Jake said quietly. "You're tired."

"Oh, I'm way beyond tired."

"I'll go." He got slowly to his feet, although Cassie didn't move. "Will you be okay?" he asked. She looked up at him, and the sorrow in her eyes tore through his heart.

"Yes, I'll be fine."

"I can stay a little longer, if you want me to."

"No, it's okay. I'm used to being quiet and by myself. You need to get back to your dad. Talk to him, Jake." She paused, just for a moment. "He needs you." That seemed an odd thing for her to say, but he didn't ask what she meant. She was done talking, that much was clear.

"I'll see you tomorrow?" he asked, just before he turned to go.

"Yes." Her voice was distant. He wanted to stay, but she was right. There was a lot to talk over with Ben, and it was getting late.

As he walked back down the lane, he thought about what she'd said. Well, she'd said a lot over the course of the evening, but the thing that stuck in his mind was that she was used to being quiet and alone. That sounded damn lonely… and, while he'd admitted he felt that way himself, the thought of Cassie being lonely made him shiver.

He let himself back in through the kitchen door. The light was on, like it had been when he'd left, but the living room was still shrouded in darkness and he wondered for a moment if his dad had already gone to bed, until he noticed him sitting in the chair, still staring out the window, just as he had been a couple of hours ago.

Jake went and sat opposite him again, leaning forward, his elbows on his knees.

"How long have you known?" he asked quietly. "About Maddie being mine, I mean."

"Kate told me just after Maddie was born." Ben sounded tired too.

"Why didn't you tell me?"

Ben turned and looked at him. "Because she asked me not to."

Jake felt his mouth drop open and tried to control his voice. "And you went along with that? Jeez, Dad. Was her friendship more important to you than your own son?"

"Kate wasn't just a friend," Ben murmured.

Jake let the words settle for a moment. "What do you mean?" he asked slowly.

"We'd been lovers for nearly four years," Ben said simply. "Since you and Cassie left." He turned to look at his son. "She was a beautiful woman, and she was only in her early forties when we got together." He smiled, just gently. " I'm not exactly an old man myself either."

Jake let out a slight laugh. "I get it, Dad," he murmured. "You don't need to justify it to me."

"I'm not. I'm just telling you. She'd been a friend for a long time after your mom died, and then one day I realized I was in love with her. I wanted more, but she didn't, not back then. We thought you and Cassie would both be coming back when you'd finished college and Kate didn't want either of you to feel awkward or embarrassed… so I told her I'd wait for her, until she was ready to accept we were meant to be together. It was only after you and Cassie left for good that she came to me."

"Cassie knew about this, I take it?"

"No. Kate didn't want either of you to know. She was still worried how you'd react."

"Well, I wouldn't have minded." Jake explained.

"That's what Cassie said too."

"So she knows now?"

"Yeah. I told her when she came back."

Jake paused for a moment. "I still don't get it," he said quietly. "What made you agree to keep Maddie from me? I'm your son."

"Yeah, you are. But Kate told me what you'd done."

"What I'd done?"

"That you'd slept with Alice Hammond. How could you do that?"

"I didn't. I didn't sleep with her, Dad." Ben looked up at him. "That was a misunderstanding. It wasn't Cassie's fault. It was other people."

"And does Cassie understand it now?"

"Yes. She's getting there, anyway. She's agreed to give me a chance with Maddie, so it's a start."

"Okay. That's good, but you were still an unreliable, childish, selfish kid. You wouldn't have had a clue how to raise a child; how to put them first."

"I know. That's all completely true. But I'm different now. I've changed."

"That's easy to say, son. Less easy to prove."

"Then I'll prove it. Cassie told me I have to show Maddie I'm worthy of her. I intend to. I won't let her down."

"And Cassie?" Ben asked.

"She says it's about Maddie. I'm not sure she wants anything to do with me now."

"And if she does?"

"I'm here. I'm not going anywhere. But I don't even know if she's single. She might have another guy in her life… wherever that is."

"She lives in Portland."

"She didn't go far, then?"

"No, just far enough to lose herself in a bigger town, and to escape the gossips."

Jake stared at his own hands. "And does she have someone else? Another guy?"

"I'm not sure."

"But, surely Kate would have known. And she'd have told you."

"No. Kate and I didn't talk about it."

"What? So she told you about Maddie being born and you never talked about her again?"

"No, son." Ben took a deep breath. "We didn't talk about *Cassie*. I kept her secret, because Kate asked me to, and because she could give me a good reason for it. But I didn't like it. You're right, you are my son and, whatever you'd done, I still felt you were entitled to know. I agreed not to tell you, because, as far as I could see, it was better for Maddie…"

"Not to have me in her life?" Jake's voice was barely audible.

"Yes. At the time, that's what I felt. You broke Cassie's heart – broke mine too when you left here the way you did. You were too damn destructive back then. I didn't want you to do that to your daughter. But, like I say, it wasn't an easy decision. Kate and I argued… badly, and then we agreed we wouldn't talk about it."

"So it just never came up?"

"Maddie did, but not Cassie, or her personal life – and not you. Kate told me when Cassie got her job with a publisher, and that she writes, but that's it. Apart from that, we only talked about Maddie. Cassie used to send her mom photographs every couple of weeks by e-mail. Kate gave me copies."

Jake's eyes widened. "You've got pictures?"

"Yeah. Do you want to see them?"

"Yes, please."

Ben got slowly to his feet and went over to the bookcase, turning on the table lamps as he went. He pulled the box from the bottom shelf and came back, handing it to Jake.

"They're in order," he said softly. "Start at the bottom and work up."

Jake took the lid from the box and pulled out the pile of photographs. He turned them over, one by one, his eyes resting on each one, as he took in the first few weeks of Maddie's life, in an incubator. Looking at her like this, she seemed to grow and develop quickly, from a tiny scrap of life, into a recognizable, beautiful baby. He progressed forward, to pictures of her smiling, eating a banana – and getting in a mess, by the looks of things – and standing, holding onto the side of a pale gray couch, which he guessed was in Cassie's apartment.

"She's so beautiful," he whispered.

"Yep."

"There are no pictures of Cass here," Jake said, continuing through them, to Maddie as a toddler, grinning at the camera.

"No."

"Why not?"

"She's taking the pictures."

"Get with the twenty-first century, Dad… she could take a selfie."

"I know that. But these aren't about Cassie, Jake." Ben sighed. "They're about Maddie. It's always been about Maddie."

Jake nodded his head. "She seems like an incredible mom."

"Oh, there's no seeming about it. That young woman is remarkable. She's the best there is," Ben finished and they sat in silence for a while, staring at each other. Ben spoke again first. "I did ask her, just the other day, whether she had someone…"

"And?" Jake leant forward, unable to hide his curiosity.

"I was asking if there was someone she might have left Maddie with, in Portland… I hadn't even met Maddie at that stage, and I wasn't sure she'd brought her here…"

"Yeah? What was her answer, Dad?"

"She said she only ever leaves Maddie with Emma, and… and Kate." He paused. "She didn't say there *wasn't* another guy, just that there's no-one she chooses to leave Maddie with. But that might be because the relationship is quite new, or maybe he works. Who knows?"

Jake slumped back in his seat. "Yeah," he sighed. It wasn't the definitive answer he'd hoped for… or needed.

"If she is single though, and if she's willing to give you a second chance, you'll be a lucky man," Ben whispered. "Cassie's one of a kind."

"I know." Jake looked up.

"So don't screw it up."

Ben sat back and wiped his hands down his face. He looked older than his years and the enormity of their conversation struck Jake, like a hammer blow.

"Christ," he said, putting the photographs to one side. He got up and moved across to his dad, crouching down in front of him. "I can't even imagine how you feel. We're sitting here talking about Cass, and whether I've got a chance with her... But you've just buried the woman you love – for the second time," he murmured. And then he remembered something else. "You found Kate's body, didn't you?" he asked.

Ben nodded.

"What happened?"

Ben looked at him. "I used to go down there for breakfast," he explained. "Kate wasn't willing for us to live together, but she liked to have breakfast with me, especially this time of year... out on the porch, listening to the ocean." Ben took a breath. "When I got down there, she was lying on the kitchen floor, naked."

"Naked?" Jake was surprised.

"Yeah. I'd spent the evening down there. We'd been to bed..."

"You don't need to explain, Dad," Jake said softly.

"When I left, she said she was going to make herself a cup of tea. It was a warm night, so she didn't bother putting anything on. I kissed her goodnight in the kitchen, and came on home. I reckon she died within minutes of me leaving. There was a broken teacup beside her on the floor..."

"Oh, Dad."

Ben cleared his throat and took a breath. "I covered her over and called Doc Cooper. Once he'd worked out it was a heart attack and not foul play, or anything, we put her into a bath robe, so no-one would know... You know what this place is like, and Kate would've hated anyone to gossip about her."

"Does Cassie know?"

"No. She knows I found Kate, but not the circumstances. And I'm not gonna tell her."

"Cassie wouldn't judge, Dad. Not either of you."

"I know that, but I think Kate would have wanted it this way. I wanted to stay with her that night, but she said no – she always said no.

If only I'd stayed…" Ben's voice cracked, and Jake fell to his knees and pulled his dad into a hug. He felt his shoulders shaking as the tears fell.

"I'm sorry, Dad," he mumbled. "I should've been here today, for you too. I wish… I wish we'd all spent more time together as a family. I wish things had been different."

"No use wishing, son," Ben said, clearing his throat, leaning back and wiping his eyes. "Doing is the only thing that counts."

"Then I'll do, and I'll think, and I'll get it right this time around. I won't let you down again… any of you."

Chapter Twelve

Cassie

It was the feeling of being tugged that woke Cassie.

"Good morning," she said, while signing at the same time. Maddie returned the sign, then clambered off the bed, pulling Cassie with her.

"I guess we're hungry," Cassie said to herself, as she let Maddie haul her into the kitchen. They stopped and Cassie made her right hand into a fist, extending her forefinger, and moving it along under her chin, like a worm. "Cereal?" she said, at the same time. Maddie shook her head and held up her flat left hand, tapping it with the index and middle fingers of her right hand, firstly on the back and then the front.

"Okay, toast it is," Cassie nodded her head and made the 'okay' sign.

She pulled out a chair at the table and Maddie climbed up, while Cassie fetched some bread and put it in toaster, before filling the kettle, placing it on the stove and getting a beaker from the cupboard. She half-filled it with juice and put it on the table, but Maddie shook her head again. Cassie tilted her head to one side and Maddie raised her right hand, making a squeezing motion with her fingers.

"You want milk?" Maddie never had milk at breakfast, except on her cereal. "Okay." She took away the beaker of juice and replaced it with one of milk, which Maddie drank down.

The kettle whistled, the toast popped out of the toaster… and breakfast was ready.

After their shower, which they took together, Cassie dried first Maddie's hair and then her own, and they got dressed.

While she was pulling on her shorts and top, watching Maddie struggling obstinately with her socks, she remembered how good it had felt to be held by Jake the night before. His arms were definitely stronger than before, his chest and back definitely broader and more muscular. She shook herself out of that thought. He may have held her, he may have comforted her, but that didn't mean he wanted her. He probably had women falling all over him back in Boston, or maybe he had one special woman. Whichever it was, she couldn't compete.

Besides, despite his kindness, she knew he'd find it hard to forgive her for what she'd done. She was finding it impossible herself – so how must he feel? She'd got it wrong… spectacularly wrong. He hadn't slept with Alice. Okay, he may have been unreliable, and he may still have a few things to prove, but he hadn't betrayed her. And she'd have to go a long, long way before she could even begin to feel good about herself again.

Once Maddie had finished with her socks, Cassie helped her with her shoes and then took her hand, leading her out through the kitchen door, which she closed and locked behind her, and down the porch steps.

She didn't want to think too hard about what she was about to do. She'd decided before getting into bed the previous night, that she was going to invite Ben and Jake for dinner. And, Maddie having woken up so early meant she'd probably be able to catch Ben before he went out to do whatever he had to do this morning. She could put the invitation to him… it would be easier. He was due to come round and finish fixing the roof that afternoon anyway, and Jake could join them for dinner later on. She had it all planned in her head, so thinking about it anymore wasn't really necessary, and it was just making her more nervous, which was ridiculous. This was just Ben… well, Ben and Jake.

They arrived at Ben's yard and she helped Maddie up the steep steps at the side of the garage, which led to the office above, then knocked on the door. She turned and looked back down into the yard and, only then, noticed that Ben's truck was missing. There was a sleek, black BMW… but no truck. Ben must have already left for the morning.

She let out a sigh and prepared to lift Maddie to carry her back down the steps again. She could always talk to Ben when he came around later. It wouldn't be too late to go to the store and get whatever they needed for dinner, if he and Jake wanted to come. Now all she had to do was sneak back out of the yard without Jake seeing her... He was probably still in bed, she imagined. He was never one for getting up too early, if he didn't have to.

She raised Maddie into her arms, just as the door to the office swung open, nearly hitting them.

"Sorry," Jake said automatically.

Cassie felt herself blushing. "No. I'm sorry."

"Cass?" He sounded surprised. "And Maddie." He put his right hand to his head and gave a salute. "Hello," he said.

"You... you learned, 'hello'?" Cassie said.

"Yeah. And goodbye," he replied. "You said those were the first things everyone learned, so I thought I'd start there."

"That's..." She was at a loss for words.

"Surprising?" He helped her out.

"I was going to say, impressive."

He chuckled. "Don't be too impressed." He ran his fingers through his hair. "I got myself in such a muddle."

Cassie lowered Maddie to the ground again, but she raised her arms up, wanting to be lifted.

"Can I?" Jake asked.

"If she'll let you." Cassie crouched down and turned Maddie in Jake's direction. "Hold out your arms to her, so she knows what you're gonna do," she explained to him. Jake followed her instructions. Cassie looked at Maddie and made the 'okay' sign, tilting her head to one side, like a question. Maddie nodded her head enthusiastically. "Guess she likes that idea," Cassie said, and Jake leant down and lifted Maddie into his arms.

"Thanks." He looked at Cassie.

"Like I told you last night, Jake – it's about her. She's happy, so that's okay." Cassie swallowed hard as Maddie rested her head on Jake's shoulder. "So…" she continued, trying to ignore the lump rising in her throat. "How did you get yourself into a muddle?"

He looked at her for a few seconds, then seemed to remember what they'd been talking about. "Oh yes, the signing." A smile formed on his lips. "You'd said everyone knew 'hello', and 'goodbye' and how Maddie asked for a drink, and the bathroom." He paused for a moment. "My dad gave me the name of the website he uses to learn from, so I settled down in bed last night with my laptop. 'Hello' and 'goodbye' were easy," he continued, "and I was thinking this was gonna be a breeze, and if I kept going, I'd have it cracked by, maybe two in the morning." He let out a laugh. "Only then I realized that Maddie might not just ask for a drink… she might be more specific." He looked at Cassie. "I kinda worked out for myself that she wasn't likely to ask for a whiskey and soda…" Cassie couldn't help but laugh. He grinned down at her. "But that still left me with water, and juice and milk as the bare minimum. So I started learning those, but then I kept getting confused, except with milk – that was easy to remember." He stopped talking and leaned a little closer. "And that was before I even started on the bathroom… I mean, does she say specifically what she wants to do, or does she just say she needs the bathroom?"

"It depends where we are. If she's somewhere familiar, she'll usually just tell me she's going to the bathroom, and take herself off. If we're out, or somewhere she doesn't know – like here – she'll usually say what she needs to do."

"Okay, so I need to learn all of that." He looked a little overwhelmed.

"Don't expect do learn it all overnight, Jake," Cassie said.

"I didn't. I gave up around two-thirty."

"Two-thirty?"

"Yeah…"

"But it's only just after eight now. You can't have had much sleep."

"No, but it's fine. I wanted to get my day's work finished by the time dad gets back from Doc Cooper's place. I'm just using dad's office while he's not here."

"Have you got plans for later, then?" Cassie could feel her own disappointment rising.

He seemed surprised. "Well, yeah. Dad told me he was coming down to see you this afternoon, to finish fixing your roof." He paused. "I thought I'd tag along and help out… if you're okay with that."

She wondered if her relief was visible on her face. Her slowly forming smile must be. "Yes… I'm fine with that," she murmured.

"Good." He smiled back, and she felt herself being drawn into his deep green eyes. She didn't think she physically moved toward him, but she wouldn't have been surprised if she had.

"How is Ben?" she asked, clearing her throat.

He blinked a couple of times. "He's… well, he's not good. We talked last night. He told me about your mom and him being lovers. It's a shame they couldn't have been more open about it though… you know, been a proper couple. I can't imagine your mom would've enjoyed sneaking around."

Cassie smiled. "No. It wouldn't have been her style at all."

Maddie shifted in his arms. "Does she want something?" Jake asked.

"No, she's fine. She'll let me know if she isn't."

"How did Maddie handle the funeral?" He lowered his voice.

Cassie didn't correct him, or tell him not to bother doing that. She often found herself doing it too. "I don't think she understood any of it," she replied. "She's never been here, so to her this is just a vacation by the beach, and she's having a great time. Yesterday probably felt like a big party, with lots of people coming to the house and fussing over her – which she loved."

"And the church service… the coffin?"

"I don't think that meant anything. She didn't associate it with mom, anyway. She doesn't know this is where grandma lived, so there's no connection. Grandma visited us in Portland." She raised her eyes to his. "That's where we live," she explained.

"I know. My dad told me last night."

Cassie nodded her head. "Mom used to come and visit every few weeks," she continued. "I guess it's only going to register with Maddie when we get home and grandma doesn't come visit." Her voice cracked as she finished speaking.

Jake reached out and touched her arm.

"When you tell her… when you have to explain it," he said. "I'll be there, if you need me."

"I've already told her," Cassie murmured, "or tried to, but I don't think the words meant anything."

Jake's eyes darkened. "I remember my dad telling me," he muttered, "about my mom. But I was older."

"Did it register right away?"

"You know it did, Cass. I came straight to you."

She swallowed as she recalled him running to her, tears falling down his cheeks and how he'd blurted out the words, like they were caught in his throat and he had to spew them out before they choked him. She nodded slowly.

"I remember the only thing I thought about for ages was that I'd never see her again, that she'd never put her arms around me, and tell me everything would be okay… but then you did that, Cass. You told me it would be okay."

She felt a tear fall onto her cheek. "And was it?" she whispered.

"Hey… don't cry." He moved Maddie slightly and pulled Cassie close to his chest, his free arm around her shoulders. "Please don't cry." She felt Maddie's hand on her head, patting gently, as Jake held onto her.

"What do I do without her?" she mumbled into him.

"You get by, and you keep on getting by," he said, "and one day, you'll find the getting by just gets a little bit easier."

"Does it?" She looked up at him. He was staring down at her.

"Yeah, it does. It's early days, Cass. Give it time."

She swallowed down her tears and pulled back her shoulders, pasting a smile on her face for Maddie's benefit as she turned to her.

"We came down here to ask you and Ben to have dinner with us," she said.

"Tonight?" he queried.

"Yes… why? Do you have to go back?"

"No, not until tomorrow morning. But why don't I take us all out somewhere?"

Cassie shifted from one foot to the other. "I'm not sure I'm ready for the town gossips." She looked up at him. "I mean, everyone who was at the funeral yesterday is going to have worked out that Maddie is yours. And you're back, and I'm back… but…"

"It's okay, Cass. We can go somewhere out of town, if you want."

"Or you can just stay on with us and have something to eat, once you've finished working on the roof. We can open a bottle of wine, and you can put Maddie to bed… if you want."

"Well, when you put it that way…" He smiled down at her. "We'd love to come."

Jake

He was still reeling from having Cassie in his arms again. He'd wanted to hold her for longer; he'd wanted her to hold onto him too, because he'd been fairly sure she needed someone, or something to hang onto. He wanted to do more for her, but he didn't know how appropriate that was. If she had a guy in Portland, waiting for her, then he should probably leave her alone… except when she was crying, because there was no way in hell he wasn't going to hold her when she was crying.

"I think it's helping Ben to spend time around Maddie," Cassie pointed out.

"I don't doubt it."

She looked down, and he wondered for a moment if she was blushing… she certainly seemed to be.

"What's wrong, Cass?" he asked.

"I… I just wondered what to cook," she said. "Do you still eat the same things?"

He smiled. "Pretty much. If it used to have legs, or wings, I'll eat it… and don't bother too much with green stuff." Cassie laughed softly. God, he loved her laugh.

"So nothing's changed then."

"Nope." He shook his head. "But why don't I cook?"

"You? Cook?"

"I can, you know…"

She couldn't hide her doubt. "Yes, I'm sure you can."

"Really, Cass." Maddie started fiddling with the buttons on his shirt. "I live alone. I have done since we broke up." He watched her closely and he was sure her eyes widened and maybe, just maybe, her lips parted when he said that. Or was that wishful thinking? "I either learned to cook, lived on take-out, or starved to death. I tried the take-out route for a while, but it got real boring and I was putting on weight… so, I learned to cook."

"You live alone?"

She'd picked up on that, so perhaps it hadn't been wishful thinking after all. He wanted to know whether she had anyone waiting at home – maybe if he told her about himself, she'd reciprocate? "Yeah," he responded, not taking his eyes from hers. "There's no-one in my life right now."

She nodded slowly. "And… and how far do your culinary skills stretch? I mean, what are we talking here? Boiling an egg and burning the toast… or can you *really* cook?" He was disappointed she hadn't taken the bait, but hid it well.

"Take a risk and find out," he teased. "Let me bring dinner tonight."

"Won't it be easier if I cook?"

"I won't poison you, Cass… honest."

"That's not what I meant." She smiled up at him. "I just thought that, with you and Ben working on the house, it'd be easier if I did the cooking."

"It'll be fine… but what does Maddie like to eat?"

"If you really want to win her over, cook her pasta."

"Spaghetti?"

He tried to stifle a laugh as he said the word, but Cassie couldn't. She let out a full-on giggle, which ignited tiny sparks over every nerve in Jake's body. "You remember the mess I used to get in eating spaghetti?"

He nodded, chuckling. "Hell, yeah… I remember it could get real ugly."

"Well, Maddie takes after me when it comes to her inability to keep it on her fork, while getting it to her mouth. So, you can cook spaghetti if you want to," she said, "but you're clearing it up afterwards."

He shook his head. "I don't have that long. I've gotta be back in Boston tomorrow. How about lasagna?"

"She loves lasagna."

"That's fine then. I'll make it this morning and we can bring it with us. Cass… I'm really—" His phone rang, interrupting what he was about to say. He pulled it from his pocket and checked the screen. It was Erica. He could ignore the call, or cancel it, but that would look odd… and she'd probably only call again. "Excuse me," he said. "I should probably take this."

Cassie reached out and took Maddie from him.

"We'll go," she whispered as Jake went to connect the call. He held up a finger to her.

"No… please wait." He pressed the button on his phone. "Hello?" he said, his voice more businesslike.

"Hi, Jake… It's me."

"Yes?" He watched Cassie. She knelt beside Maddie, who she'd put down on the floor. She was signing something, although he didn't know what it was. He really needed to get up to speed.

"I thought I'd better check in with you," Erica was saying in his ear. "Why?"

She gave a delicate cough. "Well, just to see if your weekend went okay. You didn't take my calls yesterday."

"No. I was in a meeting with Mitch."

"Oh… I see." He swore he could hear the relief in her voice and wished he could set her straight.

He saw Maddie nodding her head, and Cassie looking up at him. He wondered if something was wrong.

"Wait a second," he said into the phone and put his finger over the mouthpiece. "Is everything okay?" he asked Cassie.

"Sorry," she replied. "Maddie needs the bathroom."

He smiled and reached into his pocket, handing her his keys. "Let yourself into the house," he said. "You know where everything is."

She took his keys and lifted Maddie into her arms, carrying her quickly down the steps and across the yard.

"Was that it?" he said into the phone again.

"No," Erica replied. "I wanted to let you know that tomorrow's meeting has been moved."

"To when?" he asked.

"It's been brought forward by an hour."

"So… twelve o'clock?"

"Yes." He thought he heard a slight hesitation in her voice.

"Okay, I'll be there," he said.

"And did your weekend go okay, Jake?"

"Fine, thanks. Look, I've got visitors. I need to go."

"Oh, okay. I'll see you tomorrow then."

"Yeah."

"Bye, Jake."

"Bye." He hung up quickly and ran down the stairs, just as Cassie and Maddie came back out through the kitchen door.

"Everything okay?" he asked.

"Yes, thanks." She handed him back his keys.

"I was going to say I'm really grateful to you for saying I can put Maddie to bed tonight. You'll have to let me know her routine, so I don't get anything wrong."

"Since we've been here, because she's running around and spending so much time by the sea, she tends to just crash out."

"So, she doesn't have bedtime story?" Even as he said the words, Jake realized his mistake. "No, of course she doesn't. Sorry, Cass. That was a stupid thing to say." He sighed. "It's so sad she doesn't get to hear all those great stories we grew up with."

"Why?" She looked up at him. "Why is it sad? She likes stories. They may not be the ones we grew up hearing, but she enjoys them." He looked at her, really confused now. How could Maddie hear a story?

"I don't understand…"

She reached out and touched his arm. He jumped. He couldn't help it. Her touch was like a bolt of electricity.

Cassie didn't seem to notice. "I'm no Mark Twin, or C.S. Lewis, but we do okay…"

"How do you mean?" He took a step closer.

"We make up our own stories," Cassie explained. "They're usually spread over several evenings, because they take a while to sign."

"You sign stories to her?"

Cassie nodded her head. "I write them out during the evenings, when I've got a spare half hour… I create different characters and scenes and storylines to go with them. I draw pictures too and then I simplify the language so I can sign them to her. She went through a phase of liking stories with magicians in them – which was fun, because I could do anything I wanted with magic, but now she's into princesses."

Jake was staring at her… and he knew it. But then why wouldn't he? She was everything he'd ever wanted – she always had been – but she was also a whole host of things he'd never realized he'd needed, until he didn't have them anymore… and he knew he was more deeply in love with her than he'd ever been.

"Is that yours?" Cassie asked, nodding toward his BMW.

"Yes."

"So you got rid of the Jeep?" Unlike most people, Cassie wasn't impressed by his shiny new car. She had a wistful look in her eye, and Jake knew why.

"Yeah," he replied, "but not that long ago. I only bought this at the beginning of the year. I hung on to the Jeep for as long as I could, and I was real sorry to see it go." He gazed into her eyes and knew they were both thinking the same thing. They were both remembering the times they'd made love in the back of his Jeep… which was why him having Alice, or anyone else, in there would have been even more of a betrayal as far as Cassie was concerned. Like the beach, his childhood bedroom, her childhood bedroom, and their tiny apartment near the college, the Jeep held a lot of very special memories… and they were all about Cassie.

Cassie swallowed hard and looked back at the sleek black car. "You bought it?" she said.

"Yeah."

"Construction workers must get paid well."

"I'm not a construction worker."

Cassie turned to him. "Oh yes. I remember you saying you had meetings. I just assumed you'd go into construction. It's what you always planned..." Her voice faded.

"I did. And then I got promoted a few times. I'm overseeing a project now and if I make it work, I'll be the Head of Corporate Construction for Eldridge Holdings."

Cassie's eyes widened. "I've heard of them," she whispered.

"Yeah... they are quite big."

"And you're gonna be a department head?"

"Only if I bring in this latest project. There's a lot riding on it... more than just my promotion and pay rise." She tilted her head to one side. "The client's reputation, his money, my boss's faith in me..." he explained. "It's a lot of pressure."

"Do you enjoy it though?"

He smiled. "Yeah, Cass, I really do. What I'm doing now, and the head of department job... that's what it was always about. That's what I've been working so hard for."

Chapter Thirteen

Cassie

"I've made some lemonade," Cassie called as she came out of the door and onto the porch.

"I'll be down in a minute." She could hear Jake calling from above, on the roof. He'd refused to let Ben go up there again, despite his father's protests that he did roof work all the time.

"Not when I'm here you don't," Jake had said, and was up the ladder before Ben could stop him. Ben had spent the afternoon working on the dilapidated garage instead.

"Did I hear you say 'lemonade'?" Ben asked, coming around the corner of the house.

"You did."

Maddie was already sitting on the swing seat, with a plate of cookies beside her.

"How do I sign cookie?" Ben asked.

Cassie put the tray of lemonade down on the table, then held out her left hand, palm side up. "Imagine this is the cookie dough," she said. Ben copied her. "Then make like you're cutting cookies with the other hand." She demonstrated, twisting the fingers of her right hand into the palm of her left.

"Hey… no private lessons," Jake called out to them, as he approached from the other side of the porch. He was smiling as he walked up the steps and joined them. Cassie turned, and her breath caught in her throat. When he'd arrived earlier, he'd been wearing jeans and a white t-shirt and she'd had to admit, he'd looked good, but now, he'd removed the t-shirt, and the jeans were hanging low on his hips, and he looked so much better than good. She'd been right, his body was more toned, more muscular… and much harder. She couldn't help but stare, admire, and reminisce over what had once been hers. "What were you doing?" he asked, walking slowly toward them.

"Cassie was showing me how to sign 'cookie'," Ben explained, demonstrating. He glanced at Cassie. "Was that right?"

"Um… Yes," she stuttered, trying to regain her composure.

Jake copied too and then they turned and looked at Maddie, who was holding out the plate to them, a resigned expression on her face. They all laughed.

"I guess she's worked out she's not going to get them all to herself," Cassie said, going over and hugging her daughter, grateful for the diversion. She put her hand on her chin and moved it away, like she was blowing a kiss, then with a clenched fist ran her thumb down her jaw. Maddie nodded her head, smiling.

"What did you say to her?" Jake asked, coming over and sitting down beside Maddie.

"I told her she was a good girl." Cassie signed 'good' and 'girl' again, for Jake's benefit.

"Show me once more?" Jake said, and then copied Cassie's movements.

"Don't expect to remember all of this," Cassie warned him. "There's a lot to take in."

"I'm working that much out already."

Ben was standing looking at Cassie. "I'm confused," he said, biting a chunk out of the cookie he'd taken from the plate.

"Why?" She went over to him.

"'Good' looks a helluva lot like 'thank you' to me."

Cassie smiled. "It is."

"Oh, hell." Jake put his head in his hands. "You mean there are signs that look the same?"

Cassie laughed now. "No-one said this was easy." She demonstrated the difference between 'thank you' and 'good'.

"So you just rotate your hand?" Jake asked.

"Yes. Vertical is 'thank you', horizontal is 'good'."

"And how do you remember that?"

"You just do, after a while. And with 'thank you', you tend to direct your hand toward the person you're thanking, whereas with 'good' you just kinda lower your hand."

"Jeez, Cass."

"Wanna give up, son?" Ben looked at him, his eyes hardening.

"No, of course not. It's just…"

"Hard work?" Ben supplied.

"Yeah. And I feel like I'm getting nowhere…"

He looked a little despondent. Cassie went back to him and leant over, her hand on the arm of the swing beside him. She was close enough to touch him, but she didn't. "I've had a lot longer doing this," she said. "A couple of days ago, you didn't even know Maddie existed." She lowered her eyes. She felt ashamed of her decisions and her mistakes; as well as confused by her feelings for Jake. She'd expected him to hate her, to despise her for what she'd done; she certainly hadn't expected his warmth, his kindness, or to see that smoldering desire she was almost certain she caught a glimpse of in his eyes every so often.

She felt Jake's finger beneath her chin, raising her face to his.

"I know," he said. "Thanks, Cass. I'm just being a girl."

"Nothing wrong with that." Cassie smiled at him. "In case you haven't noticed… Maddie and I, we're both girls."

Jake's eyes penetrated hers. "Oh, I'd noticed, Cass—"

"And how do you sign girl?" Ben asked him, interrupting the moment.

Jake glowered over at his dad. Cassie leant a little closer, calmed herself, and whispered, "Thumb, jaw," and recognition dawned on Jake's face as he raised his thumb to his jawline, running it from ear to chin.

"Is that right, Cassie?" Ben asked. She straightened and nodded her head. "See, you can do it, son," Ben continued. "Just have a little faith in yourself… and be patient."

Jake glanced up at Cassie. "I will," he said and winked at her, and Cassie couldn't help but wink back.

They ate dinner on the porch, sitting around the rectangular table. It was too warm to eat inside.

"This is good," Cassie said between mouthfuls. Jake really could cook and, judging from Maddie's expression, she was enjoying it too.

Late in the afternoon, Ben and Jake had gone back home to quickly shower and change, returning with the lasagna – which just needed to be baked – some salad, garlic bread and a bottle of red wine. While Jake prepared the meal, Cassie had bathed Maddie, and now she was sitting in her pale pink pajamas, next to Jake.

"You brought green stuff?" Cassie said, helping herself to more sliced peppers and tomatoes from the salad bowl.

"There's green, red and yellow in there," Jake observed. "It's a positive rainbow."

"Yeah, but it's all kinda healthy, isn't it?" Cassie teased.

Ben smiled, watching them, as he slowly ate his food and poured some more water into Maddie's beaker.

"I thought Maddie should have some green stuff," Jake replied. "Doesn't mean I'm gonna eat it."

"Not even to show a good example?" Cassie was really struggling to keep a straight face.

Jake stared at her. "Aw hell, Cass. Okay, pass the salad." Cassie burst out laughing, and picked up the bowl, passing it to him. "The things I do for you," he grumbled, putting a few leaves of lettuce and some sliced peppers onto his plate.

"Not for me," Cassie corrected, "for your daughter."

He stilled and glanced up at her. "That sounded good."

"What?"

"When you said 'your daughter'."

"Well, she is."

"I know. It just sounds good when you say it."

They stared at each other until Ben gave a slight cough and Cassie turned, realizing that both he and Maddie were looking at them. She flushed the same color as the tomatoes and glanced back at Jake, who was grinning – *damn him*.

Maddie soon asked for a second helping of lasagna and, once she'd finished that and everyone else had completed the meal, they all cleared away and returned to the porch to finish the wine. Maddie sat on Jake's lap on the porch swing. Although she still had no idea who he was, Cassie was relieved she'd taken to him. She seemed very comfortable, both in his presence and his arms and rested her head on his chest while he rocked her.

"If you want to put her to bed while she's still awake," Cassie warned him, "you'd better stop doing that. She's gonna be asleep in a minute."

"Shall I take her through then?" Jake suggested.

"If you like."

He got to his feet, taking Maddie with him and she looked up at him.

Cassie came over and signed that it was time for bed. Maddie rubbed her eyes and went to get down, but Jake kept hold of her. Cassie caught Maddie's attention and explained that Jake would be taking her. The little girl smiled and relaxed again, putting her arms around Jake's neck and snuggling down into him.

"What did you say?" Jake asked.

"I just told her you'd be putting her to bed tonight," Cassie said.

"And that made her smile… like that?"

"Evidently."

She saw the glow spread up his face, and felt tears stinging behind her eyes. It was going to be the first time in Maddie's life that she hadn't put her to bed, and she wasn't sure how she felt about that.

"Come with us," Jake said. "I can't do this by myself."

Cassie's eyes locked with Jake's. She expected to see helplessness, but what she saw instead was a familiar longing that matched her own, and any sadness she'd felt at relinquishing Maddie's bedtime ritual to him quickly vanished. They were going to put their daughter to bed together, and that was right; that was exactly how it should be. She smiled up at him, then turned and led the way through to her bedroom, holding the doors open and pulling back the comforter for Jake to lower Maddie down onto the bed.

As he pulled the cover back up, Maddie grabbed his hand.

"She wants you to stay," Cassie explained, when he glanced at her for guidance.

He squatted down on the floor beside the bed.

"How do I tell her 'goodnight'?" Jake asked, looking up at Cassie again.

She came and sat on the bed and demonstrated.

"Remember the sign for good?" she asked.

"Like blowing a kiss?"

Cassie smiled. "A little." She showed him again and he nodded. "You add 'night'," she said, holding her left hand horizontally across her body. "Think of this hand as being like the horizon," she explained. "And your right hand is the setting sun, going over it." She cupped the fingers of her right hand and raised it up over her left.

"And then you put them together?" Jake asked, trying it.

"Yes…" She watched him. "That's right. Make sure you face Maddie, so she knows you're talking to her." Jake turned and signed 'goodnight', and Maddie signed back to him, then settled down in the bed.

He reached up and stroked her hair gently. Cassie watched his face for a few moments, but the emotions she saw there were too much for her and she stood up, crossed the room and waited for him by the door. She knew he was thinking of how many times he'd missed out on doing this, and she knew that it was all her fault.

It only took a few minutes for Maddie to fall asleep, but Jake stayed, gently stroking her hair for quite a while.

Eventually though, he got up, turned and came to stand beside her in the doorway.

"Thanks," he whispered, his voice barely under control.

"Don't thank me, Jake." Cassie could hear her own emotion.

"Hey…" He clasped her shoulders and turned her to face him. "I mean it. Thank you for letting me do this… and for helping me with the signing. Especially earlier. I know dad was testing me, with that 'girl' thing, and I hadn't remembered it."

"Neither had he."

"That's not the point," he insisted.

"You don't have to remember everything first time, Jake."

"I know. But I'm gonna work real hard to get it right, I promise, Cass."

He was so close she could feel his breath on her cheek and she focused, just for a second, on his lips, recalling how hard his kisses could be when he really wanted her, so hard her own lips were sometimes left bruised. She'd always liked that intensity, that need in him.

"We should probably get back to your dad," she said, still feeling overwhelmed by guilt at what she'd taken from him.

His shoulders dropped, just a fraction, or at least she thought they did. "Okay," he murmured.

She led the way back to the kitchen, where Ben was already washing up. They joined him and, before long, everything was tidied away.

"Shall we have coffee outside?" Cassie suggested.

"Sure." Jake smiled broadly, and Ben agreed.

"You go get comfy," Cassie said. "I'll bring it out."

As she stood waiting for the kettle to boil on the stove, Cassie wondered – not for the first time – how her life might have been different, if she hadn't screwed it up so badly. One thing was for sure, being around Jake again, she knew she loved him as much today as she'd ever done – and maybe more so, after seeing him with Maddie.

Jake

Waiting for Cassie to bring out the coffee, Jake sat in silence with his dad. He'd found it really hard to keep it together while he was putting Maddie to bed. Stroking her hair and watching her fall asleep had seemed like such an easy thing to do, but it was all he could do not to break down.

She'd already stolen his heart and now, as he stared, unseeing out across the ocean, he had no idea what he was going to do when Cassie sold the house and went back to Portland – to her normal life. He assumed he'd have allocated weekends with Maddie, maybe time during the school breaks, and he'd have to learn to live with that… How? He had no idea, because he wasn't even sure he could go home tonight, ten minutes down the lane, let alone live over an hour away from her.

He was still haunted by the idea that, somewhere in Portland, there was a guy who, maybe, got to put Maddie to bed some nights, who got to sit and watch TV with her, and take her to the park, and who knew how to sign 'goodnight' without having to be shown… *And* who got to kiss Cassie, and hold her, and touch her. He sighed. Yeah, of course it was about Maddie, but as far as he was concerned it was also very much about Cassie. He didn't want there to be a guy who got to see her crying, got to wipe away her tears and tell her he could make it better… because he couldn't. No-one else could make it better – only Jake could do that.

He leant forward, resting his elbows on his knees, his chin on his clenched fists. Being in Cassie's room again, with her, had felt weird. He couldn't help but remember the times they'd sneaked around as teenagers, snatching whatever moments they could, just to be together. He'd made love to her on that bed countless times; especially when her mom was at work during the long summer vacation, when they'd come back from college and they'd had the house to themselves. God, those were good days… making love for hours, swimming in the ocean, eating whatever Kate had left for them in the refrigerator, Cassie falling asleep in his arms, a book lodged between them; then waking up to her warm, sleepy kisses. His want, his need for her had always been overpowering. It still was.

Outside Cassie's old room, just a few minutes ago, he'd realized that. He'd had to reach out and touch her. She didn't want his thanks, but he needed her to hear it anyway. Feeling her skin beneath his hands was like being scorched, and he'd thought she felt it too. Her eyes had dropped to his lips and he'd seen that look on her face; the one she used to get whenever she wanted him to kiss her – real hard; when she wanted him to crush his lips to hers and leave them swollen. He'd thought about it too; thought about leaning in, reclaiming her, but she'd moved away and suggested going back to his dad. So, maybe he'd been wrong... except it didn't feel like it. It felt like she wanted the kiss, like she wanted him, just as much as he wanted her, but something was holding her back. Another commitment, perhaps? He felt his muscles clench. He really didn't want her to have someone else. He didn't want allocated weekends, or school breaks with Maddie. He didn't just want Maddie. More than anything, he desperately wanted Cassie too. He wanted both of them, together, because together they were a family. They were his family.

"You okay, son?" Ben asked.

"Hmm?" Jake looked over to where Ben was sitting at the other end of the swing seat.

"I asked if you're okay?"

"Yeah..."

"Anything you wanna talk about?"

Jake shook his head and leaned back, trying to relax a little. "Not right now."

He turned his head as the screen door swung open and stood to help Cassie with the tray, taking it from her and placing it on the table. She poured the coffee, handing out the cups and they all sat together on the swing, Cassie between Jake and his father.

Jake took a sip of coffee, barely noticing the scalding heat. What he did notice was that Cassie's bare leg was pressed against his, and he thanked the Lord he'd changed into a shirt and left it untucked. At least she and Ben couldn't see he was bone hard.

He ached to touch her, but what if she wasn't free?

For a while, nobody spoke, but Jake had questions... questions that needed answering if he was going to stand a chance of getting any sleep at all, especially as he was going back to Boston the next morning. He needed to know if there was any hope for them at all, or whether this really was just about Maddie.

"Dad told me you work in publishing, and you write?" Jake said, thinking that maybe her career was a neutral place to start.

"Yes." She looked up at him.

"What does that entail?" he asked, twisting a little, and pulling his shirt down to ensure he was covered still.

"I'm a freelance editor," Cassie replied. "I work mainly for a small publisher in Portland, but I've picked up a few clients of my own in the last year or so – mainly self-published authors, who pay me to edit their novels."

"How do you manage to do all that when you've got Maddie?" He put his arm along the back of the seat, behind her head.

"It's not too bad. I work from home, and I just go into the office when I have to, for meetings. My boss is really good and she lets me take Maddie with me." Cassie smiled. "She's so quiet, no-one really knows she's there."

"And the writing? Your writing, I mean." He hoped she'd been able to fulfill that ambition; that she hadn't been held back. It was something she'd dreamed of for as long as he could remember.

She lowered her eyes. "I—I've got my first novel coming out soon," she whispered. "It's part of a series, that was picked up by a New York publishing house. It's not a big publisher, but…"

"Really?" He was overjoyed and he didn't bother to hide it. "That's great, Cassie."

She looked up at him. "It's not that impressive."

"It damn well is."

She sighed. "I always wanted to write something meaningful, cerebral and thought-provoking," she murmured, twisting her cup in her hands.

"And?" he prompted.

"And I've ended up writing chick-lit."

"Chick-lit?"

"Romantic fiction," she clarified. "I realized very quickly through my editing work, and through talking to Veronica – my boss – that the best-selling genres at the moment are romance and thrillers, or murder mysteries. I couldn't write the last two… I'd be awful at that, so I decided to try romance. Veronica read my first manuscript and gave it to a friend of hers in New York, and she took it on."

Jake leant into her. "Well, I'm really proud of you," he said. He hoped that didn't sound patronizing, because that wasn't how he meant it. He really was proud of her, for doing what she'd wanted, and dealing with everything else life had thrown at her – well Jake had thrown at her, really.

He'd never read any romantic fiction, but he'd seen the covers when browsing online. From what he'd seen, books like that usually seemed to fall into two categories. Some featured nearly naked bodies – either men, or women, or both – while others showed pretty, wholesome-looking women, being held in the arms of handsome, rugged men, maybe on a beach or in a field of flowers. He wondered if she'd gone for raunchy or romantic, and what she used for her inspiration. Did *she* have a handsome, rugged man, whispering in her ear, or a hot crazy sex life to stimulate her imagination? God, he hoped not. He didn't like the sound of either of those options. He was going to have to try and get hold of a copy of her book, when it was launched, so he could find out.

"Is it hard?" he asked. "Writing a novel, I mean?" He was fishing now, and he knew it.

"Yes and no." He looked down at her, waiting for her to explain. "You have to put so much of yourself into a novel," she said, "and that can be quite tough sometimes."

"Especially with romantic fiction, I should think…"

"Why?"

"Because romance is such a personal thing," he qualified.

She looked up at him through her long eyelashes. "Yes, it is." Although dusk was now descending, there was enough light coming from the kitchen and the setting sun for him to see her cheeks flush. She looked adorable. "It might be hard," she continued, "but I'd rather write than edit. I can lose myself in my stories…" Her voice trailed away to a whisper and he was left contemplating what type of worlds she created to lose herself in.

Ben coughed quietly at the other end of the seat and Jake glanced at him over the top of Cassie's bent head. He'd almost forgotten his dad was there.

"Have you thought any more about the kitchen and the bathroom?" Ben asked, returning Jake's gaze, but addressing his question to Cassie.

"What about the kitchen and bathroom?" Jake inquired, before Cassie could answer.

"They need work," Ben replied.

"And I'm not sure whether to do it or not." Cassie turned to face him again. "I know I'll get more money if I do, but it's a lot to spend."

"It'll take more time too," Ben pointed out.

"Time isn't the problem," Cassie explained. "We can stay for the summer."

Jake felt his heart skip a beat. They could stay for the summer. Would she agree to do that so easily if she had a guy in Portland? He doubted it.

"What about your work?" Ben asked.

"I can work from anywhere," Cassie said. "I've got a couple of manuscripts to edit, and I'm working on the fourth part in my series of novels, but it doesn't matter where I am… and Maddie doesn't start school until September, so we can stay until then. It's not the time, Ben – it's the money. I've got some savings, but they're probably not enough. Besides, they're for Maddie. I don't want to touch them."

"I understand that," he replied.

"Selling this place, even without the kitchen and bathroom being modernized, I should make enough to be able to buy a small apartment in Portland," Cassie continued. "We don't need anywhere big… it's just the two of us, and I need a space to work, but it'd be nice not to worry about paying rent every month. I think it's gonna have to be enough."

It was just the two of them… she wasn't living with anyone. She might have a casual boyfriend, but Cassie didn't really do casual. He felt himself relaxing, and moving just a little closer to her, and then he registered the other thing she'd said… She was worried about making the rent each month. He didn't like that. He didn't like that at all.

Ben was nodding his head slowly. "Makes sense, I guess," he murmured.

Jake had a lot to think about, but for now, he wanted to change the subject. "Can you show me how to sign 'good morning'?" he asked Cassie. "I know 'hello', which is fine, but I want to know 'good morning' too."

Cassie put her cup down by her feet and demonstrated to them both, watching them while they copied her. They came up with other words they wanted to learn and the next hour or so was spent watching, copying, and laughing as Jake and Ben frequently messed up.

When it was time to leave, Cassie walked with Ben and Jake to the top of the steps.

"Thank you for a lovely evening," Ben said. "I'll be round tomorrow." He leant forward and kissed Cassie on the cheek, then let her go and walked down the steps and around the corner of the house, leaving Jake alone with her.

"It's been really special," Jake whispered, taking a step closer to her. Cassie nodded, but didn't reply.

"I *won't* be round tomorrow," he added. "I'm going back to Boston first thing in the morning." He saw her face fall. "I'm coming back on Saturday," he continued. "Would it… would it be okay if I came to see you?"

She looked up, her eyes widening. "Of course," she murmured.

"Good. I'll see you then. Give Maddie a hug from me." She nodded her agreement and reluctantly, he turned to go, wanting to kiss her, but still feeling uncertain of his reception. He started down the steps, hoping she'd call him back for some reason… anything to give him hope.

"Jake?" Cassie called after him as he reached the bottom step. He stopped and flipped around.

"Yes?" He looked up at her.

"Thank you."

"What for?"

"Bringing dinner, the wine, being here, being so kind… oh, just everything." He heard her voice crack, and quickly climbed back up the steps to stand in front of her, pulling her close into his arms.

"It's okay, Cass," he whispered. "It was just a lasagna."

Her shoulders shook as she laughed through her tears, and she smacked him lightly on the arm. "You're an idiot, Jake Hunter."

"Made you laugh, though." He smiled down at her. She nodded, resting her forehead on his chest. "It gets better. I promise."

"I wish…" she murmured into his shirt. "I wish…"

He pulled back a little further. "A very wise man told me not that long ago that there's no point in wishing. He told me doing is the only thing that counts."

"And what if there's nothing I can do?" She raised her face and looked up at him. "I can't go back, Jake. I can't take back my mistakes. I can't give you and Maddie all the things you missed out on with each other. Oh God… I got it all so wrong, didn't I?" she sobbed.

"Stop it, Cass." He took a deep breath. "Maddie doesn't look to me like she's missed out on anything by not having me around. You've done an incredible job with her…"

"And what about you, Jake? What about all the things you didn't get to see and do and feel?"

"Cass, please… You can't keep blaming yourself for all of that. I got it wrong too. But that's in the past and just because we got it wrong, doesn't mean we can't try and make it right again."

"How?"

He leant in close, so his forehead was touching hers. "We're already trying, Cass," he whispered. "We're here, aren't we? So we're already trying."

She pulled back just a little and glanced from his eyes down to his mouth, just like she had earlier. His heart, and his body might have been yelling at him to crush his lips against hers, but his brain was screaming at him to back off, to give it more time; yelling at him not to rush her, and risk screwing it up, and maybe losing her… again. So, he tried something he'd never been very good at in the past. He compromised. Leaning into her, he brushed his lips just gently across hers, with a featherlight touch. He held them there, for a moment or two, savoring her sweet softness, and then he pulled back. Her eyes were closed, her face raised… God, he wanted more and he thought, maybe she did too. But he'd wait until he knew for sure. He wasn't prepared to take the risk of getting it wrong. He had too much to lose... and he wasn't thinking about Maddie.

He pulled her into his arms again and felt her relax into him.

It was some time before he finally let her go, said goodnight again and joined Ben in the lane.

"You okay?" Ben asked him.

"Yeah."

"And Cassie?"

"She was upset," Jake told him, "but she's okay now."

"Upset about her mom?"

"Yeah..."

"And?"

"And about what happened with Maddie. About not telling me," Jake explained.

"She told you that?"

"Yeah. She said she thought she'd got it wrong."

"And what did you tell her?" Ben looked up at him.

"I told her getting it wrong doesn't mean we can't make it right... I got it wrong too."

Ben smiled. "Sounds promising," he murmured.

"I hope so, Dad... I sure hope so."

"After that talk you had earlier, I got the impression she's on her own, didn't you?"

"Yeah."

"So do you think there's any chance for the two of you?" Ben asked.

Jake looked at him. "I really want there to be. But she needs time."

"Then give her time, son."

They started walking home.

"This thing with the kitchen and the bathroom, and the money," Jake said, sliding his hands into his pockets.

"What about it?"

"How bad is it? I mean, are we talking a total refit, or just some cosmetic work?"

"A total refit. The bathroom in that place is a disaster. It needs ripping out and starting from scratch."

"And the kitchen?"

"The same, really. All the units need replacing, the floor and walls need work, and she's gonna have to get all new electrical items. The cooker in there is older than you are."

Jake let out a half laugh. "I noticed. I guess she's looking at… something like seven to ten thousand to fix it?"

"I don't know. I can probably bring it in for a little less than that. I'd have to price everything up."

"Than price it up and give me the figures"

Ben stopped walking. Jake carried on for another couple of paces, then he stopped too and turned to look at his father. "Why?" Ben asked.

"Because I'll pay for it," Jake replied. "But I don't want Cassie to know," he added quickly.

"Why not?" Ben was surprised.

"Because she'll refuse to accept it."

Ben started walking again, and Jake fell into step beside him.

"So you want to lie to her?" Ben mused.

"No. I want *you* to lie to her." Ben stopped again. "If I do it, she'll know," Jake continued. "I could never lie to her."

"And you think I can?"

"For a good cause… maybe."

"What am I supposed to tell her?" Ben asked.

"You could say you picked everything up cheaply… maybe a cancelled job, or something?"

Ben nodded his head. "Might work, I guess. And I could make the cabinets for the kitchen myself. That'd keep the cost down. Then you'd only be paying for the bathroom, and the electrical items, which I can get discounted."

"Tell me how much it is, and I'll transfer the money into your account," Jake said.

"I'm gonna need more than money to get this finished by September. I've already got a full workload as it is."

"I'm gonna be here all summer, and I haven't forgotten how to use a hammer."

"So I saw," Ben agreed. "You did a good job on that roof today."

"Thanks."

"And you don't want to say a word about this to Cassie?" Ben asked, after a moment's pause.

"Not a word."

Ben smiled at him. "Why are you doing this?"

"To help out with the house."

"So it's got nothing to do with making the job take longer, so she has to spend the whole summer here too?"

"Why? Do you have a problem with your granddaughter being here for a couple of months longer?"

"Of course I don't, but I wasn't talking about Maddie…"

Jake looked at him. "I know you weren't," he murmured.

Chapter Fourteen

Cassie

Cassie sat in the window seat and stared out at the pouring rain. Maddie was curled up beside her, a blanket over her legs. Just because the bad weather had been predicted, that didn't make it any easier, and it had been a trying day. Maddie had been moody and difficult since she'd woken up. Cassie knew it was hard on Maddie, but that didn't excuse some of her behavior, and she was transported back to her own childhood, when she and Jake had listened to music, played computer games, or watched TV to while away the colder, wetter months… until they'd grown up a little, and found other things to occupy them. She let out a sigh and stroked Maddie's hair, remembering Jake putting her to bed and his emotional reaction… and his kiss. She'd been surprised by that. Being held by him when she was crying was one thing, but that kiss? That was a whole different thing altogether. At least Cassie thought it was, but what did Jake think? Would she ever know? He'd be back in Boston by now and, by the time he returned, he'd probably have forgotten all about it.

She rested her head in her hand and wondered what he'd be doing in the city. He'd had a midday meeting, she knew that, because he'd wanted to stay and have breakfast with them, but he couldn't, because he had to leave at eight. She wondered if his meetings were informal, or if he wore a suit. She'd never seen him wear one – well, not since his mom's funeral – but she could imagine he'd wear it well. She couldn't really picture him working in a big corporation. To her, Jake was a guy who wielded a hammer, or a wrench, whose jeans were usually covered in paint and dust, and who was more at ease on a ladder or scaffold than in an office… but people could change.

The knocking on the door woke her from her daydream and she moved Maddie to one side, signing that there was someone at the door. Maddie pulled her blanket away and jumped down from the seat, following behind Cassie to see who'd come calling.

"Hi, Cassie." It was Ben.

"C'mon in… you're soaking."

"Yeah, and I drove down here." He entered the house and signed 'hello' to Maddie, who came up and hugged his legs.

"I hope you're in the mood for playing, or coloring," Cassie said. "She's fed up."

"And her mom?" Ben looked down at her.

Cassie raised her face to his. "A little, I guess." She shrugged.

"Well, why don't you make some tea? We can have it with these cakes I picked up for us." He held out a white bag with the coffee shop logo on the side. "I got Emma to put them to one side for me," he explained. "You know how fast they can sell out."

Maddie went to grab the bag, but Cassie crouched down and, holding out her right hand, she snapped the first two fingers down against her thumb. "No," she said, at the same time. Maddie tried to turn away, but Cassie pulled her back, using both hands out in front of her, with her palms facing outwards, she swished them back and forth, from side to side. "Behave," she urged, with a warning note in her voice that she knew Maddie couldn't hear. She stared into the little girl's defiant eyes, as Maddie folded her arms across her chest. Cassie took a deep breath and got to her feet.

"She'll come round in a minute," she said to Ben. "I'll start on the tea." She went over to the stove and picked up the kettle, keeping an eye on Maddie the whole time.

"Been having a rough day?" Ben asked, sitting down at the table and putting the bag down in front of him.

"You could say that. I think she's gotten used to all the attention she's been getting, what with the funeral, the wake and Jake being here a lot of the time, doting on her." Cassie replaced the kettle on the stove and switched it on.

"He's just making up for lost time, Cassie."

She turned to him. "I'm not blaming him, Ben. I'm just saying." She sighed. "It's hard…"

"I know."

She glanced across to Maddie, who'd now sat down on the floor, with her legs crossed. "I thought we'd bake cookies this morning," Cassie said, fetching cups from the cabinet. "And she threw the dough across the kitchen, then she wouldn't eat her lunch, and now this… on top of everything else…" She leant back on the countertop and put her hands over her face, trying hard to swallow back her tears. Why did this have to be so difficult? Losing her mom was hard enough, but her confused feelings over Jake were making it worse, and now Maddie playing up as well… It was all too much, especially when Jake wouldn't be back until the weekend to help, or hold her, or kiss her again – if he even wanted to – or just make it all seem a little bit better.

She felt a tug on her jeans and moved her hands away. Maddie was standing by her feet, looking up. The little girl rubbed her fist in a circular motion across her chest. Cassie smiled and nodded her head, then leant down and picked up her daughter, and kissed her on the cheek.

The kettle whistled, but it was Ben who got up and took it off the heat.

They sat at the table and ate their apple cakes, drinking tea – well, milk for Maddie – and Ben started telling Cassie that he might have a solution to the kitchen and bathroom problem.

"I met an old friend of mine this morning," he began. "He's in my line of work, but further up the coast." Cassie nodded her head and brushed the crumbs from the table and onto her plate. "He was telling me about this difficult client he's got."

"Oh yes?"

"Yeah. He was fitting out a house for the guy, and right at the last minute he changed his mind about what he wanted. No expense spared, he decided to ditch the original plans and start afresh."

"His client must have more money than sense."

"That's true," Ben said. "Anyway, cutting a long story short, my friend has got a load of bathroom fittings and some kitchen equipment going spare, if you want it."

"Spare?" Cassie stared at him. "You mean he doesn't want anything for it?"

"The client's already paid for it, and this guy owes me a favor… so no."

Cassie could hardly believe her luck. "And will it fit?" she asked.

"I think so. I drove over there at lunchtime and at first glance, it looks like it'll do the job for you."

"Oh, Ben… that's just perfect."

"So, you wanna go ahead with it?"

"Of course. It was only the money – not being able to afford it – that was holding me back." She hesitated.

"What's wrong?" he asked.

"I was going to talk to you about something else." He waited. "I'm thinking about ripping out the units in mom's bedroom and redecorating it. You're already doing so much for me, but do you think you could build me something a bit more modern? Just a small built-in closet in that alcove by the window…?"

"Sure. I'll take a look later and get some measurements. Seems like a good idea," Ben replied. "It's real dated in there." Cassie didn't need to ask how he knew that. The answer was obvious and she didn't want Ben to dwell on his memories.

She looked around the kitchen. "This place will be completely transformed by the fall," she murmured. "I'll be sorry to sell it."

"I wish you didn't have to."

"I know. So do I. But at least we'll have one last summer here."

Despite her sadness, the thought of a summer in Somers Cove brought a smile to her lips. Not only did Maddie seem to love it at the beach, but it would give her a chance to get to know her father, and for

Jake to spend time with Maddie too. And, of course, the prospect of seeing more of Jake herself was… exciting. After less than twenty-four hours without him, she knew she was still completely in love with him, and that she wanted him back more than she'd ever wanted anything.

Jake

"I must've made a mistake," Erica curled her auburn hair around her forefinger and looked up at Jake. "I'm sure dad said twelve o'clock."

Jake had always assumed that Rich's ex-wife, Erica's mom, must have had auburn hair, because Rich himself had almost black hair, graying at the temples, but still almost black. He'd also assumed that Rich must've come off better in the divorce, because Erica had lived with him since she turned eighteen – and knowing Erica, she was always gonna follow the money. As Rich's only child, she stood to inherit his business, which was worth a fortune.

Jake tried really hard not to show his frustration. If he'd known he had an extra hour, he could have stayed in Somers Cove and had breakfast with Cassie and Maddie, maybe even stolen another kiss, like the one that had kept him awake last night, and which he could still feel, even now. Instead of which, he'd left early, without even seeing them.

"So the meeting's still at one?" he asked.

Erica nodded her head slowly, and took a step toward him. "I guess we could find a way to kill the time," she murmured.

He dreaded to think what she had in mind.

"I've got work to catch up on," he said quickly, sitting down at his desk and hoping she'd take the hint.

"At least have lunch with me. You need to eat, Jake." She came and stood in front of him, leaning over his desk. She'd undone enough buttons on her gray silk blouse that it was impossible not to see the top of her white lacy bra and the ample cleavage she was displaying... presumably for his benefit.

"I'll eat later." He kept his voice neutral, just shy of abrupt. "Now, if you'll excuse me, I've got calls to make."

She stood up, clearly put out by his dismissal.

"I'll see you in an hour then," she said, turning to go.

"I guess so" He didn't look up.

Erica worked in the marketing department. Why was she needed at a planning meeting? The answer to that, of course, was that she wasn't.

"Jeez," Jake said under his breath, putting his head in his hands. "How much more?"

He opened his laptop and checked his messages, answering a few of the more important e-mails from that morning. He replaced lunch with a couple of cups of coffee and filled in the time until the meeting going over the revised plans Mitch had sent through, after they'd met at the site on Monday.

There were nine people in the boardroom, including himself, Rich and Erica. The suits, sat around the large glass table, nodded to Jake as he entered and Rich looked him up and down.

"Dressing down today, are we?" He was smiling as he spoke.

"I've come straight from home," Jake replied.

"Home?" Rich queried.

"Somers Cove," Jake corrected. "I haven't had time to go back to my apartment yet."

"Well, it's your brain we want, not your designer labels."

"I don't wear designer labels." Jake helped himself to a coffee and sat down in his usual seat, on Rich's left. Erica was, unfortunately right beside him.

"You'd look good in them, if you did," she whispered.

Rich coughed gently and looked around the room. "Well, now we're all here, Jake can fill us in on how things are progressing up there in Maine."

Jake held the floor for the next half hour, explaining to everyone around the table how the project was progressing and the changes

Mitch had suggested to the plans. Then he fielded questions, ranging from his choice of suppliers to the budget and scheduling. The grilling went on for over two hours, at the end of which Jake just wanted to get back to his apartment, except there was something he needed to say first.

Once everyone but Rich and Erica had left the room, Jake turned to his boss.

"Can I have a quiet word?" he said.

"Of course, Jake. What's troubling you?" Jake nodded pointedly at Erica. "You can speak freely," Rich continued. "I've got no secrets from Erica."

Jake shrugged. "You told me, when I brought in Mark Gardner as a client, that you were going to set up a Corporate Construction department and give me free reign to run it. I think your precise words were 'no interference'."

"Yes?" Rich looked up at him.

"This doesn't feel like 'no interference' to me."

"That's because this isn't the Corporate Construction department yet. You're still on trial, Jake."

Jake stared at him. "So… I've got to answer to the board for every screw and nail, have I?"

"Yes." Rich leant forward, his elbows resting on the table. "This is a huge risk, both for us and Mark Gardner."

"I know that."

"And I'm not prepared to just let you fly with it… not yet. You've still got to prove yourself."

Erica leant across him, toward her father, running her hand up Jake's leg beneath the table. He flinched. "Don't be such a bear, daddy," she simpered.

Rich smiled at his daughter. "I'm not being a bear, Pumpkin," he replied. "I'm just protecting your interests."

Jake got to his feet, releasing himself from Erica's grip. "Okay," he said. "I'll report to the board; I'll do it your way. And when I've made it a success… will you leave me alone to run the department?"

"Yes. That was what I said I'd do… and I'll do it."

"Fine."

Jake went over to the door and was about to leave when Rich called him back. "I meant to say, we're having a barbecue on Friday evening. We'd like you to be there, wouldn't we?" He winked at Erica, who nodded.

"I can't, sorry."

Rich turned to face him. "You can't?" He seemed taken aback.

"I'm going back to Somers Cove. I'll be leaving straight after work on Friday." Jake had already decided he wasn't going to wait until Saturday to drive up there. He didn't care how late he got there on Friday night, he wanted as much of the weekend as possible with Maddie… and Cassie.

"You're going back?" Erica spoke before her father could even open his mouth.

"I didn't think you were going there again until the beginning of June?" Rich added.

"My plans have changed. I'll be spending all my weekends there between now and when we break ground, and then I'll live up there until September, as we discussed."

They were both looking at him as though they expected an explanation. He wasn't sure he owed them one. His weekends were his to do with as he pleased… or so he thought. But saying nothing didn't seem to be an option. He didn't want to tell them about Maddie, or Cassie. He wanted to keep that to himself for now.

"I've made things up with my dad," he murmured.

"But, that's great," Rich said, getting up and coming over to him.

"Yes, it is," Jake replied. "I'm trying to rebuild our relationship, and I can't do that from here."

"No… no, of course you can't." Rich patted him on the shoulder and looked him in the eye. "I'm proud of you, son," he said. "You've grown up a lot in these last four years. It takes a man to revisit his mistakes and put them right."

"Yeah… I'm working that out." Jake wasn't talking about the same thing as Rich, but that didn't make the comment any less valid.

"And I am impressed with your work on the Gardner's project, Jake. I don't want you to think I'm not. Just let me watch over you for this one, and then I'll leave you alone. I promise."

Jake let himself into his apartment, closed the door and dumped his bag.

He glanced around. The furnishings were very modern and – he supposed – quite masculine, which wasn't that much of a surprise. He went into the kitchen, opened a bottle of red wine and poured a large glass, taking it with him into the living room.

He sat back in his soft leather couch and stared around the room. There was something missing. He looked at the full bookshelves, the large, widescreen television, the driftwood coffee table and the polished oak floor – something was definitely missing. He knew exactly what it was without even having to think about it. The 'something' was his family. Maddie… and Cassie. Would Cassie fit in here, he wondered. He doubted she'd have chosen this apartment herself. It was kinda impersonal, with its white painted walls and shiny surfaces. She'd have made something of it, but it wouldn't have been her choice… She belonged in that house by the coast, even if it was worn around the edges. Trying to take her away from there had been his first – and his biggest – mistake.

He sighed, finished his wine, then went to take a shower, coming back out into the living room wearing just a bathrobe.

He picked up his tablet and started browsing the Internet, looking up various websites relating to deaf children, signing, medical advances and education. Getting another glass of wine, he sat back down and started doing some more serious research. He found himself getting more and more confused. There was so much conflicting advice. Some people maintained – quite vociferously – that deaf children should be educated in mainstream schools to get a more inclusive experience. Others said that route led to a feeling of *exclusion*, and advocated special schools. After nearly two hours, he threw the tablet down on the couch beside him, in despair. He was no further forward and was, if anything, more bewildered than when he'd started. He'd have to discuss this with

Cassie when he got back to Somers Cove at the weekend. He needed to be sure she'd made the right choice for Maddie. She might already be booked into a school for deaf children in Portland, but it wasn't too late to change, if that was in Maddie's best interests.

He phoned through to his regular Chinese take-out and placed an order, and while he waited for it to be delivered, he sat back and looked around his apartment again. It might have only been a day since he'd seen her, but he missed Cassie. He really missed her. He flipped his phone over in his hands. Of course. He was being an idiot. He scrolled through his contacts list – which mainly featured business acquaintances – until he got to the letter 'R'. Cassie's number was still there, filed under her surname. He'd never deleted it, and he wished now that he'd dialed it at some point in the last four years. He'd thought about doing it often enough, and if he had, maybe they'd have worked things out sooner. Still, as his dad had said, there was no point in wishing… doing was what mattered. He pressed the connect button and waited.

It rang five times, then went to voicemail. He couldn't hide his disappointment.

"Hi, Cass. It's me… Jake." He thought he'd better clarify that. "I just wanted to… um… check in with you… make sure Maddie's okay." *Bullshit*, he thought. He really wanted to hear her voice, but he didn't want to say that to her voicemail. "Call me back if you pick this up. Bye."

God, that had sounded really lame. He threw the phone down on the couch and switched on the television. The Red Sox were playing the Texas Rangers and, although Jake preferred football, he left the game on. His phone rang almost immediately. He checked the caller ID, and his heart flipped in his chest.

"Hi," he answered straight away.

"Hello." God, her voice sounded good. "Sorry, I didn't pick up. Your name didn't come up on my screen, and I don't answer to unknown callers."

"Who does?" he said. "You didn't keep my number then?" he asked. He knew it was a little childish, but that kind of hurt.

There was a pause. "No," she replied, her voice really quiet.

A thought occurred to him. "Then how were you gonna contact me?" he asked.

"Sorry?" She sounded confused.

"You said you thought about contacting me – when you were in labor, and since. How were you gonna do that, if you didn't keep my number?" He wondered if maybe she'd written it down somewhere, just in case, and hope flared that she hadn't completely given up on them.

"Emma's still got it," she replied softly. "But I gave her strict instructions never to tell it to me – even if I asked her to."

"Seriously?"

"Yes."

"And did you – ask her?"

"No." Her voice had faded to the point where he could hardly hear it.

"Oh." He found it hard to hide his disappointment. She really had cut him out of her life.

The line was silent for a moment, then her heard a faintly whispered, "I'm sorry, Jake."

"It's okay, Cass." He tried his best to sound reassuring. He didn't want her to feel any worse than she evidently already did. It wasn't her fault... "I hurt you."

"Yes, but I'm still sorry." He could hear the emotion in her words, even from nearly two hundred miles away.

"Don't be sorry. I do understand. You thought I'd cheated. You didn't want anything to do with me. It makes sense you'd delete my number."

"You didn't delete mine though…?"

"No." He hoped, in a way, that she wouldn't ask why. He wanted to tell her the reason – that he loved her and he'd never stopped loving her, and deleting her number would've meant admitting and accepting that his love for her was over... and he'd never found a way to do that. But he wanted to say all of that to her face, not over the phone.

She didn't ask why. She just said, "Oh," in a really soft voice, that made him shiver.

"How's Maddie?" he asked. It was safer ground.

"She's been bored today," Cassie replied. She sounded kinda bored herself – or at least fed up, anyway.

"Oh? Why?"

"The weather's been awful. She wanted to play outside, but she couldn't, so she threw a tantrum."

Jake couldn't help but laugh. "Oh dear."

"She threw cookie dough across the kitchen," Cassie explained.

"Did she hit anything?" he asked.

"Jake… it's not funny."

"No." He stifled his laugh. "No, I know it's not."

"Then stop laughing." He could hear her smile, despite her words.

"Sorry." He took a breath. "I take it you didn't bake cookies, then."

"No, your dad came over with cakes. That helped."

That thought sobered Jake up real fast. He wished he could've spent his afternoon there with them, sitting around the table in the kitchen, instead of defending his every decision in the board meeting.

"Good," he managed to say. "Has she gone to bed now?" he asked.

"Yes."

"Okay." He paused. "I guess I'd better let you get on with your writing then."

"I'm editing tonight."

"Oh… well, I'll let you do that then." He hesitated. "Can I call you again tomorrow?" he asked.

"Sure," she replied. "I've put your number into my contacts list now, so I'll answer it."

He smiled. "Good."

When he climbed into bed much later on that evening, Jake wished Cassie could be lying next to him. He wished he could hold her in his arms, stroke her hair and feel her breath on his neck as she held onto him.

He missed her – a lot. Every time he closed his eyes, all he saw was Cassie. It was as though she was there with him… except she wasn't.

And he needed her. More than he'd ever needed anything.

Chapter Fifteen

Cassie

Maddie sat on the bed while Cassie braided her hair. She'd insisted on showering separately today, so once her hair was done, she was just going to have to sit on the bathroom floor while Cassie took her shower. With the mood Maddie had been in over the last few days, another tantrum was bound to ensue, but there was nothing Cassie could do about that; she could hardly leave her daughter to herself, not with the ocean right on their doorstep.

She smiled to herself, just a little, as she remembered Jake's reaction to her telling him about Maddie having tantrums. She really wasn't surprised that he'd found that funny. She knew he'd be the first to indulge Maddie in whatever she wanted, but she also knew how impractical that was. She recalled her own pleasure when she'd picked up his message and heard his voice, realizing he'd taken the time to call her – even if it was only to check up on his daughter, and not because he wanted to talk to her. He'd called her the following night too, as they'd arranged, and they'd talked for over half an hour – again mainly about Maddie. He'd told her then that he wouldn't be able to call last night, but he'd not given her a reason, and she didn't feel she could ask for one. He might have been prepared – even willing – to tell her he lived alone and had done for the last four years, but that didn't mean he didn't have a life. Cassie sighed and then realized she wasn't smiling anymore. In fact, she was blinking back tears.

It didn't help that she was exhausted. She'd been up really late the night before. She'd finally been in the mood for finishing off her fourth novel, and after she'd put Maddie to bed, had sat at her computer for hours, tapping away until it was done. Her head filled with images of Jake, she'd managed to write a really romantic ending to the story. She knew it was fiction – well, fantasy, really – but it was also her best work yet. Having Jake in her life again had proved inspirational. She hadn't had to plumb the depths of her memory, trying to recall how it felt to be held in the arms of the man she loved, to be wrapped up in him, like her own personal safety blanket. Unlike with the first three books, there had been no struggling to remember the feeling of his lips on hers, his hands touching her skin, that breathless hope and anticipation. And she'd found it a simple task to imagine his voice. Her writing was so much better, and she knew it, even though the thoughts and emotions he was evoking in her were far from fictional.

She's just finished tying up Maddie's hair, when she heard someone knocking at the kitchen door, and then a familiar voice called out, "Hello? Is anyone home?" *Jake?* Cassie glanced at the clock beside the bed. It was a few minutes after eight… How on earth had he got here so early? She signed to Maddie that someone was at the door and, before she could stop her, Maddie had jumped down and run out of the room. Cassie leapt up and followed, in time to see Maddie launch herself up into Jake's outstretched arms, a broad grin on her face.

Jake looked over toward her and she could have sworn his eyes widened. "Um… Hi," he murmured, looking her up and down. And it was only then that Cassie remembered she was still wearing her very, very short cotton pajamas, and matching skimpy top.

"Hi," she said, feeling self-conscious.

"Sorry I'm so early," Jake replied, still staring at her. "I drove back here last night, because I wanted to surprise you with breakfast. That's why I couldn't call you."

"You could've warned me," Cassie said, thinking that at least she'd have been able to get up earlier, and get showered and dressed before he arrived.

"Yeah, but then it wouldn't have been a surprise." He nodded to the countertop, where Cassie noticed a large bag from the coffee shop. "I brought muffins, and cinnamon rolls, and pastries," he carried on. "I wasn't sure what Maddie liked."

"It's got sugar in it, so she likes all of it." Cassie smiled over at him.

"Yeah… it's not the healthiest of breakfasts, but it's the weekend."

"I'm not complaining," Cassie smiled. "I know how good those cinnamon rolls are." His eyes were still burning into her. "I'd just finished getting Maddie dressed," she continued, "but I haven't had a shower myself yet… I don't suppose you could watch her?"

"Of course. Breakfast can wait a while."

"I'll only be five minutes," Cassie said.

"Five minutes?" Jake smirked. "You used to take at least fifteen… usually closer to thirty."

"Yeah, well that all ended when Maddie came along. I became the queen of the quick shower."

"Well, you can take your time today. I'll watch her and you can… well, you can do whatever you need to do." He smiled at her in a kind of knowing way.

Cassie felt herself blushing, and turned to go. "Call me if you need anything," she said over her shoulder.

"We'll be fine," Jake replied.

Cassie was tempted to take longer in the shower, but she knew Jake's signing abilities were still limited, and she worried he'd get into trouble, so she showered quickly, braided her towel-dried hair loosely behind her head, put on jeans and a t-shirt and went back out into the kitchen, which was empty.

She looked around, but they were nowhere in sight. Feeling herself start to panic, she went out through the screen door and onto the porch, looking around the garden, but there was still no sign of them.

"Jake!" she called.

"Yeah?" The reply came from the direction of the beach, and she looked over to see them playing ball on the sand. He picked up Maddie and put her on his shoulders and, kicking the ball in front of him, made his way back toward the house. "What's up?" he asked as they walked up the garden path.

"Nothing," Cassie said, trying to hide her relief. "What made you think anything was up?" She did her best to sound nonchalant.

"Oh… just that small hint of total fear in your voice." He stared at her. "She's safe with me, Cass," he said, climbing up the porch steps and depositing Maddie next to her mother.

"I know." Cassie felt embarrassed, and a little ashamed. "I'm sorry, it's just she's never normally out of my sight, and after the other day… her walking off into the ocean… well, I panicked."

"I get it," he replied, leaning toward her. "But try and trust me, please?"

"I do," she said quietly to his retreating back, as he went into the house. He glanced over his shoulder and gave her a slow, sexy smile, that fixed her to the spot and melted her from the inside out.

"Good," he murmured.

Maddie tugged on Cassie's jeans and she tore her eyes away from Jake's and looked down. "Say 'excuse me'," Cassie said, holding out her left hand, with the palm upwards and running the fingers of her right hand along it. Maddie rolled her eyes, and copied the sign. Cassie raised her right hand, made a fist at shoulder height and bobbed it up and down. "Yes?" she said and Maddie lay her left hand across her chest, then brought her right one underneath, hinging it at the elbow and bringing her right and toward her mouth, then tapping her fingers on her lips.

"What's going on?" Jake asked, looking confused..

"Well, firstly, I'm trying to teach her some manners. She has to learn not to interrupt, or just grab hold of me for attention, and to say 'excuse me'… and secondly our daughter would like some breakfast," Cassie replied, signing, 'okay', with a smile, and taking Maddie's hand.

"Okay," Jake replied, smiling broadly. "Can you show me all of that again later?"

"Sure."

He held the screen door open and they went back into the kitchen. As Cassie passed, he leaned toward her. "You know," he whispered to her, "I think I even prefer you saying '*our* daughter' to '*your* daughter'."

Maddie was overjoyed with the selection of breakfast treats, which they enjoyed together around the kitchen table.

While Cassie was making a second pot of coffee, she explained to Jake that she was going to be staying in Somers Cove for the whole summer.

"Oh?" he said, sounding surprised. "What changed?"

"Your dad has managed to get hold of the supplies we need for the bathroom and kitchen," she explained. "I won't have to pay for them, so we're going to fix up the rest of the house." She turned and leant back on the countertop. "He said he's going to need some help…" She looked over at him.

"I'll happily lend a hand," he said, not really waiting to be asked.

Cassie smiled. "Thank you."

"You don't have to thank me, Cass. If it means I get to spend more time with you and Maddie, then I'll do whatever it takes."

She stared at him, unsure whether she'd understood his meaning. She didn't want to make a big deal of it, in case she'd overreacted and he was really just meaning he wanted to be with Maddie.

She came and sat back down again, bringing the French press with her.

"So, what are your plans for the day?" Jake asked.

"Ben's coming over later," Cassie explained. "I'm not sure what he's got in mind, but for this morning, I was just going to catch up with the laundry and do some chores."

"I could keep Maddie occupied, if it helps," Jake offered.

Cassie sighed with relief. "It would help enormously."

They finished breakfast, cleared away and Jake took Maddie out onto the beach again, while Cassie put on some music, made the bed and cleared up the kitchen and living room. It made a real change to be able to get things done, without having to keep a constant vigil, and she found herself dancing around the room while she swept the floor.

"Eh-hem…" Jake's fake cough broke the spell and she turned, blushing. He was standing in the doorway, grinning and holding Maddie's hand. "She needs the bathroom," he explained, as Maddie let go of him and ran through to the back of the house. "Great moves," he smirked, once they were alone, and he stepped closer. "But then you always did have great moves, Cass." His voice became more serious, resonating through her body. She lowered her eyes to the floor, but felt his finger beneath her chin, raising her face to his. "Don't," he whispered. "Don't be embarrassed in front of me. You never used to be…" She looked up into his eyes and felt herself leaning toward him, just as Maddie came running back into the room.

Cassie snapped back to reality, looking down at Maddie, who was signing that she wanted a drink.

"That's 'drink', right?" Jake asked, seemingly calm. How could he do that, when her whole body was a churning mass of emotions?

"Y—Yes." Cassie tried to sound normal, despite the turmoil going on inside her. "Do you want to try and find out what she wants?"

"Oh, hell," Jake said, scratching his head. "I can't remember 'juice'."

"Can you remember 'milk'?" Cassie asked.

"Yeah, that's like milking a cow."

"Right. So, if you can't remember 'juice', ask her if she wants milk. If she doesn't, she'll probably say she wants juice, and your problem's solved. Meanwhile, I'll make us some tea." Cassie turned toward the stove.

She hadn't even finished filling the kettle with water before Jake called out to her, "Help, Cass. I'm pretty sure that's not juice, but I don't know what it is."

Cassie came over, knelt down and put her left hand out, palm upwards, and tapped her bent right hand into the centre of it. Maddie held up her right hand and separated her first three fingers, then tapped her forefinger on her lips, and Cassie nodded, then stood up.

"She wants water," she said to Jake. "The beakers are in the cabinet next to the refrigerator."

"And what did you do?" he asked.

"I just said 'again'," Cassie replied, going back to the stove, while Jake fetched a beaker. "I find it's the quickest way to get her to repeat something."

"God, I've got a lot to learn."

"You're doing really well," Cassie replied. "It takes time."

Jake handed Maddie her beaker of water and leant back against the sink, folding his arms across his chest. "I was gonna talk to you about some research I was doing while I was in the city."

Cassie turned to face him. "What research is this?" she asked.

"About schools. I wanted to ask if you're really sure about this place you've got Maddie booked into. There's a hell of a lot of information out there… and although most of it's conflicting, it seemed to me that a lot of people came down on the side of mainstream schools and maybe we should look into that a bit further before reaching any final decisions."

Cassie took a step toward him, then stopped. "Excuse me?" she said quietly. "I've done the research, Jake. I didn't just pick a damn school out of thin air, because I felt like it. Mainstream schools are fine for some kids, but a lot of profoundly deaf children end up feeling excluded. Specialist deaf schools offer the best education for kids like Maddie…" She took a deep breath. "If it's all the same to you, could you not second-guess my decisions."

Jake pushed himself away from the sink. "I'm not criticizing, Cassie, and I'm not second-guessing, but you've had a helluva lot longer to do the damned research and to get used to everything. This is all new to me and I want to find things out for myself." He ran his fingers through his hair. "For Christ's sake, Cass, if we'd been in this together from the beginning, this wouldn't be happening, would it? We'd have been working things out together… except we're not, because you decided not to tell me I've got a daughter."

Cassie felt the tears stinging behind her eyes. "You… you can't throw that at me whenever something comes up."

He huffed out a sigh. "Why the hell not? It's the truth."

"That's as may be, Jake, but I've already admitted I got it wrong. I've already said I should have told you about Maddie. I—I thought you understood. But obviously not. What do you want from me? Do you want me to spend my whole life on my knees apologizing? Do you want the right to guilt-trip me every time we disagree? Or do you just want to use my mistakes as an excuse to get your own way?" She took a deep breath. "Why did you even need to start looking into Maddie's schooling? Don't you trust me to make the right decisions for her? Is that what it is? Cassie screwed up by not telling you, so Cassie can't be trusted to get anything right? Is that it, Jake?"

He stared at her, his eyes darkening. "I'm going," he said quietly, "before I end up saying something we both regret."

He turned and walked quietly out the door.

Cassie felt the first tear fall before the screen had even closed behind him, and then she felt a hand come and pat her on her leg, and she glanced down to see Maddie beside her. She picked up her daughter and held onto her as she cried. It seemed it didn't matter how much she wanted Jake, or how drawn to him she was… nothing had changed.

Jake

He'd only taken a few steps down the lane before Jake felt his mistakes weighing on him. He should never have brought any of that up in front of Maddie; he shouldn't have queried Cassie's choices in the way he did, because he knew she'd always do whatever was best for their daughter; and he certainly shouldn't have thrown the fact that she'd kept Maddie from him in her face, not when she'd already admitted her regrets over that decision, and apologized for them – repeatedly. That was really childish of him.

He felt like a jerk. Again.

He stopped, already nearly halfway home. Should he go back and apologize to her, ask her to forgive him? He turned around and took a couple of steps, then stopped again. No. If he went back now, he had a feeling she'd probably be too mad at him to listen properly to what he had to say. It'd be better to wait a little while, let her calm down and then go back, and invite her and Maddie for dinner tonight, so they could talk, and he could try and make amends.

Jake sat at the kitchen table, nursing a lukewarm cup of coffee and opened his laptop. There were a few messages, including one from Mark Gardner that needed his attention. Mark had some questions that required answers, and had also revealed he wasn't going to be able to make the ground breaking, despite his best attempts at rescheduling his diary. Jake didn't think it really mattered. It wasn't like they were having a ceremony, or the press in attendance, or anything, being as the client was anonymous. He started typing out a reply. Maybe working for a while would take his mind off Cassie and how angry he was feeling – with himself, not her.

"You must've got here early this morning," Ben said, as he came in the door.

"Yeah," Jake replied absent-mindedly, while still typing. "I wanted to surprise Maddie and Cassie."

"I see." Ben came and sat opposite him, not saying another word, until Jake felt obliged to stop working and look up. "And?"

"And we had breakfast together."

"And then you came back here?"

"Yeah. I've got some work to do."

"I see." Ben repeated, still looking at him. As far as Jake was concerned, Ben could look all he wanted. He wasn't about to reveal what an idiot he'd been and get a lecture for his trouble. He knew he'd screwed up, and he would put it right in his own way.

Ben stood again. "Well, I'm gonna go down there and do some more work on the garage," he said. "I'm picking up all the bathroom fittings on Monday, so I'll need to be ready to start on that."

"Cassie mentioned she'd be staying." Jake looked up at his dad.

"Yeah, I wasn't entirely comfortable lying to her, but it's in a good cause."

"She believed you?"

"Seemed to. She's agreed to stay, so I guess she must've done."

Jake nodded his head.

"You coming?" Ben asked.

"I'll be down soon." Jake turned his attention back to his laptop. "I just need to finish this."

"Okay, son." Ben let himself out and closed the door gently, and Jake wondered whether he'd fooled his dad at all.

He finished typing his long e-mail to Mark, sent it and closed his laptop, sitting back in the chair and sighing. He realized Cassie could be talking to Ben right now, telling him that Jake had let her down, yet again. He really hoped not though. He hoped she'd let them try and work it out between the two of them, and not involve his dad. He leant his head forward, resting it on his closed laptop, wishing he could turn back the clock by an hour or so, train his mouth not to start speaking before he'd activated his brain, and maybe also to take his chances a little better. He smiled, just slightly. She'd looked so cute dancing around the kitchen, and he'd come real close to kissing her… real close. Why did he have to be such a jerk?

Someone knocked on the door behind him and he sat upright, getting to his feet and going over to open it. Cassie stood on the step, looking up at him. He could tell from the redness around her eyes that she'd been crying. That feeling of self-loathing that had been festering deep inside him instantly got a lot worse.

"Hi," he said softly.

"I've left Maddie with your dad," Cassie explained, lowering her eyes, "so I can't be long… but I didn't want her to see us fighting again."

"We're not gonna fight again, Cass," he replied.

"Aren't we?"

"No. Come on in." He stood back and let her enter the kitchen, closing the door. Then he turned to face her. "I don't want to fight with you," he whispered.

She opened her mouth to speak, then closed it, took and deep breath and tried again. "I've brought some paperwork for you," she said, holding out a large brown envelope. He took it from her and glanced inside. It contained maybe thirty or more sheets of paper. He looked back up at her. "It's the letters from Maddie's doctors," Cassie continued, "the consultants I went to see, and all the information I gathered together, when I was trying to decide which school to register her with."

Jake nodded his head. "Thanks," he said.

"You need a balanced perspective," Cassie carried on, "and those documents will give you that. Some of them say deaf children are better off in mainstream schools, and others don't, but what you need to focus on are the parts that relate to profoundly deaf children, because that's what Maddie is. After I'd seen the doctors and sought their advice, I went did a whole load more research by myself. I spent weeks on it, and I spoke to other parents of deaf children to get their points of view. I even visited with a couple of them in their homes, which was very helpful. I went to mainstream schools that had deaf students and spoke to them and their teachers to see how they coped, and how they fitted in. I wanted to know how they felt, but also how the other kids reacted to them. And then I visited the school that Maddie's going to be attending – before I enrolled her. I looked at both angles. I did everything I could think of, Jake, before I made the decision. But each child is different, and I know this is what's best for Maddie." She took a breath. "I was wrong," she added. "You have every right to be involved in Maddie's future, so read the literature; ask me anything you want…"

"And if I disagree with you?"

"Then we'll talk it through."

He put the envelope down on the table. "I'll read it all," he said, "because I want to understand. But I'm not gonna disagree with you. And I'm not gonna ask you to change your decision either. I know you'd only do what's best for Maddie. And you know her better than I do. You know what she needs. I can see how much effort and time you've put into this, just like everything else to do with her, and I know you've done it all by yourself—"

"Which I suppose you're gonna tell me was my choice," Cassie interrupted.

"No. I wasn't gonna say that. I was going to say, you're doing a great job. I just want to be involved, Cass, that's all."

"I get that, Jake." She took a step nearer the door, putting her hand out toward the handle. "That's why I brought you the damn paperwork."

"Hey…" He grabbed her arm and pulled her back, blocking her way out. "Please…" He paused. "Please don't leave. Not like this."

"How do you want me to leave, Jake?"

"I don't want you to leave at all, but if you must, then at least let me apologize first… properly." She stared up at him. "I'm sorry," he began. "I'm sorry for second-guessing you, and for arguing with you in front of Maddie. I'm sorry if I seemed to doubt you. I know it's been hard for you, and I'm really sorry if I said anything that hurt you." He looked down at her, taking a step to come even closer to her. "We were having such a lovely morning, until I screwed it up."

She blinked back her tears. "You didn't."

"Am I forgiven?"

She nodded her head, just once.

"Good." He wanted to take that final step, so he was close enough to kiss her, but now was probably not the best time. It'd look like he was taking advantage of the situation. "I've just gotta change into some old clothes and I'll come down and help out with the house," he said. "Do you want to wait for me?"

"I'd better get back," she said. "Your dad may be struggling with Maddie by now."

He nodded, but didn't move. He wasn't sure whether to ask his next question, but somehow it seemed important. "Just before you go… did you tell my dad why you were coming here?" he murmured.

"I told him I needed to let you have some papers about Maddie's school."

"But did you tell him we'd fought?"

"No." She shook her head. "I love your dad, Jake, but I think we need to work things out by ourselves sometimes, don't you?"

Jake nodded. "Yeah." He closed the gap between them so their bodies were almost touching. "Thanks, Cass," he whispered. "I wasn't in the mood for having him tell me I'd screwed up again."

"He means well."

"I know he does, but I know I screwed up. I don't need the reminder."

She reached up and gently cupped his cheek in her hand. "You didn't screw up," she said. "I overreacted."

"No…"

"Yes." She let her hand fall to her side again.

He sighed. "Let's call it quits and say we both got it wrong."

"Again." Cassie added.

He smiled. "Yeah, again."

"And can we agree to try real hard not to get it wrong again?" she added, a note of real hope in her voice.

"Yes," he replied. "Yes, we can." He wanted to kiss her, to show her how much he meant that, and how much she meant to him.

"I'd really better be going," she said. "Maddie's probably running rings around Ben by now." The look in her eyes spoke of regret. At least he thought it did.

"Oh… Okay." He was disappointed, but didn't let it show. "I'll get changed and be down there as soon as I can."

Walking back down the lane a few minutes later, in his paint-stained jeans and a dark blue t-shirt, Jake was relieved Cassie had forgiven him so quickly. But then, remembering back to when they were together, they would always make up quickly after a fight… usually having spectacular sex, and they'd both forget why'd they'd been arguing in the first place. That's how it had always been with them, at least until the last time, which was so different. That's why he'd struggled so much with Cassie running away – that just wasn't like her. Even when he acted like a kid and disappeared on her to think things through, she'd wait for him to come back, and they'd talk it out and make up – and make love. Cassie didn't leave. She'd never just leave. Except she thought he'd cheated, and cheating was the one thing they'd both agreed they could never forgive. So he kind of understood why she'd run. She'd have been hurting, and scared and alone. If only she'd spoken to him… No, if only he'd never left her at that damned party in the first place.

He came around the side of the house and his breath caught in his throat. Cassie and Maddie were standing, painting the cladding, Maddie doing the lower planks – getting more paint on her clothes than the wood – and Cassie the ones above. What really caught his eye, and his breath, was the way Cassie looked. She was still wearing tight jeans and a t-shirt, with her hair loosely braided, just like earlier, but her t-shirt had ridden up, exposing the soft silky skin of her midriff, and he wanted, more than anything, to kneel before her and kiss that delicate flesh and, maybe, undo her jeans, peel them off of her and… *Whoa*. He needed to stop those thoughts, right now. Maddie was there.

There was no denying that Cassie was sexy as hell. She was even sexier than when they'd been together before, and as far as Jake was concerned, she was, and always had been 'the one', but he needed to show a little self-control and restraint around his daughter.

And he needed some time alone with Cassie… real soon.

They spent the whole day working on the house. Jake used a ladder to paint the higher parts of the walls that Cassie couldn't reach, while Ben worked on the garage.

Later, once everyone had showered and changed into clean clothes, and Cassie had managed to get most of the paint out of Maddie's hair and changed her into her pajamas, they barbecued some chicken and burgers.

"I've had an idea," Jake said, standing by the barbecue. Cassie handed him a beer and looked up at him. "Being as you've decided to stay for the summer, and we've had a good day today and got a lot done, why don't we all award ourselves a day off tomorrow?"

"A day off?" Cassie replied, grinning. "What's that?"

He moved a little closer to her. "It's a day where you let me take you and Maddie out, and you let me treat you right."

Cassie stared at him. "I like the sound of that," she whispered, not taking her eyes from his.

"And would it be okay if dad came with us?" he asked.

"Sure," Cassie replied.

"There's… there's something I want to show you – all of you. And I'll bring a picnic," he added."

"Maddie will be so excited."

"And Maddie's mom?"

"She'll be pretty excited too."

He swallowed hard, his eyes dropping to her lips. "God, I hope so," he whispered. "I really hope so." He leaned in and kissed her gently on the cheek.

As he pulled back, he felt her sigh and he began to hope that maybe she might want him – just a little. And right now, he'd settle for that.

Chapter Sixteen

Cassie

"Try and picture the main building over here," Jake said, pointing toward the flat area of land set further back from the cliff.

"Facing which way?" Cassie asked, looking around.

Jake turned, with Maddie in his arms. "Straight out to the ocean," he replied. "Most of the guest rooms will have a sea view, and we're using a lot of energy efficient glass on this side to give a panoramic effect."

"Energy efficient?" Cassie queried, looking up at him and squinting against the sun.

"Yeah… most of the heat in a building is lost through the windows, so we're using special glass to reduce that. The whole building is as efficient and sustainable as I could make it, allowing for the practicalities of it being a hotel on the Atlantic coast." He smiled down at her.

Ben leant over the hood of Jake's car, staring down at the plans Jake had laid out, holding them flat with the palms of his hands.

Cassie turned and looked out at the ocean. "It's beautiful here," she whispered.

"Yeah, I know," Jake replied. "The client didn't take a lot of persuading to build here, not once he'd seen the view."

"I don't understand," Ben said, interrupting them. Jake and Cassie moved to face him.

"What, Dad?" Jake asked, wandering over to the car.

"These plans…" Ben continued, "they don't seem complete."

"They are." Jake became a little defensive, and Cassie came over to join them.

Ben looked up. "You said this was a high-end hotel complex, right?"

"Yeah." Jake glanced down at his plans. He looked worried.

"Well, I'm not the world's greatest expert on places like that, but don't they usually have a couple of restaurants, maybe a coffee shop, a beauty salon… a spa?"

"Yeah, they do."

"Your plans don't show any of that, son… except the main restaurant on the first floor." Ben tapped the papers on the hood.

"No, that's right." Jake seemed to let out a breath of relief.

"But surely, if it's an upscale hotel, the guests will expect that kind of thing, won't they?" Cassie asked.

"They'll get as much luxury as I can pack into this place," Jake replied. "But when I pitched this project to the client, I told him that as part of its sustainability we should avoid putting any local companies out of business. He agreed with me. He didn't like the idea of the local economy suffering… Besides, people won't want to come here if the nearby towns are all closed up – it would be a bit self defeating."

Ben stood up straight, bringing the plans with him and holding them out at arm's length as he moved around the site. Jake watched him closely. Cassie could tell he was nervous, worrying about his dad's good opinion. Whenever he was worried, he bit at his bottom lip, and he was doing it now. Instinctively, she came and stood beside him, offering unspoken support.

She felt Maddie's hand on her arm and leant in closer.

Maddie cupped her hands together in front of her, and bounced them up and down, while moving them away from her body. Then she pointed out to the horizon.

Cassie looked, then turned back and nodded her head, smiling.

"What did she say?" Jake asked, turning his attention away from his father.

"She was just pointing out the boat over there," Cassie replied.

"Oh," he said. "Can you show me again?" Cassie repeated the sign and he smiled. "It's kinda like a boat, bobbing on the water."

"Yes."

Maddie touched her mother's arm again and pointed to herself and Jake, then Ben and Cassie. Then, with both hands, she pointed toward the ocean, and finally she put her hands out, with the palms facing down, then pushed them forward, pitching them up and down a little.

Cassie nodded her head, and held her own hands out, with the palms up, wiggling her fingers. She noticed Maddie's shoulders dropping before she slumped into Jake, resting her head on his chest.

"What's wrong?" he asked.

"It's nothing," Cassie replied.

"It's clearly something," he said. "Tell me."

"Maddie wants us to go to the beach."

"And?" Jake said, seeming confused.

"I told her she had to wait."

"Oh… well, she doesn't. We can go now."

"But your dad's still looking at the plans."

Ben was standing close to where the entrance of the hotel was going to be. Jake called him and Ben looked up. "We're going down to the beach," he yelled. "You coming?"

"Maddie can wait," Cassie said, as Ben started walking back.

"We're pretty much done here," Jake replied, strapping Maddie back into her car seat. "It's just a flat piece of land – it's not very exciting for her…" Cassie couldn't really argue with that, although she didn't like the idea that Jake gave in so easily to Maddie every time she asked for something.

Ben rolled up the plans as he walked and handed them back to Jake just as he closed the car door.

"I'm impressed," he said quietly, going around the other side of the car to get in next to Maddie. He looked across the top of the car, making eye contact with Jake and holding it. "Very impressed."

Cassie could feel the warm glow coming from Jake, and she smiled.

Cassie sat on the rug and watched Ben, Jake and Maddie splashing in the shallows, a smile forming on her lips.

Maddie rocked with laughter as Ben covered Jake with water, almost from head to toe, and Jake froze, staring at her, before he and Ben started laughing too, and Maddie moved forward and started splashing Jake some more. Cassie was glad she'd thought to bring a change of clothes for Maddie, and she'd noticed Jake packing a bag into the car – which she hoped contained some spare clothing for himself and Ben, because they were all soaking wet, their shorts and t-shirts sticking to their skin.

Maddie was enjoying herself so much and her affection for Jake was obvious, even though she didn't yet know who he was. Cassie wondered when would be a good time to tell her daughter that the man she'd become so attached to was her father. Once again, she wished Jake had been there since the beginning, and that Maddie had always known her daddy.

Cassie felt her smile fading. How much had they all missed out on, because of her? She stared at the horizon, her mind filling with regret for all the wasted years, all the loneliness, all the time she'd spent wishing things could've been different. How many other Sundays like this might they have shared? Jake, her and Maddie, Ben… and her mom, who'd have loved it here. The view started to blur as tears filled her eyes.

"Hey." Jake's voice brought her back to reality. She looked up at him. "What's wrong?" he asked, sitting down beside her.

"Nothing," she said.

"Okay," he replied. "Except we both know that's not true."

Cassie turned to face him. He was looking down at her, his eyes filled with concern.

"Tell me, Cass…"

"I was just thinking about all the wasted time," she whispered. "All the times we could have been doing this together. All of us, including my mom." Her voice cracked as she said the last word.

Jake let out a sigh and put his arm around her.

"You're wet," Cassie said, pulling away a little.

"So what? It's just water." He held onto her for a while, not saying a word and they stared out at the ocean. Ben and Maddie were slowly working their way along the shoreline, picking up shells. The silence stretched out, and just as Cassie thought Jake wasn't going to say anything, he twisted her around so they were facing each other. "Try not to regret it too much," he said quietly.

"But I do," she murmured. "I'll always regret not telling you."

He smiled, just lightly. "I wasn't talking about that," he said. She tilted her head to one side. "I meant, try not to regret the time you didn't have with Maddie and your mom. She wouldn't want that. What was it she used to say?" He thought for a moment. "Oh, yeah… 'Make every day count…'."

"'Because you won't get it again.'" Cassie finished the sentence for him.

"She was right," Jake said. "And I'm sure she had some great times with you and Maddie."

"Yeah, she did." Cassie smiled.

"Then don't feel sad about it. Just remember what you had together. They're the best memories."

She looked up at him, leaning in a little closer. "What about us though? I don't have any memories of us…"

A furrow formed on his brow. "Um… Yeah, you do. You must have. I've got hundreds…"

"Not of you with Maddie."

"Oh… I see." He pulled her closer and they watched Maddie walking up the beach toward them, her hand in Ben's. "But that's what we're doing now, Cass. We're making new memories… for all of us."

"You brought so much food," Cassie remarked, lying back on the blanket with her hand over her stomach. "I've eaten too much."

"Well, I wasn't sure what Maddie would like…"

Cassie raised her head, looking up at him. "You could have just stuck with the fried chicken and potato salad, and she'd have been happy."

"So the green stuff was a bit wasted then?" Jake smirked.

"No. Although I was surprised you bothered."

"Just setting a good example, like you said."

"It all tasted incredible, Jake. Thank you."

"My pleasure." He smiled at her, holding her gaze for a moment until she felt herself blushing and looked away.

"You must've been up all night preparing that."

"No, but he did get up awful early this morning," Ben put in.

Maddie picked up her bucket of shells and pulled Ben to his feet.

"Well, I guess lunch is over," he said. "Looks like we're off shell hunting again."

"There are some rock pools along there." Jake pointed down the beach. "We'll just clear everything away and we'll come find you."

Ben and Maddie wandered off down the beach, while Cassie and Jake stood and started to pack away the picnic.

"Maddie seems to love the beach," Jake said.

"She does. I wish I brought her back here before now."

"What did I say earlier?"

"No regrets…?"

"Yeah, no regrets."

"It's kinda hard."

Jake came over, standing right in front of her. "I know, Cass."

"Thank you for today," Cassie murmured. "It's been fun."

"It's been my pleasure," Jake replied.

She still couldn't help feeling a little sad as they loaded everything back into the car.

"Now," Jake said, closing the lid on the trunk and turning to her, his eyes dark and mischievous. "You're the only one who hasn't gotten wet today, and I think we need to do something about that."

"Jake…"

Cassie went to run but, even as she tried to dodge him, Jake was too fast for her and he grabbed her, bending at the same time and throwing her over his shoulder before setting off down the beach.

"Put me down!" she squealed.

"I will… in a minute." She knew he was smiling, even though the only view she currently had was of his rear. And a very nice view it was too.

"Jake! I don't have any dry clothes."

He stopped. "You don't?" he said.

"No. So put me down."

To her surprise, he lowered her down his body to the ground. She sucked in a breath, as she felt his chest against her breasts, just for a moment, before he pulled back slightly and looked down at her. The mischief had gone from his eyes, but the dark intensity was still there, heating her from within.

He reached out and pushed a stray hair from her face.

"You might not have any dry clothes, but I've got a couple of spare t-shirts," he whispered. "And one of my many memories is how fabulous you used to look wearing my t-shirts… and nothing else." His voice lowered and deepened as he said the last few words.

"I can't wear just a t-shirt, Jake, not with your dad and Maddie around."

"I know. And that's the only reason I'm not still walking you into the ocean."

Maddie fell asleep in the car. They'd stopped off at a seafood restaurant on the way home and she'd enjoyed eating out for the first time, especially when the waitress made so much fuss of her. Cassie had been embarrassed, explaining to Jake and Ben that she'd never taken Maddie to a restaurant before – it wasn't something she could really afford. Ben had made understanding comments, but she'd felt Jake's eyes on her for some while after that.

Jake drove the car all the way down the lane to Kate's house, so they could put Maddie into bed without waking her too much.

"I'm gonna walk home," Ben said as they all climbed out of the car and Jake unstrapped Maddie from her seat. "I've had a really great day," he added. "Thanks for inviting me."

"Oh, you're welcome," Cassie replied, coming over and hugging him. "We enjoyed having you with us."

"I'll be picking up your bathroom fittings tomorrow," he said, "so I'll bring them down in the evening and we'll look at making a start, maybe Tuesday?"

Cassie nodded her head. "Thanks, Ben."

Jake lifted a sleeping Maddie into his arms. "I'll be home later, Dad," he said quietly. "I'm gonna help put Maddie to bed." He glanced at Cassie. "And maybe have a coffee with Cass."

"Okay, son. I'll leave the kitchen light on," Ben called over his shoulder as he walked away.

"Shall I take her through to the bedroom?" Jake asked Cassie as they climbed the steps up to the porch.

She opened the door and felt the stale heat breathe out of the house. "Yes, please."

They went through the house together, and then Jake held onto Maddie while Cassie gently undressed her and put her into a nightdress.

"I think we wore her out," Cassie said, as they pulled the door closed. "She barely noticed what we were doing at all."

"You sure it was us wearing her out and not the other way around?" Jake smiled.

"Why? Are you tired?" she asked. "If you'd rather get home to bed, don't feel like you have to stay with me for coffee."

He stared at her for a long moment. "I'd like to stay, if that's okay with you."

"Sure." She smiled up at him. "But can we make it a glass of wine, rather than coffee?"

"Sounds perfect."

She led the way through to the kitchen and poured them both a glass of wine, handing one to Jake, before guiding him out onto the porch. They sat on the swing seat, looking out at the ocean.

"It's a real shame you have to sell this place," Jake said after a while. "Maddie so obviously loves the beach, and the house'll be great when all the work's done."

"I know," Cassie replied, unable to keep the wistful note out of her voice. "I wish I didn't have to sell too. I've always loved it here. I've always felt safe here… but I don't have a choice. The money I make from selling the house will mean I can buy us somewhere much nicer to live. And Portland's a better choice for Maddie. It's closer to her school – I could hardly take her there every day from here."

"No…" Jake seemed thoughtful and they sat quietly for a minute or two. "Tell me about where you live now," he said.

"We've got a small two-bed apartment," Cassie explained. "It's cozy, I guess, but the rent's just been put up, which is a worry."

He moved along the seat, much closer to her and turned so they were facing each other. "That's not the first time you've mentioned worrying about money, and paying the rent," he said. "I don't like that idea. Listen, if you need help, you only have to ask, Cass."

She leant back, putting as much distance between them as the arm of the seat would allow. "You're not responsible for me," she said. "Just because you're Maddie's father doesn't mean you owe me anything. And I can take care of us…"

"I know you can." Jake replied gently. "And it's got nothing to do with being Maddie's father. It's got everything to do with you."

Cassie could feel herself blushing, and she stammered out a "Thank you," which felt inadequate, although she had no idea what else to say to him.

Jake took a sip of wine. "Tell me about your work," he said. "Have you been able to get much done since you've been here?"

"I finished my latest story the other day," Cassie replied, and smiled up at him, grateful for the change of subject, although she then recalled how much his reappearance in her life had inspired her writing, and felt her cheeks coloring again.

"What's it about?" he asked her.

"It's the next part in the series," she explained.

"Do the stories all follow on?"

"No. They're separate stories, but the characters cross over a little." She felt herself smiling. "That's where I go wrong a lot of the time."

"How?" he asked.

"Because I keep forgetting things."

"Such as?"

"Oh… I change their personalities from one book to the next. Or their hair or eye color."

"Oh dear."

"Yeah. I find it hard to concentrate sometimes."

"I'm not surprised, not when you've got to watch Maddie the whole time."

"Well, I like spending time with her. I thought tomorrow we'd try and make something with the shells she brought home. There are lots of plain wooden picture frames around the house. I was thinking we could stick shells on them. Maddie would have fun doing that, and then we could take them back to Portland when we go and hang them there... to remind us..." her voice faded.

He leant into her. "That sounds like a good idea," he told her. They finished their wine staring out at the dark ocean, their heads almost touching. "I guess I'd better be getting back," Jake said eventually, getting to his feet. His reluctance to leave was obvious.

"We'll see you next weekend?" Cassie couldn't hide the disappointment in her voice that he'd be gone from them for so long.

He nodded down at her. "Of course you will. And would it be okay if I came over in the morning?" he asked. "I'm not leaving until nine. We could have breakfast together."

She smiled, taking his offered hand and letting him pull her to her feet beside him. "That would be nice," she replied. "Maddie would like that. She's become really attached to you."

"I'm pretty attached to her too." They walked slowly down the porch steps and toward his car. "I'll be down about eight?" he suggested.

"Sure."

He unlocked the car and opened the door, throwing his keys onto the seat.

"Thank you for a lovely day, Jake," Cassie said.

"You don't have to thank me. I had a great time." He seemed to hesitate, just for a moment, then put his hands on her waist and pulled her into him, leaning down and kissing her gently on the lips. "Yeah," he murmured, staring into her eyes, "I had a really great time." He released her, then brought his hand up to cup her face, his thumb brushing against her cheek. "Goodnight, Cass," he murmured.

"Goodnight."

As Cassie lay in bed, struggling to sleep, she wondered why Jake had ended the kiss so quickly. The way he looked at her, the way he spoke to her made her think he wanted her… but his kisses were so restrained, so brief. There was none of the passion she remembered from before. Was she reading it wrong? Was he really not interested in her? Maybe he wasn't finding it so easy to forgive her as he said. Maybe he never would. Now she'd been in his arms, felt his lips on hers, spent time with him, heard his soft words… she wanted him back in her life again, for good. The thought that he might not want the same thing filled her with cold fear, and a tear trickled down her cheek as she wondered how her future would feel without him.

Jake

He lay in the dark of his bedroom, staring up at the ceiling, reliving yet another too chaste kiss. What was wrong with him? Why couldn't he just follow his heart and claim her back? His whole body ached to be with her… but still, whenever they got close, his head would always win out, raising the nagging doubt in the back of his mind that she wasn't ready, that he needed to work harder on building the trust again, reminding him if he got it wrong this time, he'd maybe risk losing Maddie, and he'd definitely lose Cassie for good… and he couldn't bear that thought.

He turned and stared out the window at the glittering stars in the deep purple sky and smiled as he remembered how Cassie used to love sitting on the beach, watching the night sky, holding hands, talking, kissing, and making love. He'd told her, just that afternoon, not to harbor regrets for things she'd missed out on with her mom, and here he was, about to start doing just that himself. It was hard not to though… It was hard not to think about all the Christmas mornings, all the birthdays, all the vacations they could have shared. And all the nights he could have fallen asleep with her in his arms, and the mornings he could have woken up with her beside him.

He wondered what he'd have done if she hadn't deleted his number four years ago... If she'd called him instead and told him she was pregnant. He'd have come back for her, he knew that much. But where would they have lived? He'd have wanted her to return to the city with him, so he could follow his dream. But she'd have wanted to stay here, in Somers Cove, with her mom, where she felt safe. And was that really so unreasonable? She'd have wanted her mom near her at a time like that, wouldn't she? Except she didn't get to have her mom on hand, because she'd had to leave and do it all by herself.

God, she'd given up so much... and what had he done? Nothing. He'd had time to date other women, to build his career, to buy his apartment and his car, to have a social life with his friends. And meanwhile Cassie had raised his daughter by herself, with no support, no friends, and very little money. And when he'd found out, the first thing he'd done, and kept doing, was to blame her for not telling him, to assume she'd *chosen* to keep him in the dark because it made her life easier. Easier? He had no idea.

The more he thought about it, the closer he came to deciding that, in her shoes, he'd probably have done the same thing.

"I don't know where Emma gets those cinnamon rolls," Cassie said, licking her fingers, "but I've got to tell her to stop stocking them."

"Why?" Jake asked, struggling not to respond as Cassie's tongue slowly worked over her fingertips. "You like them, don't you?"

"Yes. I like them too much. At this rate, I'll be enormous by the time I go back to Portland," Cassie replied.

He leant over and took her hand in his. "And you'll still be beautiful," he whispered. He saw her swallow, and her cheeks flush. "Can I call you?" he asked, changing the subject for both their sakes. "Like I did last week?"

Cassie nodded her head. "Yes, I'd like that."

He checked the time on his watch. "I've gotta go," he said, gulping down the last of his coffee. "I've got a meeting this afternoon, and I haven't prepared a damn thing yet." He smiled at her as he got to his feet.

Cassie stood up at the same time as him, and Maddie followed suit. Cassie leant down and signed to Maddie that Jake was leaving and she looked from her mother's face to Jake's, and then started to shake her head vigorously from side to side. Cassie tried to take Maddie's hand, but she shook herself free and went over to Jake, holding up her arms, to be lifted. He bent down to pick her up and she clung to his neck, and he felt tears against his skin.

"What's wrong?" Jake asked.

"Isn't it obvious?" Cassie replied. Jake stared at her. "She doesn't want you to leave. I explained it to her earlier… you know, that you were going, but you'd be back at the weekend. She got upset, but I thought she was okay again. I guess not."

"Oh…" He held Maddie closer. "Oh, God. I'm sorry, Cass."

"Why are you sorry? You have to go. We knew that. It can't be helped."

"Yeah, but if she's upset, that means you're gonna have to cope with her by yourself."

"Which I'm used to," Cassie replied.

"Even so…" Jake looked at her. "I feel bad about it."

"There's nothing you can do, Jake. It's not your fault. She just likes having you around."

"I like being around." He thought for a moment. "It'd be easier for her, maybe, if she could join in our calls."

"Jake… seriously?"

"Wait. I'm not being dumb," he explained.

"Really?"

He smiled. "Yeah, really. Why don't we Skype, instead of phoning? I know Maddie won't be able to hear me, but she'll be able to see me and I can try and sign with her, and then she'll know I haven't forgotten her, especially if we try and make it about her."

Cassie looked at him and he saw a new softness in her eyes, and then he noticed them glistening. "That's… that's a lovely idea, Jake," she murmured.

He took the few steps to stand in front of her. "Please don't cry, Cass. I can handle one of you breaking up on me, but not both of you. Okay?"

Cassie smiled up at him. "Okay."

"I should finish work around six tonight, so I'll get back to my apartment by around six-fifteen. Can we Skype then?"

She nodded. "Yes. We can use my laptop."

"Good. I'll try and call at six-fifteen each evening, but if I get held up in a meeting, I'll text you and let you know."

"Okay."

"And I'll be back next Saturday."

"Is that your office?" Cassie's voice came through loud and clear on his laptop.

"Yeah," Jake replied. "My meeting overran even longer than I thought."

"Your text said you'd be home by seven. What happened?"

Jake didn't want to talk about how Rich and Erica had held him back, for no good reason that he could see, other than Erica flirting with him and Rich looking on, which had felt weird and awkward. "My boss needed to speak with me afterwards," he said. "I only got away a couple of minutes ago, and I didn't want to miss seeing Maddie before bedtime, so I thought I'd just call you from here instead of going back to my place."

"Oh... I see. Well, it gave me a chance to give Maddie her bath. So, she's ready for bed once we've finished the call."

"Would you like me to show you around?" he offered. "My office is nowhere near as exciting as my apartment, but you might as well see where I spend most of my time." He recalled Cassie's responses to his home when they'd had their first Skype call at the beginning of the week. She'd made all the right noises, but he got the feeling he'd been correct in his assumption – it wouldn't have been her choice of somewhere to live. They'd kept their calls each night about Maddie as much as possible, although Cassie had told him she'd finished editing a book for a client and had sent it back. He'd marveled that she found the energy to work as well as look after Maddie, learn to sign and keep house. He was exhausted. He hadn't had time to do anything all week, except work, Skype with Cassie, do a little shopping, and fit in learning a few new words of sign language so he could try and communicate better with Maddie during their calls. He hadn't even had time to ask Cassie how the house was progressing, although judging from the view he got behind her each evening, it didn't look like much had changed... not in the living room, anyway.

"Sure," Cassie replied, pulling Maddie closer on her lap. "We'd love to see where you work." She signed something.

"What are you saying to her?" Jake asked, getting up from his desk and bringing his laptop with him.

"I'm just telling her this is your office."

He turned his laptop around which meant he couldn't see them anymore and slowly rotated it, so they could view where he worked.

"Wow... It's really big."

Jake stifled a laugh. "It's been years since I've heard you say that, Cass."

"Jake!" He could tell she was smiling, and he thought she was probably blushing, even though he couldn't see her.

"Sorry."

"No you're not."

He laughed. "No, not really."

"Stop a second." Cassie said abruptly.

He paused. "Why?"

"Maddie's just signing something." There was a short silence, then, "She's saying she likes the picture on your wall."

Jake looked up at the painting on the wall opposite the full length windows. It was of a seashore at sunset. He'd bought it when he'd been given his own office, to remind him of home... and Cassie. He'd thought about moving it to his apartment when he'd moved in there, but he spent more time in the office anyway, and he liked looking at it while he was working.

He sat back down, putting his laptop on the desk in front of him. He could see Cassie and Maddie on the screen again.

"It's lovely," Cassie said.

"The office, or the painting?"

"Both. And it is much bigger than I'd expected."

Jake couldn't help but grin.

"Stop it, Jake." Cassie was smiling too.

"I didn't say a word."

"You didn't need to."

Jake leant forward, resting his elbows on the desk.

"I'm not gonna be able to call you tomorrow night," he said. "Can you tell Maddie for me? I'm not up to that level yet."

"Sure. Is there a reason?"

"Yeah… I've just found out this evening, my boss is giving a party tomorrow, and I can't get out of it. I tried, because I wanted to drive home straight after work again so I could be with you on Saturday morning, but my client – the guy who owns the chain of hotels – he's gonna be at this party, so I kinda have to be there too."

"Okay. I'll explain it to Maddie when we've finished."

Jake nodded. "I'm sorry," he said.

"It can't be helped." Cassie shrugged.

"I'll drive up early on Saturday, though. I won't be there for breakfast, but I'll get to you as soon as I can."

"Please take care, Jake…"

He smiled. He liked the concerned tone of her voice, and her words. She really cared… "I will, don't worry."

Erica's dress was so short, it was almost embarrassing, and she was certainly attracting plenty of male attention, although not from the one source from which she desired it… namely, Jake.

He'd spent the entire evening so far talking to Mark Gardner in Rich's large garden, and trying to keep as far away from Erica as possible. Mark had been a friend to Jake before he became a client, the two men having met nearly three years earlier at a charity function. Neither of them had really wanted to be at the event; although they hadn't realized it at the time, they were both nursing broken hearts. Jake was still getting over Cassie and Mark never revealed exactly what had happened to him, although Jake got the impression it was something to do with a holiday romance gone wrong. On top of that, Mark's parents had been killed in a car accident about a year beforehand and he was still struggling to cope. They'd spent the evening getting very drunk together, Mark's driver had taken them back to Mark's townhouse, and their friendship had blossomed. Now, they met regularly over a beer, or to watch the Patriots, if they were playing at home, being as Mark had VIP seats. Mark guarded his privacy fiercely, and Jake respected that. In turn, Mark was grateful that Jake let him be himself.

"You know how obvious it is, don't you?" Mark murmured.

"What?" Jake looked up at Mark, who, at six foot five, was an inch or two taller than him.

"The boss's daughter's obsession. She hasn't taken her eyes off you all evening."

"Yeah, I know." Jake struggled to keep the frustration out of his voice.

"She's not bad looking, I guess…" Mark mused.

Jake glared at him. "She's not my type. And besides, I'm already taken."

Mark almost dropped his wine glass. "You are? This is news. I haven't seen you with anyone."

"That's because she's not from around here. And just so you know, you can't tell Rich… or Erica."

"Oh? Why?" Mark looked confused.

"Because it's complicated." Jake looked up just in time to see Rich approaching, with Erica in tow. "I'll tell you about it later," he whispered.

"I can't wait…" Mark muttered under his breath, as he smiled over at Rich.

"Mr Gardner." Rich approached, holding out his hand. "I'm glad you could make it. I know you're a bit of a recluse, but I was starting to doubt your existence." He laughed at his own joke. No-one else did. "I hope Jake's been looking after you," he added.

"Jake always looks after me, Mr Eldridge." Mark shook Rich's hand.

"Glad to hear it." Rich turned towards Erica. "Allow me to introduce my daughter, Erica."

"Pleasure," Mark said, taking her hand and giving it a light shake.

"Erica works in our marketing department, doesn't she Jake?" Rich added.

"Yeah, she does."

"At least for now, anyway."

Jake looked up, feeling hopeful all of a sudden. Had Rich finally seen the light and realized his daughter had no talent whatsoever? Was he about to move her somewhere else? Maybe they could open an office in Alaska… "Is she moving on, then?" he asked.

"Well, I'm sure she'll settle down one day soon. Maybe get married, and give me some grandchildren…" Rich moved closer and put an arm around Jake's shoulder. "You know how important family is to me, son." Jake felt his blood turn to ice, and glanced up at Erica, who was smiling at him. "She could do with a dependable man in her life, don't you think?" Rich continued. "Someone with good career prospects." He gave Jake a wink, then released him and turned back to Mark.

"It's been nice meeting you," he said, then took Erica's hand in his. "C'mon, Pumpkin… we need to circulate…"

Jake held back his groan until he was certain they were out of earshot.

"What the hell was that about?" Mark asked.

"I think that was a hint – a not very subtle hint – that Rich sees me as a future son-in-law."

"Oh… oh dear."

"That's one way of putting it."

"Well, we're in fairly polite society…" Mark took a sip of his wine. "You can't marry her, Jake, no matter what your boss wants. You'd be miserable."

"I've got no intention of marrying her."

"Why don't you just tell them both you're with someone else?"

"Because I'm not… well, not really."

"But you said…"

"Yeah. I know. I also said it was complicated." Jake glanced around. There were some chairs set out on the edge of the lawn. "Shall we?" he suggested.

"Sure."

The two men sauntered over to the quiet area and sat down. Jake sighed deeply. "It started four years ago…" he paused. "No, that's not true, it started twenty years ago."

"Wait a second… Is this the girl you told me about when we first met? The one who ran out on you and broke your heart?"

"Yeah, except she didn't run out on me."

"But she broke your heart?"

"Yeah, but that was my fault, not hers."

Mark looked confused. "But I remember you telling me, you went back for her and she'd left town, without a word."

"Yeah… well, it turned out she had a reason for doing that."

"Which was?"

"She was pregnant."

"Shit." Mark leant forward, resting his elbows on his knees. "I'm assuming it was yours?"

"Yes. Of course it was."

"Okay, don't jump down my throat."

"Sorry." Jake tipped his head back and looked up at the dusky sky.

"But you had no idea?" Mark asked, leaning back as well. "I mean, you've never mentioned having a kid."

"That's because they didn't tell me."

"Who's 'they'?"

"Cassie, her best friend, her mom and my dad."

"Even your dad didn't tell you? Man, that's harsh." Mark exhaled.

"Not really. I was an asshole back then."

"Even so…"

Jake looked across at Mark and shrugged.

"So, what's happened?" Mark asked him.

"I went back home a couple of weeks ago, to try and mend a few fences with my dad, and discovered I've got an incredible daughter.

She's three and a half, and she's beautiful. She's absolutely adorable. Her name's Maddie... and she's deaf."

Mark's head dropped, but he didn't say a word for a moment. Then he turned to Jake. "And your girlfriend? Cassie, was it?"

"Oh, she's beautiful too."

A slow smile formed on Mark's lips. "I see. And you wanna get back together with her?"

Jake nodded. "More than anything."

"You're not angry with her that she kept your daughter from you?"

"I was, when I first found out. I was mad as hell with all of them. But now, I've realized Cass did the right thing... the right thing by Maddie, anyway. They both deserved better than the guy I was back then."

"And how does Cassie feel about the idea of getting back with you?"

"I'm not entirely sure. We haven't gotten that far yet. I'm gonna be living up there for the summer and... well, I'm hoping to convince her that I've changed, that I'm worthy of them both."

"So, you're not exactly 'taken' then..." Mark surmised.

"Yeah. I am." Jake looked at his friend. "There's no-one else for me. So, as far as I'm concerned, I'm taken."

Mark turned to face him. "I hope it works out for you, man," he whispered.

"Thanks." Jake paused. "One thing's for sure, I don't need this shit." He nodded in Rich's direction. He was now talking to another man, near the double doors into the living room of his enormous house, with Erica still standing by his side, although her eyes were fixed firmly on Jake.

"Just ignore it," Mark suggested. "Spend the summer with your family. By the time you come back, it'll probably have blown over. And if it hasn't... well, hopefully you'll be with Cassie by then, and it'll be irrelevant what Rich wants."

"And if I don't have a job anymore?"

Mark shrugged. "Then Rich is an idiot. But, honestly, if that does happen, come see me."

Jake stared at his friend. "Are you serious?"

Mark patted him on the shoulder. "Always, Jake. 'Serious' is my middle name. I thought you knew that…"

Jake let himself into his apartment and turned on the lights. He glanced around at the angular furniture, the stark empty surfaces, the shiny floor, the blank emptiness of it all, and went straight through into the bedroom.

He didn't care that it was already eleven-thirty. He didn't care that it would be nearly three am by the time he reached Somers Cove. He was leaving tonight. Right now. Well, as soon as he could pack a bag, anyway. He had a key to his dad's place. He'd let himself in, quietly, and get a few hours' sleep. And then he'd surprise Cassie and Maddie in the morning. He smiled at the thought.

Chapter Seventeen

Cassie

Work had progressed well on the house since Ben collected all the fittings for the bathroom and kitchen. The only problem was that, on Friday, he had to turn off all the water, and because he had so much work on, he had no idea how long it would be before he could get the bathroom re-fitted and turn everything back on again.

"It's really not gonna be practical for the two of you to carry on living here," Ben remarked, looking around the bare shell that had once been the fully tiled bathroom.

"With no toilet, shower, or running water... you have a point." Cassie moved Maddie from one hip to the other.

"Here, let me take her," Ben said. "She's tired, and heavy, and you need a rest."

Ben wasn't wrong. Cassie hadn't slept well all week... and she knew why. She was missing Jake, although she wasn't about to admit that to anyone else.

"I suppose I should've realized this would happen," Cassie mumbled, scratching her head. "But where are we going to live? I can't afford the motel..."

"You don't need to. I've got plenty of room, and it'll only be for a week or two."

"You're saying we can stay with you?" Cassie turned to him.

"Of course. I'd love to have you both come stay. You and this little bundle can share the guest room... if that's okay with you?"

"It's fine." Cassie smiled. "We're sharing a room here anyway."

"Well then…" Ben leaned over and switched off the light, plunging the empty room into darkness. "Why don't you pack up some things, and we'll head on back there now. I'll cook us some dinner, and you can give Maddie her bath."

Cassie leant into him, resting her head on his shoulder. "What would we do without you?" she murmured.

"Learn to like camping?" He grinned and Cassie couldn't help but laugh.

She sat up late with Ben, talking over plans for the house, his ideas for her mom's bedroom, and the kitchen, and how much quicker he thought everything would go once Jake was there full time.

"He'll be able to help out in the evenings, too," Ben suggested, "as well as weekends."

"I guess we should tell him that I'm staying here," Cassie said, picking up her phone. "I can text him. He's at this party his boss is giving, but I'm sure he won't mind."

"There's really no need," Ben replied, giving her a smile. "He's not coming back until tomorrow morning, sometime just before lunch, I think. We can just tell him then."

Cassie didn't want to push it. She didn't want Ben to know she was just looking for an excuse to contact Jake. And he was right, Jake would be there in just a few hours anyway. She could wait that long…

Maddie rolled over and tugged on Cassie's arm.

"It can't be morning – not yet," Cassie whimpered quietly to herself. She opened one eye, then the other and was appalled to see that it was, indeed, morning. It was yet another bright, sunny morning. She turned and looked down at Maddie, who was smiling up at her.

She signed, 'good morning'.

Maddie made a 'drinking' sign, like she was taking a drink from a glass. Cassie raised her eyebrows, tilted her head to one side and waited. Maddie made the sign again and started tugging on Cassie's arm, but Cassie stayed firm and shook her head. Maddie flopped back down on the bed for a moment, then sat up, made the sign again and then, with her right hand held flat, she moved it around in front of her chest.

"That's better." Cassie nodded, signing 'good girl', while she spoke. "Saying please gets you a lot further."

She climbed out of bed and quickly went over to the window. Ben's truck was gone. He'd obviously gone to do some work somewhere, or had gone into town for some reason. At least she and Maddie had the house to themselves and could wander around as they were for the time being, which was just as well, because she'd forgotten to bring a robe with her. Maddie was waiting for her by the bedroom door and the two of them went out together.

Ben's house was much larger than her mother's. There were four bedrooms, two on either side of the stairs, which ran up the centre of the property. Cassie and Maddie were in the guest room, which had its own bathroom and was situated next door to Ben's room. Jake's bedroom was opposite, and beside that was the smallest of the bedrooms, which Ben used for storage.

Cassie led the way to the top of the stairs with Maddie following close behind. She was looking forward to seeing Jake later on, and spending some of the day with him. She turned at the top of the stairs, and was about to take Maddie's hand, when the door to Jake's bedroom opened.

Cassie let out a yelp of surprise and leapt backward, losing her footing. Then she screamed, fearing a headlong dive down the full height of the staircase, but Jake quickly stepped forward and reached out, grabbing her flailing arm with one hand and placing the other firmly around her waist, pulling her back into the safety of his bare chest.

"Cass?" he said quietly, holding on to her. "Are you okay?"

She stared up at him. He looked sleepy and disheveled, and gorgeous. "Y—Yes," she muttered. "Sorry. I'm fine, Thank you." She pulled away, just slightly, although Jake kept an arm around her. "You… you saved me," she muttered.

"I'll always save you," he replied gently. She flushed and he looked from her down to Maddie. "Well… This is a surprise," he said, smiling.

"Right back at you," Cassie said, gathering her scattered wits back together.

Letting Cassie go, Jake crouched down in front of Maddie and gave her a salute 'hello'.

Maddie looked a little shy, and glanced up at Cassie, who gave her a nod.

She turned back to Jake and repeated the salute back to him, then she spread out all the fingers of her right hand and tapped her extended thumb on her forehead. Jake looked up at Cassie.

"I got the 'hello'," he said, "but what was the other bit?"

Cassie looked down at her feet. "Well," she mumbled, "when I was explaining to her that we were gonna talk to you on the computer, and that she'd be able to see you, she got really excited…"

"That's sweet," Jake replied.

"Yeah, it was. But then, as the week went on, each time I was getting the computer set up, and I was telling her we were gonna talk to you, I realized it was wrong for me to say we were gonna speak to 'Jake' each night. Because to her, you're not 'Jake'." She looked down at him. "So, I told her who you are."

Jake stood up. "You mean you told her I'm her daddy? Is that what she was signing? 'Hello Daddy'?"

Cassie nodded her head.

Jake bent down and lifted Maddie into his arms, his eyes closed as he held her to his body. When he opened them again, Cassie noticed they were sparkling with unshed tears. "Thanks, Cass. Thank you so much. I know this is a big deal… a really big deal. It means a lot."

"I know it does." Cassie swallowed down the lump in her throat as Maddie nestled into Jake's bare chest. "If I didn't know how much it meant to you, I wouldn't have done it."

Jake stared at her for a moment, then took a step closer, just as Maddie started to sign. Cassie laughed, just gently.

"What?" Jake asked.

"That might have been a momentous event for you… but your daughter's hungry."

"*Our* daughter, Cass," Jake whispered, leaning in and kissing her gently on the cheek. "Our daughter."

Jake turned to Maddie. "I guess we'd better find some breakfast then," he said.

"I guess so."

Jake led the way down the stairs, carrying Maddie, with Cassie close behind. As they got into the kitchen, he put Maddie down on the floor and went over to the refrigerator.

"Scrambled eggs and bacon okay?" he asked.

"Maddie doesn't like bacon," Cassie replied, "but she'll eat scrambled eggs, with toast."

"She doesn't like bacon?" Jake seemed incredulous. "Are you sure she's mine?"

Just for a moment, Cassie was unsure whether to laugh or cry, but she was erring toward crying. "Yes, I am," she mumbled.

Jake came over and stood in front of her. "I know," he whispered, staring into her eyes. "I'm sorry. That was a bad joke…" Cassie felt herself leaning toward him, just as Maddie tugged on her hand.

"We're not going to get a moment's peace until she's been fed," she managed a laugh.

"Evidently not." Jake turned and pulled down a pan from the many hooks above the wide stove. "Sit down," he said. "Breakfast's on me, and while I'm making it, you can explain why I opened my bedroom door to find my two most favorite people in the whole world standing right outside at eight o'clock on a Saturday morning."

"We're staying here," Cassie explained, fetching a coloring book and some crayons from the rucksack she'd packed for Maddie, and putting them out on the kitchen table.

"You are?" Jake turned and looked at her.

"Yes. There's no water at our house, as of yesterday afternoon. So, your dad suggested we stay here until the bathroom and kitchen are fixed."

Jake came over, with two eggs in one hand, and a knife in the other, and leant over the table until his lips were just a couple of inches from hers, and whispered, "Damn wise man, my dad."

Cassie giggled, and blushed as he turned away. She let her eyes roam down his toned back to the shorts that hung low on his hips, and then further down to his strong legs, and she sucked in a breath. "Speaking of surprises," she said, bringing herself back to reality, "we weren't expecting you back till much later this morning."

"No…" He finished breaking the eggs into a bowl and started to whisk them, turning and leaning back on the countertop. "I got back from the party last night and, well, I didn't want to stay in the city any more. So, I drove up here… got in about three-fifteen, I guess, and just fell into bed."

"Three-fifteen… So, you've had less than five hours' sleep?"

"Yeah. It'll hit me later." He smiled.

"I was gonna say, the Jake I used to know couldn't survive on less than eight hours… preferably ten."

"Yeah, he's still in here." He grinned across at her. "I'll probably fall asleep on you sometime around four this afternoon."

She liked the sound of that… a lot, and she let her mind drift back to the days when Jake would study late, then fall asleep the next day with his head on her shoulder, or her breasts, or her stomach, and she'd caress his hair. She'd sometimes read a book, or just listen to his breathing, until he woke up and would sleepily kiss her, and make love to her gently and tenderly.

"Breakfast's ready." Jake's voice broke into her dreams and she sat bolt upright, blushing. "You okay?" he asked, bringing over two cups of very hot coffee, one for each of them, and a glass of milk for Maddie.

"Hmm? Yes… I'm fine." Cassie didn't dare make eye contact with him, so she cleared away Maddie's coloring things and set out her knife and fork, just as Jake was putting down her breakfast in front of her.

"You gave her bacon?" Cassie said.

"She my daughter. She's gotta like bacon." Jake smiled. "It's just one slice. If she hates it, she can leave it. If she likes it, there's more keeping warm in the oven."

"But you refuse to just take my word for it that she won't eat it?" Cassie glared at him.

He stopped in his tracks, looking down at her. "It's just bacon, Cass." He glanced at Maddie, and then burst out laughing. "Oh… oh dear."

"What?" Cassie turned and looked at her daughter, who was helping herself to her food, and had already quietly eaten the slice of bacon that Jake had given to her. "The little…" Cassie muttered under her breath.

"It's obviously how I cook it."

"You'll be wearing it if you don't stop gloating," Cassie countered.

Jake laughed loudly and leant over, kissing her lightly on the lips. "Me? Gloat? Never…"

They decided to have lunch together on the beach, so Jake drove them into town and they went to the store together – daring the tongues to wag – and bought what they needed for a picnic. Back at Ben's, Cassie made sandwiches and, once everything was ready, they carried it all down the lane to the beach. It was odd, coming back to her own home, but not going inside. She felt like a visitor, and it made her a little uncomfortable.

Once they'd eaten, Jake and Maddie played ball, while Cassie sat and watched them. It had been a lovely morning. Maddie had behaved herself better than she had all week, which didn't really surprise Cassie, being as Jake was back. It seemed Maddie only played up when Jake wasn't there these days. During the course of the morning, like after breakfast, when they'd cleared away together, Jake had bumped into her a few times in the kitchen, and he'd kissed too, but his kisses were still so brief, so light, she was almost starting to believe she'd imagined them.

Jake

It had been a spectacular day. So much better than he'd imagined, and well worth the loss of sleep that driving up overnight had entailed.

The highlight, so far, had to be finding out that Cassie had told Maddie who he was. He was still struggling to take that in, just over twelve hours later. It was a huge thing for her to have done… and something he didn't expect Cassie to commit to yet. It gave him so much hope. More hope than he wanted to admit to, even to himself.

And although that was the highlight, he had to admit, he could't stop thinking about how good Cassie had looked that morning when they'd stumbled on each other outside his bedroom door. He wasn't sure if she knew how little her pajama top concealed, but he'd been more than aware of her nipples peaking through the thin material. Luckily, the sight hadn't distracted him too much, and he'd been able to grab her and stop her from falling down the stairs. Pulling her into his arms, and feeling her against his chest had been a bonus… a really great bonus.

It was just a shame Cassie had been so quiet all afternoon. They'd had a really nice lunch on the beach, but after that, she'd gone kind of remote on him, and he had no idea why.

Now, they'd had dinner together, Ben had gone over to the office above the garage to catch up on some paperwork, and Jake had just finished putting Maddie to bed, with Cassie's help, of course. Coming out of the room she was sharing with Cassie, they stood at the top of the stairs.

"I meant what I said earlier, Cass," he whispered, although he didn't know why. "Thank you for telling her about me. It really does mean so much."

"And I meant what I said," Cassie replied, starting down the stairs. "You are her daddy, it felt wrong to call you anything else. And I know you appreciate it."

They got to the bottom of the stairs.

"Do you feel like a glass of wine?" Jake offered.

"Hmm… I need one."

"Go and sit in the living room," he suggested. "I'll bring them in."

He joined Cassie a few moments later. She was sitting in the corner of the sofa and, rather than sit at the other end, Jake put the wine on the coffee table and came and sat right beside her, taking both of her hands in one of his. He placed the other on her cheek.

"Do you know?" he murmured. "I've wanted to have you to myself all day."

"Why?"

"To do this…"

"Do what?"

He leant in a little.

"Jake… wait." Cassie pulled back from him and he sat up.

"What's wrong?" he asked. "Don't you like my kisses?"

She looked down at her hands, still entwined with his in her lap.

"I don't understand your kisses," she said quietly.

"Sorry?"

"I said I don't understand them," she repeated. "They're so brief… so platonic. It feels like you're not sure about whether to kiss me, or not."

"That's because, most of the time, that's exactly how I feel," Jake replied.

"In which case…"

"But only because I don't know how *you* feel," he added quickly. "Cass…" He moved even closer still. "I want to kiss you so much, and sometimes I think you want that too, but other times, you seem… I don't know… kinda distant. I know we can't just take up where we left off. Everything is different now. And I don't want you to think I'm pushing you for anything you're not ready to give. More than anything, I know I've got to earn your trust again, and that's a long road. But I want you, Cass. I think I want you even more now than I did four years ago. And I wanted you like my life depended on it back then…"

"You did?" She seemed surprised.

"Yeah, I did." Had he never told her that?

He looked into her eyes and decided to take a chance. Closing the gap between them, he covered her lips with his, and held them there, just for a moment. He sensed she was waiting for him to pull away, but he didn't. He ran his tongue along her lips and, when she gasped, he delved inside, just gently, exploring her. She was exactly as he remembered – sweet, tender and soft. He brushed her cheek with his thumb, letting his fingers move up into her hair, and she moaned, just ever so slightly, into his mouth, her tongue responding to his, twirling against him. He groaned and, releasing her hands, he reached behind her and pulled her closer, feeling her breasts against his chest. He needed to stop… soon… just not quite yet. He changed the angle of his head and kissed her a little deeper and he felt her hands come up his arms, resting on his biceps for a moment, before they passed up, and along his shoulders, and around his neck. Her fingers played in his hair. He really was gonna have to stop… now…

He pulled back and let out a long sigh.

"I want us to be together, Cass," he murmured, resting his forehead against hers. "Nothing's changed, not as far as I'm concerned. Everything's just the same as it always was… except I think I want you even more."

He heard her suck in a breath. "I never stopped caring about you," she whispered. "But Maddie comes first, which means I have to be sure."

He put his finger under her chin and raised her face to his, forcing their eyes to connect. "I know," he told her. "I get it. I'll always be there for Maddie. I'm her father and I'm not going anywhere, you can be damn sure of that. But can I just tell you one thing, Cass? Even if we didn't have her, if I'd come back here and found you on your own, with no Maddie, I'd still want you in my life again. I get that it's about Maddie, I really do… but it's also about you. At least it is for me. It's always been about you." He kissed her again, just gently, his tongue running along and around her lips, and into her mouth, until she was breathing hard and moaning. Then he pulled back.

"We'll do this however you want, Cass. If you want to take it slow, we'll take it slow. I'll wait as long as you need, and I'll do whatever I have to, to prove I'm worthy of your trust. But, I need to know I've got a chance. I need to know there's hope for us. I don't care how long it takes, but can you just tell me… do you want me back?"

He watched Cassie raise her eyes to his once more, then slowly nod her head. "Yes," she whispered. "Yes, Jake."

He pulled her into his arms and kissed her again.

Later – much later – when it was time for bed, they stood outside her bedroom door once more.

"Goodnight," Cassie whispered.

Jake leant down and kissed her, just quickly.

"Goodnight," he repeated.

As Cassie opened the door, he pulled her back.

"I wish it didn't have to be like this," he murmured. "I wish I wasn't saying goodnight to you, at least not like this. I wish…"

"I know, Jake." She ran her hand down his cheek and, standing on tiptoes, she kissed him. "I know."

"If you put that one in the corner," Ben said, pointing to the furthest corner of the kitchen, "then the longer one will go over there." He nodded toward the wall by the window, where the sink used to be. "At least I think that's how I planned it."

Jake rolled his eyes and carried the heavy cabinet over to the corner, putting it down where Ben had indicated. Cassie held her thumbnail between her teeth… God, she looked cute.

"Do you want some help?" she offered.

Jake looked over to her. "No, it's fine." He smiled.

Ben gazed around the room. "It's coming together," he said.

"Yeah, Dad…" Jake replied, "as long as you ignore the fact there are no doors on any of these cabinets."

"I'm getting there," Ben retorted, going into the corner of the room and getting out his tape measure again.

Emma was standing near the door, holding Maddie's hand. "I think we'll go down to the beach for a while," she said. "It'll keep Maddie occupied and out of the way…"

"Thanks, Em," Cassie replied.

Emma knelt down and signed to Maddie that they were going down to the beach. Maddie jumped up and down, clapping her hands.

"I guess she likes that idea," Jake said, smiling.

As Emma stood again, she turned to Cassie. "I meant to ask, when are your books being delivered?"

"Monday morning, between eight and eight-thirty."

"Very precise!" Emma joked.

"Well, it's lucky they are being precise. I'll have to come down here specially. They're still being delivered to this address. And I don't want the guy to take them away, just because there's no-one here."

"What books are these?" Jake asked.

"My books," Cassie explained. "I get ten copies free, from the publishers."

"What? Is this your novel we're talking about?" Jake came over to her.

Cassie nodded.

"We'll be off," Emma announced, taking Maddie's hand and going out through the screen door.

"See you in a while, Em," Cassie called after her.

"Your novel's out on Monday?" Jake said, standing in front of Cassie.

"Yes."

"And when were you going to tell me this?"

"Um… Why did you want to know? I wouldn't have thought you'd want to read it. It's hardly your thing," Cassie murmured.

"I want to know because I'm proud of you."

"For writing a romance novel… hmm, a great achievement."

"Hey." Jake put his arms around Cassie and pulled her into his chest. "Stop putting yourself down."

Ben turned and looked at them, clasped together. "I'm going back home," he said. "I'm gonna fetch down a couple of the doors and see how they fit."

"Want a hand?" Jake offered.

"No, son," Ben grinned. "You've got yours full already."

Cassie tensed and pulled away from Jake as Ben made his way out.

"What's wrong?" he asked, as soon as they were alone.

Cassie looked down at his chest, avoiding his eyes.

"Cass, tell me."

"Your dad's comment," she murmured.

"What about it?"

"I don't know… it makes me feel…"

"What?"

"Like people are watching us."

"So what if they are?" Jake pulled her close again, and although she was stiff, she let him. "And anyway, it's just dad… and he's on our side. Besides, I don't care who's watching us, or who knows about us."

"Who are you… imposter? And what have you done with *my* Jake Hunter?" Cassie looked up at him, smiling. Had she really just called him hers?

"I mean it, Cass." Jake was still serious. "I don't care about any of that anymore. It's not important. You're what matters. You and Maddie. If other people wanna gossip about us, let them. As long as you're mine and I'm yours, and Maddie's safe and happy, I really couldn't give a damn about anything else."

She rested her head on his chest and let her arms come around his waist, sighing into him.

"And just so you know, I'm still your Jake Hunter," he murmured into her hair.

On Monday morning, they all got up early. Cassie had thought she'd go down to the beach house and wait for the books to be delivered, but Jake said he'd go, in case they were heavy. He didn't need to leave until nine… or nine-thirty at a push, so Cassie cooked breakfast while he was gone and he returned, with the box under his arm, just as she was putting the toast on the table.

"They're here!" he announced, putting the box down on the countertop.

Everyone gathered round, including Ben, who'd waited behind for the big 'reveal'.

"I'm so nervous," Cassie said. "Can't you all just turn around, or something."

"Hell, no," Jake said, handing her a sharp knife to cut through the tape that held the box together.

Cassie sighed and took the knife from him, while Jake lifted Maddie into his arms. She ran the blade along the tape, then pulled back the sides of the box, and lifted out a book, holding it in her hands. Whatever she'd said, he could tell from the look in her eyes that she was pleased. She turned it around, showing off the cover and Jake sucked in a breath. The image was of a man's torso. He was wearing a shirt that was completely undone revealing a muscular, tanned chest. He smiled to himself. It seemed Cassie had gone for raunchy, not romantic, then. He looked at the title, which was '*Destiny*' and wondered what it was about, and then let his eyes wander down to the bottom of the book…

"Um… I think they've made a mistake, Cass," he said.

Cassie turned the book around and looked at the front cover.

"No. I don't think so."

"Well, unless you've changed your name…" Jake pointed.

"Oh, no, that's my pen-name," Cassie replied.

"Your pen-name?"

Cassie started to blush. "Well, yes. I didn't want to write under my own name," she said. "Not this kind of thing, anyway. It's too…" She glanced at Ben. "It's too embarrassing."

Jake couldn't help but smile. "I see," he murmured. "They look great," he added.

"Really?"

"Yeah, really." He leant down and kissed her on the cheek, then kissed Maddie too. "But I've only got twenty minutes now until I have to leave, so can we have some breakfast?"

Cassie put the book back in the box and moved it onto the floor. "Yes, sir." She smiled over at him.

'Brett wandered across the sandy beach, his tanned body on show for all to see, his muscles taut and rippling. And yet, there was no arrogance to his stride. He didn't strut, he just sauntered casually, his dark green eyes taking in the surroundings, and settling at last on Isabel, her long blonde hair catching in the wind as her baby blue eyes raked up and down his perfect form. She wanted him…'

Jake let out a half-laugh. He'd stolen a copy of Cass's book from the box before leaving the house than morning and now, in the still quiet of his apartment, after he'd finished his Skype call with Cassie and Maddie, and eaten a bowl of stir-fry, he was lying on his couch, with a glass of wine, reading… and now smirking to himself, because, if Cass had drawn an actual picture, or taken a photograph, she couldn't have more obviously portrayed these two characters as the two of them. Brett was clearly Jake, albeit more muscular and toned – and handsome – according to her description anyway, because there was no way Jake would have described himself in those words. But the eyes, the hair color, the smile and even the sense of humor – they were all Jake. And as for Isabel? She was Cass, through and through. Except Isabel had hang-ups and insecurities about her appearance that Cass had never had… had she? No. Cass was the hottest girl in town. If anyone had hang-ups it was Jake, who'd gone through puberty terrified that Cass would come out of school one day and tell him she'd fallen for some ten foot tall football player. Once they started dating, and then – later on – sleeping together, he'd been constantly aware of how other guys looked at her, and how lucky he was that she loved him, and no-one else. And she had loved him, until he blew it, that is…

He read on for a little while. Then, after a couple more chapters, he sat up, leaning forward and concentrating even harder on the words before him…

'He looked down into her eyes, shining in the clear moonlight and whispered, "Are you sure?" His voice was so quiet, she struggled to hear him over the sound of the waves lapping on the shore beneath them. She didn't need to hear him, though… she knew what he was asking. And she knew what her answer would be.

She nodded slowly, her hands resting on his arms, as he slowly entered her. She cried out in pain, her eyes snapping shut and he stilled, until she opened up again, to find a look of such anxiety on his face, she knew she'd never stop loving him. Not as long as she had breath in her body.

"It's okay," she murmured.

"Really?" He seemed uncertain. "We can stop, Izzy. I don't want to hurt you."

"You won't. I know you won't."

She felt him slowly inching inside her, stretching and filling her until they were completely connected.

"You feel so good," he muttered.

"So do you."

And he started to move…'

Jake put the book down beside him for a moment, leant back and stared at the ceiling.

She'd recreated it. The scene was identical. Well, it was told from a female perspective, but the waves, the moonlight, the actions, even the words... Hell, that was exactly what he'd said to her, all those years ago on the beach, when he'd taken her virginity. He'd asked her if she was sure, and then when he knew he'd hurt her, he'd asked if she wanted to stop. He picked up the book again. Had she really felt like that?

'... she knew she'd never stop loving him. Not as long as she had breath in her body.'

So much strength of feeling. But he'd honestly thought it was just him who'd felt like that...

He lay back, taking the book with him.

As the story progressed, he recognized more scenes, more situations, more conversations, more jokes. He read the sexual encounters with interest, and not just because they turned him on – which they did. Each one was a recreation of something they'd done. He laughed out loud at her description of them having sex in the back of his Jeep – although, unlike his Wrangler, she'd given Brett a Toyota Land Cruiser – but the scene was still the same, at least the first time they'd tried it, when Cassie had got her foot stuck in the open window and, in trying to help her out, they'd gotten tangled and she'd ended up smacking him in the face with her elbow, cutting his lip open. He hadn't been able to kiss her properly for nearly a week after that, and as for explaining it to his dad...

He continued through the book, which wasn't their story, despite the similarities in character and scenes. Brett and Isabel were older than Jake and Cassie had been. At twenty-five, they were just a year younger than Jake and Cassie were now. And, rather than it being the story of two childhood sweethearts, whose lives went wrong, this was the tale of a couple who met on vacation, shared a torrid couple of weeks and then went their separate ways, only for each of them to realize they couldn't live without the other, but to then work out they had no means of getting in touch. The second half of the book was a series of hilarious misunderstandings, silly confusions and sad disappointments until, in the end, the couple were reunited, quite by accident on an airplane, both heading back to the resort where they'd fallen in love.

As he finished the story and set the book down on the table in front of him, several things struck Jake. Firstly, he felt flattered that Cassie had portrayed him like that. Not only had she made the hero so obviously Jake, and then embellished *all* his attributes, she'd also made him out to be some kind of stud. In the book Brett and Isabel had sex all the time they were together. Literally *all* the time. He thought back… Yeah, he and Cassie used to have a lot of sex too, but that had nothing to do with him. It had everything to do with Cassie, and the fact that she was so completely perfect, so utterly gorgeous that he couldn't keep his hands off her.

He smiled. The sex scenes… They were just like Cassie. The words were 'proper', as he'd have put it. There was sex, there was a lot of sex, but Isabel's language was feminine and coy. He let out a snicker as he remembered that Cassie would never have said the word 'cock'. If she referred to his penis at all, she usually just said 'it'. But she used to get turned on as hell when Jake's language got a little raw. When he told her – in graphic detail – all the things he wanted to do to her, she'd be practically begging him to take her. That was one of the best things about Cass… As Jake always used to tell her, she was a heady combination of sensual reticence. It was a powerful turn-on.

Jake checked the time. It was gone two in the morning. He really needed to go to bed, even if he was still feeling a little wired from the experience of reading Cass's book.

He got up and switched off all the lights, and took the book with him through to his bedroom.

Lying in bed, he wondered if Cassie felt she'd missed out. She'd made Brett the image of Jake in most ways, but Brett was considerably more romantic than Jake had ever been. Had she wanted that? He guessed she must've done… He sighed deeply, knowing it was another way he'd let her down; taking her for granted and not telling her often enough how much he loved her and what she meant to him.

He turned over and wished Cassie could be with him, so he could tell her now, just like he'd done at the weekend. He smiled… Okay, so he may not have been demonstrative before, but they'd been real affectionate with each other on the couch at his dad's on Saturday night. He'd told her what she meant to him, and how much he wanted her. He hadn't held back at all… and it hadn't even been like he was trying. Those words had just come naturally.

He may have let her down before… and she might have wanted more, but it was a 'more' he'd be more than happy to give her now, and it would come right from his heart. Jake knew he'd changed a lot in the last four years and, although he was very far from being Brett – he wasn't that damn perfect – he knew he liked the newer version of himself a lot more than the guy he used to be. His only hope was that, once she really got to know him again, Cassie would agree.

Chapter Eighteen

Cassie

Cassie disconnected the call, unsure whether to scream with laughter, or tears.

"What's wrong?" Ben came into the room and looked up at her.

"Is it that obvious?"

"Well, you look like someone just told you your pet dog died, so yeah."

"Oh. Well, I don't have a pet dog."

"It's a metaphor, Cassie."

"I know… I'm the writer, remember?" She put her phone down on the countertop. "I've got a problem."

"What?"

"That was my publisher in New York."

"And?" Ben asked

"And my book's been selling really well, all week."

"That's great, isn't it?"

"Yes, it is…" Cassie paused.

"Then what's the problem."

"She's managed to get me a slot on one of the radio stations in Portland as a promotional thing."

"And this is bad news? Sounds good to me."

"It is, except I'd rather have a bath in boiling oil than talk publicly – and live on air – about my books. But that's not the problem."

"Then what is?"

"Maddie," Cassie explained. "What am I going to do with her?"

"When is it?"

"Monday lunchtime."

"This coming Monday?" Ben ran his hand through his hair.

"Yes."

"I'm out all day Monday, but what about Jake?"

"Jake?"

"Yeah. He's coming home tomorrow night after he finishes work, and he won't be going back on Monday morning like he normally does. He's gonna be up here until the fall—"

"I know all that, but I don't see how it helps."

"Let him look after Maddie for the day," Ben explained.

"How can I, Ben? He can't sign very well."

Ben came over and put his hands on her shoulders. "They'll get by. It'll do him good… and maybe her too."

"What if he has to work though?"

"Then let him deal with it. He's her daddy. Let him take some of the responsibility for once."

Cassie nodded, even though she wasn't convinced.

As Cassie lay awake later that night, listening to Maddie's soft breathing, she wondered what the interview would be like. What would they ask her? And how would she answer them? She couldn't tell them the truth; that the characters in her book were based on Jake and herself. That would be far too embarrassing. She'd have to make something up. Still, she had the weekend to think about it. She felt odd knowing people had been reading her book all week. She'd written it to be read, obviously, and she was thrilled it was selling, but the idea that people were reading her thoughts and feelings and emotions, things she'd struggled for so long to get down on the page… that was a little strange.

The only thing she was grateful for was that Jake hadn't read it… and given the genre, he was unlikely to. She'd die of embarrassment if he knew how much of them she'd put into the characters. It wasn't like she had much choice – she didn't know any other men well enough to describe them in that much detail, so Brett had to be Jake, and if Brett was Jake, then Isabel had to be Cassie, because she really didn't want to describe Jake having sex with anyone but herself, even in fiction.

That thought made her whole body tingle. Last weekend had been very special. Jake's words had taken her by surprise. She'd had no idea he still felt the same way about her. Come to that, she'd had no idea he'd felt like that about her back then. Before, he'd always been very physical, but now he was more... much, much more. He was sweet, romantic and considerate, as well as loving and attentive and caring. She turned over and looked out the window. She missed him. She missed him a lot.

"I told you not to wait up," he whispered, leaning over and gently tucking a stray hair behind her ear.

She opened her eyes and looked up at him, then sat up on the couch and stretched her arms above her head.

"I know," she muttered, "but I didn't like the idea of you coming back to a quiet house."

"It was still quiet, Cass," Jake replied. "You were sound asleep. If you hadn't left the light on, I'd never have known you were in here, and I'd have just gone straight up to bed."

"Sorry."

"Hey..." He pulled her up to her feet and into his arms. "Don't be sorry. I like that you stayed up. Even if you didn't."

"What time is it?" She yawned.

"It's just before midnight. I had a lot to finish up before leaving, so I didn't get away until nearly nine." He leant down and kissed her. "Which is why I told you not to wait up."

"Do you want a coffee?" she offered.

"No, thanks. I stopped and had one on the way."

"Glass of wine?"

"Sure, if you want."

She went to go to the kitchen, but turned around on the threshold. "I'm not ready to say goodnight yet," she explained. "You've only just got here."

"Well, you could always come to bed with me." He smiled over at her. "Then you wouldn't have to say goodnight."

"I would, when we went to sleep."

"You're assuming I'd let you sleep."

She felt a pool of heat settle in the pit of her stomach.

"We… We're meant to be taking it slow, remember?" she whispered.

"Damn, and there was me hoping you'd have missed me so much you wouldn't be able to resist."

She laughed and continued into the kitchen. She was just reaching up to the top shelf for the wine glasses, when she felt his hands on her waist.

"Did you miss me, Cass?" he asked. He sounded worried, like he thought she might not have done.

She grabbed the glasses and turned around in his arms so she was facing him. "Yes, I did."

"Good. I missed you too."

He took the glasses from her and put them down on the countertop, then placed his hands on her cheeks and pressed his lips to hers. She opened up to him immediately and their tongues met. He moved his feet either side of hers, their bodies fused and she felt his long, hard erection pressed against her hip.

She instantly pulled back, wide-eyed. "Is this your idea of taking it slow?" she whispered, catching her breath.

"It's about as slow as I'm able to go right now," he replied, leaning in and capturing her bottom lip between his teeth, nipping at it gently.

"Oh, God…" she muttered.

"I want you," she heard him whisper as he trailed kisses along her jaw toward her ear. When he got there, he murmured, really softly, "But I'll wait," and she let out a long sigh, at least some of which was tinged with disappointment.

He took a step back, but she grabbed his arm and held on. "I want you too, Jake. I'm just…"

"I know," he said softly, running his thumb across her bottom lip. "I know."

They didn't drink the wine. By a kind of silent mutual consent, they seemed to agree it would be better for both of them if they went to bed – separately.

They kissed goodnight outside Cassie's bedroom door. It was a kiss that left her wanting more.

Maddie's excitement at seeing Jake the next morning was a joy to see. They all had breakfast together – even Ben, who for once on a Saturday morning, didn't have any odd jobs to do.

They decided they'd spend the morning doing the grocery shopping and tidying up, and head down to the beach house in the afternoon to varnish the kitchen cabinets.

Over lunch, Cassie decided to ask Jake about looking after Maddie.

"I need to ask you a favor," she began, tentatively.

"Then ask," Jake replied, taking a bite from his sandwich.

"I've got to go to Portland on Monday."

"You have?" He put his sandwich back down on the plate and focused on her. "Um… Why?" He looked worried, and she wondered what was going through his mind.

"I've got an interview on the radio to promote my book."

"But that's great, Cass." He seemed genuinely pleased, and maybe a little relieved.

"Hmm. The problem is, I don't really want to take Maddie. I think she'd be bored, and I won't be able to concentrate if I'm worrying about her."

"Leave her here with me then," Jake replied.

"Are you sure? I mean, I know you have to work…"

"And so do you." He reached across and took her hand. "I was just gonna be doing paperwork on Monday anyway. I'm not due on site until Tuesday, so she can sit in the office with me."

"Oh, good luck with that." Cassie smiled.

"We'll be fine," Jake reassured her. He paused for a moment. "And, Cass?"

She looked across at him. "Yes?"

"If this happens again, you don't need to ask me as a favor, okay? If you need me to have Maddie for an hour, or a day even, while you get things done, then just let me know. I'll move things around."

"Thank you."

"Don't thank me, Cass." He picked up his sandwich and took another bite, and she wondered if she'd offended him.

Jake held her hand as they all walked down the lane together. It was a hot day, really hot – maybe the hottest of the year so far – but the trees gave them shade. Ben and Maddie had gone on ahead a little way and Jake slowed the pace, hanging back.

"I'm sorry if I was a bit abrupt earlier, about Maddie," he said.

"You weren't," Cassie replied. "I probably just phrased it wrong."

"No… It's just, well, when you said you were going to Portland, I wondered if you were going to meet someone. It kinda scared me."

"Who would I be going to meet? Apart from the woman who's going to interview me, of course."

"I don't know… A guy, maybe?"

"What guy?"

"I have no idea who's in your life, Cassie," he explained.

"Well, there are no men, that's for sure. I—I told you I want you back, Jake. I wouldn't have done that if I was with another man, would I?"

"No, I guess not… Sorry. I just over-reacted. I didn't like the idea of you with someone else, that's all. It made me cranky. I'm sorry."

"It's okay."

He smiled. "And I don't want you thinking that Maddie's your responsibility and you have to ask me to do my share. You're not on your own any more. She's *our* responsibility now, so I meant what I said. If you need me to take her, then I'll work around it."

"And I meant what I said. Thank you. And I don't mean thank you for looking after her, but thank you for being considerate."

"Was I really that much of an ass before?"

Cassie didn't answer straight away. She took a breath, then turned to him. "I prefer the way you are now," she murmured.

"Nicely put." He smiled down at her then he stopped and pulled her back. "I'm sorry if I was less than you wanted me to be."

"Don't be. I wasn't complaining."

"Maybe you should've done." He rested his forehead against hers. "I want us to spend as much time together as we can over this summer, Cass."

"We will."

"No, I mean just the two of us. Don't get me wrong, I want to be with Maddie too, but we need to get to know each other again, by ourselves. And that's not me pressuring you. We can go as slow as you need to, as long as we're together."

"We are together, Jake."

She heard his sigh, just before his lips touched hers.

They all stood outside the house.

"We'll give it a little while longer to cool off," Ben said, taking a handkerchief from his pocket and wiping it around his neck. "It's too hot in there to work. The house has been closed up for too long in this heat."

"Are there any more windows we can open?" Jake asked.

"Nope... that's the lot," Cassie replied. "But once the air starts flowing through, it soon cools off."

"Why don't we varnish the kitchen doors while we're waiting?" Ben suggested. "We can set up the table in the shade, over there..." He pointed toward the big oak tree that stood to one side of the house.

"Good idea," Jake replied and headed off to the garage, where Ben had stored all the tools and fittings, now that he'd finished repairing the building itself.

Once they were set up, and Maddie was happy coloring, it didn't take long before the doors had all received a coat of varnish and were left to dry.

"The house must be cool enough by now," Jake said.

"I'll try it," Ben suggested, wandering over to the door.

Cassie felt Maddie tug on her t-shirt. She held out her left hand and signed 'excuse me'. Maddie folded her arms across her chest. Cassie repeated the sign and waited. After a moment or two, Maddie copied the sign.

"What's happening?" Jake asked.

"Hang on," Cassie replied, not turning to him. She was a little abrupt, but Maddie was trying her patience.

Cassie raised her right fist up to shoulder height and bobbed it up and down, saying "Yes," at the same time.

Maddie put her hands out, palms down and then pushed them forward, moving them up and down.

Cassie shook her head, and, crouching down, she held her own hands out, with the palms up and wriggled her fingers. Again, Maddie folded her arms across her chest, her face forming into a scowl, and she turned toward the ocean, taking a step.

Cassie grabbed her arm, holding onto her and, with her right hand, she took her index and middle fingers, snapping them down onto her thumb. "No!" she said out loud, but Maddie continued to struggle.

"Cass?" Jake said, "What's going on?"

"Jake… not right now, okay?"

Cassie repeated the 'No' sign a couple more times, still holding on to Maddie, who was now glowering at her mother.

"Cass…" Jake said.

Cassie stood up. "She wants to go out onto the beach. I told her she has to wait, and she didn't like that answer."

"Is that it?" Jake seemed surprised. "She just wants to go down and play on the beach?" Jake came over and crouched down in front of Maddie. "Well, I can take her down there for a little while…" He smiled and went to pick up Maddie, but Cassie grabbed his shoulder.

"No, Jake, stop it."

He got to his feet again. "What?" he asked. "What's the harm? She's bored, she wants to go play. It won't hurt if I take her down there for a half hour."

"Jake, for crying out loud."

"What's the problem?"

"You really need to ask?"

"Yeah… looks like it." She saw the color of his eyes change and, out of the corner of her eye, became aware of Ben, coming across the lawn toward them.

"Well, for one thing, if I say 'no' to her, you can't say 'yes'. You already did it once, when we were at the hotel site and she wanted to go down to the beach while your dad was still busy looking at the plans. You gave into her when I'd said 'no'. That was bad enough, Jake, but this… If you keep doing it, she'll wise up, real fast."

"Well, excuse me," Jake rounded on her. "I'm sorry I'm not the perfect parent. I guess I'm just not as practiced at this as you are. But then I wouldn't be, would I, being as I didn't know I was a parent until a couple of weeks ago. Maybe, just maybe, Cass, you could consider cutting me some slack."

"You're gonna do this again?" She heard her voice crack. "You said you wouldn't, Jake."

"Yeah, well we can all say things we don't mean." He glared at her and then turned, grabbed a pot of varnish and headed for the house.

Cassie stared after him for a moment, then looked down to see Maddie crying silent tears, and she bent and picked her up, holding her close and swaying her from side to side while her own tears fell silently too.

Jake

"Feel better now, do you?"

Jake turned and dumped the pot of varnish on the table. Ben was standing by the door, watching him. "Leave it, Dad."

Ben sighed and took a couple of steps into the room. "No," he said. "No, I won't leave it."

Jake felt his shoulders drop. He felt bad enough already, he didn't need a guilt-trip. "I'm not in the mood for a lecture right now."

"Really? And you think Cassie was in the mood for you letting off at her?"

"*Me* letting off at *her?* That's rich."

"Oh, I'm sorry, I forgot. This is all about you, isn't it?"

"Dad…" Jake's voice was a little more threatening. "Leave it."

Ben came and stood by the table, at the opposite end to Jake. "You seriously need to grow up, son."

"You wanna talk to me like I'm five as well now, do you? You think it wasn't bad enough getting that from Cassie?"

"She didn't talk to you like you're five, but you're sure acting like it." Ben pulled out a chair and sat down, looking up at Jake. "She was dead right, you know – kids are real clever. Give them a chance and they'll play their parents off against each other to get whatever it is they want. Hell, you did it all the time…" Ben stopped and smiled, just a little. "I remember when you were little, and your mom would have been having a tough day with you, and I'd come home from work and just give you whatever you were asking me for, because it was easier than saying 'no', and dealing with the tantrum. And then later, when you'd gone to bed, your mom would lay into me. Man, would she go for me, because she knew the next day would be twice as bad for her. I took the easy route, but all Amy wanted was for me to be on her side. You've gotta be united, Jake, all the time. And that's all Cassie was trying to tell you."

"Why did she have tell me off like that." Jake sat down and looked at his father. "She made me feel like I was the child, not Maddie."

"You want me to repeat myself?" Ben asked. Jake stared for a moment longer, then looked down at his hands. "You've gotta remember, Cassie's been the good guy and the bad guy to Maddie all her life."

"That was her choice, Dad," Jake replied, looking up again.

Ben's features hardened and he fixed his eyes on Jake. "You wanna go there? Again?"

Neither man spoke, until Jake looked away again.

"It's hard work raising a kid your own, Jake," Ben continued, his voice softening a little. "But it's been even harder for Cassie these last few weeks. You've come on the scene and, because you're excited about Maddie, you're giving her whatever she asks for. But sometimes that's just not practical. Sometimes, you have to say no. That's how kids learn. I imagine Cassie's trying to think about the future too. Maddie's got to learn to accommodate other people and not always get her own way. She'll be going to school soon and she needs to be able to get along with other kids, and other adults. I know her wanting to go to the beach might seem like something real small, but it's the principle. She has to learn to wait until Cassie says it's okay – or until you do – not just expect to get what she wants all the time, just because she wants it."

"I couldn't see the harm in her spending half an hour on the beach. It would've kept her quiet for a while and then we could have got on with working…"

"I'm sure Cassie had her reasons."

"Yeah, disagreeing with me. Because heaven forbid I should have an opinion."

Ben stared at him again. "No-one said you're not entitled to an opinion, Jake."

"Oh, really?"

"Yeah, really. All I'm saying is, if you do disagree, you need to do it quietly, away from Maddie. Work it out together and do it differently the next time. Cassie's not unreasonable, Jake. She never was. And if you've got a valid point, she'll listen – but arguing in front of Maddie is never gonna win Cassie round. Even if Maddie can't hear you, she still gets it, and it just makes everything ten times worse, especially for Cassie… and especially right now. She's going through enough already, without you adding to her problems."

"Is she okay?" Jake sat up a little.

"Neither of them are okay, Jake."

"Shit…" Jake got to his feet, running his fingers through his hair. "I've fucked up, haven't I? Again."

Ben nodded, just once.

"Can you…?" Jake moved around the table toward the door. "Can you sit outside with Maddie while I talk to Cass?" he asked, although he didn't really wait for a reply.

"Sure," Ben replied, getting to his feet and following Jake out onto the porch.

They walked across the lawn. Jake could see Maddie was now sitting at the table. She had two dolls, both dressed as princesses and, with one in each hand, she was playing, quite contented, the earlier upset all forgotten. Cassie had her back to him. She seemed to be clearing up the brushes, her shoulders hunched over. He walked up behind her and put his arms around her.

"I'm sorry, Cass. I'm a jerk." She turned in his arms and he saw tears rolling down her already stained cheeks. "Oh… Cass." He pulled her close and held onto her. "Forgive me?" She didn't respond.

Ben came and sat down beside Maddie and Jake pulled back a little from Cassie. "We need to talk," he said. "Dad'll stay with Maddie." He took her hand. "Come with me." He brought her back toward the house and, although she was reluctant, she followed.

Once inside, he pulled her into his arms again. She looked up into his eyes. "I can't keep doing this," she whispered and Jake felt cold fear grip him.

"You can't keep doing what, Cass?" *Please don't let her end it… not before it's even begun.*

"I can't keep walking on eggshells, Jake." She wiped her cheeks with the backs of her hands. "I'm not sure you've really forgiven me for keeping Maddie from you. And sometimes, I really doubt you ever will, but I can't live like that. I don't want to. I—I mean, I'm finding it hard enough to forgive myself, and live with what I did to you, but I can't keep having it thrown at me every single time we disagree about something." She swallowed down her tears. "We have to be here for Maddie, not fighting each other all the time."

"We don't fight all the time," he countered. "And I'm the one who needs to be sorry." He rested his hand against her cheek, gazing into her soft blue eyes. "I got it wrong. I promise, I won't use it against you, ever again. That was really childish of me. I apologize, Cass. You don't need to feel like you're walking on eggshells. Not with me." He moved a little closer so their bodies were touching. "But I do wish things could've been different. I wish I'd been there from the beginning."

Her eyes darkened, and she took a step back. "You're doing it again, already," she choked, fresh tears falling.

"Hey… no I'm not. Really, I'm not." He kept hold of her, even though she was stiff in his arms. "I'm just saying, I wish I'd done things differently. Leaving you at that party, it might have seemed like nothing much at the time, to both of us, but in reality, it became something huge. It was the beginning of the end, and everything went wrong from that moment on. But that wasn't because of you, Cass. It was because of me."

"I still could've contacted you. You can't tell me you don't blame me for that…"

"Yeah, I can. I don't blame you. I'm sorry I said the things I said to you outside." She started to shake her head and opened her mouth to speak, to give him another reason to blame her. "Stop it, Cass. Please," he begged. She looked up at him and he moved closer, so his lips were poised above hers. "Forgive yourself, Cass. Just let it go…" And he kissed her.

A while later, breathless and more turned on than he'd been in years, he pulled back again. "I wish we weren't here." He smiled. "I wish we were in my bed, or on the beach, or anywhere but here… And I really wish our daughter and my dad weren't right outside, because I'm not in the mood for going slow – not right now."

Cassie smiled back at him, and he got the feeling she wasn't either. "Maybe we'd better go back outside, then."

"Hmm, maybe. Otherwise I'm very likely to take you into your old room back there and completely forget about going slow… for at least an hour or two." He grinned.

"And you don't think your dad or Maddie might miss us?"

"I don't think I care." He shook his head slowly, then took her hand and led her back out through the door. "I promise, Cass, I won't disagree with you in front of Maddie again," he said, as they walked along the porch.

"Do you even understand?" she asked.

He stopped and turned to her. "My dad explained… well, kind of."

"And what did he tell you?"

"That kids are manipulative, and we need to be on the same page. Well, that was the gist of it, anyway."

"He's right… but did he explain why I didn't want Maddie going to the beach?"

"No. I assumed it was because we're busy with the house. I think he did too."

He saw her shoulders drop. "I'm not a tyrant, Jake. I know it's boring for her, watching us working. Sure, she's got dolls and toys and coloring books, but she wants attention too, and that's fair enough."

Jake was confused. "In that case…"

"It's too hot," she said. "It's the hottest part of the day, and there's no shade on the beach." Cassie looked up at the sky. "Give it another hour or so, and she can go and play out there for a little while, but right now… no." Cassie shook her head. "It's too hot for her."

"I didn't realize."

"You didn't give me time to explain – to her or you."

"I'm sorry."

"Surely, you know I'm not like that. I'm not gonna spoil her fun just for the sake of it."

"I know… I should've realized. Hell, I should've thought for myself." He looked across to where Maddie and his dad were sitting in the shade of the big oak tree. "Does she get it now? Did you explain to her?"

"Of course I did. Once you'd stormed off. And then we got her dolls and she's been playing happily ever since."

"Why were you crying, Cass?" he asked, moving a little closer.

"Isn't it obvious?"

"Was it just because I hurt you?" Something told him there was more to it. "I mean, I know I hurt you, but there's something else, isn't there?"

"It's been real hard these last few weeks, Jake." The words just fell out of her. He took her hand and pulled her down to sit on the porch steps.

"Tell me." He'd hoped having him around would've made things easier, but obviously not, and he wasn't sure what he could do about that, because he certainly didn't want to go.

Cassie took in a deep breath, then let it out slowly. "I guess it's just the next phase," she said.

"The next phase?" He was confused.

She turned to him. "Yes. When Maddie came home from the hospital, we got into a kind of routine… you know?"

He shrugged. "Not really, no." He smiled, just to make sure she knew he wasn't holding the past against her.

"Well, I guess all babies are different anyway, but we got into our own routine. And I'd just gotten used to it, and Maddie changed the rules."

Jake chuckled. "How do you mean?"

"Oh, I'd just gotten into the habit of her wanting to be fed every four hours, and she switched out a feed… then I'd get used to that, and she'd cut out one of her sleeps during the day. The routine was always changing."

"So it wasn't really much of a routine, then?" He chuckled.

"No, not really." Cassie smiled up at him and he leant into her. "Then, as she got older," she continued, "we got into more normal mealtimes, bedtimes, bath times… and the stories."

"Okay." Jake didn't see where this was going.

"And then she started with not wanting to eat certain things…"

"Like bacon, you mean?"

She narrowed her eyes at him, although her lips curved upward. "Yeah, like bacon… And now, she's just a mass of tantrums. She seems to have forgotten how to say 'excuse me', or 'please', or 'thank you'. And when I tell her off, she looks at me like she hates me." He heard her voice catch.

"Hey…" He pulled her into his arms again. "I'm here now…"

She looked up at him. "Oh, and you're gonna make it better, I suppose?" He ignored her sarcasm. He knew she didn't really mean it like that.

"No," he replied calmly. "But I can be the bad cop too. You don't have to do it all yourself."

She sighed. "I don't want you to be the bad cop, Jake. You've only just met her, and she worships you."

He smiled. "And you don't think she worships you? I'm not just here for a vacation, Cass. She's gotta get used to the idea that I'm here to stay, and being her daddy isn't just about having fun. Hell… what do you think I'm gonna do on Monday if she's naughty? Wait for you to get home and let you tell her off?"

Cassie let herself sink into him a little. "I guess I'd better spend tomorrow teaching you how to sign 'no' and 'stop' then."

"Looks like that might be useful." He twisted, so he was facing her and put his arms around her. "You're not saying 'no' or 'stop' to me though, are you?"

"No." She seemed surprised. "Whatever gave you that idea?"

"Just now, when you said you couldn't keep doing this… That scared me."

"Oh. I'm sorry."

"Don't be sorry. Just don't say 'no', or 'stop' to me."

"Not ever?" He noticed the corners of her lips twitching. "That's a bit dictatorial, isn't it?"

"Okay… You know I'd never force you to do anything you don't want to, so you can say it in the bedroom."

"Just the bedroom?" She was trying so hard not to smile.

"And the shower." He moved closer still, his voice a low whisper. "Anywhere else?"

"I can think of all kinds of places," he murmured.

"And you think I'm gonna say 'no', or 'stop' to you in these places, do you?"

He stared at her lips. "The option's always yours, Cass. You can tell me to stop any time you want, and you can always say no, but I really really I hope you don't."

Jake heard the kitchen door open, and felt himself sag with relief, even though he knew that was a little pathetic. He'd only been alone with Maddie for just over six hours, but it felt like six days. Maddie was sitting beside him on the couch. He patted her leg and she looked up at him, then he spread out the fingers of his right hand, tapping his thumb on his chin, before holding out both of his hands in front of him, so he was looking at the back of them, then moving his right one, and folding it out, so it looked like a door opening. Maddie grinned, then jumped down and ran through to the kitchen. He'd taught himself a few words during the course of the day. 'Mommy' and 'door' had been two of them, in anticipation of Cassie's return.

Jake got up and started to follow his daughter, whispering to himself, "I guess you're as pleased to see your mom as I am."

Maddie was already clasped in Cassie's arms by the time he got into the kitchen.

"She's missed you," he said, leaning against the doorframe and watching them.

"I missed her too." Looking over at her, he was amazed by how much *he'd* missed Cassie, and not just because Maddie had been a handful all day. He'd *really* missed her.

"And I missed you more." He smiled. His voice had dropped a little, and he wondered if she knew what he meant.

"Has it been that bad?" Cassie looked over at him, settling Maddie on her hip. Evidently she didn't understand. She thought he was talking about Maddie. Oh well…

"Let's just say, if you'll have her for the next hour, so I can think straight and get some work done, I'll worship you until the day I die." He thought for a moment. "Actually, I'll do that anyway, but you get what I mean."

"Oh… it's been *that* bad." She smiled, and he thought she looked a little shy, and very cute.

"No, it's been okay. Well, kinda okay. But I've got a couple of urgent emails I need to reply to. So, can you…?"

"Sure, but…" She looked worried.

"What's up, Cass?" He moved into the room.

"If it's been that bad, you probably don't want me to tell you I've got a book signing to go to, and I'm gonna need you to look after Maddie again."

"It's fine," Jake was relieved it was nothing serious. "When is it?"

"It's in a couple of weeks. It's on a Saturday though, so at least work shouldn't interfere, and your dad might be able to help out."

"I'll be fine, Cass. A book signing? I'm impressed." She blushed, and he went to move closer just as his phone rang. He pulled it from his back pocket and checked the screen. It was Erica – again. She'd called twice already today. He'd ignored her, and he was going to ignore her this time too. He put his phone back, letting it go to voicemail.

"You don't need to take that?" Cassie asked.

"No," Jake replied. "It's just someone from the office. They can wait. If it's important, they'll leave a message."

"We mustn't stop you working," Cassie said, smiling. "You'd better get on with your emails, and check your messages." Her smile became a grin as she stood to one side to let him out, obviously assuming he'd need to go out to the office.

"It's fine. My laptop's in the living room." Jake pointed back over his shoulder. He went to leave, then turned back again. "I heard you," he said, "on the radio."

"Oh." Now she seemed *really* embarrassed.

"You were good." He gave her a quick wink, then went back into the living room and settled down on the couch, his laptop in front of him.

Jake closed the oven door and set the timer, then took a sip of wine.

"Is that bolognese sauce I smell," Cassie said, coming into the kitchen, with Maddie's hand in hers. The little girl was bathed and ready for bed, in bright yellow pajamas.

"It is." Jake handed Cassie a glass of wine. "For you," he said.

"It doesn't come in bigger glasses, does it?"

He laughed. "No, but I'll keep it filled up, if that helps."

"Definitely." She took a sip and closed her eyes. "You're seriously going to feed our daughter spaghetti bolognese?" Cassie said, opening her eyes again and sitting down at the table. Maddie went over to Jake and held up her arms. She was tired. He bent down and lifted her up.

"Well, not exactly," he replied, leaning back on the countertop. "We went shopping today and I let Maddie choose what shape pasta she wanted… so we've got Conchiglie."

"Shells…" Cassie nodded her head. "Why am I not surprised?"

"Well, I figured there'd be less mess with shapes than with spaghetti?" Jake hoped he'd done the right thing. "And I've mixed it all together and put cheese on top and it's baking in the oven. It's kinda like a messy lasagna, I guess. I'm making it up as I go along."

"Sounds delicious."

"Well, it'll only be another ten minutes."

"Good, because a certain little girl is getting tired."

"I know."

"Where's your dad?" Cassie asked.

"He's gone out with a couple of buddies."

"That's good," Cassie replied. "I mean, it's good he's going out."

"It was always a regular Monday night thing. They called round earlier and talked him into it."

"Well, I'm glad they did. He needed to get out."

"Yeah, I think he did. He'd been moping a bit." They stared at each other for a moment.

"What did you do with her today?" Cassie said, breaking the tension and taking another long sip of wine.

"Well, first I tried working," Jake explained.

"I bet that went well," Cassie laughed.

"Not really. Maddie wanted to play, so we played for a while. Then I tried working again, but she got hungry, so we had lunch. And then she wanted to go down to the beach." Cassie opened her mouth, then closed it again. "It's okay," he said, "I told her it was too hot, so we went and played ball in the garden out back, under the trees, and went down to the beach for a while just before you came home. We'd just finished our milk and cookies when you got in…"

"Milk and cookies?" Cassie smirked.

"Yeah. I like milk and cookies."

"You're just a big kid, Jake Hunter."

"Only when it comes to milk and cookies…"

"How do you do it?" Jake asked, as he pulled the door closed on Cassie and Maddie's bedroom.

"Do what?"

"Get anything done?" Cassie led the way downstairs and through to the living room, sitting down on the couch. Jake followed, bringing the wine through from the kitchen on his way.

Cassie smiled up at him, taking her glass. "Who said I get anything done?"

"Well, your work… your writing. When do you do that?" Jake sat down beside her.

"In the evenings, once Maddie's gone to bed. I usually work until around midnight, sometimes a little after."

"Every night?"

"Yes, including the weekends."

Jake put his glass down on the table and turned to face her. "That doesn't leave a lot of time for a social life."

Cassie laughed softly, although he sensed it contained irony, rather than humor. "What's a social life? I haven't had one of those since I left here. I can't, not with Maddie."

Jake didn't really know what to say and for a moment he sat, just staring at her. "You mean… you mean there's been no-one in your life at all since we broke up?"

Cassie shook her head, looking down at her glass. "No… no-one."

He felt sure his relief must be visible, even though he knew it was unfair of him to feel like that. He'd had a life, while she'd been alone. "Did you want someone?" he asked tentatively. "Was it just Maddie keeping you from getting together with another guy?"

She looked up at him. "To be honest, I don't know. I hated being on my own, but I didn't like the thought of being with anyone else either."

"Were you lonely?" He wanted to know.

"Oh God, yes. All the time. Having a child around isn't the same as being with someone."

He moved closer, so their legs were touching, then reached across, taking her glass from her hands and putting in down on the table next to his. "I'm not gonna lie," he murmured, leaning into her, "there's a part of me that kinda likes the idea that you haven't been with anyone else. In some ways I haven't changed at all, and I'm still kinda selfish. I like knowing I'm still the only man who's seen you naked, and touched you, and tasted you, and been inside you." He heard a very slight moan coming from her parted lips. "But if you were lonely, Cass, then I don't like that idea quite so much."

"It wasn't that easy to just date someone," she whispered.

"Why? Because you had Maddie to take care of? You could've left her with your mom, or Emma while you went out. You could've dated." He didn't like the thought of her with another man, but…

"No, I couldn't."

"Why not? Why didn't you wanna be with someone?"

She turned away and mumbled, "Because they wouldn't have been you, Jake."

He wasn't sure he'd ever felt so full of hope in his life. He reached across and turned her face back toward his. "Is that why you used me as the character in your book?" he asked.

Her head shot up. "You've read my book?"

"Yeah. I snuck one out the other day and took it back to the city with me. I stayed up nearly all night reading it and thinking about it."

Cassie covered her face with her hands. "Oh, God," she muttered. "I'm so embarrassed."

"Why?" He pulled her hands away, but she still wouldn't look at him. "Why, Cass?"

"Isn't it obvious?"

"What? Because you made Brett like me and Isabel like you, and you described some of the things we did together?"

"Well, yes."

"Why's that embarrassing? And why did you tell that radio interviewer you'd invented the characters?"

"You didn't actually think I was going to tell her, and all her listeners, that those two characters were based on us, did you? I mean, the things I describe in the book… they're personal."

He chuckled. "Not anymore they're not."

She sighed. "Do you mind?"

"Mind what?"

"That I used us, and the things we did, in the book?"

"No. Why would I mind?"

"*Because* it's personal," she insisted.

"I guess it is, but I like the fact that you used those things."

"I could hardly use anything else. I've got nothing else to base it on."

"How do you mean?"

"Exactly what you just said, Jake. You're the only man who's ever done all those things to me. You're the only man I've seen naked. I had no idea how to describe anything, other than to describe you."

"Yeah, but you made me out to be a lot more than I really am, Cass." He grinned at her.

"I did?"

"Yeah… I'm really not that impressive."

Cassie looked down at her hands. "I always thought you were," she whispered. "I was just working from memory."

"Then your memory is a little rose-tinted, baby."

She raised her head and looked into his eyes. "I remember all of it, Jake. Every single second, and none of it's rose-tinted." She paused for a moment. "I still can't believe you've read it…"

"I enjoyed it," he said. "Where did you get the names?"

"Brett and Isabel?" He nodded. "There's a listing on the Internet, of the one thousand most popular names, or something. Brett was the one next to Jake, so that was easy…"

"And Isabel? Was that next to Cassie?"

"No, I just wanted a name that Brett could shorten to make a pet-name."

"Like I call you Cass, you mean."

She nodded her head. "I've always loved the fact that you're the only person I know who does that."

"Hmm, me too."

"So why did you make Brett almost exactly like me – even down to the sense of humor – but give Isabel all those hang-ups and insecurities? That's not who you are, Cass."

She stared at him. "Yes it is, Jake. That's exactly who I am."

Chapter Nineteen

Cassie

"But… but that can't be right." He stumbled over his words.

"Why not? You always knew how unsafe I felt unless you were with me."

"Yeah, but that was different."

"No. I needed the reassurance of knowing you were there. Without that, I always felt like I was nothing."

He put his hands on her shoulders and twisted her around to face him. "Nothing? *Nothing?* Cass, you were everything. I was the one who was terrified – terrified of losing you. Terrified you'd wake up and realize you could've done so much better than being with me. Hell, you were – you still are – the most beautiful girl in this town. I wish I'd known. I wish I'd worked out you felt like that. I'd have done so much more to make you feel safer."

"You did…" She could feel her cheeks reddening again. "God, I'm starting to wish I'd written a murder mystery now," she said, just to try and lighten the mood.

Jake laughed, loudly. "A murder mystery? That would never have worked."

"Thanks."

"Well, let's face it, whenever you read one, you could never work out who the murderer was, sometimes not even once it had been revealed." He had a point, she had to admit. "Besides…" He leaned in again. "You write a mean romance, and a really hot sex scene."

Her cheeks burned as he gripped her upper arms, pulled her close and kissed her. She sucked in a breath, feeling his tongue tickle along her lips and she opened up to him willingly, arching her back and pressing her breasts into his chest. She didn't know if it was all the talk of sex scenes and the past, or whether it was what he was doing to her right now, but she wanted him more than she'd ever wanted him before, and she wasn't sure she could tell him to stop, or even slow down. She snaked her arms around his waist, up under his t-shirt, and grazed her nails gently over his skin, hearing his deep groan reverberate through her body.

He pulled away, staring into her eyes. "I'd really like to take you down the lane and out onto the beach, and I'd like to lay you down on a soft rug and recreate that scene, just like it is in your book, just like it was the first time."

"It can't be like the first time, Jake. We can't go back. Besides, we can't leave Maddie here by herself…"

"I know. I still want you though. I want to see you and touch you. I want all of you, Cass. You're mine."

She bit her bottom lip. She wanted him too, but not like the first time. There was no point in trying to recreate what had gone before. This had to be about here and now, not what they'd had in the past.

"I love you, Cass," he whispered, his voice echoing across her senses. "I love you so much. I always did. I've never stopped loving you. Not for one single day."

"I love you too, Jake." She saw his eyes widen, felt his arms tighten around her and his lips twitch into a smile.

He stood up and, leaning over, he lifted her into his arms.

"What are you doing?" she squealed.

"I'm taking you to bed, Cass. If we can't go to the beach—"

He was deadly serious and, to Cassie, it was like a cold shower. He needed a reality check. "Put me down, Jake."

He looked down at her, his eyes showing his confusion, together maybe with a little hurt. "Why? Don't you wanna go to bed with me? Is this too fast for you?"

"It's not that…"

"Then what is it?" He held her in his arms still.

"Life's not a romance novel, Jake. You don't have to sweep me off my feet and carry me to your bed. Life's about caring for Maddie, paying rent, cooking, cleaning, doing the laundry… and being alone." Even Cassie heard her voice crack on the last word.

He lowered her to the floor, standing her on her feet right in front of him. Then he placed his hands on her cheeks, his eyes boring into hers.

"I know life's not a romance novel, and I'm no romantic hero, Cass. But I can cook, I'm okay with laundry, and I'm quite capable of cleaning up around the place too. And, from now on, it's not about being alone. You'll never have to be alone again; not unless you want to be… to have some time to yourself, while I look after Maddie, so you can have a break. I want us to share everything, including the laundry, the cleaning, the shopping, and looking after Maddie. But more than anything I want us to share each other. I want us to share our love, Cass." He moved a little closer, his lips just an inch from hers. "Do you want that too?"

She nodded her head.

"Good." He bent down and picked her up again.

"Jake…"

"I know. This is nothing to do with romance novels. I just want you in my arms for as long as possible… starting now."

He kicked his bedroom door closed behind them and carried her across to his bed, setting her down gently on the mattress.

Cassie glanced around the room. Even in the moonlight, she could see how much it had changed. His football posters and old pine closet were gone. There was a bookcase, a couple of landscape pictures on the wall opposite the window and a large built-in closet, with mirrored doors took up the whole wall at the end of the bed.

"This is different," she said.

"Yeah. Dad remodeled it after I moved away."

"It's more… grown-up."

"Well, I guess it had to happen." He smiled down at her, then sat down beside her on the bed, leaning across and kissing her. She felt his hand come up and caress her breast through the thin material of her t-shirt, and the lacy bra beneath it, and she sucked in a breath at his touch. Without breaking the kiss, his fingers slowly moved down, to the waistband of her jeans, unbuttoning the fastener and then working the zipper downwards.

He pulled back, just a little, nuzzling into her neck, kissing her jaw and working upwards, biting gently on her earlobe.

"Are you still on birth control, Cass?" he whispered. "If you're not, it's okay."

What did that mean?

He was leaning back, looking down at her, waiting for an answer. "It's fine," she murmured, feeling confused. "My periods are still just as painful as they ever were… the pill helps." His lips twitched upward and then he laughed, his head rocking back. She slapped his arm, just lightly. "Painful periods aren't funny," she admonished. "You wanna try having them one day."

"I'm sorry." He calmed down. "It's just you always used to tell me everything. I kinda like that."

Cassie laughed too now, her confusion forgotten. "I know. Do you remember when I was twelve and my periods first started…?"

"Yeah, and you decided I needed to know all about it. I had no idea what to say when you told me that. I wasn't sure whether I was supposed to be pleased for you, or commiserate."

"Given how painful they can be, I think commiserate."

He put his hand on her cheek, just gently. "I really did love it that you shared everything with me." He leant across her, toward the lamp on the nightstand.

"No, Jake. Please…"

"What's wrong?" He moved back, looking at her. "I was just gonna turn the light on. I want to see you."

"That's the whole point. I don't want you to…" She let her head drop.

"Why not? You're beautiful."

"No, I'm not."

"You are, babe."

Cassie breathed out slowly. "Maddie might have been born early, Jake, but I still gained some weight while I was pregnant, and that last ten pounds has never gone. I don't look the same as I used to."

"No, I think, if anything, you look better. And I never thought that would be possible."

"You don't know how I look. You haven't seen me."

"I've seen you in your shorts and your skimpy tops, and your sexy pajamas. And I've got a great imagination… I've got a really good idea how you're gonna look, Cass. And anyway, I don't care if you don't look the same. I don't care if you've gained a little weight."

"But, you look so much better," she whispered.

"Oh, really? You've been looking, have you?" he teased.

"It's been hard to miss. You have been wandering around half naked."

He turned her to face him. "If you really don't want the light on, that's fine. I can see you well enough in the moonlight, and you look incredible. Okay?"

She looked into his eyes and knew he meant it.

He got up and pulled her to her feet, lifting her t-shirt over her head, then he let out a half-laugh. "What's funny?" she said, raising her arms to cover herself.

"Hey, nothing." He pulled her arms away again, holding them by her sides. "I was just thinking how unlike a romance novel this is. I don't remember anywhere in your book where Brett and Isabel discussed weight gain, painful periods, housework, laundry, childcare and how the bedroom was decorated, before they even got undressed."

She laughed. "No…"

"The only thing they talked about was birth control," he added. "But I guess your characters have to be responsible."

Cassie's smile faded and she looked down at his chest, her earlier uncertainty returning.

"What's wrong?" Jake asked.

She looked up. Even in the moonlight she could see the concern in his eyes. "What did you mean when you said it was okay if I wasn't still on birth control."

"Just that you don't need to worry about it. I've got condoms."

"You have?"

"Well, I thought I should be prepared."

"You assumed this would happen tonight?"

He put his hands on her waist, pulling her close. "No. I didn't assume anything. I've wanted you since the first time I saw you again, so I *hoped* this would happen, but the timing was always down to you. Even now, if you wanna stop, then we'll stop. And I'll wait until you're ready."

She looked up into his eyes. "I don't wanna stop," she whispered.

He smiled. "Good. Let's just forget about everything else for a while and concentrate on us. I've been dying to taste you for so long…" She gasped, and he swallowed the sound into his mouth, claiming her, delving into her with his tongue. "I want you underneath me," he murmured, "with your legs wrapped around me, and I wanna be buried so deep inside you." She put her hands on the back of his head, squirming against him and deepening the kiss, his words setting her every nerve on fire.

She felt his hands come around behind her, unfastening her bra. He pulled away a little, releasing her breasts, letting her bra drop to the floor, and then he gently pinched her nipples between his thumbs and forefingers.

"Oh… Oh… Yes!" she whimpered. His mouth returned to hers, his tongue more urgent, more possessive, until he broke free again and knelt down, placing his thumbs in the top of her jeans and pulling them down, bringing her panties with them.

"Step out," he said, holding her hand, and she did, letting him pull her clothing to one side. She was naked before him and he leant forward and kissed the tops of her thighs, before standing and walking her backward, until her legs hit the bed. With one hand behind her, he lowered her, and moved her further onto the soft mattress, then stood and looked down at her.

"You're beautiful, Cass." His voice was hoarse, filled with emotion.

He knelt between her legs and leant forward, kissing her stomach and moving upward to her breasts, swirling his tongue across her extended nipples. She rocked her head back, relishing the contact as he sucked and licked her, then gently nipped each bud between his teeth, groaning deep in his throat.

He kissed his way slowly down her body, to the neat triangle of soft blonde hair. Then, nestling between them, he parted her legs, pushing them upward, exposing her.

"God, I've wanted this for so long," he said, and bent his head forward, running his tongue along her swollen folds. He used his fingers to part her, opening her up to him and then grazed his tongue across and around her clitoris. "You taste so good," he muttered into her, sucking on her nub and slowly inserting a single finger into her.

"Yes…" she hissed between her clenched teeth. "Oh, Jake… yes."

"You're so wet, baby." He circled his finger inside her, rubbing against that delicate area on the front wall of her vagina, and she felt the quiver deep inside.

"Please, Jake… more…" she begged.

He inserted a second finger, increasing the intensity of his movements, while his tongue worked over her, harder and faster. She brought her hands down onto the back of his head, bucking her hips up into him and, as he twisted his fingers one more time, she closed her eyes and let out a low plaintive cry, the bolts of pleasure rushing through her body, wave after wave pouring over her.

"Stop…" she pleaded. "I can't take it." He didn't listen, but kept up his movements as she arched and writhed, her juices pouring out onto his hand, soaking him.

Finally, she began to calm, gulping in great breaths.

"That was…"

"Something else." He finished her sentence, getting to his knees and pulling his t-shirt over his head. She let her eyes roam over his chest in the moonlight. "You felt incredible, Cass," he said, undoing the buttons on his jeans, then getting up and taking them off, and staring at her, just a moment longer, before lowering his trunks.

Cassie couldn't help but let her eyes drop, and she felt herself tingle with anticipation.

He climbed back on the bed, kneeling between her legs again, his hand clamped around the base of his erection.

"You okay?" he asked gently.

She nodded, feeling him press the head of his arousal into her. Then he was stretching her, filling her as he pushed slowly inwards.

"You're... you're so tight, Cass." She could see the struggle etched on his face.

"It's been a while." She ran her hands up his arms, letting them rest on his rigid biceps.

He smiled down at her, stilling. "And still all mine," he murmured.

"Still all yours..."

He leant down and kissed her, inching further inside until she'd taken his whole length, then he rested for a moment before gradually pulling out again, almost to the tip, and then pushing deep inside once more. She brought her legs up, wrapping them around his waist as he built a slow, steady rhythm, gradually increasing the pace, and the depth, taking her a little harder with each stroke, until she arched off the bed once more, crying out his name as she detonated around him. She heard him groan, saw him throw back his head, and her name left his lips in a long low howl as he filled her, over and over, his whole body shuddering.

Eventually, he slumped down, just keeping his weight off her.

"I love you," he breathed, between shallow gasps.

"I love you too." She cradled him, her legs still wrapped tight around him.

He turned them both, keeping them connected, so they were on their sides, looking at each other.

"Was it me," he murmured, "or was that even better than it used to be?"

"It was better." She smiled, sleepily. "Much better. Not that there was anything wrong with before..."

"No, I know. But that was..."

"Yes, it was."

They lay still for what seemed like hours, just looking at each other. Jake caressed her hair, her cheeks, her face. He kissed her tenderly, and all the while, he kept them connected, still hard inside her.

Staring at him, Cassie knew she had to ask the question that had been going through her mind ever since they'd broken up. She knew she'd probably regret it, but like a car crash happening in slow motion, there was nothing she could do to stop herself…

"Can I ask you a question?" she said quietly.

"Sure." Jake pulled her a little closer in his arms.

"I told you there's been no-one in my life since we broke up. Can I ask if you've been with any other women?"

She saw his eyes close and knew she should've kept her mouth shut, left the question unasked and tried to live with not knowing, because it seemed that knowing was going to be so much worse.

"I can't lie, Cass," Jake replied eventually. "There have been a few women over the last four years. But none of them have been serious…"

"So, you didn't sleep with them?" She almost didn't dare let herself hope.

"Yeah, I slept with them… well, I had sex with them," he clarified.

She felt herself stiffen and pull back from him slightly. She didn't mean to do it… it was involuntary and instinctive.

"Don't," he said gently, holding onto her. "Please don't. Believe me, Cass, none of them mattered, not like you."

Full realization of what he was saying dawned on her and she pulled away completely now, releasing herself from him.

She stared at him, unable to believe what she was hearing. "You've… you've slept with other women?" she whispered.

"Yes."

"And you've just… done what we did?" She couldn't say the words.

"Yes." He seemed confused, like he didn't understand her point.

"Then how do I know it was safe? How do I know you're clean?" She went to move away, shifting across the bed, but he pulled her back.

"Because I am," he said. "I always used protection. Every time." He tried to pull her closer but she resisted still. "Don't you know me better than that, Cass? I'd never risk your health. Never."

She looked down at this chest. "I'm sorry," she mumbled. "I shouldn't have doubted you."

He leant back. "It's okay." He loosened his grip on her and she took advantage, moving away from him.

"I need to go back to my own room," she said, turning and sitting up on the edge of the bed. "I have to be there in the morning, or Maddie will wonder where I am."

"It's not morning yet." Jake sat up, looking over at her. "Are you going because you've just found out I've been with other women?" he asked.

She got to her feet, suddenly feeling self-conscious that she was naked in front of him. She folded her arms across her breasts. "No, of course not," she said, trying to sound light-hearted. "I never expected you to live like a monk, Jake." She forced a smile onto her lips. "It's fine."

"Yeah, sure it is." He got up, walked around the bed and stood in front of her. He was close… close enough for Cassie to feel his erection pressing into her. "Talk to me," he said.

She looked down at his chest. "Is… is sleeping with lots of other women how you came to be such a good lover now?" she whispered, almost to herself.

"I didn't sleep with *lots* of women," Jake replied. "There weren't that many. And if I'm a better lover than I was when we were together before, that's because of you. You make everything better. You make me want to be better." She looked up at his face. His eyes were soft, sincere, filled with love. "I'm sorry, Cass," he said.

"It's fine… it really is." She took a step back and moved away, going around the other side of the bed to pick up her clothes. Clutching them in her hands, she turned back to him. "When I was on my own, for all those years, I always knew you'd be with someone. I knew you were too special to be on your own…" She couldn't finish her sentence; she couldn't say how much that thought had always hurt.

He came closer, standing at the end of the bed. "I'm not sure I like what you're suggesting, Cass." She stared at him. "You seem to be implying that you ended up on your own because you're not special, not worthy in some way."

She shrugged. It had often felt like that, it was true; but she'd never expected him – or anyone – to see through her loneliness and pain so easily. He moved forward and stood right in front of her again.

"Oh, Cass…" He pulled her into his arms. "I thought you'd be with someone too. I thought you'd be married, with kids, because I knew you were too beautiful, too loving, to spend your life by yourself." He leant back just a little and ran his fingers down her face. "Do you have any idea how much I hate the idea of you being lonely?" he asked.

"I think so. Probably about as much as I hate the idea of you making love to someone else."

"Not making love, baby. That was always just you."

"But you said…"

"I said I had sex. There's a difference."

She scoffed. "That's semantics."

"No… no, it's not. I never felt a damn thing for any of them. Whereas you, you're my whole world and when I'm with you, it's like I'm finally complete. I know who I am; everything makes sense when we're together. We belong, Cass."

"Tell me I've got nothing to fear… please, Jake?" She needed reassurance.

"You have absolutely nothing to fear, baby. You're so safe. Nothing's gonna hurt you. I promise."

"And… and they're all in the past now?"

He held onto her, really tight. "Of course they are. You're my present. You're my future. I swear to you, on Maddie's life, there's no one else but you. I love you, Cass. I only want you… you and Maddie."

She smiled up at him and stood back. They needed to move forward, not keep looking back and wondering what might have been. No matter how much the thought of him with other women hurt, she had to try and put it behind her. "I love you too, and I want to leave the past where it belongs, and focus on us, and the future."

He grinned. "Me too."

"But I seriously had better get back to my own room," she murmured, pulling her t-shirt over her head.

"Can I come with you?" he asked. "I get that you need to be there for when Maddie wakes up, but I want to sleep with you, Cass." He paused and she could see him thinking for a moment. "At the risk of talking about the past just for a minute, I have to tell you… you're still the only woman I've ever spent a whole night with. You're the only woman I've ever slept with."

She felt tears pricking behind her eyes, but she blinked them back. Hearing that helped, just a little. "We can't," she said. "Maddie and me, we're sharing a bed."

"Oh." She could feel his disappointment. "That's a shame. I'd love to wake up next to you in the morning." He put his hands on her hips, moving her back toward the wall, then placed his hands either side of her head and leant down, his lips almost touching hers. "You always did like to make love in the mornings… long, and slow, and real hard." His voice made her shiver.

"I know…" She let her hand rest on his chest. "I really need to sleep with you too," she murmured. "I need the reassurance of you."

He leant back, just a little. "Whatever you think you need reassuring over, you don't. You really don't."

As usual, Maddie woke Cassie early.

She stretched, and remembered the night before. Jake's hands, his tongue… the feeling of him deep inside her. His words… they all came back to her and she felt herself tremble with pleasure and the anticipation of seeing him again…

She also remembered crying herself to sleep, feeling grateful that Maddie couldn't hear her. The idea of Jake with other women haunted her, but what really got to her, what was really breaking her up, was that she and Jake hadn't needed to be apart in the first place. If only she'd spoken to him, listened to him… waited for him, none of this would have happened. He'd have been there for her and Maddie, there wouldn't have been any 'other women', and nights like last night would have been her every night…

She tried to shake off her feelings of guilt, grabbed Maddie's hand and led her out of the bedroom. Jake's bedroom door was slightly open, so Cassie crossed the landing, with Maddie in tow and poked her head around. The room was empty, the bed made. She felt her shoulders sag with disappointment. Maddie tugged her hand and signed that she wanted breakfast. Cassie smiled. Of course. Jake was probably downstairs making them something to eat. They went down together, but the kitchen was empty. The whole house was empty. There was no sign of him.

He'd gone…

Jake

He glanced at his watch. It was a little before seven-thirty. He'd been on site for nearly half an hour and he was already wishing he could go back home and see Cassie.

The site was a hive of activity and Jake was relieved they were finally under way with the project. He climbed the steps into the site office and sat behind the small desk at one end, leaning back and closing his eyes for a moment.

He was worried – not about the project, that was going just fine. No, he was worried about Cassie. There was no doubt about it, she'd been upset when he'd told her about the women he'd had sex with while they'd been apart. He wished she'd never asked the question in the first place, but she was bound to, he supposed. He'd been intrigued by her past too, and once she'd asked, he had to tell her; he couldn't have lied to her. His only hope now was to convince her that she was the only one he wanted, that she always had been. Because that was the truth. It was the reason he'd never spent a whole night with any of them. He'd never wanted to wake up next to any other woman.

He opened his eyes again, recalling the previous night. He'd never had sex like that in his life, not even when he was with Cassie before. It wasn't that they did anything different, it was just that it felt so different. Jake had to admit, he might not have been the most considerate of lovers in the past. Sure, he'd always been able to make women come, and none of them had ever complained, but last night, he'd realized – for the first time – that he wanted to watch Cassie climax. He wanted to feel her orgasms, and when he did, they were sensational. He didn't really care about his own fulfillment – he got more than enough from pleasuring her. He wondered now, why he'd never realized any of this before.

He picked up his phone and went to his message app. He knew Maddie couldn't read, and Cassie was unlikely to let anyone else read her texts, so he decided to tell her exactly how he felt.

— Good morning, beautiful. Sorry I had to leave before you got up. I miss you and I can't stop thinking about you. I'll be home as early as I can. Come to bed with me again tonight? I love you, always. Jake xx

He pressed send.

He put the phone down on the desk and tried to concentrate on some work for a while. After a half hour or so, he still hadn't had a reply, so he typed out another message.

— Still missing you. Still wanting you. Still loving you. Jake xx

Again he pressed send.

After another hour, he realized Cassie wasn't going to reply. She must be busy with Maddie, or maybe she'd gone out and forgotten to take her phone. Still, he sent a third message, smiling to himself as he typed…

— I keep getting hard just thinking about you. Can't wait to be inside you… Hope you're wet thinking about me too. Love you. J xx

He chuckled as he pressed send, knowing how embarrassed she'd be when she read his words.

Then later, as he ate his lunch, he typed out a fourth, more romantic this time…

— *Aching for you… longing for you. Be mine again tonight… please? J xxx*

Well, it was kind of romantic, anyway…

The day had gone well. There were no snags; nothing went wrong and they'd made good progress. Erica had called and, this time, he'd spoken to her. The pretext she gave was that Rich wanted an update, so he told her what was going on and then made an excuse to end the call as quickly as possible, hoping she'd get the hint. Somehow he doubted it.

He was tired, but then he hadn't had much sleep, having lain awake for over an hour after Cassie had gone back to her own room, and he'd been up since just before six.

The drive home was easy and he pulled up outside his dad's house and climbed out of the car, stretching his aching muscles. The house was open, but there was no-one in sight… He wondered where they all were, but then he heard the sound of laughter coming from the back garden and he went around the side of the house, rounding the corner just as a soaking Maddie turned the garden hose on Cassie. Ben roared with laughter again, and Jake joined in. Hearing him, they turned and, as Maddie spun to see what they were looking at, she brought the hose with her, dousing him in freezing water. Jake gasped at the chill, then took off toward her, ducking the wild spray of water as she tried to get away, before he plucked her into his arms and spun her round, soaking the whole garden, including Ben and Cassie.

As he lowered Maddie to the ground again, out of the corner of his eye, he saw Cassie wander around the side of the house, her head bent. She seemed to be wiping at her face with the backs of her hands. Was she crying? He glanced at Ben and raised an eyebrow.

"What's wrong?" he asked, nodding toward Cassie, who'd now disappeared into the house.

"No idea. She's been real quiet ever since I got back. We came out here to water the garden. I assumed it must be something to do with her mom and I was trying to get her to talk to me, but Maddie got hold of the hose and things got a little out of hand."

"So I see." Jake smiled. "Can you watch Maddie, Dad? I'm gonna go see what's happened."

"Sure."

Jake followed in Cassie's footsteps, dripping water in through the kitchen. She wasn't there, but the trail of wet footprints led up the stairs, which he took two at a time. Her door was closed, so he knocked.

"It's me, Cass," he called. "Can I come in?" She didn't reply, so he opened the door, just a crack. "Cass?" he said. He poked his head inside. She was standing by the window, water dripping onto the wooden floor, as she stared down into the garden below. "What's wrong?" he asked, coming into the room.

"Nothing." Her voice was flat.

"Run that by me again." He came and stood right behind her. "Only this time, try the truth."

"You left…" She spun around and he saw she really was crying, tears streaming down her cheeks.

"I left?" He reached out to her, but she pulled away from him. He was confused. "What do you mean, I left?"

"You weren't here this morning. I thought… I thought you'd left."

He sighed, closing his eyes, just for a second. "You thought I'd left… you mean, left *you*?" he asked. She nodded her head, another tear dripping onto her cheek. He pulled her into his arms. She was stiff, reluctant. "Cass, I had to be on site at seven. I left at six-fifteen. I wasn't gonna come in here and wake you that early in the morning. Not after last night. You didn't leave my room until well after midnight."

"How was I supposed to know any of that?"

"I'm sorry. I should've explained. I told you I had to be on site today. I guess I just assumed you'd know the kind of hours I keep. I should've thought. It was inconsiderate of me. But surely, after everything we did, everything we said last night, why would you think I'd leave?"

She shrugged. "I wasn't sure…"

"What about?" He looked down at her and held her gaze.

"How I compare…" He felt himself sag into her.

"Christ, Cass. There is no comparison." He tightened his grip on her. "You always were the best. Always. None of them could compare with *you*… But now, it's just so much better, even than it was before."

He leant down and kissed her, very gently, very tenderly, his lips brushing softly against hers.

"I've had such a horrible day," she muttered, leaning back into his arms. "I thought I'd lost you… again."

"You didn't think to check your phone, then?" he asked, smiling just a little.

"My phone?"

"Yeah…"

Cassie glanced over at the nightstand, where her phone was sat, alongside the alarm clock. "I haven't even looked at it all day," she admitted. "Why?"

Jake released her. "Go take a look," he said, and watched as she walked slowly over to the bed, standing beside it and picking up the phone. She pressed a few buttons, then her eyes settled on the screen, reading slowly. He'd sent four more messages during the day, making eight in total, all along the same lines, although some were longer than others, so it took her a while to read through them. When she looked up, her eyes were filled with tears again.

"Don't cry, Cass," Jake said, going over and hugging her tight. "They're meant to make you happy."

"They do. I just wish I'd seen them earlier, and replied. What on earth did you think when you didn't hear back from me?" She looked worried.

"Well, I thought you were probably busy with Maddie, or you'd gone out, or just that you hadn't had time to read them. I sure didn't think you'd assumed I'd left you. If I'd realized that, I'd have called. Hell… I'd have come back and convinced you in person."

"God, I wish I'd known."

"So, you would've replied?" he asked. "If you'd seen them?"

"Yes, of course."

He moved closer. "And what would you have said?"

"That I missed you too… a lot. That I want you." She paused. "That I'm always yours. I always have been…" Her voice cracked a little and he bent his head and kissed her. He kissed her for a long, long while.

Finally pulling back, he looked down at her.

"We'd better get out of these wet clothes, don't you think?"

"What about Maddie?"

"She's fine; she's with dad." He moved his hands down and slowly started to undo the buttons on her blouse, not taking his eyes from hers, even for a second. He let her top fall to the floor, then undid her bra and bent down, sucking and licking over first one nipple, then the other. She sighed and brought her hands up behind his head, her fingers twisting in his hair, holding him there, while he undid her jeans and pushed them and her panties down her legs. Her jeans were wet and stuck to her and he couldn't help laughing.

"What's wrong?" she said.

"I can't get your jeans to budge," he replied. "They're so wet."

"Oh."

"It's fine." He knelt down and gave them a tug. Cassie giggled. "Hang on," Jake said, and got up again, going through to the bathroom and returning with a white fluffy towel. He knelt down again and, helping Cassie out of her sodden clothes, he started rubbing the warm dry towel over her damp skin. "Our daughter's a mean shot with that garden hose," he said.

"Yeah, she was having fun though."

"Evidently." Jake looked up at her. "Turn around," he whispered. She did and he continued to dry her. Leaving the towel on the floor, he stood again, close behind her, his hands on her bare shoulders. "I want you," he murmured into her ear. "Now."

"We can't," she said, leaning back into him. "We have to get back downstairs."

He turned her around to face him. She was biting her lip, doubtful. "We can make it quick." He grinned.

She hesitated, and he saw in her eyes the moment she decided, just before she nodded her head in agreement.

"Turn," he whispered. "Kneel on the bed." Cassie did as he said, perching right on the edge of the bed, her shoulders and breasts pressed firmly into the mattress. He smiled at her. "You remembered," he muttered.

"Of course." He'd always loved to take her like this, with her ass in the air, hard and fast. He quickly pulled his shirt off over his head, and undid his pants, pulling them and his trunks down. He was bone hard already and he moved in behind her, entering her in one swift move.

"Jake!" she yelled.

He stilled. "Sorry… is that too much?" Had he hurt her?

"No…" she whimpered. "It's not enough."

"You want more?" He grinned.

"Hmm… please…"

"You got it, baby." And, placing his hands on her hips, he started to move…

Maddie and Ben were sitting at the kitchen table. Ben was chopping onions and mushrooms, Maddie was mixing something in a bowl. Ben was still in damp clothes, but Maddie was wearing fresh pajamas. As Jake and Cassie walked down the stairs together, Ben looked up at them.

"We're making pizzas," he said, raising an eyebrow at Jake, who just smiled in return.

Cassie went over ahead of him. "You are?" She was wearing clean, dry shorts and a t-shirt, her hair loose around her shoulders. Jake had gone back to his own room and changed too, into jeans and a casual short-sleeved shirt, but only after he'd come, real hard inside her. Cassie had bitten down on the comforter to stop herself from crying out as her own climax overwhelmed her, and then they'd both collapsed on the bed and lain in each other's arms, just for a few minutes to catch their breath. It had been glorious.

"Yes," Ben replied.

"And what are we having on these pizzas?" Jake asked, joining them.

"Pretty much everything in the refrigerator," Ben joked. "I let Maddie choose, so be prepared."

They all laughed, and Jake sat down beside Maddie.

"You wanna take over here while I go get changed?" Ben suggested.

"Sure. Thanks for watching her," Jake replied.

"Anytime." He turned to Cassie. "I found Maddie's PJs in the dryer. I hope that's okay?"

"Of course it is. Thanks for changing her."

"Well, she was getting a little chilly out there."

Cassie bit her bottom lip. "Sorry." She couldn't look at Ben.

"It's fine. You guys needed to um… talk."

"Yeah, we did, Dad," Jake put in, trying to help Cassie out. "Thanks."

Ben stood and went up the stairs, and Jake got up and went over to Cassie, who was leaning back against the countertop. "Don't be embarrassed," he said.

"I'm sure he knows what we were doing," she replied.

"I'm petty sure he does too, but what does it matter?"

"He's your dad, Jake."

"And…?" He put his hands on her waist, his feet either side of hers. "I'm Maddie's dad… doesn't mean I can't think like a guy when I'm around you. My dad's just a regular guy too. *And* he's actually pretty cool. Besides, I think he's kinda worked out that we're a bit more than friends." Cassie stared at up him. "He's got a granddaughter as evidence."

She put her arms around his neck and let him hug her, just for a moment.

"I think we'd better supervise," she said, pulling away again. "Three year olds, and tomato sauce aren't a great combination… oh… oh dear…" She started to giggle, and Jake turned to see Maddie's face, smeared with dollops of red sauce.

"How?" He looked from Maddie to Cassie. "How did she do that, in just a few minutes?"

"She's three, it's tomato sauce… what can I say?"

"Oh, hell…" Jake went over to her, but didn't really know where to start. As well as covering herself, there was sauce on the table and some dripping onto the floor.

Cassie came up beside him. "I'll take Maddie upstairs and dunk her in the shower." Cassie picked her up. "God, she's even got it in her hair." She smiled at Jake. "You clear up down here, and maybe make a fresh batch of sauce?"

"Sure…" He looked around at the devastation his daughter had wreaked, then went over to the sink and started running the hot water.

Jake could hear Cassie drying Maddie's hair. He'd tidied up, washed down the table and the floor and made some more tomato sauce by the time Ben reappeared.

"What happened?"

Jake explained about Maddie and the mess, and Ben laughed. "You took your eye off the ball, didn't you?" he said, looking at Jake.

"Yeah."

"Too busy with Cassie?" Ben smiled.

"Yeah… busted."

"You wanna grate some cheese?" Ben suggested, handing him the block from the refrigerator.

"Sure." Jake set to work, while Ben sliced some peppers.

"You're not messing her around, are you?" Ben asked suddenly.

"Who…?" Jake looked up at him.

"Cassie."

"No. Of course I'm not. What the hell gave you that idea?"

Ben stopped chopping, put down his knife and looked at Jake. "When I came home last night, Cassie was in your room…"

"Yeah? And?" Jake held eye contact with his dad.

"I—I heard you."

"Shit. Sorry, I mean… Really? I thought we were being quiet."

Ben chuckled. "Um… No. You weren't quiet at all."

"Sorry." Jake wasn't really sure why he was apologizing. He just felt he should.

"It's fine, really," Ben replied. He seemed a little uncertain, then he carried on speaking. "But then, after a while, she went back to her room. And a little later, I heard her crying."

Jake felt cold all of a sudden. "You did?"

"Yeah. Her room's right next to mine. She was quiet, but I know what I heard. Look, if you're messing with her…"

"I'm not, Dad. Honest. I love her. She went back to her room because of Maddie, not me."

"So why was she crying?"

"I don't know."

"Then I suggest you find out."

"I'm going to…"

"She's given you a second chance, son. If you screw it up again, you won't get a third… I can promise you that…"

"I think she'll sleep well tonight," Cassie said, as Jake closed the bedroom door.

"She's exhausted," he agreed. "She barely managed to stay awake through dinner."

"The pizzas were good, though." Cassie led the way back down the stairs and into the kitchen, where Ben was clearing up the kitchen still.

"What did you and Maddie sign to each other when I was putting her into bed?" Jake asked, gathering up the dishes from the table.

"I love you."

He turned to her. "But I thought…"

"What?"

"Well, isn't that…" He pointed to himself. "I," he said. Then he hugged his arms across his chest. "Love," he added. And then he pointed to Cassie. "You." He smiled at her.

"Yes." She smiled back. "That's the long version."

"There's a short one?" Cassie nodded her head. "Show me…" he asked.

Cassie raised her right hand, holding up her thumb, her pinkie and her index finger, leaving her middle two fingers down. With her palm facing Jake, she shook her hand from side to side, just slightly. "I love you," she said, staring at him.

He moved closer so they were just a foot or so away from each other, studying her hand, then he mirrored the sign himself. "I love you," he replied.

He let his hand fall, then pulled her into his arms. "Thank you," he said.

"It's just a sign, Jake." She leant back a little, looking up at him.

"I don't mean that. I mean thank you for letting me into Maddie's life."

He saw her eyes fill with tears and she pulled away from him, running from the room, out the door and into the lane.

Jake turned to Ben. "Get after her, boy," his father said. "I'll stay with Maddie."

Jake didn't need telling twice. He took off after Cassie. At the end of the driveway, he looked right and left and, in the twilight, he saw her running toward the beach. He ran – fast – and caught up with her halfway down the lane.

"Cassie!" He grabbed her, turning her around to face him. "What's wrong?"

"Everything," she cried, and he pulled her close and let her sob into his shirt.

When her tears started to subside he looked around and noticed they were near to the oak tree – the one under which he'd first asked her to be his girlfriend. He pulled back from her, took her hand and led her across, underneath its wide branches.

"Talk to me, Cass," he said, leaning her back against the gnarled bark of the thick, strong tree trunk. He stood in front of her, one hand by her head, the other on her waist, looking into her eyes.

"I can't stop thinking about it," she began.

"Thinking about what?"

"About all the wasted time, about how much we all missed out on. About how I got it so wrong. If I'd just waited for you, listened to you, none of it would have happened. We'd have stayed together, you'd have been there when Maddie was born, we'd have been happy together…" She paused, swallowed hard, and then sobbed out, "And there wouldn't have been any other women…" And she started to cry again. She was in so much pain, and she was taking all the blame on herself, for everything.

"Cass," he said gently. "Please look at me." He waited until she raised her face to his. "You did the right thing." She started to shake her head, but he clasped her chin in his hand and held it. "You did the right thing," he repeated firmly. "I wasn't ready to be a dad back then." He shrugged. "If you'd contacted me, sure, I'd have been there for you, but I don't think I'd have coped with it all, not like you have. I think when the going got tough I'd have done what I always did; I'd have run away... And I think that might well have been worse, for all of us, because eventually you'd have gotten fed up with me being so unreliable and we'd probably have broken up for good. What's happened... it's not your fault. I got you pregnant, and then I made you doubt me. I should've been more of an adult, more reliable, and trustworthy, so you could turn to me with certainty, knowing I'd do the right thing. Instead, you had to leave town, go to a strange place and live on your own, with no friends and no family around you... and that was my fault, Cass, not yours. I was a selfish idiot, but I've changed. I've really changed." She was sobbing hard, gulping in great breaths, her shoulders heaving. "Is that why you were crying in bed last night?" he asked.

"How did you know?" she stared up at him.

"Dad heard you. He told me. He was worried I was messing you around. Is that why you were crying?" he repeated.

"Yes."

He sighed and leant forward a little more, tracing around her lips with his fingertip. "I know you regret what happened and I know it's bothering you that I slept with other women," he whispered. "And I'm sorry that happened. I truly am. I meant it last night, when I said they didn't mean anything. They didn't. I didn't love them. I've only ever loved you, but I was so damn lonely without you. And I know that's pathetic of me, but I was. As far as I was concerned back then, you'd left me and I thought you didn't love me anymore, so after six months or so, I—I met a girl, and we ended up together."

Cassie stopped crying for moment and mumbled, "Did... did you live with her?"

"No, baby." Jake moved in closer. "I wasn't making it up last night when I said I'd never spent the night with anyone else. I haven't. I dated her for a couple of months… and, yes, I did have sex with her a few times. It wasn't like when I'm with you though. With you, I can't get enough. I want you all the time. The moment we've finished making love, I want you again. With her, with all of them, I saw them once or twice a week, and that was enough. I didn't want any more, because being with them just reminded me how much I missed you… So, I broke it off with her. I told her it was to do with work, but it wasn't. I ended it because she wasn't you. It seemed unfair to tell her that, so I lied instead. I lied to all of them. I broke up with all of them because none of them were you, Cass. When I came back to Somers Cove, I didn't expect to find you here. I was thinking I could use the summer to try and finally forget you, to lay your ghost to rest, so I could actually get over you and move on with my life; stop being so damn lonely, maybe meet someone and stop comparing them with you. Finding you here was… I don't know… I guess it was the answer to a prayer. Because, deep down, I think I knew I could never forget you, or get over you, and I was kidding myself thinking I could ever love anyone else… because it's always been you. Always."

She stared up at him. "Please," he continued. "Please stop this. Please forgive yourself, Cass. I need you to. I need you to forget the past, mine *and* yours. We've got an incredible future lying asleep back there." He nodded back down the lane toward his dad's house. "I wanna enjoy every moment I can spend with her, and with you. And I hate you feeling like this about yourself… I hate the thought of you crying yourself to sleep. I know we can't share a bed yet, but if you ever feel unsafe, I want you to come to me, not cry alone. Never cry alone, Cass."

He leant in, and paused, his mouth just a couple of inches from hers, and he waited for her to close the gap. She did, and while the kiss started gentle and soft, it quickly became heated, intense, passionate, filled with pent-up need and desire.

"I want you, in my bed… now," he whispered, his hands creeping up under her t-shirt, his fingers grazing over her soft skin.

"Hmm…" Cassie moaned into his mouth.

"I'll take that as a yes." And he bent down, placing his arm around her thighs, and lifted her over his right shoulder.

"Jake!" she giggled.

"What?" He started to walk quickly back toward Ben's house, Cassie bobbing up and down on his shoulder.

"Put me down!"

"No… not yet."

"I can walk," she squealed.

"I know."

"Then put me down."

"No."

She patted his ass through his jeans. "Jake!"

He stopped dead. "Did you just spank me?" He was grinning.

"Um… yes." She sounded doubtful and part of him wished he could see her face.

He raised his left hand and brought it down on her ass cheek, none too gently.

"Ow! That hurt."

"I'll kiss it better, in a minute. Right before I make you come…" He started walking again.

"Promises, promises," he heard Cassie mutter.

"Yeah, and I always keep my promises," he replied, and sped up a little.

Chapter Twenty

Cassie

Standing at the kitchen sink, Cassie felt Jake's arms come around her. She turned and looked up into his face. "You look tired." He did. He looked exhausted.

"That's because I am," he whispered, leaning down and kissing her.

"You need to slow down, Jake. You're gonna make yourself ill."

"I'm fine, Cass."

"No, you're not."

"It's just been a tough week, babe, that's all." He leant his forehead against hers. "You know how much this means to me…"

"Everything?" she queried.

"No, not everything. You and Maddie mean everything…" He paused. "But I've worked damn hard these last four years for this. This is my one chance to get it right. If I can just make this work, then everything I've worked for will pay off." He let his head fall back again, looking up at the ceiling. "And it's not just about me. Rich has a lot riding on this, and so has the client."

"You're putting a lot of pressure on yourself."

He looked back at her again. "It's fine, honest. I'm just tired."

"Look, why don't we give it a miss tonight?" she suggested, leaning back a little. "We don't have to make love every night… I don't mind. And you could do with the sleep."

His face darkened, just a little, but he pulled her closer. "I'll pretend I didn't hear that," he murmured. "Besides, you *do* mind, and so do I. And anyway, it's the early mornings that are killing me."

"Coupled with the late nights, Jake."

"The late nights are fine." He smiled. "Just fine…"

Over the last two weeks, they'd gotten into a routine. After Maddie had gone to bed, Cassie would work until eleven, or just after and then she and Jake would go to bed – his bed. They'd make love until gone midnight, sometimes much later, and then Cassie would return to her own room. Jake would get up at five-thirty, shower and dress, and leave for work at six-fifteen. He refused to wake Cassie, even though she said it was fine. Instead, he sent her text messages, or left her notes, telling her he loved her. During the last weekend, he'd managed to get a few hours' sleep during the day, but this week had been hard. They'd hit a few snags on the site, and he'd had to bring in some extra men to keep on schedule.

She sighed into him. "Well, at least it's Friday. It's the weekend, and you can have a rest."

"Maddie gets that concept, does she? It's your book signing tomorrow… I'm not expecting much rest."

"There's always Sunday…"

"Yeah, I wanted to take you both out on Sunday."

"You need to relax, Jake."

He kissed her again. "Yes, ma'am." He moved his feet either side of hers, letting her feel his arousal. "Do you feel like coming upstairs now?" he asked. "I can't think of anyone who helps me relax better than you… especially when you're underneath me, and I'm buried deep inside you."

She blushed; his words always did that to her. "We can't. Your dad's taken Maddie to the store, but they'll be back any minute."

"Oh, okay." His disappointment was obvious.

"I do have some good news, though." She looked up at him.

"You do?" He raised his eyebrows, expectantly.

"Your dad finished the bathroom today," Cassie told him.

"At your house, you mean?" Cassie nodded. "And?" He didn't seem to understand.

"And that means we can move back down there."

"How? The kitchen's still a long way from being completed."

"I know. I asked Ben to stop the kitchen and get the bathroom done first, because I wanted us to be able to move back, and we couldn't do that without a bathroom. We can eat here, but we need a bathroom."

She felt his shoulders sag. "I thought… I thought you said it was good news."

"It is." She smiled up at him.

"But… I mean, don't you like living here?" He seemed genuinely upset.

"Of course I do, Jake."

"Then why'd you wanna move out again?"

She sighed and pulled his hands from her waist, taking them in hers. "You misunderstand," she said. "While your dad's been working on the bathroom, I've been finishing up my mom's old room. It's pretty much done now, at least, it's done enough…" She took a breath, hoping he was going to like her suggestion. "Maddie can go back to sleeping in my old room – she sleeps on her own when we're at home in Portland, so she's used to that, and she normally comes in to me in the morning when she wakes up…" she continued. "And… and I thought we could sleep in my mom's old room."

"We…?" His face lit up.

"Yes… we. I've repainted the furniture, and your dad's built the new closet. I need to finish the redecoration still, but that won't take long, and won't stop us from sleeping down there. It's nothing like it used to be, so there won't be any memories… well, except the ones that we make. But we can sleep in there… If that's what you want?"

"Want? God, Cass… I'd love it." She smiled, and he covered her mouth with his, kissing her hard, and deep.

The sound of Ben coughing behind them broke them apart. They turned and saw Maddie and Ben standing by the kitchen door, both smiling over at them.

"Sorry to interrupt, but we bought ice cream. We need to put it in the deep-freeze."

"Don't let us stop you," Jake replied.

Maddie ran across to him and raised her arms up. Jake bent down and lifted her, kissing her cheek and giving her a salute 'hello'. She returned the greeting and rested her head on his shoulder.

"Cassie's just been telling me the bathroom's finished down at the beach house," Jake said to his dad.

"Yeah… I got the last of it done today." Ben closed the freezer door and turned around.

"So…" Jake pulled Cassie into his free arm. "We're gonna sleep down there from now on."

"You'll have to wait until tomorrow, I'm afraid," Ben replied.

"Why?"

Cassie looked up at him. "I didn't say we could move down there tonight," she explained.

"You didn't?"

"No. Your dad hasn't turned the water back on yet."

"And before you ask, it's best to do it in daylight, just so I can make sure there's no leaks." Cassie felt Jake deflate. "It's only one more night, son." Ben grinned. "I'm sure you'll manage."

"I wish I was." Jake's arm squeezed her tighter and she leant into him.

"You and Maddie can pack up all our things tomorrow, while I'm out," she suggested, "and even start moving them back, if you have time. I'll explain it all to Maddie after dinner tonight."

"Sounds like a plan," Ben added.

Cassie went over to Ben and stood in front of him. "Are you sure you're okay with this? I feel kinda guilty moving out, and coming back here for meals. I feel as though we're treating your house like a diner, even if I will be doing most of the cooking."

Ben put his hand on her shoulder. "I don't mind one bit," he said. "You need your own space." He glanced across at Jake. "You're a family now… you need to start being one. And anyway, I'll have the kitchen finished in a couple of weeks – hopefully – and I'll come eat with you…"

"You'll always be welcome to eat with us…" She turned to face Jake, the realization dawning on her that 'always' wasn't going to be for that long. Come the fall, she'd be moving back to Portland, and he'd be going home to Boston. And she had no idea how they were going to make things work.

∽

Jake

The plan for the morning had been that Cassie would get up early, being as she had to leave by six-thirty, and let Jake and Maddie sleep in. She'd explained to Maddie that, when she woke up, she should go into Jake's room to wake him.

Before Cassie had gone back to her own room, the night before, Jake had held onto her, telling her he couldn't wait for them to be able to sleep together the next night, although he told her he didn't expect them to get much sleep…

However, this morning, Jake had woken early – before Cassie – and had crept downstairs and made her a cup of tea. Bringing it up, he heard her in the shower, and stole into her room, sitting on the bed and watching her dress. After she'd kissed him goodbye and left, he'd snuggled down next to Maddie and snatched another hour's sleep, before she'd woken him again.

They'd packed up Cassie and Maddie's clothes, and Jake put the bags into his car, driving them down the lane to the beach house, with Maddie strapped into her seat. Ben was already down there, working on the kitchen.

"Hey." Ben looked up as they came in through the screen door. Jake put down the bag he was carrying and looked around. He was stunned by the change in the room since he'd last been in here. Although there were no electrical items yet, the doors were all fixed to the cabinets; and the pecan slab countertop was fitted. Ben had left the front edging natural, allowing the beauty of the wood to really show.

"This is amazing, Dad," Jake said.

"It's coming along." Ben got to his feet, arching his back.

"That countertop is something else."

"You're paying for it…" Ben smiled over at him. "I thought you'd want something good. I just need to oil it."

"It's amazing to think you built all this…"

"Why's it amazing, Jake? This is what I do."

Jake stared at him. "I know. I just…"

"You just think things have to be on a grander scale? I get as much satisfaction from doing this as you do from building your big houses and hotels."

Jake looked at the floor between them, feeling ashamed of himself.

"I'm proud of you, son. You've achieved a lot." Jake looked up again. He saw nothing but honesty in his father's eyes.

"I know where I got it from now…" Jake murmured.

"What?"

"That… that need to build things. To take pride in creating something, and doing it well."

"It's a good feeling."

"It sure is." They stared at each other for a moment, before Maddie tugged on Jake's hand. He looked down. "I guess I'd better get unpacking. A certain person is quite excited at the idea of having her own room." He picked up Maddie's bag.

"Yeah… and her daddy's not too unhappy at that prospect either."

Jake laughed and led Maddie down the corridor to the bedrooms at the back of the house.

"Hi, Emma!" Jake called. "We're gonna sit out here." He helped Maddie into a chair and sat down opposite her.

"That's fine," Emma replied, as she finished clearing the table nearest the door. "I'll be back out with you in a minute."

"No rush." Jake pulled his phone from his back pocket and set it down on the table, checking first to see whether Cassie had sent any messages. She hadn't, but that was good news as far as Jake was concerned. They'd agreed she would only contact him if she was going to be late back. It was nearly one o'clock and her book signing should have finished over half an hour ago. He'd brought Maddie to the coffee shop for lunch, just to fill in the last hour or so of time before Cassie got back, and then he thought they could spend the afternoon on the beach. He planned to take them out to dinner that evening, and then, once Maddie was asleep, he was going to take Cassie to bed, and stay with her, all night long. The anticipation was killing him.

Emma came over and gave Maddie a salute 'hello', accompanied by a hug.

"What can I get you?" she asked.

"I didn't think this through," Jake said, suddenly realizing. "I don't know how to sign enough food items yet..."

Emma laughed. "Oh... I'm not that great with food myself." She thought for a moment. "Hang on, I've got an idea." She held out her hand to Maddie, who took it and jumped off her chair. "We'll be back in a minute," Emma called over her shoulder, taking Maddie into the coffee shop. Jake looked around. Main Street was bustling, which wasn't surprising for a hot mid-June Saturday. He could understand why Cassie had always preferred the town in the winter. As much as the locals and their gossip had always annoyed him, the influx of tourists was much worse.

Maddie and Emma soon returned, and he got up and helped Maddie back onto her seat.

"Where'd you go?" he asked Emma, sitting back down again.

"I took her into the kitchen and showed her the food... well, some of it. I didn't get far."

"Why not?" He looked up at her, shielding his eyes from the bright sun.

"I didn't need to. She saw the Mac 'n' Cheese and that was it."

"I should've guessed." He grinned.

"And what can I get for her father?" Emma asked.

"I'll take the turkey sandwich, without the lettuce… extra mayo. Thanks, Em."

"What bread would you like?" she asked. He gave her a look. "Okay, white," she said, shaking her head.

"If Cassie can't get me to eat healthy, no-one can," he said.

Lunch was good. While they were eating, a couple of people stopped to talk to them – locals who'd seen them sitting there and wanted to know whether Jake was moving back for good, how Cassie was, where Cassie was… Basically any excuse to catch a little tittle-tattle. Jake gave as little away as he could – just because, deep down, he still felt like it was none of their damn business.

Not long after they'd finished, Maddie caught his eye. She made a kind of fist with her right hand, but with her thumb between her first and second fingers, and then shook it from side to side.

"Oh… now?" He had no idea how to sign that, but he said it anyway.

Emma was just giving the check to a customer nearby, so he called her over.

"Can you help?" he asked.

"What's wrong?"

"Maddie needs the bathroom…"

"Well, you know where it is, Jake. You've been here before."

"I've never taken her," he replied, looking sheepish.

Emma smiled. "Okay," she said, tucking her pencil behind her ear. "I'll take her…" She held her hand out to Maddie again.

"Thanks," he called after them as Emma took her inside.

He needed to speak to Cassie about this. It had been this same this morning, when he'd had his shower. Cassie had told him that Maddie often showered with her, or at least stayed in the bathroom, but he'd felt uncomfortable about that, so he'd asked Ben to mind her. He knew he should be fine with having Maddie around him, but he wasn't sure how Cassie felt about it, or how Maddie would react to seeing him completely naked, if she'd even react at all. He'd have to speak to Cassie and go with whatever she thought was best in future.

Now he thought about it, there were a few things he needed to speak to Cassie about. Most importantly, they needed to start thinking about what they were going to do in the fall. Cassie would be putting the beach house up for sale soon and then, come September, she'd move back to Portland, and he'd be returning to Boston at around the same time. Except hell would have to freeze over before he'd live away from them, so they needed to talk it through and come up with a solution. As far as he was concerned, the answer was obvious. Maddie had to come first. So, they'd live in Portland… And he'd just have to commute nearly two hours into work and back each day. It'd mean he'd see less of them, but he couldn't think of a way around it. Of course, that was always assuming Cassie wanted them to live together – it hadn't occurred to him before that she wouldn't…

The red sports car pulled up outside the coffee shop, but Jake hardly noticed it, he was so preoccupied, worrying about whether Cassie might not want to live with him. It was only when he heard his name being called in a worryingly familiar voice, that he looked up and saw Erica climbing out of the brand new open-top Mercedes-Benz SLC. Her leather skirt was so short that it left nothing to the imagination, and her top barely covered her ample breasts, which she'd clearly decided didn't warrant the encumbrance of a bra. In between these two insufficient items of clothing, she displayed a fair amount of tanned midriff… All in all, her appearance was that of a high class hooker, but the 'high class' tag was only earned by the car from which she'd just stepped. Other than that, she just looked like a hooker. She flashed a grin at him as she walked over, moved a chair right up beside his and sat down next to him.

"What are you doing here, Erica?" he asked, his defenses going into overdrive. As well as showing off too much skin, she was way too close.

"I've been calling you for the last two weeks." Her voice was a soft purr, and she ran her fingers up his arm as she spoke. "And you haven't taken a single one of my calls."

He wanted to yell at her that she should really try and get the message, but she was his boss's daughter. He didn't want to lose his job. "I've been busy," he replied.

"I thought so." She smiled. "So I decided I'd drive up here and see what it is that's been keeping you so occupied."

"You know why I'm here, Erica." He tried not to sound as impatient as he felt. "I'm working."

"Not all the time, Jake. You could've come home at weekends…"

"This is my home," Jake replied. "My family is here." He wasn't lying.

"It hasn't been the same without you." Erica flattened her hand, letting it rest on his bicep and sucking in a breath.

"Does your father know you're here? he asked.

She laughed. "Of course he does. It was daddy who suggested I come up here… He knows how much I've been missing you."

Jake wondered how she could be missing something she'd never had, but he didn't say anything. So, she was here with Rich's approval – even his encouragement. *Damn.* She'd been calling him several times a day and – as she'd said – he'd ignored every one of her calls, hoping she'd take the hint. It seemed he'd misjudged her, and the situation. Far from his absence cooling her ardor, it seemed to have enhanced it.

All his instincts were telling him to get rid of her – now – and he wanted to remove her hand from his arm, push her away and tell her to leave him alone. But Maddie might come out at any minute. It wouldn't look good if she saw him pushing a woman. But then it wouldn't look great if Maddie came out and saw a strange, scantily-clad woman touching him either… He had to do something, the problem was, what?

Chapter Twenty-One

Cassie

Cassie sang along to the music on the car radio. Justin Timberlake always made her want to dance, even when she was driving.

The book signing had gone really well, much better than she'd thought. She hadn't really known what to expect, but she certainly hadn't anticipated a line of people stretching out through the door of the bookstore and along the sidewalk.

She couldn't help smiling… It had been a good day. Once the signing was over, she'd grabbed a quick sandwich and set off for home, and her smile became a grin as she thought about what the rest of her day held in store. She wasn't sure if Jake would have been able to move all her and Maddie's things back into the beach house, but if not, they still had the whole of the afternoon to get that done. And then tonight, she hoped to persuade him to go out for dinner, maybe somewhere up the coast, away from the town, and then, once Maddie was tucked up and sound asleep, she and Jake could go to bed. She knew he was tired, and she didn't really mind if all they did was sleep. What she was really looking forward to was the morning… Because Jake was so right. She'd always loved sex in the mornings, and she couldn't wait.

Cassie had pulled off the Atlantic Highway and was only about ten miles from Somers Cove, when her phone rang. She pulled over to the side of the road, turned down the music, and answered it.

"Cassie?" It was Emma. She sounded worried.

"What's wrong?" Cassie asked.

"Where are you?"

"About ten miles out of town," Cassie replied. "Why? What's wrong, Em?"

Cassie was starting to worry herself now.

There was a moment's silence, then Emma spoke again. "Jake brought Maddie into the coffee shop for lunch," she began.

"Yeah." Cassie couldn't see why that would be a problem.

"And Maddie needed to use the bathroom…"

Cassie smiled. "Oh… let me guess, he didn't know what to do about that." She could imagine the situation, but she still couldn't see why Emma was calling her about it. If Jake had to work out how to take his little girl to the bathroom, it was hardly the end of the world. She just wished she could've been there to see him handle it.

"That's not why I'm calling, Cassie," Emma continued. "I brought Maddie in to use the bathroom because Jake chickened out…"

"Coward." Somehow Cassie wasn't surprised he'd found someone else to help him out.

"Cassie…"

"What, Em?"

"I was just gonna take her back out to him, but I can't."

"Why not?" Surely he hadn't left without her. He wouldn't… would he?

"Because… because there's another woman sitting with him."

Cassie felt an icy chill creeping over her skin, a sick feeling settling in the pit of her stomach.

"Another woman?" she repeated.

"Yes."

"Where's Maddie now?" Cassie tried to focus, despite the pain and fear that were spreading through her body.

"She's here, with me. I couldn't take her back out there, Cassie. The woman… she's all over Jake, like a rash. I couldn't let Maddie see that. She be so confused."

The pain flipped to anger. Blind anger. "Keep her with you, Em. If this woman goes, and Jake doesn't go with her, if he comes in to collect

Maddie, I don't care what he says, or does, you keep her, Em. Don't let him take her... I'll be there as quick as I can." She ended the call, dropped her phone onto the passenger seat, slammed the car into drive and floored the gas.

Cassie made those last ten miles in just over ten minutes, but then she was speeding all the way, only slowing as she turned into Main Street. She took a left between the florists and the bookstore, into the narrow road that led behind the buildings to the private parking area for the store owners and their staff, and pulled up in one of the bays behind the coffee shop.

Jumping out, she went in through the kitchen door, much to the surprise of Noah, the chef, and Patsy, one of the waitresses, who were talking together and both leapt out of their skins when Cassie stumbled in.

"Sorry," she said. "I'm looking for Emma."

"She's out front, honey," Patsy replied, nodding to the swing doors that led through to the front of the shop.

Cassie nodded her thanks and followed Patsy's directions, going through into the café, where she found Maddie sitting in a booth, with Emma beside her. She glanced over to the front window. From where she was standing, there was a pillar in the way, but she could see Jake's back. She didn't want to see anything else, and certainly not another woman.

"Hi," she said. Emma turned.

"Hi." She looked serious.

Cassie saluted 'hello' to Maddie, giving her a broad smile. "I'm gonna take her home," she said to Emma.

"Home here? Or home Portland?" Emma's eyes betrayed her concern.

"Here, for now. At least for tonight." Cassie blinked back her tears. "I need to think... And thanks for doing what you did," Cassie added. "Keeping her from seeing... that." She nodded toward where Jake was sitting.

Emma got to her feet, letting Maddie out of the booth. "I'm here if you need me." She pulled Cassie into a hug.

Cassie took Maddie's hand and led her back through the kitchen and out to her car, strapping her into the back. She didn't have Maddie's seat – it was in Jake's car, damn him. Still they didn't have far to go, and she'd drive more carefully now.

She climbed in behind the wheel, gripping it tight, her knuckles whitening. She mustn't cry, not yet. She had to get them both home first…

She reversed out of the parking bay and drove back down the road and out onto Main Street. As she passed the coffee shop, she glanced to her left, and all her good intentions flew out the window. Jake was sitting with with his back to the window facing a beautiful redhead, who was leaning into him, her hand resting on his chest. Cassie wondered if the woman could be wearing any less, and whether that was the kind of thing that now appealed to Jake. It never had before, but then – as he kept telling her – he'd changed.

The cry that left her lips was involuntary. How could he do this to her? How could he?

Jake

Her hand shifted across to his chest and she leant in a little closer. Jake turned to face her, taking in the perfect makeup, the painted red lips, the way her eyes grazed over his features.

"Why are you here, Erica?" he growled. He was getting beyond fed up now.

"You know why…"

He let out a sigh and turned away again, catching sight of a bright blue Toyota driving past. That looked like Cassie's car. He sat forward.

Fuck… That *was* Cassie's car. She'd been at the wheel, looking right at him. *Seriously… Fuck…*

He jumped to his feet, knocking the table forward and shoving Erica to one side.

"Jake?" she cried, grabbing hold of him. "What's wrong."

"Let go of me." He shook himself free.

"But, Jake…?"

"Enough, Erica!" he yelled, and tore across the wide sidewalk, ripping open his car door and leaping inside. A huge truck was passing and he had to wait before he could reverse out of the parking bay, then he threw the car into drive and took off down the road.

If he'd bothered to look in his rear-view mirror, he'd have seen Erica jumping into her car and following him.

He didn't bother stopping at his dad's place… Cassie's car wasn't there.

He drove straight on past and screeched to a halt at the beach house, alongside her blue Toyota. His dad's truck was there too. He leapt from the car and sprinted, not even bothering to close the door behind him. There was no-one in sight, and he ran up the porch steps, yanking open the screen door, to be faced with Ben, blocking his way.

"I think you'd better leave," his father said. He looked so disappointed, as well as angry.

"Not a chance." Jake looked around the room, but there was no sign of Cassie… "Where is she?"

"She doesn't want to see you."

"Cass!" he called out. There was no reply, so he called her again, a little louder.

"I said…" Ben started to say, but he stopped and they both turned at the sound of a door opening behind them. She didn't close it, but came out into the corridor.

"Cass," Jake said, trying to get to her. Ben wouldn't move. Jake looked down at him. "Please, Dad," he begged.

"It's okay, Ben." Cassie's voice was calm… scarily calm.

Ben stepped to one side, and Jake walked quickly to Cassie. "I can explain," he said as soon as he got to her.

Cassie stared at him. "You swore to me, on Maddie's life, that there was no-one else…"

"There isn't. I'm not with Erica. I never have been. She's my boss's daughter. She's been chasing me for ages, over a year now. But I promise you, there's nothing going on."

"Really?"

"Yes, Cass. You've gotta believe me. You've gotta trust me…"

"Do I?" She glared at him. "Where's Maddie, Jake?"

He felt his blood turn to ice.

"Oh, shit…" He clasped his hands either side of his head. "I left her." He felt sick. "It's okay, I promise. She's safe, Cass. I left her with Emma." He turned. "I'll go get her… I'll go now."

"You don't need to," Cassie said, and he stopped. "She's here." Jake was confused and he guessed it must show. "Emma called me," Cassie explained. "She saw you with… that woman. She didn't want Maddie to see what you were doing, so she kept hold of her until I could get there. She's in the bedroom. She's safe, Jake, but it's no thanks to you. You were so busy doing whatever the hell it was you were doing with that woman, you forgot your own daughter. How could you do that, Jake? How c-could you?" Her eyes blazed into his, tears overflowing onto her cheeks as she turned and went back into the bedroom, closing the door quietly behind her.

He crouched down, before his legs gave way, resting one hand on the floor, the other pushing back through his hair.

"Jake?"

"Not now, Dad. Not now." He could hear the cracks in his own voice. How could he have forgotten Maddie? His only thought had been to get to Cassie and stop her from thinking the worst of him. He'd panicked, and left his own daughter behind. Whatever happened, Cassie would never forgive him for that.

He slowly stood up, running his hands down his face and, without looking in Ben's direction, he went back out through the screen door, and onto the porch.

He had no idea where he was going, or what he was going to do, but there seemed little point in hanging around here.

He went back around the side of the house and groaned as he saw Erica's red Mercedes parked up behind his own car.

"What the fuck?" he muttered under his breath.

She climbed out from behind the wheel, standing with the door open, her hand resting on the top of the windshield.

"Just go, Erica," he said wearily, before she had the chance to even open her mouth.

"But, Jake…" She still had that soft purr to her voice, and her lips tilted upward. Christ, even now, she was still flirting with him.

He slammed his car door shut as he passed between his and Cassie's car, and moved toward her. "How many times?" He raised his voice a little. He came and stood in front of her, the shiny red door between them. "How many times do I have to turn you down?" he said. "Get the message, Erica… I'm not interested. I never have been, and I never will be."

"Jake, you don't mean that."

"Yeah, I do. I really do. I don't care if it costs me my job, my apartment and everything else I've worked for. I've got more important things to worry about right now. So if you need to go home to your dad and tell him what a shit I am, you go right ahead and do that. And if Rich wants to fire me for not fucking his daughter, then you tell him from me, I couldn't care less. Personally, I think it's damn weird anyway."

She glared at him for a long moment. "You'll pay for this," she hissed.

"I'm sure I will…" He sighed. "Just leave, Erica."

She hesitated for a moment, then lowered herself back behind the wheel and turned her car around with some difficulty, before she drove off at speed.

"Well, I guess that makes it a full house," Jake muttered under his breath.

"What's that?" Ben's voice cut into his thoughts.

Jake turned and saw his dad standing, leaning against the side of his truck.

"I'm guessing you heard most of that?" he said.

"I heard all of it."

Jake put his hands in his pockets and looked down at the ground. "Well, I'm not in the mood for a lecture about swearing at ladies, so don't even think about it."

"That was no lady," Ben replied.

"How's Cass?" Jake looked up again.

"I don't know. I followed you." He pushed himself off the side of the truck and moved over toward Jake. "I'm guessing that's your boss's daughter then?"

"Yeah. That's Erica."

"Wanna tell me about it?"

Jake shrugged.

"C'mon," Ben suggested. "Let's go for a walk along the beach." He started walking slowly and, after a moment, Jake fell into step beside him, and they walked down to the shore, strolling along the water's edge.

"She's been making my life a damn misery. I've heard of infatuation before, but this has been ridiculous… She just wouldn't accept I wasn't interested. Everywhere I turn, she's there, like my fucking shadow." He let out a breath.

"Has this been the whole time you've worked there?" Ben asked.

"No. It wasn't too bad to start off. She was at college, so I only had to deal with her during vacations, but she finished college about a year ago, and since then…" He left the sentence hanging.

"What's her dad got to do with it?"

"I didn't think he had anything to do with it, until a few weeks ago, when he started dropping not very subtle hints about how she needed to settle down with a guy who had good career prospects, while looking at me, in this knowing way. I got the distinct impression my job – or at least my promotion – might have become dependent on the two of us getting together."

"But I thought this guy said you'd be promoted for bringing the hotel project in."

"Yeah, he did. Like I said, his attitude changed toward me a few weeks back. I think Erica had a word with him, pointed out what she wanted out of the deal and I became the prize... or the sacrifice."

"What are you going to do?" Ben asked.

"What about?"

"About your job?"

"Leave, if I have to. I mean, there's always the chance he'll fire me first, of course..."

"Can he do that?"

"Probably not. But I'm not sure I'd fight him. I don't wanna work for someone who treats me like that."

"You need the money now, Jake. Don't be hasty. You've got Cassie and Maddie to think about."

Jake stopped walking and turned to his father. "Have I? You honestly think she's gonna forgive me for this? You said it yourself, she gave me a second chance already, she sure as hell won't give me a third. I'm not sure she'll ever let me near Maddie again. Not after today."

"She's mad with you, Jake."

"She has every right to be." He sighed. "I left our daughter behind."

"You think that's what this is about?" Ben asked him.

Jake stared down at his father. "Of course it is. That's what she was yelling about..."

"Hmm... Don't be so sure." Ben stared across the ocean. "Parenting's not easy, Jake. Cassie gets that. She gets that everyone makes mistakes." He smiled. "Do you know, I left you on a bus once."

Jake turned to him. "You did?"

Ben nodded. "Yeah. It was when your mom was still alive. You were only little, I was worrying about work and I clean forgot about you... I thought Amy was going to kill me. Luckily Doc Cooper's wife, Louisa, she was on the same bus and she brought you home, or God knows what might have happened."

"I never knew that."

"Well, it's not something I boast about, son. And unlike most of the women around here Louisa Cooper isn't one to gossip. If it'd been anyone else, trust me, you'd have heard about it. The point is, we all make mistakes. You've just gotta learn something from them, that's all."

"If I get the chance. Like I say, I don't know if Cassie will let me have Maddie again."

"She will. I think you need to be more worried about the other thing."

"Erica?"

"Yeah…"

"She didn't seem nearly as bothered by that as she was about Maddie," Jake said, kicking his feet in the sand. He was surprised she wasn't, but he knew the idea of harm coming to Maddie was enough to push everything else to one side.

"Do you know what she said to me when she came in?" Ben looked up at him.

"No?"

"She just came through that door, and when I asked why she was crying, she looked at me and said, 'Jake's with another woman'. No mention of you leaving Maddie, or anything else, just that you were with another woman."

"I should go and talk to her," Jake said, turning back. "I need to explain, get her to understand."

Ben grabbed his arm. "No. Leave her for a while. She needs time to calm down. You go and talk to her now, you'll just make it worse."

"How the hell does it get any worse, Dad?"

"Just give her till the morning, then go talk to her."

Jake hesitated for a moment, then let his shoulders drop, and they carried on walking.

Much later, as the sun was starting to set, they drove their cars back to Ben's house and parked up. There had been no sign of Cassie at the beach house, and Jake heeded his father's advice and controlled the urge to knock on the door.

As Jake was following his dad into the kitchen, his phone beeped. He wondered if Cassie had maybe seen him walking back to his car and sent him a text message and he pulled it out of his pocket straight away.

"Great," he muttered, reading from the screen. "Life just gets better."

"What?" Ben asked, turning on the lights.

"It's from my boss. He wants me back in Boston tomorrow at noon."

"A Sunday?"

"Yeah…" Jake sighed.

"Can't you tell him you'll see him Monday?"

"This isn't the kind of message you argue with. Besides, he knows I can't be away from the site on Monday… assuming I still have a job by then…"

Chapter Twenty-Two

Cassie

Cassie opened the bedroom door and crept out, with Maddie just a pace behind. She walked slowly down the corridor to a silent house. Jake and Ben had both left.

It was probably for the best. She wasn't in the mood for talking to Jake, that was for sure. She was in the mood for yelling at him, but that wasn't going to get her anywhere.

Maddie tugged on her hand and Cassie was just too tired to get her to sign 'excuse me', so she looked down and tilted her head to one side. Maddie signed that she was hungry and, only then did Cassie realize she had no food in the house. Not only that, she had no means of cooking anything either. She'd intended to persuade Jake to take them out for dinner, and afterwards... She felt the tears welling again.

"No, dammit," she muttered to herself, "I'm not gonna cry anymore."

Still, she needed to do something about their evening meal.

She went over to the couch and pulled her phone from her purse, calling Emma, who answered on the second ring.

"Hey," she said. "Are you okay?"

"No."

"What happened."

"He came back here," Cassie explained.

"I know. He took off. He didn't even pay his bill..."

"I'm sorry."

"Don't worry. That's not important. What matters is you… you and Maddie."

"And food," Cassie added.

"Food?"

"Yeah. We're back at the beach house," Cassie explained, "but we've got not stove, no refrigerator… no food."

"Oh. Well, d'you wanna come to me? I'll make us all something."

"Would that be okay?" Cassie had been hoping Emma would ask. She didn't really have anywhere else to go. Ben's was obviously out of the question, but as much as she didn't want to talk to Jake, she also didn't want to spend an evening by herself.

"I'd love to have you both come over."

"Can we come now?" Cassie asked.

"Sure. I've just closed up for the night. You can help me cook."

"How can I trust him again, Em?" Cassie took a sip of wine, leaning back against Emma's countertop while she chopped mushrooms. She was making a sauce to go with the chicken.

Maddie was on the living room floor, playing, under Cassie's watchful eye.

"He said she was someone he worked with?" Emma asked, putting down her knife and turning to Cassie.

"Yeah. He said she was his boss's daughter, and she'd been chasing after him for over a year."

"And did you believe him?"

"I don't know what to believe. She was all over him and he didn't seem to be doing a lot to put her off, not from what I could see."

Emma returned to her chopping.

"What are you going to do, Cassie?"

Cassie took a longer sip of wine. "My instincts are telling me to leave," she replied. Emma dropped her knife with a clatter.

"Leave?"

Cassie looked her in the eye. "Yes."

"But you can't."

"Yeah, I can. I've been thinking… Most of the house is done now. I could ask Ben if he'll complete the kitchen for me, and I can put it up for sale from Portland as soon as it's ready. I don't need to be here, not really."

"And Jake?"

Cassie swallowed hard. "I won't stop him from seeing Maddie. I can't do that to either of them, but I'm not sure I can be with him. He could see her on the weekends…" Her voice faded as she thought about the reality of that.

"Why, Cassie? He didn't do anything, not really."

"But would he have done? If I hadn't come back when I did, would he have? I went out of town for one morning and, the minute my back was turned, he's in the arms of another woman. I—I can't do it, Em," she sobbed. "I can't live like that, constantly waiting for the next woman. I'm really starting to think my mom was right…"

"What about?"

"When she said 'once a cheat, always a cheat'."

"Except Jake didn't cheat, Cassie. He didn't cheat with Alice and it doesn't sound like he cheated with this woman from his office either. This is more about your insecurities than Jake, isn't it?"

Cassie nodded her head. "But that doesn't make it any less real," she said.

"I know." Emma came over to her and put her arms around her shoulders. "Will you do one thing for me?"

Cassie looked up at her. "What?"

"Will you try and remember how much you regretted your actions last time, and then speak to him, before you decide?"

They stayed with Emma until late. Maddie fell asleep on the couch and Cassie and Emma talked. They didn't talk about Jake… well, not all the time, anyway. By the time they left, Cassie had decided she would talk to him, and then she would make the decision about whether to return to Portland, or not. However she looked at it, she felt like the dream had been shattered – she just needed to work out what to do about that.

When she got home, she put Maddie to bed in her room, and went across the hall to her mom's old bedroom. She'd had such different plans for tonight, and they certainly hadn't involved going to bed on her own in here. Or crying herself to sleep.

Maddie woke her at eight o'clock the next morning, which was late by Maddie's standards, but Cassie was grateful as she'd been crying until the early hours. A quick glance at her reflection in the bathroom mirror told her everything she needed to know. The lack of sleep and hours of weeping had taken their toll. She'd definitely wait a few hours before going and talking to Jake. She didn't want him seeing her like this, that was for sure.

Maddie signed that she was hungry and Cassie took her out to the kitchen, unlocking the door and leaving it open. It was another bright, sunny day, and Cassie stretched her arms above her head, taking in the fresh air. Luckily, Emma had sent them home the night before with a bag of pastries, and they had water... so at least they had something for breakfast.

She was just setting things out on the table when she heard a knocking on the door. She turned and saw Jake, standing on the other side of the screen.

"Hi," he said quietly. "Can I come in?"

Maddie noticed him and jumped down from the table, breakfast temporarily forgotten. She pushed open the screen door and pulled him inside.

"I guess that answers that question," Cassie muttered.

Jake allowed himself to be pulled into the room and over to the table, where Maddie sat back down again. He stood awkwardly beside her, his hand resting gently on her head for a moment.

"I'm sorry, Cass." His voice was soft, and he looked really tired still. She felt drawn to him, despite everything. He looked at her and she remembered she was just wearing her pajamas... Why did this keep happening to her?

"Let me go and get dressed," she whispered.

"Please don't, Cass," he replied. "I haven't got long."

"You don't?" She was surprised. He wasn't going to stay and talk? Wasn't this important to him?

"No. I've gotta go back to Boston."

"You're leaving?" she queried, her anger rising.

"No, not in the way you mean. I told you, I'll never do that to you again. I'm coming back. I've just gotta go into the city to meet someone."

"Right now?"

"Yeah."

An awful thought flashed through her mind. "Are you going to see her?" She hated herself for feeling so jealous, so possessive of him, but she couldn't help it.

He looked at her, long and hard. "I don't know."

"J—Jake…?" Cold fear crept over her. How could he not know? What was he saying? "W—What are you telling me?"

"I've been ordered back to meet with my boss," he explained, taking a step closer. "I can't say for sure whether Erica will be there, or not. That's what I mean, that's all I'm saying. I'm sure as hell not gonna go looking for her, if that's what you're asking." She heard him sigh. "I know you're not sure about me right now, but I love you… You and Maddie. You're my family, Cass."

"How do I know can I trust you, Jake?" Seeing him, hearing his words and the feeling behind them, she knew she wanted to trust him, and she looked up at him, her eyes pleading with his. She felt scared and she wanted, more than anything, for him to make her feel safe again.

"By remembering I haven't done anything since your mom's funeral to make you doubt me, and that includes what's happening now. What Erica did, turning up here, I had no control over that."

"Maybe, but you could control what happened once she was here, Jake. You were hardly fighting her off…" She tried hard not to remember the scene outside the coffee shop, the woman's hands on Jake, how close together their heads had been.

"You wanted me to manhandle a woman, knowing Maddie might come back out at any minute? You wanted her to see me do that?"

"No, of course not, but I didn't want her to see you with another woman practically in your lap, either. And it was only thanks to Emma that she didn't."

"Again… I couldn't control what Erica was doing. You haven't met her. She's headstrong, putting it politely. I was trying to work out how to get rid of her without creating a scene when I saw you drive past, and I ran straight after you," he tried to explain.

"Leaving Maddie behind."

"Yeah. But you need to remember, I only found out about Maddie in the first place because you took your eye off of her and let her walk out into the ocean. I didn't blame you for that. I still don't. You were preoccupied… Shit happens, Cass."

"So it seems."

"Don't give up on us," he pleaded. "You are, aren't you? Giving up, I mean…" He seemed so sad.

"I don't know." It was the truth. "I don't know how I feel, other than confused, and bone tired… and hurt." Again, it was the truth. She looked up at him. "Did you lie to me, Jake?"

"No. I haven't lied." He looked bewildered.

She tilted her head to one side. "Are you sure? You told me you're single and you don't have anyone. But, after what I saw yesterday, I'm wondering if that was a lie?"

"No, it wasn't, but… well, I'm not single, not anymore."

"Oh…" The sob rose in her throat, and she covered her mouth with her hand. "Oh my God." She grabbed the back of the chair.

He took the few paces he needed to stand right in front of her. "I didn't lie to you. But I'm not single, Cass, because as far as I'm concerned, I'm with you." He reached out and cupped her face in his hand, brushing her cheek with his thumb. Cassie couldn't help but lean into him, just a little. "Other than you, there's no-one in my life. There never has been. Not really…" He glanced down at his watch. "I've gotta go," he mumbled. "I'm sorry, baby."

He let her go and headed for the door and Maddie turned round, seeming confused.

"Can you tell her I'm going, and I'll be back soon as soon as I can," he asked. "It'll be quicker if you do it."

Cassie signed the message to Maddie and she ran over to him, giving him a hug. He picked her up and held her for a moment, then put her back down again. He looked up at Cassie, held her gaze for a long moment, then turned away and went out through the screen door.

As he reached the bottom of the porch steps, he turned back.

Maddie had wanted to follow him, so she and Cassie were standing together by the railing and Cassie looked down as Maddie raised her hand, her thumb, pinkie and index finger extended, and shook her hand from side to side. She wondered if Jake would remember what that meant and looked up to see him return the sign and mouth 'I love you' back at Maddie. His eyes moved to Cassie and he paused for a moment, then pointed to his chest, hugged his arms to himself, then pointed to her, his eyes filled with such sincerity, it hurt... It really hurt. She stared at him, tears spilling down her cheeks, until he shook his head, just once and turned away.

Jake

Had he really expected her to sign back? Not, probably not. Had she believed him? He wasn't sure. Did she trust him? He had no idea, but it didn't feel like it. Would she still be there when he got back...? He gripped the steering wheel. God, he hoped so, because he had no idea whereabouts in Portland she lived. Would he ever see them again? Of course he would. She wouldn't just disappear on him, he knew that. She'd never take Maddie away from him, not now. She couldn't hurt either him or Maddie that much. He was as sure of that as he was of taking his next breath. Was it just about Maddie now though? Was Cassie done with him? Fear gripped him. Was he going back in time...? Was she going to leave him? He wanted her to stay, for them, not just for Maddie. He wanted her to want him and love him, and to need him, like he needed her.

When he pulled into the parking lot at the office, he wondered for a moment how he'd gotten there. None of the journey came back to him at all. He hadn't focused on the road, other vehicles, signs or signals. All he'd been able to think about, the only thing that had been inside his head throughout the whole three and a half hour journey, was Cassie.

As he climbed from the car, he pulled his phone from his back pocket and tapped out a message to her:

— *Wait for me. Please. I know you're hurting. I know that's my fault. I want to make it better, and I will. I'll be back as soon as I can. We'll work it out, Cass, I promise. I love you. Just please don't leave me. J xxx*

He waited a few minutes, hoping she'd reply. Nothing happened. He checked the time at the top of the phone. He had just a few minutes to get into Rich's office, so he switched the phone to silent, put it back into his pocket, hoping to feel the gentle vibration at some point in the very near future, and went inside.

"Sit down." Rich indicated the chair opposite his own.

Jake sat, grateful at least that they were alone. There was no sign of Erica. Rich's face, however, gave him little cause for gratitude, or even optimism. He looked like thunder.

Rich waited for a moment, letting Jake settle, took a deep breath, then, in a calm voice, asked, "What did you think you were doing?"

"With regard to what?" Jake had a good idea, but he wanted Rich to spell out his distorted plans for his own daughter.

"Erica... what else?"

"I wasn't doing anything."

"So you think it's perfectly acceptable to lead a young woman on, do you?" Rich's eyes bore into his.

"I did *not* lead her on."

Rich leant back in his seat. "Oh, really? Then why is it she came back here yesterday, completely distraught? It took me the whole evening to calm her down."

"I'm sorry about that, Rich, but that was Erica's doing, not mine."

Rich's shoulders dropped. "There's nothing worse than seeing your own child unhappy, Jake. If you had kids of your own, you'd understand what I'm talking about…"

"I understand better than you think," Jake countered. "But I can't manufacture feelings I don't have." He paused for a moment. "Can I speak frankly?" he asked.

Rich stared at him, blinked a couple of times, then nodded his head.

"I didn't lead Erica on, Rich. Whatever she's told you, it's all in her head. She's pursued me to the point of it being… well, embarrassing, to put it mildly. Her behavior's so inappropriate, I'd already just about reached breaking point before I left for Somers Cove and, if she hadn't been your daughter, I'd probably have been looking to have her fired for sexual harassment. I was hoping that with me not being here, she'd take the opportunity to fixate on someone else." Jake stopped for a moment. Rich's face was giving nothing away and Jake was fairly sure he'd probably already lost his job, so he may as well finish what he had to say. "I'm sorry, Rich. I know you love your daughter, but she's not the woman for me. She never was and she never will be. I've got someone in my life already. She's someone I've known since I was six, and we got together in high school—"

Rich snorted. "You seriously expect me to believe that? If that's the case, how come I've never met this woman. You've never brought anyone to any social events, not once in the four years I've known you. You've never even spoken about her. You're making that up to save face…"

"No, I'm not. Cassie and I broke up four years ago, when I moved here. But we're back together now. We got back together just a few weeks ago, and we're staying together, whatever Erica thinks or does, because I love Cassie, and because… we've got a daughter."

"How the hell have you managed that in a few weeks?"

"We haven't. Maddie's three and a half."

Rich looked confused, but Jake wasn't about to offer an explanation. "She was pregnant when you broke up?" Rich asked eventually.

Jake nodded.

"You abandoned your pregnant girlfriend?" Jake could see Rich was shocked.

"No, of course I didn't. I had no idea Cassie was pregnant when we broke up."

"But she didn't let you know? She didn't tell you you had a daughter?"

"No." Jake shook his head. "And I don't blame her. You know what I was like when I came here, Rich. I was selfish, irresponsible, unreliable. Cassie did the right thing."

"And now?"

"I'm trying to build a life with them."

"Don't you think it might have been better if you'd be honest about your girlfriend and your daughter from the start, rather than letting Erica think she stood a chance with you?"

Jake sighed. "I've always been straight with Erica. I always told her I wasn't interested, and that she didn't have a chance. I tried everything I could think of. I was blunt, I was even rude. I tried ignoring her, telling her to leave me alone. I couldn't have been more straight if I'd tried. She chose not to listen."

Rich's eyes narrowed, and Jake wondered how long it would be before he was packing up his desk. "I saw you as a future son-in-law," he murmured, almost to himself. "I knew you had a bad relationship with your own dad. I thought you could be the son I never had."

"I'm not insensitive to that, but I already have a father. I don't need another one. My dad's a great man in his own right, I was just too dumb to appreciate him back then."

Rich seemed genuinely upset. "I had such plans for you and Erica. I—I thought you and she could get married, make a team and take over from me one day…" he murmured.

"Then maybe you should've told me. I could've put you straight a long time ago. Marriage to Erica… well, it was never gonna happen. If you'd bothered to ask me, I'd have told you that," Jake replied. He leant forward. "I can't stay here now, Rich."

The older man looked up sharply. "You can't leave. Not now. We've got a contract with Gardners. You brought the damn thing in, and I've got no-one else who can take it over."

"You can do it, can't you?" Jake suggested.

"No. I don't have time. I've just taken on a new housing complex north of the city. This is your project, Jake. You need to see it through."

"I can't work with Erica here, Rich. She's already caused more trouble than I wanna think about. I've gotta go home and try to straighten out my life, thanks to her. I'm not gonna let her ruin everything I've ever wanted."

Rich stared at him. "You can't expect me to fire my own daughter… and besides, I thought *this* was everything you wanted." He waved his arm around his office.

"So did I, until Cassie came back into my life. And I'm not asking you to fire Erica, but if I have to choose between this job and Cassie. I'll choose Cassie… every damn time."

Chapter Twenty-Three

Cassie

The sound of footsteps brought Cassie out of her dream. Maddie had been in bed for nearly an hour and she'd spent all of that time sitting on the swing, just staring out across the ocean. She turned her head to see Ben standing at the top of the porch steps. She hadn't seen him all day, even though there was still work to be done. She guessed he'd left her alone to think, to heal a little.

"Feel like company?" he asked.

Cassie wasn't sure she did, but she shifted along the seat and nodded. He'd done so much for her, it felt rude to turn him away.

He came and sat down beside her and, for a while, neither said anything.

"Do you want to talk about it?" he asked her eventually.

"I don't know." She wasn't lying. Part of her did want to unburden. She'd spent the whole day silently going over everything in her mind, pitting logic against emotion, finding that neither carried the balance. Maybe talking about it would help. But at the same time, was Ben the right person to talk to?

"Are you still mad at him?" Ben's voice interrupted her thoughts.

"No… yes. Maybe a little." She heard him chuckle.

"You're just like your mom," he sighed. "Indecisive." He turned in his seat. "You know me, Cassie. I'll always be impartial, even when it's Jake. He may be my son but, if I think he's done something wrong, I'll call him on it, and this time, I really don't think he's to blame…"

"For which part?"

"His boss's daughter. That's the bit that really bothers you, isn't it?"

Cassie wasn't sure she wanted to admit it, so she countered with, "He left Maddie behind," knowing it sounded pathetic.

"Yeah, and you know how easy it is to make a mistake. She was safe. Even if you hadn't already collected her, she would've been fine. She was with Emma. He didn't leave her…" He paused, evidently trying to think of somewhere dangerous Jake could have abandoned his daughter.

"To wander into the ocean by herself?" Cassie supplied.

He looked at her. "We've all done it, Cassie. And we both know that's not what's eating at you."

"She was practically in his lap, Ben."

"But he didn't put her there, or even invite her."

"He didn't move her off either."

"From what he's told me, he did once he saw you. He practically dumped her on her ass on the sidewalk."

She turned away, focusing on the golden sun as it descended toward the horizon.

"Is it always going to be like this?" she murmured.

"Like what?"

"Women… chasing after him…"

"Maybe. He's a good looking boy – gets that from his mom." Cassie turned to him and smiled. "The point isn't who chases after him… it's what he does about it. You've gotta trust that he'll be faithful to you."

"And how do I know he will?"

"Because he's not gonna risk losing what he's only just found."

Cassie felt her heart sink. Of course, Jake's main concern was Maddie. He'd do anything to keep her in his life. That was understandable.

"And I'm not talking about Maddie," Ben added, as though he'd read her mind. "He loves that little girl with everything he's got, but he loves you so much more." He got to his feet and looked down at her. "That's something else you've got in common with your mom," he said, putting his hands in his pockets. "She had no self-confidence either. I guess that's because of what your father did to her. And it didn't matter how many times I told her, I'm not sure I ever convinced her that I loved her just as she was, that she was everything I wanted." His voice dropped to a whisper. "She always doubted that…"

Cassie stood too. "Thank you for loving her," she said.

Ben coughed and looked up at her, blinking quickly. "It wasn't hard. But that's not what I'm trying to tell you," he continued. "What I'm trying to say is, you're the same, you and Kate – in all kinds of ways. For some reason I can't fathom, you're convinced you're not good enough for him." He put a hand on her shoulder and looked into her eyes. "You're way too good for him, if the truth's told. But you've gotta stop expecting him to leave… or to cheat. He won't. He won't ever do that to you. But if you keep on believing he will, one day, you'll get to my age, and all you'll find is that life's passed you by. It will all have happened around you, while you've been waiting and worrying. You'll have wasted a lifetime, when you could've been happy, living it with a man who really loves you."

Cassie hadn't slept very well… again.

Another whole day had passed. It was six-thirty the next evening and she'd still not heard anything from Jake. He'd said he'd be back, and she believed him – if for no other reason than she knew he'd never just walk out on Maddie. The problem was, he hadn't said when.

As it was Monday, she wondered if he'd had to go to the hotel site for the day… but then he'd have been back by now. He usually got home around six, or just after and, while she hated to admit it, she was starting to worry.

They were at Ben's house, and Maddie was helping him made a salad. Cassie was aware of him watching her, looking over in her direction every so often, and she tried to smile across at him. He smiled back.

"He'll get here," he said, reassuringly. "Whatever's keeping him, he'll have a good reason."

As long as it's not Erica, Cassie thought, and wanted to slap herself even as the words ran through her head. Ben had been right, and so had

Emma. It was her own negative thoughts that were the problem. Even now, when Jake was probably just held up somewhere, she was assuming the worst. She needed to stop it. She also needed to see him, and talk to him. If he'd just come home…

Part of her wondered why he hadn't sent her a message, letting her know what he was doing, and when he'd be back, but then she kept reminding herself that she hadn't replied to his message the previous day, and it was such a sweet message too. She also hadn't signed that she loved him, and she did love him – so why would he contact her? Why would he keep sending messages to get no response back? There was only so much any man could take. If she wasn't careful, no matter what Ben said about Jake's loyalty, she was going to drive him straight into the arms of another woman.

She picked up her phone from the table, went on to her message app and typed:

— When do you think you'll be home? Will it be tonight or tomorrow? C

She held onto the phone for a few minutes, waiting, but nothing happened. A few minutes stretched to five and then ten, and still he hadn't replied.

Ben brought the salad bowl over to the table, together with the potato salad. Then he helped Maddie sit in her chair.

"Sorry." Cassie looked up. "I'm not being of much use, am I?"

"It's okay. Everything's ready." He brought the roast chicken out of the oven. "You started the cooking, I'm just finishing it."

"I put a chicken in the oven and made a potato salad." Cassie shrugged, looking down at her phone again.

Ben started to carve. "He'll reply," he said. "Just—"

The loud beep interrupted him.

"Do you mind?" she asked, looking up.

"Go ahead." He nodded.

She got up from the table and went to the door, going out and sitting down on the step before she opened the message and started to read…

— Sorry, I was driving. Had to park up. Coming home now. Should be back around nine. Sorry it's too late for Maddie, but can I see you? J xx

She sighed, looked up at the sky, then back at her phone and started to type.

— Yes. We need to talk. C

His reply was immediate.

— Why do I feel so scared? Shall I come to your place? J xx

She paused, then wrote back:

— I don't know. Why do you feel scared? Can we meet on the beach? C

— I'm scared because I think you're gonna tell me you're leaving me. Whereabouts on the beach? What about Maddie? J xx

— Usual place. I'll ask Ben to sit with her. C

— Okay. I'll be there. I've gotta know. Are you leaving me? J xx

She sighed again. She didn't want to do this by text, but she didn't want him to drive home worrying either. She typed one word and pressed send.

Jake

He stared at the screen, at the word 'No', and for the first time since Saturday lunchtime, he let himself hope. He quickly typed out a reply.

— Back soon. xx

And, putting the car into drive, he set off for home.

Jake managed to get home at just before eight-thirty. His dad was out, but Jake guessed he'd already be down at Cassie's. He took fifteen minutes to grab a quick shower and change into clean jeans and a t-shirt, before heading down to the beach.

He didn't bother to go near the house. Cassie had said to meet on the beach, so he went straight on past, onto the shore and turned right, going around the headland and into the cove. He could see her, sitting by the rocks, her long legs stretched out on the blanket in front of her, and as she leant back on her hands, he felt his heart flip in his chest. She was gazing out to sea, her hair catching in the light breeze and she hadn't spotted him yet.

"Hi," he said gently as he approached.

She looked up. "Hello."

He hesitated, just for a second, then sat down beside her, bending his legs and resting his arms on his knees. The sun had almost set, but the last rays were casting golden sparkles on the still water.

"I'm sorry," Cassie said, not looking at him.

"You've got nothing to be sorry for," he replied. He turned, just as she did and, as she raised her face to his, their eyes locked. "I get it," he whispered. "I get how seeing me with another woman like that would've hurt you. I'm the one who's sorry."

"Except you didn't do anything wrong. I understand that." The sense of relief almost overwhelmed him. "I'm just…" she continued, "I'm finding this difficult, that's all."

His relief disappeared in an instant. "What's difficult? Is it Maddie?" he asked. "Is it because I forgot her. I know that was unforgivable."

She put her hand on his arm and he felt the warmth seep into him. "No. It's got nothing to do with that."

He turned and knelt beside her, facing her. "Then tell me what's wrong. Tell me what you're struggling with."

"That there's always going to be a woman throwing herself at you…"

"It really doesn't happen that often, Cass." He tried to laugh.

"It's a reminder. A reminder I don't need, that I'm not good enough for you…" He felt her sigh and wondered how hard she'd found it to say that. He knew it was no good telling her that her fears had no foundation. They were her fears, which meant they were real to her –

even if she was so far off base, she wasn't even in the same ball park as him.

"Have I ever done anything to make you think you're not good enough for me?" he asked her gently.

"Ever?" she queried.

He smiled and shrugged. "Okay, since I came back here. We both know I sometimes got it wrong when we were younger."

Cassie turned and looked out across the ocean, as though she was thinking.

"No," she said eventually.

"I think I've said this before," he whispered, reaching out and cupping her chin in his hand, turning her face back toward him, "but I'm gonna say it again. You're it for me, Cass. If you'd decided to give up on us, I'd have come after you——"

"I couldn't take Maddie from you. I couldn't do that to you, or her," Cassie interrupted.

"I'm not talking about Maddie," Jake clarified. "I know you'd never take her from me. What I mean is, if you'd decided we couldn't be together, if you'd left me, I wouldn't have just walked away like I did before. I'd have pursued you, relentlessly. I'd have worn you down. I'd have used everything, every trick I could think of, every secret I've ever known about you, to win you back. I'd have come after *you*, Cass. I've spent the last two days living in fear that you'd be gone when I got back here, and knowing that would break me."

"I—I did think about going back to Portland, on Saturday evening."

He felt his mouth dry. "You did?"

"Yes. I was scared."

"If you're scared, you need to be with me, not on your own."

"I know."

"Tell me what you're scared of." He sat back, leant over and took her hands in his. "Tell me, Cass."

"Sometimes I wonder if you're just with me for Maddie. Sometimes I wonder if you just want to recreate the past, you know, go back and make it like it was before. And I'm scared that if you can't have that, and

309

if all you want is Maddie, then we'll fall apart… Maybe not now, but one day in the future."

He sighed deeply. "I love our little girl," he said. "She's everything I could want and I wouldn't change a thing about her. But I've already told you that, even if she wasn't in the picture, I'd still want to be with you. I said that to you. I've tried living without you – I wasn't very good at it. I don't want to do it again. This is all about you and me. It's about us, because without us, there is no Maddie. You've gotta believe me. There's nothing I wouldn't do to be with you… Nothing." He leant a little closer. "Which is why I've been such a long time in Boston…"

"What do you mean?"

He brushed a loose hair away from her cheek. "I spoke to my boss yesterday lunchtime," he began. "It was a surprising conversation in some ways."

"Why?"

"Because he had ideas that didn't coincide with mine. He… he was looking to me to take over his business."

"Really?"

"Yeah. Don't sound so proud, or pleased though… There's a catch." He squeezed her hands a little tighter. "He wanted me to become his son-in-law first."

Cassie sat bolt upright pulling her hands from his. "Oh my God. He wants you to marry her?"

"Well, that was his plan, yeah."

"But—" She went to get up, but Jake grabbed her and pulled her back down to her knees.

"I'm not gonna marry her, Cass. I've resigned."

"You've… You've resigned?" Her voice was a whisper.

"Yeah. I told Rich I couldn't stay there working with Erica. He obviously couldn't fire his daughter, so me resigning was the best solution."

"But… your job, your career? It means so much to you, and you've worked so hard for it."

"It means nothing, if me working there hurts you." He knelt up in front of her, so they were facing each other. "I don't wanna work for someone who thinks they can just plan my life for me. I'm the only one who gets to do that… well, with you."

"So, what are you going to do?" Cassie asked him.

He smiled. "That's why I've been gone so long. I had things to deal with. When I resigned, Rich went into a kind of melt down." Jake smiled as he remembered the look on his boss's face. "We're under contract to the hotel chain, and I brought the deal in, so he kinda needs me."

"So?" He could see the confusion on Cassie's face.

"So, we reached a compromise."

"Which is?" She sounded nervous.

"I'm gonna stay on until the hotel is completed – which will be early next year. It's scheduled to complete at the beginning of March."

"So you'll still be working with Erica…" It wasn't a question and he heard the disappointment in her voice.

"No I won't. I've agreed to oversee the build. I've told him, I won't go into the office. I'm gonna be working as a contractor, not an employee."

"So, where will you be based? Here?"

He looked at her. "No. Portland. If that's okay with you?"

"Portland?" she whispered.

"Yeah. Let me explain." He took her hands in his. "I've had a busy day," he said quietly, "which is why I didn't text you, or call at all. I'm sorry about that, by the way. I had every intention of sending you a message, to let you know what was going on, but it's been non-stop."

"Non-stop what?" She looked at him.

"Meetings and making arrangements." He held her gaze. "I met up with the hotel client first thing this morning." He looked up at the sky for a moment. "God, I wish I could tell you his name, it'd make life so much easier… Anyway, I told him what had happened, and to start with, he was so mad with Rich, he wanted to pull out of the contract altogether, but I explained the new position and the legal ramifications of getting out of the contract, and he came around. He's not happy about it, but he's going ahead with it."

"So you're still going to be working on the site?"

"Until September, yeah… I'll be there every day, just as I always planned, and then I'll just be there for a couple of days a week until the build is complete."

"And after that?"

"After that, I've got a new job lined up."

"Already?"

"Yeah. That's the other thing I spent a lot of this morning talking to my client about. He's offered me a job."

"Doing what? He's a hotelier, isn't he?"

"Yes, which means he owns a lot of buildings. He wants me to go around them all, looking at ways of making them more environmentally friendly. And he's also found another potential site for a new build, although I'm not allowed to say where yet, because he's still negotiating. If it goes through, he wants me to design and build that hotel too."

She smiled up at him. "So… I guess you're asking if you can move in with me, are you?"

"No."

He saw her shoulders slump. "But you said you wanted to be based in Portland. I thought…"

"That's the other thing I've been doing today. I've been meeting with a realtor. I've put my apartment up for sale."

"You have?"

"Yeah. I want us to buy somewhere together. So I'm not gonna be asking if I can move in with you, but I am…" He held her hand a little tighter. "I am asking if we can move in together." He saw her eyes glistening. "Don't cry, Cass," he murmured. "I wanna buy us somewhere beautiful, where we can live together and raise our gorgeous daughter."

"We can buy it, Jake. I'll put the money in that I get from selling the beach house."

He leant closer to her. "I don't want you to sell the beach house. I want you to keep it, so we can come here at weekends. Maddie loves it here, and so do you. You belong here."

"But you hate Somers Cove."

"I don't hate it. I just don't love it like you do. But I want you to be happy. And you're happy here. I know we can't live here all the time because of Maddie's school and my work, but I want you to keep your mom's house."

"Can we afford that?"

He chuckled. She'd said 'we', and that, quite simply, made his heart sing. "Yeah, we can."

"You'd do all that for us?"

"For *you*, Cass, yeah. I'd do that, and more."

He leant forward and kissed her, really gently, running his tongue along her lips and, when she opened to him, delving inside, tasting her soft sweetness.

"I want you," he muttered.

"We can go home," she whispered.

"No. I want you here. Now."

She pulled back, looking up into his eyes. Even in the moonlight, he could see the doubt in hers. "I thought I explained, I thought you understood. We can't recreate the past," she said quietly.

"And I don't want to," he reasoned. "I don't wanna recreate your book either." He reached in between them and undid the button on her jeans, pulling them down a little.

She gasped out his name.

"Shh." He pulled her t-shirt over her head and unclipped her bra, removing it and releasing her breasts before laying her down gently on the rug and pulling off her shoes and jeans, so she was lying before him in just her thin lace panties. "I seem to recall taking it slow real when we did this the first time around." He moved between her legs, looking down at her. "I've got no intention of going slow… not this time. I want you, right now." He parted her legs with his own and pushed her panties to one side, inserting two fingers inside her. He closed his eyes. "Fuck, Cass," he whispered. "You're so wet."

She was panting with want already, raising her hips off the rug.

"Please Jake," she murmured. "Please."

He stood, not taking his eyes from hers, and tore off his own t-shirt, undid his jeans and let them drop to the floor, kicking them and his shoes to one side. He hadn't bothered with underwear after his shower, and his erection stood proud.

He knelt back down and placed one hand on her panties, his fingers tucked in the top. "These aren't particular favorites of yours, are they?" he whispered, but didn't bother to wait for an answer before he ripped through the thin lace, tearing them from her. Her eyes were locked with his as he rubbed the head of his cock against her and, without pausing, entered her – hard.

He let out a long gasp. "God, you're so tight," he muttered, and he started to move real fast. She matched his rhythm, bucking into him, her eyes locked with his as he took her deeper, his strokes becoming longer, her groans rivaling his as he pounded into her, over and over. He felt her hands come up his arms, resting on his biceps, and she lifted her legs, wrapping them around him.

"Please, Jake!" she cried.

"Come for me," he called out, and his words pushed them both over the edge into ecstasy.

They took a while to calm.

"It's… it's never been like that." Cassie seemed to be struggling to talk.

"No." He smiled down at her. They were still joined and Jake was reluctant to part them.

"You were…"

"What?"

"Forceful?" She smiled up at him.

"Not too forceful? I didn't hurt you?"

"No. I know you'd never hurt me."

He closed his eyes, just for a moment, and when he opened them again he felt a stronger connection to her than ever before. His love for her completely overwhelmed him. "I have done, Cass. I know that, but I'll do my best to never hurt you again. I'll put you first, and I'll keep you safe. Always."

He saw her eyes fill with tears.

"Don't cry, baby." He lowered himself down to hold her in his arms. "Will you do something for me?" he whispered.

She nodded.

"Will you promise to always talk to me, and always tell me when I'm screwing up. Help me get it right, Cass."

"Only if you do the same with me…"

He leant back and stared down at her again. "When do you screw up?" he asked.

"All the time. I'm not perfect, Jake."

"You are to me." He moved forward, already hard again inside her, and kissed her tenderly. "Can you do me one other favor?" he said, resting his forehead against hers. He felt her nod her head. "Please don't write any of this into a book. I don't mind you sharing some things, but I'd like to keep what's happened over the last few days to ourselves."

Her hand came up and gently cupped his face.

"Of course I won't write it. I'd rather forget all about it, to be honest."

"Even what we just did?" he smirked.

"No," she smiled back. "Not that. I won't ever forget that."

"Oh, you don't need to worry about forgetting it," he murmured as he started to move inside her again. "I won't ever let you. I'm gonna keep doing that… over and over."

She let out a slight laugh.

"What's funny?" he asked.

"I was just thinking… I'm not sure I could write what we just did anyway. I don't think I have the vocabulary."

He chuckled "I can always help with words, and descriptions. Between us, I think we could make your books even hotter. I can give you a guy's perspective of what it feels like to make love to a woman who just makes everything right, who gives him everything he needs and makes his life complete, just by being there, by his side." He kissed her deeply. "And that's you and me I'm talking about, Cass. It's always been you and me."

Epilogue

∽

Early November

Cassie

"Man, it's cold," Jake lifted Maddie from the car, hugging her tight and wrapping her into his jacket. She was sleepy, but that wasn't unusual after the drive up from Portland on a Friday evening.

"I'll open the door, so you can get her inside and straight to bed," Cassie said, running up the porch steps ahead of him.

"Hopefully dad remembered to come down and turn the heating on." The wind was whipping in off the ocean and Cassie agreed. The idea of a chilly night didn't appeal, although she knew she wouldn't be chilly for long, not in Jake's arms. Almost as soon as she opened the door, she felt the warmth seep out.

"He remembered." She held the door open to let Jake pass through and he disappeared down the corridor to the bedrooms at the back of the house, passing the new staircase he'd put in, which led up to the guest bedroom, and the office he'd spent the last few months installing.

Once they'd decided to keep the beach house, Jake had wanted to extend up into the attic. Initially they'd toyed with creating a big den up there, but he needed somewhere to work. There was too much space to just have an office, so they'd decided to add a guest bedroom as well. It was fairly small, but functional, with a neat little adjoining shower room. Ben had helped with the work, and they'd completed it a couple of weeks ago – finishing it off during their weekend visits.

"She's fast asleep," Jake said, coming back out into the living room. He wandered into the kitchen area and opened the refrigerator. "Dad's stocked us up with vital supplies," he smiled, pulling out a chilled bottle of wine. He raised an eyebrow at Cassie.

"Oh, yes," she replied to his unasked question. He chuckled.

"I'll pour…"

"And we'll take it to bed…?" She finished his sentence.

He came over to her, leaning down and kissing her gently. "You took the words right out of my mouth."

"What are your plans for Maddie's birthday?" Emma asked. It was due to be Maddie's birthday the following week.

"She's having a party," Cassie replied, "with half a dozen of her very best friends from school." She smiled. "And she's already wound up with excitement. Jake's bought her more presents than any four year old really needs, naturally."

"Well, I guess it's like her first birthday to him."

"Yeah, I guess." Cassie looked through the misted coffee shop window. They'd finished breakfast and Jake was outside, talking on the phone to his hotel client, who'd just called. He was pacing up and down, looking concerned. She'd have liked to keep on staring at Jake, but then she remembered she had a question to ask Emma. "We thought you and Ben might like to come over tomorrow to celebrate. I've brought a cake with us, so she'll be having two birthday cakes in a couple of days, but what the hell. You can never get enough birthday cake, when you're four, can you?"

"Um, you can't get enough when you're twenty-six either," Emma joked. "I'd love to come and eat cake. I just wish I could make it down to you on Tuesday…"

"So do I. I'm not looking forward to having seven little girls running around the house."

"Is Jake gonna be there?" Emma asked.

Cassie nodded. "The party was his suggestion. I wasn't going to let him get away with not being there."

"Are his signing skills up to dealing with seven little girls?"

Cassie smiled indulgently. "Probably not, but he'll just charm them into doing what he wants."

"So it's not just Maddie who worships him then?"

"No, all of her friends do too. And as for their moms…" Cassie rolled her eyes. "It's embarrassing sometimes how obvious they are, even when I'm right there with him."

"And you're okay with that now?"

"I wouldn't say I'm okay with it. I honestly don't see why they need to behave like that, but I know he won't take them up on any of their offers, or do anything to hurt me, and that's what matters."

"I'm glad you two straightened everything out." Emma smiled at her and they drank their coffee in silence for a moment, Emma helping Maddie color in her book. "I miss you guys," she said, all of a sudden.

"We miss you too," Cassie replied.

Emma looked up. "No… I mean, I *really* miss you." She took a breath. "It's quiet here now." She glanced around the coffee shop. There were only three other customers in, which was why she was able to sit with Cassie and have a break. "And, if I'm honest…" she continued, "I'm lonely."

Cassie was taken aback. "Oh, Em," she said, reaching across the table and taking her friend's hand. She noticed Emma's eyes were glistening. Were things really that bad?

"Seeing you two getting back together," Emma carried on, not looking up, "it makes me realize what I'm missing out on."

"You don't have to miss out. You're beautiful, Em. Any guy would be lucky to have you."

"Hmm… now we just have to convince them of that." Emma looked up and smiled across the table, but Cassie could tell her heart wasn't in it. "Do you remember the guy I told you about? The one from a few years ago?"

"You mean the one you were seeing when I had Maddie?"

"Yeah. I was thinking about him the other day. I quite often think about him, especially at this time of year. It's almost exactly four years ago that he came to town…"

"And stayed for a week… and broke your heart."

"Yeah." Emma lowered her head.

"I wasn't much use to you then, was I?" Cassie said, feeling guilty.

"You'd just given birth prematurely," Emma reminded her. "You had other priorities than helping me get over a broken heart."

"And did you?" Cassie watched her friend closely.

"Did I what?" Emma looked up slowly.

"Get over it? Get over him?"

They stared at each other. "No. I may have only known him for a week, but I always thought he was 'the one', you know?" Cassie nodded. "Still, I guess he didn't." She sighed. "And I think it's about time I moved on."

"Good for you." Cassie tried to sound enthusiastic, which would have been a lot easier if she had, for one second, been able to believe that Emma meant a single word of what she was saying. She remembered the guy Emma was talking about. She'd never met him, but he'd come to town for a week's vacation and spent most of it in Emma's bed – at least according to Emma, anyway – and when he'd left, he'd taken her heart with him, promising to return. Only that was the last she'd ever seen of him. She studied Emma's face. Her sadness was almost overwhelming and, as much as she wanted to ask her friend why she was suddenly feeling so low, she didn't think now was a good time. Jake might come back in at any moment, and Maddie was there. They needed some time alone, so she could really talk to Emma.

"I know we're seeing each other tomorrow," she said, "but that's about Maddie. So, why don't we do something next Sunday? We could go for a picnic, or something…?"

"A picnic? In November?"

"Sure, why not?"

Emma thought for just a moment, then shrugged her shoulders. "I suppose you're right… Why not?"

Jake had stopped pacing outside. Now he was standing, looking up at the sky. Seeing Emma like this and hearing her speak of her loneliness, made Cassie realize how lucky she was to have him in her life, and how close she'd come to losing him for good. Their home in Portland was beautiful and she loved every moment they spent there, but she cherished their weekends at the beach house – the solitude and memories were special to them both.

To begin with, when they'd first moved back to Portland, Jake'd had to stay away quite a bit; there had been a few issues with the hotel construction and he'd needed to be on site, so he'd stayed with Ben, leaving Cassie in Portland, sometimes for two or three days at a time. While she'd found it hard being away from him, it had one advantage: the sex when he came back home, or when she drove up to Somers Cove at the weekends, was incredible. It was like meeting up again for the first time, every time. It almost made it worth being apart… almost.

Her books were selling well. The second and third parts of her series were now out, and the fourth part was due out in a couple of weeks. She'd begun work on her second series and, she had to admit, having Jake back in her life, was proving to be an inspiration – in more ways than one. She knew her writing had improved. Just as he'd said he would, Jake was helping her to see things from a male perspective, and not only so far as sex was concerned, but also emotionally. From the things he said and the way he said them, she knew beyond any doubt that he loved her completely.

As far as she was concerned, he was everything he always had been. But he was also so much more.

Jake

"I really need you to come up and check things over," Jake said into his phone. It was chilly outside, but he didn't want to talk in front of Cassie and Emma. He hated his business intruding into their weekends anyway, but to have a work conversation on the phone in the coffee shop felt like the height of bad manners. He gazed through the steamed-up window. He could just about make out Cassie, sitting in the booth where he'd left her with Maddie and Emma. She looked beautiful, as ever.

"I'm not sure I can make it…" He heard the doubt in Mark's voice, intruding into his thoughts. Mark hadn't been to the site since he'd given his original approval, all those months ago. Jake knew he was busy, but this was getting ridiculous. He'd turned down over half a dozen invitations to come and see the progress of the build.

"We've got to go through the interior design plans," Jake persisted. "I still need your approval on several items and we're due to start in a couple of weeks. If you don't come up here soon, it's gonna hold up construction." He heard Mark sigh. "I get that you're busy, but why don't you come at the weekend… next weekend, maybe? You could come up on Saturday and stay over with us at the beach house until Sunday. We can go and inspect the site, and Cassie and Maddie can come along. Cassie would love to meet you, and I'd really like for you to meet them too." Although Jake and Cassie had been back together for several months now, he hadn't been able to find time for them all to get together.

There was a long silence.

"Mark, what's wrong?" Jake asked. "You haven't been up here for months. I haven't even seen you for ages – which I know is my fault as much as anything. I've been busy with Cass. But this is a good chance to get some business done and for you two to meet up. You'll really like her, I know you will."

"I'm sure I will, Jake."

"Then what's the problem?" A thought occurred to Jake. "Are you having second thoughts?" he asked tentatively.

"What about?" Mark sounded confused.

"About employing me once the construction's completed."

"No," Mark replied quickly. "Of course not. I can't wait to bring you on board. I've got so much lined up for you to do, it can't happen soon enough as far as I'm concerned."

"Then why on earth…?"

"Because I'm trying to avoid going anywhere near Somers Cove, that's why." Mark blurted out the words, then fell silent.

"I—I didn't know you'd even been to Somers Cove before."

There was a moment's hesitation before Mark said, "Yeah. A few years ago."

Jake laughed. "Look, I'm not that keen on the place myself, but it's not *that* bad, not really. What have you got against it?"

"It's not the town itself…"

"It's someone in the town?" Jake hazarded a guess.

"Yeah." Mark sighed again, and Jake leant back against the lamp post. "I went to Somers Cove on vacation about four years ago." He paused. "Actually, it was almost exactly four years ago. I spent pretty much the whole week with the most beautiful woman I've ever seen. It was a very… um… romantic week." Jake smiled to himself as Mark continued, "She was incredible. I've never met anyone like her, and no woman since has ever come close to comparing with her. Trust me, I've tried." Jake's smile turned to a grin. "I'm worried," Mark carried on, "I'm worried that, if I come up there, I'll meet her again, and I can't do that…"

"Why not? If she's as good as you say, surely meeting her again wouldn't be a bad thing," Jake suggested.

"It would be disastrous. I… well, let's just say I let her down – badly. I'm not sure how she'd react to seeing me, and I don't think I can do that to either of us…" Mark's voice faded to a whisper.

"Oh." Jake took a deep breath. "Well, I wouldn't worry too much about it. Whoever she was, she's unlikely to be here still. Most people leave, given the chance. And even if she is here, the beach house is fairly remote. If you came to visit, you wouldn't have to stop in the town at all, you could just drive straight through and on to the house. And on the Sunday, we'll all be at the site anyway."

There was another short pause. "Are you sure?"

"Yeah, I'm sure."

"Okay. I guess it'll do me good to get away for a couple of days… And besides, I'd like to meet the woman who finally tamed you." Jake heard the smile in Mark's voice.

"I'm not the one who needed taming."

"I'm not *that* bad," Mark countered.

"Hmm… I believe you," Jake laughed. "So you'll come up next

Saturday?"

"Yeah, I'll drive up there after lunch."

"Okay. We'll look forward to it."

They finalized their arrangements and ended the call. Jake put his phone back into his pocket and made his way into the coffee shop, sitting down next to Cassie, and putting his arm around her.

"Everything okay?" she asked.

"Yes." He leant over and kissed her. "It is now." He smiled.

"That was a long phone call."

"I had to persuade him to come up for a visit…"

"He needed persuading?"

"He's a busy man." Jake didn't think Mark would appreciate Cassie and Emma knowing about his past fling in the town. They might even be tempted to try and guess who the woman was, whereas Jake didn't really care.

"And is he coming?" Emma asked.

"Yeah." Jake picked up a red crayon and started coloring the sail of the boat in Maddie's picture. Maddie grinned up at him as she completed the scales on the mermaid's tale, alternating them in pink and pale blue. "He's gonna come up next Saturday and stay over." He leant into Cassie. "I thought we could all go visit the site together on Sunday. You haven't been down there for ages."

"Oh." Cassie seemed disappointed, and Emma's face had fallen too.

"Have I done something wrong?" Jake asked.

"It's just Emma and I have been arranging to spend next Sunday together."

"So?" Jake looked from one of them to the other. "Emma can come too, can't she?"

"You really think your multi-millionaire client wants to come on a family picnic?"

He laughed. "You were planning a picnic – in November?"

"Yes." Cassie turned to him. "There's nothing wrong with that."

"No, of course there isn't." He smiled. "Why don't we have the picnic down on the private beach at the site?" he suggested. "The client and I won't be long looking over the plans. You guys can mess around on the beach, and then we can all freeze to death having a picnic."

"We won't freeze to death."

"If you say so." He leant over and kissed her again. "What do you say, Em?" He turned to Emma.

"Sounds good to me," she replied. "As long as you're sure your client won't mind."

"He'll be fine. He's a friend, as well as a client."

"In which case, do you think I might be allowed to know his name at last?" Cassie asked. "Being as he's coming to stay?"

"I guess… I'll introduce you to him next weekend."

"You're just a tease." Cassie looked up at him.

"Yeah, and you love it."

"I really love a log fire, don't you?" Cassie rested her head on Jake's chest as they lay together on the couch. She felt good in his arms.

"Yeah. I love this place in the summer, but I think it's even better in the winter, don't you?"

"It's more romantic." Cassie twisted and looked up at him. He leant down, brushing his lips against hers, just gently.

"Hmm… sure is." Her eyes glistened in the glow from the roaring fire, which was the only light in the room. "Keeping this place was one of the best decisions we ever made," he added, pulling her further up his body, wrapping his legs around her too and holding her in place. "I'm pleased I sold my place, and I love our house in Portland… and I love our weekends here. We've got the best of both worlds, haven't we?"

"Yes, we do…" She sounded dreamy, almost sleepy.

"Mind you, if we're talking about good decisions, coming back to Somers Cove in the first place has to be right up there." He stroked her hair.

"I'm glad you did," she whispered. "I'm so happy you came back into my life."

"Me too." He tucked his finger under her chin, raising her face to his. "I've made another decision, Cass," he began, "and I really need you to agree to it." She raised an eyebrow, waiting. "I need you to agree to marry me." He heard her intake of breath. "I know it's all the wrong way around, and I should be down on one knee and everything, but I've never been overly conventional, you know that. I'm sorry this isn't more romantic, but I just know that I've never loved you more than I do now. When I'm not with you, I ache for you, and I need the whole world to know that you're mine."

"I'm yours already, Jake. I always was."

"I know." Was she going to say 'no'? "I know you are, but—"

"And I can't think of anything I want more than to be your wife."

"Really?" She nodded and he felt the smile spreading across his lips as he kissed her deeply and rolled them off the couch, onto the soft hearth rug, Cassie lying on top of him.

They were both finally back where they belonged. Together.

The End

Keep reading for an excerpt from Suzie Peters' forthcoming book
Lattes and Lies
Part Two in the Wishes and Chances Series.

Available to purchase from April 13th 2018

Lattes and Lies

Wishes and Chances Series: Book Two

by

Suzie Peters

Chapter One

Four years earlier

Emma

"You've gotta stop re-arranging the muffins." Emma jumped and looked up across the counter, straight into Nick's gray eyes. He was smiling at her. "You okay?" he asked, like he didn't already know the answer.

"Yeah, I'm fine." Even to Emma, her words sounded unconvincing, but maybe that was just her tone – her bored, dissatisfied, disappointed tone.

"Well, I believe you." Nick folded his arms across his broad chest and stared at her.

"What do you want?"

"For my sister to tell me the truth; that'd be real good."

"I *am* fine."

"Yeah, right."

She didn't reply, but picked up a cloth from behind the counter and came around his side to wipe down the tables, the same tables that she'd already wiped just fifteen minutes before. Nick grabbed her arm as she passed. "Em," he said. "You're not happy."

"Well, neither are you."

"We're not talking about me," he countered.

"Why are we talking about me all of a sudden?" she asked, biting back her tears. She glanced around the empty coffee shop. It was five-thirty. She still had another hour and a half until she could close up for the night… Her last customer had left just before five, and Nick would probably be the only other person she saw tonight. She could just tell him she was bored – it wouldn't be a lie.

"Because you've been like this since Cassie took off, and that was months ago now."

Emma glared at him, then looked down at his hand, resting on her arm, until he released her. He sighed. "Okay," he said, "don't talk to me, but Mom and Dad are starting to notice. Mom asked me yesterday what's been eating at you, and you know she's not gonna let up once she gets started. So, you can either tell me about it, or you can carry on as you are now and get the inquisition from them. Your choice."

"I'm such a failure," she mumbled.

"Excuse me?" Nick leant back on the counter, looking down at her.

Emma pulled out one of the chairs at the nearest table and sat down, facing him. Her brother wasn't like anyone else in Somers Cove, there was no getting away from that. He'd come back from law school four years ago, much quieter than when he'd left, and since then he'd worked with Tom Allen, the local attorney. He was good at his job, everyone knew that, but he didn't conform. Nick had never really conformed. He wore his dark hair long – just above shoulder length – and kind of disheveled, but with such an air of confidence, no-one ever questioned it. His eyes were light gray and piercing, and his stubble bordered on a beard, but didn't quite get there. He never wore a suit – not even in court – choosing jeans, a shirt, a tie, and a waistcoat. He had style… it was just a style unlike anyone else's. It was Nick's style.

"I said, I'm a failure," she repeated.

"I heard you. I'm just not sure why you'd say that."

Emma looked around her. "You're a lawyer, Nick. Cassie's working for a publishing company, *and* she's writing a book… and I work in the town coffee shop."

Emma didn't dwell on the fact that she'd been to college. She'd gone at the same time as Cassie and her boyfriend, Jake, and just about every other kid from their year in high school, all of whom had graduated earlier in the year - except for Emma. She didn't graduate. She hadn't even survived her first semester. She'd hated every second of college and had come home after just eight weeks. It was a subject the family avoided, because it nearly always ended in recriminations, resulting in Emma feeling like she'd let her parents down… again.

"And what's wrong with working in the coffee shop?" Nick queried. "You're providing a valuable service. Everyone needs coffee, Em."

She smiled up at him. "It's not exactly what I had planned."

Emma had always intended to go into catering. She was a brilliant cook and, in her dreams, she saw herself with a restaurant, or maybe a small hotel of her own… But they were dreams, nothing more. In reality, she worked for Mrs Adams in the coffee shop, and lived in the apartment upstairs.

Nick pushed himself off the counter and came and sat beside her. "I know," he said. "But who's to say you couldn't take over this place one day? You could turn it into whatever you want it to be."

"How?"

"You've still got the money you inherited from Grandpa Jonas. You could use that."

"Mrs Adams doesn't want to sell."

"Seriously? You've asked her?"

"Yes. When we first got our inheritances, I had the same idea."

They'd both inherited from their paternal grandfather about six months earlier. Nick had immediately bought a piece of land, about five miles outside of town. He wanted to build a house there – one day. For now, he lived on the site, in a trailer. It was something else for their parents to feel embarrassed about. But Nick didn't care about that; he just wanted a place of his own, that he'd created, in his style… and he didn't mind waiting for it.

"And she doesn't want to sell?" Emma shook her head. "That's ridiculous. She's never here. I mean, you practically run the place." It was true. Mrs Adams spent most of the cold winter months in Florida, where her son, Max and daughter, Ruth, both lived now.

"I know." Emma shrugged. "But even if she did, I don't think Grandpa Jonas's money would be enough. I'd be buying the building, *and* the business."

"Well, if she changes her mind, you should talk to the bank," Nick encouraged. "You'd have a substantial downpayment. They might lend you the rest."

"I don't know…"

"It might happen. And if it does, I'll help you with the paperwork. I'll come to the bank with you as well, if you want me to." He looked at her, holding her gaze for a moment. "That's not everything though, is it?" he asked.

"I miss Cassie," she murmured.

He leant over and gave her a hug, putting his arm around her. "I know you do. You two have been inseparable for years."

"Well, not as inseparable as she and Jake were."

Nick paused for a moment. "Yeah. None of us saw that one coming. Why *did* they break up?" he asked. "You've never said." It was a question the whole town had been asking for months. Jake and Cassie had been together for six years, but had been friends since they were six years old. And then they'd gone their separate ways when they finished college earlier in the year… just like that. They'd both left town on the same day. Jake had just disappeared without a word to anyone; Cassie had told Emma and her mom what she was doing and where she was going, but only on the understanding that they never revealed it to anyone else, and because of that promise, Emma hadn't even been able to tell Nick.

"I *can't* say, you know that. I was sworn to secrecy."

"Okay." He didn't push. "You know where she is though, so why don't you go and see her?" he suggested.

"I can't. Not at the moment. Mrs Adams has gone down to visit Ruth until after Thanksgiving."

Nick sighed deeply. "At least if you owned the place – or even ran it – you could take on more staff, and have a few days off. This way, she's got you as an unofficial manager, working every hour of the day, on a waitress's salary, with no-one to cover for you, because she decides who works here and when, while she swans off to Florida for weeks at a time."

She couldn't deny anything he was saying. Emma worked six days a week, until seven o'clock each night and had two part-time helpers. There was no doubt about it, Mrs Adams was taking advantage, but there was nothing Emma could do about it.

"Maybe you can get Cassie to come here for a visit?" Nick tried again.

"She won't be coming back," she said.

Nick stared at her. "Not ever?"

Emma shook her head. "No."

"Wow." He let out a low whistle, then leant in closer to his sister. "You're lonely, aren't you?"

She turned to face him, tears forming in her eyes. She nodded her head. "How did you know?" she asked.

He shrugged. "Takes one to know one."

"You're lonely too?" Emma blinked back her tears.

"Yeah, but like I said before, we're not talking about me." He smiled at her.

"No, and we're not talking about me either," she murmured.

Nick rested his elbows on his knees. "Okay," he sighed. "But you know where I am if you change your mind."

Emma leant into him. "Thanks," she whispered. Then she squared her shoulders and sat back in her chair, looking across at him. "Did you come in here for a reason?"

"What, you mean apart from proving that I'm the best brother in the world?"

"Yeah, apart from that…"

"Well, I've gotta work late tonight…"

"Nothing new there," Emma muttered. Nick had been really focused on his job since returning from law school, but now she knew he was lonely, she could understand that.

"Yeah, okay," he said, smiling at her. "And I was wondering if you could make me some macaroni and cheese to take back to the office."

She swatted his arm with her cloth. "It's always about food with you, isn't it?" She got to her feet and put the chair back neatly under the table. "And I don't do the cooking, in case you've forgotten?" That was another point that rankled with her. She could cook better than Noah, the chef, but she was employed to wait tables.

"It's your recipe, though," Nick pointed out.

"Yeah, but Noah gets the credit." She shook her head, just for a moment. "I'll go and ask him to make you some, and I'll bring it over to your office when I close up."

He stood up, leant down and kissed her on the cheek. "You're a star, Em."

"Yeah, I know."

Emma was running out of things to tidy. She'd sent Patsy home early; there seemed little point in both of them kicking their heels. Noah was cleaning the kitchen, and prepping for tomorrow's breakfast. Although it was quiet, Emma wasn't unduly worried. This was normal for a Thursday night in early November. People were tired at the end of the working week. They were either at home with their families, or they'd be in Mac's Bar. The coffee shop would get a little busier over Thanksgiving and, again, over the Christmas holidays and then there'd be another lull, before the tourists started to return in earnest in the spring.

She leant on the shiny wooden counter and surveyed the shop. It was a little tired, but the locals seemed to like it. The wood panelling gave it an air of old-worldliness that went well with the neat round, dark wood tables and matching ladder-backed chairs. There were booths running down one wall and, in the summer, they provided seating outside as well, along the wide sidewalk. Right now though, it felt kind of cozy in here, even if she knew she could do so much more with the place… if only it were hers.

She let out a sigh, turned and started cleaning down the coffee machine.

The door opened and closed again and, surprised by the late caller, Emma swung round… and her tongue dried, feeling like it was stuck to the roof of her mouth. The man walking toward the counter was the most gorgeous human being she'd ever seen. He was tall – very tall –

with thick dark brown hair and a strong, square jaw. He wore jeans, a gray t-shirt, and a black leather jacket, none of which hid his athletic build.

"Hi," he said, staring at her unashamedly. "Are you still open?"

"Yes," she replied, nodding her head at the same time.

"Great." He smiled, and she felt a warmth in the pit of her stomach. That was weird. She'd never felt anything quite like that before. "I'm in need of coffee."

"Okay." She came closer as he sat down opposite her. "What would you like?"

His smile widened. "A latte, thanks."

"Coming right up."

She fetched a large cup from the shelf behind the counter and prepared him a coffee, as requested.

"Are you visiting town?" she asked, not turning round.

"Yeah. I'm here until next Wednesday… on vacation."

Now she flipped her head round. "At this time of year?"

"Why not?" He smiled again, and that warmth spread a little further.

"People tend to visit here in the summer, that's all."

"Well, I like to be different."

She passed the cup of coffee over the counter and he pushed a ten dollar bill toward her.

"Being as you're not exactly rushed off your feet," he said, looking around the deserted café, "why don't you join me?" He patted the stool next to his.

Emma felt that strange heat increase again. She lowered her eyes, feeling a little shy, but when she looked back up, he was still smiling at her. "Okay," she said. "Thank you."

She made herself a latte as well and came around the counter, sitting down beside him.

"Is it normally this quiet around here?" he asked, once she was settled.

"At this time of year, yes." She looked up at him. His amber colored eyes were mesmerizing. "People – tourists, I mean – they come here for the beaches. So, the summer's our busy time." She felt like she was rambling.

"Are the beaches any good?"

"Oh, yes." She smiled. "They're…" She searched for the right word. "Beautiful – really dramatic."

"You'll have to show me." His voice had dropped a note or two, his eyes pierced hers, and she felt herself being drawn to him. That warmth had now given up spreading. It had suffused throughout her whole body and, as she watched him sip his coffee, she wondered how those long fingers, now gripping his cup, might feel caressing her skin… How was this even possible? He'd been there all of five minutes and she'd turned into a simmering mass of need and emotions. And she didn't think it was just her either. The look in his eyes was one of complete desire, and he hadn't once taken them from her. "I'm booked into the hotel up the street…" He was still talking, and she dragged her attention away from her lustful thoughts and back to his words. "But they don't serve evening meals. So, is there anywhere I can get something to eat?"

"There's Fernando's," Emma suggested. "It's at the other end of Main Street." She pointed over her shoulder.

"Sounds Italian." He grinned and she twisted in her seat, trying to get more comfortable, despite the increasing heat of his gaze, but the movement just made her even more aware of how much she ached for his touch… What was wrong with her? How could she want him this much, this quickly?

"That's because it is," she managed to say.

"Any good?" he asked, moving just a little closer.

"Not bad." She shrugged and tried not to sound too negative. "Gino and Elaine are lovely, but they're not very adventurous."

"So it's a bit… safe?"

"That's a good way of putting it."

"Well, I guess safe isn't *always* a bad thing."

"No, but it can get a little boring."

He smiled again, and his eyes sparkled, like they were burning into her. "You're sounding like a woman after my own heart," he whispered, then he paused, opened his mouth, closed it again and finally said. "Look, I know you don't know me… and I've literally just walked in off the street, but would you like to have dinner with me tonight?"

Emma stared at him. The heat, the need, and the want were still there but, being sensible, he was right. She didn't know him. "Um… I'm not sure…"

He held up his hands. "I promise I'm not a serial killer, or a madman, or an ax murderer." He smirked. "But then I guess serial killers, madmen, and ax murderers probably say that all the time." He moved his hand along the countertop, closer to hers. "I'm really just an ordinary guy."

"It's not that," she murmured. It was in part, but he seemed so genuine.

"Then have dinner with me," he urged. All of a sudden a thought seemed to strike him. "Oh, I'm sorry," he said quickly. "I should've thought. You've probably already got plans for this evening."

"No, I don't have plans. I've got no-one to make plans with." Oh, God. Had she really just said that out loud… to a total stranger? She felt herself blushing, especially when she noticed the corners of his mouth twitching upward.

"Then you've got no reason not to eat with me."

"Except I don't know why you want to." Her head dropped. If this was his idea of a joke, she'd rather know now. She didn't need anyone else to humiliate her. It seemed she was doing a perfect job of that all by herself.

She felt his finger under her chin, felt him raise her face, until she was looking into his twinkling pale brown eyes again.

"Are you serious?" he asked.

"Well, yes," she replied. She was.

He sighed. "I want to have dinner with you because you intrigue me," he murmured. Then he stood, looking down at her. "And because we've already established we've got something in common."

Emma was confused, as well as breathless. "What's that?"

He leant in closer to her, close enough for her to smell his body wash. She thought it might be sandalwood and vanilla, but whatever it was, he smelt divine. His lips were only a few inches from hers, and she couldn't help but focus on them when he whispered, "We both think safe is a little boring."

Mark

She was the most beautiful woman he'd ever seen – and he'd seen some beautiful women in his time. How on earth could she doubt he'd want to have dinner with her? She was staring up at him, her deep brown eyes gazing for a moment into his. She was utterly bewitching. And he was rock hard; harder than he'd been in… well, forever. *Please let her say yes, he thought. Even if it's just dinner. She's enchanting.*

"Thank you," she murmured eventually. "I'd love to have dinner with you."

"Great." *Thank God for that.*

"I'll meet you at the restaurant, shall I?" she suggested.

"No." It didn't work that way, not where he was concerned. "I'll come back and pick you up."

"I've got a quick errand to run when I finish work," she said.

"Okay. Give me a time. I'll be here."

"Um… seven-thirty?"

"Seven-thirty it is. Shall I wait out front for you?" She nodded and he noticed how the light caught her hair. Now she was sitting beside him, he could see it was almost black, but with brown flecks, and had a natural wave. At the moment, it was tied, quite loosely, behind her head, with a few strands hanging down the side of her face, but he wondered what she'd look like with it left untied, wild… untamed. "Great. Well, I'll see you later," he said and started toward the door.

"Wait," she called after him, and he stopped, turning to her. "I don't even know your name… and you don't know mine."

He grinned at her – he couldn't help it. "I know," he said, and he opened the door and went outside, still smiling.

He walked down the street, feeling elated. Nothing quite like this had ever happened to him before, and it felt so damned good. He'd picked up all kinds of women in the past; he'd taken them to intimate dinners, to private clubs, and usually to his bed, but they'd always, *always*, known who he was. It got boring after a while – real boring. The 'coffee shop girl'… she had no idea. And that was what felt great – well, that and the idea of spending a whole evening looking into those beautiful dark brown eyes, talking about… *Oh shit.*

What was he going to tell her about himself? He stopped and looked up a the night sky, studying the twinkling stars for a moment. His instincts were yelling at him to tell her the truth. She was really special – different – and he certainly wanted more than the usual one night stand… He wanted a lot more than that. He may have only spent a few minutes in her company, but he'd worked that much out already… and lying to her wasn't a good place to start. But could he tell her the truth? If he did, it'd be all over a small town like this before they'd even sat down in the restaurant.

He walked on more slowly, plunging his hands into his pockets.

He'd checked into the hotel as Mark Ellis, using his mother's maiden name, because he wanted a week of anonymity. If you said the name 'Mark Gardner' anywhere in New England, everyone knew immediately who you were talking about: the son of the owner of the biggest chain of hotels on the East coast, one of the hottest rising stars in the business world – set to take over from his father – and a very, very eligible bachelor. Mark was good at keeping his private life private. He was an expert at it, and he knew the press hated that, so given the opportunity, they made up stories about him, most of which were too ludicrous to be taken seriously by anyone. He saw a lot of women, but he took them to places they wouldn't be photographed, and where they could be alone, anonymous, and intimate – if they wanted to. And they usually wanted to. He rarely saw the same woman more than once though, simply because he'd yet to find a woman who wasn't more interested in his fortune than she was in him.

And he'd been burned... twice. A couple of years ago, it had been a young actress and, most recently, an up and coming model, both of whom had sold the story of their solitary 'night of hot passion' to the gutter tabloids. There had been lurid details and photographs – of the women, not him. Mark did everything in his power to avoid being photographed, but that didn't make the stories any less intrusive. His family consoled him that most people who mattered didn't read that kind of trash anyway. His friends – such as they were – consoled him that both women had been real complimentary about his prowess in the bedroom. He'd laughed; he'd made the right noises... but since the last time it had happened, back in the summer, he'd been wary. Well, he'd been more than wary. In reality, it had been over four months since he'd been with a woman...

Still, 'coffee shop girl' wasn't just your average woman.

He got back there ten minutes early, having showered and changed into casual pants and a jacket, with a button down shirt, and stood outside the now locked door to the coffee shop, which was shrouded in darkness. He waited patiently. It was cold, so he paced up and down, telling himself it was to keep warm, not because he was nervous. Since when did Mark Gardner get nervous on a date? Maybe since he was pretending to be someone he wasn't... and maybe since he was about to have dinner with a woman he already knew would forever haunt his dreams and fill his every waking thought.

At exactly seven-thirty, she appeared from a doorway just beyond the coffee shop. But... his heart sank. She wasn't alone. Walking beside her was a tall, muscular-looking guy. Even in the street lights, Mark could see the guy's hair was – frankly – messy. Although it was cold and the girl was wearing a knee-length coat, her companion was just in shirtsleeves, with a loose tie and waistcoat, over jeans, his hands shoved deep into the pockets. He looked kinda disheveled, and a little rough around the edges. *What the hell?* he thought.

They approached quickly, the girl's heels tapping on the sidewalk.

"Hello," she said quietly, as she came to stand in front of him.

"Hi." He looked from her to the man standing next to her. His eyes were steely and, although he couldn't see them clearly in this light, Mark guessed they were probably either blue or gray.

"This is my brother, Nick," the girl said. *Her brother.* Mark felt relieved and confused at the same time.

"I'm not stopping," Nick said quickly. "I just came to check you out." Well, that was honest enough.

Mark almost laughed, but managed not to. "Okay." He guessed it was a fair thing to do. He didn't know the guy's sister… Actually, at this point, he still didn't even know her name.

Nick looked him up and down. "Em told me her plans for this evening." He paused. *Em? Short for Emily, maybe? Or Emma?* Mark hoped it was Emma… it suited her perfectly. "And I told her I thought she was insane," Nick continued.

"Fair enough," Mark replied. "Would it help if I told you my intentions are entirely honorable?"

"No. I'd just call that bullshit." Mark laughed and noticed Nick's lips curl upward. "We both know a guy's *intentions* can vary enormously from his actions. If they didn't, I'd be out of a job."

Mark raised an eyebrow. "Nick's a lawyer," 'Em' explained, then she turned to her brother. "Okay," she said. "You've done your protective brother bit. Can I go and have dinner now?" She tilted her head to one side, her hand resting on her hip.

Nick looked from her to Mark, and back again. "Sure," he said, smiling. He bent down, kissed her on the cheek, and whispered, loud enough for Mark to hear, "Call me, if you need me."

She leant back and looked up at him. "Get going," she said, pointing back down the street.

Nick chuckled, shaking his head and turned away, walking slowly back the way he'd come, evidently immune to the cold.

'Em' turned to Mark. "I'm so sorry," she said.

"Hey… don't be. I think it's good you've got someone looking out for you. I'm sure I'll be the same with my sister, when she's old enough to date."

"You've got a little sister?"

"Yeah."

"How little?"

"She's not a toddler, if that's what you mean. She's ten years younger than me."

"Well, being as I don't know how old you are, that doesn't help much."

He smiled. "Sorry… she's fifteen."

"Um… I hate to tell you this, but fifteen is old enough to date."

"Yeah. I know." He smiled as he thought of Sarah. "She just hasn't gotten around to it yet, thank God." He grinned.

"Somehow I get the feeling you'll be even worse than Nick." She stared up at him.

"Probably." He took a half-step closer. "Now," he said solemnly, "I think it's time we introduced ourselves." He held out his hand. "My name's Mark…" he paused, just for a second, and made a snap decision. "Mark Ellis."

"Emma Woods." He was pleased. Emma. Just as I hoped. Her name felt right for her and he knew then that, unlike her brother, he'd never shorten it. She would always be 'Emma' to him.

She put her hand in his. Her skin was soft, delicate, and he felt the air being sucked from his lungs at her gentle touch.

"It's a real pleasure to meet you," he whispered.

They were shown to a quiet table at the back of the restaurant. There were a few people dining, maybe five or six other couples, and a group of eight, who were quite loud and – thankfully – seated as far away as possible. Emma removed her coat, handing it to the hostess – who Emma introduced as Elaine, the co-owner – and, as she turned back to Mark, his breath caught in his throat. In the coffee shop earlier, he'd noticed how her black pants had clung to her hips and he'd found it hard to ignore the way her nipples had shown through her thin white blouse. But now… Oh, my God… She was wearing a dark blue, knee-length, all over lace cocktail dress, which appeared to be see-through, but it wasn't. Mark could just make out a layer of skin colored material beneath the lace, creating the illusion. An illusion that made him hard again, in an instant.

He held her seat, pushing it forward as she sat down, and resisted the urge to touch her shoulders, or lean down and kiss her neck.

Over a 'safe' main course of spaghetti with meatballs, which they'd both ordered, Mark gazed into her brown, sparkling eyes and explained that he worked in the hotel trade. It wasn't a lie... well, not really. He did. His family owned dozens and dozens of hotels all over New England. The fact that he'd implied he worked in a particular hotel was beside the point. He avoided specifics and turned the topic of employment back onto Emma.

"So, do you manage the coffee shop? Or..." He left the question hanging. She seemed too young to own it, but she'd been the only person there, and it had felt like she belonged.

She shook her head. "No." She looked a little dejected. "I'm just a waitress."

He put down his fork and reached across the table, taking her hand in his. "Don't say 'just' like that," he told her. "You're not 'just' anything." Even as he said those words, he wondered what would happen if he took Emma home and introduced her to his family as a 'waitress'. His mom would be fine with it. Lisa Gardner was renowned among her friends as an incurable romantic. His dad? No... Michael Gardner would freak at the idea of his only son, the heir to his empire and fortune, dating a waitress. He smiled to himself. Since when did he 'date' – in the conventional sense, anyway? Or take women to meet his parents, for that matter? Never. Well, not until now, anyway. But there was something about Emma that was different... very different.

Emma was talking. "I wanted to buy the place," she was saying. "I inherited some money not long ago." She took a sip of wine, and he was momentarily distracted by her lips and the sudden urge to kiss them. "It's not enough though."

Mark sat forward. "You could borrow the rest, couldn't you? If you've got a big enough down payment, the bank would lend it to you." He'd happily give her the money, but he could hardly tell her that.

"You sound just like my brother."

"Well… couldn't you?"

"I don't know. I didn't inquire."

"Why not?"

"Because when I asked her, Mrs Adams – the woman who owns the coffee shop – she said she wasn't interested in selling at the moment, so there seemed little point in pursuing it."

"Then how do you know your inheritance isn't enough?"

"It's not just the business I'd be buying. Mrs Adams owns the building as well… so that's the shop, the apartment above, *and* the business."

Mark nodded. He didn't know how much money she'd inherited, or how much Mrs Adams was likely to be asking for the property and business, but he guessed it didn't matter if she wasn't interested in selling, and he sensed Emma's disappointment.

"Is it an ambition of yours?" he asked.

"What? Owning a coffee shop? Not really."

"Then why…?" He was confused.

She smiled. "Why even think about it?" He nodded. "Because at the moment, I *do* run the place, but I get paid a waitress's salary. And I figure I could make it so much… *more*, if I just had a free hand."

"In what way?" He was intrigued.

She sat forward in her seat, ignoring her food. "I'd redecorate, to start with; make the place more modern. And I think we should offer more home-made cakes and pastries – something a bit more unique – not the mass-produced things Mrs Adams buys in…" Her eyes lit up. "And then I'd change the lunchtime menu. I'd make it more… adventurous."

"Do you know anything about cooking?" he asked her.

"Yes… I love to cook. It's what I always wanted to do."

"Then why didn't you?"

She slumped back into her seat, her face falling. "I studied culinary arts at college," she said. "But I hated it… I only lasted half a semester and I came back home. I've been at the coffee shop ever since." She picked up her fork and started pushing her food around her plate.

"What didn't you like about it?" he asked.

"Pretty much everything." Emma didn't look up. He reached across the table and, placing his finger under her chin, just like he'd done at the coffee shop earlier, he raised her face. *Shit*. There were tears in her eyes.

"What's wrong?" he asked.

"Quitting, like I did… it's always made me feel like such a failure." She mumbled out the words, then clamped her mouth shut, like she regretted saying them.

"No-one's a failure… unless they give up on themselves," he whispered, leaning a little closer. Her eyes met his and he wondered, briefly, if she had. "You're young," he added. "You're… what? Twenty-two?" She nodded. He'd guessed right, that was something. "Most kids are just leaving college at your age, with no idea what working for a living involves. You've got huge advantages. You've got experience, understanding, expertise. You know your business, your field, your market…" He stopped, aware he was sounding too much like a businessman and not enough like a hotel employee. She was staring at him.

"Thank you." Her voice was barely audible.

"What for?"

"Apart from Nick, you're the first person to show any faith in me." She seemed to think for a moment. "Well, that's not true. My best friend was always really supportive, but she's left town now."

He wondered if she was lonely. She sure seemed to be unhappy… and isolated. It didn't sit well with her. It didn't sit well with him either.

"Just don't give up," he said. "Mrs Adams might change her mind one day, so keep the plans going. Keep thinking up the ideas."

She smiled. "Oh… I do. It's what keeps me going."

God, that was sad. Was that really all she had?

They didn't bother with dessert, or coffee. Neither wanted the former and when the latter was offered, Emma gave him an almost imperceptible shake of her head. While Elaine went to get the check, Emma explained that the coffee there was awful, which made Mark laugh out loud.

"You should know," he said, quietening down as he handed over the right amount of cash, including the tip. He didn't want to use a credit card while in town… the name wouldn't match the one he was using. And he knew it would get back to the hotel owner – and to Emma – probably before he'd even put his card back into his wallet, that Mark Gardner was in town and staying under a false name. He shook his head as he helped Emma into her coat, feeling guilty for deceiving her.

"This is me," Emma said as they approached the coffee shop again.

"You live above the shop?" he asked.

"Yes."

"And I guess that means you open up every day?"

"Seven o'clock sharp." She smiled.

"A twelve hour shift. How many days a week do you do that?"

"Six. I have Sundays off. That's when I sleep."

"And you do this for a waitress's salary?"

"I keep my own tips. And I have the apartment."

"Rent free?" he asked.

She shook her head. "No… but it's reduced."

He felt as though he'd quite like to sit down with Mrs Adams and give her a good talking to about employee relations.

Emma moved a half-step closer and he caught the scent of her perfume. It was floral, like jasmine, or something. "I've had a lovely evening," she said.

"Me too."

"I'd invite you up, but I've got an early start."

"That's okay." He moved closer still. They were almost touching. "Can… Can I see you again tomorrow night?" That wasn't a question he was used to asking.

There wasn't even a blink of hesitation before Emma nodded her head, a smile forming slowly on her lips. "I'd like that," she said.

"And… can I kiss you?" he whispered.

Again, she nodded. "I'd like that too."

He brought his hands up, clasping her face, and leant forward, gently brushing his lips across hers. At the moment they touched, his world stopped spinning. Just like that. Nothing moved or stirred… not even his heart. After a minute – probably less – he pulled back, staring down at her face as she opened her eyes, gazing up into his.

"I'll see you tomorrow," he whispered. She nodded and he let her go, watching as she went inside. Then he turned and walked away, feeling a little lost without her.

To be continued…

Printed in Great Britain
by Amazon